K.D. Richards is a na̲... who now lives outsid̲... two sons. You can find her at kdrichardsbooks.com

Katie Mettner wears the title of 'the only person to lose her leg after falling down the bunny hill' and loves decorating her prosthetic leg to fit the season. She lives in Northern Wisconsin with her own happily-ever-after and wishes for a dog now that her children are grown. Katie has an addiction to coffee and X and a lessening aversion to Pinterest—now that she's quit trying to make the things she pins.

UNDER LOCK AND KEY

K.D. RICHARDS

THE SILENT SETUP

KATIE METTNER

MILLS & BOON

First Published in Great Britain 2024
by Mills & Boon, an imprint of HarperCollins*Publishers* Ltd
1 London Bridge Street, London, SE1 9GF

www.harpercollins.co.uk

HarperCollins*Publishers*
Macken House, 39/40 Mayor Street Upper,
Dublin 1, D01 C9W8, Ireland

ISBN: 978-0-263-32249-1

1024

UNDER LOCK AND KEY

K.D. RICHARDS

Chapter One

Maggie Scott looked around the dimly lit museum gallery, exhausted but content. She'd done it. The donors' open house for the Viperé ruby exhibit had been a rousing success. The classical music that had played softly in the background during the night was silent now, but the air of sophistication and sense of reverence still filled the room. Soft spotlights lit the priceless paintings on the wall while a brighter beam shone down on what was literally the crown jewel of the exhibit. The Viperé ruby glowed under the light like a blood red sun.

Maggie stood in front of the glass case with the almost empty bottle of champagne she'd procured from the caterers before they'd left and a flute. She poured what little was left in the bottle into the flute and toasted herself.

"Congratulations to me." She downed half the liquid in the glass. Her eyes passed over the gallery space with a mixture of awe, satisfaction and pride. The night had been the culmination of a year's worth of labor. A decade of work if she counted undergraduate and graduate school and the handful of jobs she'd held at other museums before joining the Larimer Museum as an assistant curator three years earlier. It had taken a massive amount of work to ensure the success of the display and the open house for the donors and board members, who got a first look at the highly anticipated exhibit. As one of two assistant curators up for a possible promotion to curator and with the director of the British museum who'd loaned the Viperé ruby to the relatively small Larimer Museum watching her, she was under a great deal of pressure from a great many people. But the night had been an unmitigated success, so said her boss, and she was hopeful that she was now a shoo-in for the promotion.

Maggie stepped closer to the jewel, reaching out with her free hand and almost grazing the glass. The spotlight hit the ruby, creating a rainbow of glittering light around her. She raised the champagne flute to her lips and spoke, "To the Viperé ruby and all the other pieces of art that have inspired, challenged and united humanity in ways words cannot express."

She finished the champagne and stood for a moment, taking in the energy and vitality that emanated from the works around her.

Maggie was abruptly yanked from her reverie by the sound of a soft thud. She and Carl Downy were the only two people who were still in the building. Carl was the retired cop who provided security at night for the museum. Mostly, that meant he walked the three floors of the renovated and repurposed Victorian building that was itself a work of art between naps during his nine-hour shift.

A surge of unease traveled through her. She gripped the empty champagne bottle tightly and called out, "Carl, is that you?"

A moment passed without a response.

Unease was replaced with concern. Carl was getting on in years. He could have fallen or had a medical emergency of some type.

Maggie stepped into the even more dimly lit hallway connecting the rooms, the galleries as her boss liked to call them, on the main floor. The thud had sounded as if it had come from the front of the museum, but all she saw was pitch black in that direction. She knew the nooks and crannies of the museum as well as she knew her own house. Normally, she loved wandering through the space, leisurely taking in the pieces. Even though she'd seen each of them dozens of times, she always found herself noticing something new, some aspect or feature of the pieces she'd overlooked. That was one of the reasons she loved art. It was always teaching, always changing, even when it stayed the same.

But she didn't love it at the moment. The museum was eerily still and quiet.

Suddenly, a dark-clad figure stepped out of the shadows. He wore a mask, but she could tell he was a male. That was all she had time to process before the figure charged at her.

Her heartbeat thundered, and a voice in her head told her to run, but her feet felt melted to the floor. The bottle and champagne flute slid from her hands, shattering against the polished wood planks.

The intruder slammed her back into the wall, knocking the breath out of her. Before she had time to recover, he backhanded her across the face with a beefy gloved hand.

Pain exploded on the side of her face.

She slid along the wall, instinct forcing her to try to get away even as her conscious brain still struggled to process what was happening. But her assailant grabbed her arm, stopping her escape.

Her vision was blurred by the blow to her face, and the mask the intruder wore covered all but his dark brown eyes.

Still, she was aware of her assailant raising his hand a second time, his fist clenched.

Her limbs felt like they were stuck in molasses, but she tried to raise her arm to deflect the blow.

Too slowly, as it turned out.

The intruder hit her on the side of her head, the impact causing excruciating pain before darkness descended and her world faded to black.

KEVIN LOMBARD'S PHONE RANG, dragging him out of a dreamless sleep at just after one in the morning.

"Lombard."

"Kevin, hey, sorry to wake you." The voice of his new boss, Tess Stenning, flowed over the phone line. "We have a problem. An assault and theft at the Larimer Museum, one of our newer clients. Since you are West Investigation's new director of corporate and institutional accounts, that makes it your problem."

Kevin groaned. He'd only been on the job for three weeks, but Tess was right, his division, his problem. It didn't matter that he hadn't overseen the installation of the security system at the Larimer. He'd looked over the file, as he'd done with all of the security plans that West Security and Investigations' new West Coast office had installed in the six months since they'd been open, so he had an idea of what the gallery security looked like.

West Security and Investigations was one of the premier security and private investigation firms on the East Coast. Run primarily by brothers Ryan and Shawn West, with a little help from their two older brothers, James and Brandon, West Security and Investigations had recently opened a West Coast office in Los Angeles, headed up by Tess Stenning,

a long-time West operative and damn good private investigator. If he'd been asked a year ago whether he would ever
consider joining a private investigations firm, even one with
as sterling a reputation as West Security and Investigations,
he'd have laughed.

But staying in Idyllwild had become untenable. A friend
of a friend had recommended he reach out to Tess, and after
a series of interviews with her and Ryan West, he'd been offered the job. Moving to Los Angeles had been an adjust-
ment, but he was settling in.

He searched his memory for the details of the museum's
security. Despite West Security and Investigations' recom-
mendation that the museum update its entire security system, the gallery's board of directors had only approved the
security specifications for the Viperé ruby. Shortsighted,
he'd noted when he'd read the file, and now he had the feeling that he was about to be proven right.

Tess gave him the sparse details that she'd gotten from
her contact on the police force. Someone had broken into
the museum, attacked a curator and a guard and made off
with the ruby. He ended the call and dragged himself into the
bathroom for a quick shower. Ten years on the police force
had conditioned him to getting late night—or early morning,
as it were—phone calls. The shower helped wake him, and
he set his coffee machine to brew while he quickly dressed
then pulled up the museum's file on his West-issued tablet.
A little more than thirty minutes after he'd gotten the call
from Tess, he was headed out.

He arrived at the Larimer Museum twenty minutes later,
thankful that most of Los Angeles was still asleep or out
partying and not on the roads. He showed his ID to the police officer manning the door and was waved in. Officers

milled about in the lobby, but he caught sight of Tess down a short hall toward the back of the Victorian building, talking to a small man in a rumpled suit and haphazardly knotted blue tie. The man waved his hands in obvious distress while it looked like Tess tried to console him.

Kevin made his way toward the pair. In the room twenty feet from where they stood, a police technician worked gathering evidence from the break-in.

"This is going to ruin us. The Larimer Museum will be ruined, and I'll never get another job as curator again." The man wiped the back of his hand over his brow.

Tess gave Kevin a nod. "Mr. Gustev, this is my colleague Kevin Lombard. Kevin, Robert Gustev, managing director and head curator of the Larimer Museum."

Gustev ignored Kevin's outstretched hand. He pointed his index figure at Tess. "This is your fault."

"West Investigations is going to do its best to identify the perpetrators and retrieve the ruby."

Gustev swiped his hand over his brow again. "I can't believe this is happening."

The man looked on the verge of being sick.

"Mr. Gustev—" Tess started.

"You were supposed to protect the ruby."

"If you recall, we did make several recommendations for upgrading the museum's security, which you and the Larimer's board of directors rejected," Tess said pointedly.

Gustev's face reddened, his jowls shaking in anger.

"Mr. Gustev," Kevin said before the curator had a chance to respond to Tess. "We are going to do everything we can to recover the ruby. It would help if you took Tess and I through everything that happened up until the time the intruder assaulted you."

"Me? No, it wasn't me that the thief attacked."

Kevin frowned. On the phone, Tess had said the guard and the curator had been attacked.

"It was my assistant curator who confronted the thief." Gustev frowned. "She's speaking with the police detective in her office right now."

"Oh, well, why don't you tell us what you know, and we'll speak to her once the police have finished."

Gustev ran them through a detailed description of the party that had taken place earlier that night. Kevin pressed the man on whether anything out of the ordinary happened at the party or in the days before, but Gustev swore that nothing of note had occurred.

The curator waved a hand at Tess. "I have to call the board members." He turned and hurried off down the hall, ascending a rear staircase.

Tess's eyes stayed trained on the retreating man's back until he disappeared on the second-floor landing. She let out a labored sigh. "This is going to turn into a you-know-what show if we don't get a handle on it fast."

Kevin's stomach turned over because she was right. "I'm not sure we can avoid that, but I'll do my best to get to the bottom of things as quickly as possible." He turned to look at the activity taking place in the room to the right of where they stood.

Glass sparkled on top of a podium covered with a black velvet blanket. A numbered yellow cone marked the shards as evidence. A crime scene tech made her way around the room, systematically photographing and bagging anything of note.

Tess groaned. "Someone managed to break into the building and steal the Viperé ruby, a ruby the size of your fist and worth more than the gross domestic product of my home-town of Missoula."

His eyebrow quirked up. "Sounds like a lot."

"Try two hundred fifty million a lot."

Kevin gave a low whistle. "That's a lot."

Tess cut him a look. "A lot of problems for us. I'm afraid Gustev—" she nodded toward the staircase that the curator had ascended moments earlier "—is going to throw himself out of a window."

The curator was more than a little bit on edge, but who could blame him. "The thief attacked the assistant curator but left her alive?"

Tess nodded. "The night guard and one of the assistant curators were knocked unconscious by the thief, apparently."

Kevin frowned. "What was an assistant curator still doing here so late?"

"That I don't know." Tess shrugged. "But the museum had a party tonight to kick off the opening of the Viperé ruby exhibit. The board, donors and other muckety mucks, drinking, dancing and, undoubtedly, opening their wallets."

"Undoubtedly," he said, turning his attention back to the crime scene technician at work.

Tess shook her head. "The guard was out cold when the EMTs arrived. They took him to the hospital. He's on the older side, former cop, though, so he's tough. The curator is in her office. Declined transportation to the hospital."

"Sounds like she's pretty tough, too."

Tess shrugged. "Or stupid. Detective Gill Francois is questioning her now."

He frowned. He hadn't had the pleasure of working with Francois yet, but he'd heard of him. The detective was a bulldog.

Tess chuckled. "Don't do that. Gill's good people. I've already talked to him. He's agreed to let us tag along on the case, as long as we play nice and keep him in the loop regarding anything we find out."

He felt one of his eyebrows arch up. "And he'll do the same?"

Tess rolled her eyes. "You know how it goes. He says he will but..."

"Yeah, *but*." He did know how it went. He'd been one of the boys in blue not so long ago.

"Listen, I made sure West Investigations covered its rear regarding our advice to the board of directors of the museum to upgrade the entire system." Tess waved a hand in the air. "I told them that the security they'd authorized for the Viperé ruby left them open to possible theft, but they didn't want to spend the money and figured the locked and alarmed case along with the on-site twenty-four-hour security guard was enough."

"Didn't want to pony up the money?"

Tess tapped her nose then sighed. "Still, this is going to be a black mark on West Investigations if we don't figure out what happened here quickly. I know you've barely gotten settled in, but do you think you're up for the job?"

"Absolutely," he answered without reservation. "The first thing I want to do is get the security recordings and the alarm logs and get the exact time when the case was broken. We'll also need to figure out what the thief used to break the glass." He pulled the same type of small notebook he'd used when he was a police detective out of his jacket along with the small pen he kept hooked in the spiral. His tablet was in the computer case that hung from his shoulder, but he preferred the old-fashioned methods. Writing out his notes and thoughts helped him remember things better and think things through. "Of course, shatterproof glass isn't invincible, but it would have taken a great deal of force and a strong weapon to do it." He scratched out notes on his thoughts before they got away from him.

Tess cleared her throat. "The alarm went off just after eleven, triggered by the curator after she'd regained consciousness. Getting more specific than that is going to be a problem, at least with regards to the alarm logs."

Kevin looked up from his notebook. "Why?"

Tess looked more than a little green around the gills.

His stomach turned over, anticipating that whatever she was about to say wasn't going to be good.

"Because the alarm didn't go off," she said.

"The alarm didn't go off." Kevin repeated the words back to Tess as if they didn't make any sense to him. Then again, they didn't. "How is that possible?"

"That is a very good question."

He and Tess turned toward the sound of the voice.

A man Kevin would have made as a cop no matter where they'd met descended the back staircase.

Kevin's gaze moved to the woman coming down the stairs next to him, and his world stopped.

The man and woman halted in front of him and Tess.

"Hello, Kevin." The words floated from Maggie's lips on a wisp of a breath.

"Hello, Maggie."

Maggie Scott. His college girlfriend and, at one point, the woman he'd imagined spending his life with.

Chapter Two

Kevin's eyes swept over Maggie, drinking her in. Her dark hair was mussed and fell in tangled ringlets around the soft curve of her cocoa-colored cheeks. When he'd thought of her over the years, it had always been as he'd remembered her. A co-ed in jeans that hugged her voluptuous curves and CalSci T-shirts that he'd loved peeling off her. But now she was dressed in a black sheath cocktail dress and heels that accentuated long, smooth legs that had him remembering the ecstasy he'd felt having them wrapped around his waist.

"You know each other?" Detective Francois's voice pulled him back to the present. The detective's gaze darted between Kevin and Maggie.

"Yeah," Kevin answered.

At the same time, Maggie said, "We were acquaintances in college."

Acquaintances. They'd been much more than acquaintances. For a while, he thought they would spend the rest of their lives together. But then the NFL had come knocking, and he'd let hubris and arrogance turn him into a fool. He'd wanted to start his new life unencumbered, so he'd broken things off with Maggie.

It was, to date, the biggest mistake he'd ever made in his life.

Pale skin shone under the thinning wisps of hair on the top of Francois's head. Kevin put him somewhere in his early fifties, but the intelligence that sparked in the man's eyes said it wouldn't be easy to get anything over on him. It was clear he suspected there was more than a mere college friendship between Kevin and Maggie, but the detective didn't push. At least, not yet.

"What is this about the alarm not going off?" Francois looked at Maggie with suspicion in his gaze. "I thought you said you triggered the alarm when you regained consciousness?"

"I did," Maggie said, defensiveness in her tone. She wrapped her arms around her torso.

"She did," Tess interjected, "but the alarm should have gone off automatically when the intruder entered the building and when the case with the Viperé ruby was opened, but it didn't."

"And why didn't it?" Francois demanded.

Tess rubbed her temples. "We are looking into it, but it appears that someone turned the system off just before the theft occurred."

"Turned it off?" Detective Francois said. "Can someone just hit a switch and shut the thing down?"

"It's not that easy," Kevin said, his eyes straying to Maggie again. The shock he'd seen in her eyes when they'd first landed on him was gone, replaced by a guarded coolness. She had the beginnings of a shiner growing around her left eye. A bandage was affixed to her right temple.

He fought the urge to hurt the person who'd put their hands on her.

"We can discuss this further in a moment. I was just going to have an officer take Ms. Scott home." Francois nodded at a uniformed officer, who hurried over.

"If it's okay with you, Detective, I'd like to ask Ms. Scott a few questions," Kevin said.

Francois made a face. "I'm sure Ms. Scott is exhausted. Maybe it can wait until tomorrow?"

"It's okay," Maggie said. "I'll do whatever I can to help. I can't believe someone stole the Viperé ruby."

"Let's start there. I'm sure you've told Detective Francois already, and Tess of course knows about the ruby from having set up the security, but would you mind telling me about the gem?"

"The Viperé ruby from the Isle Bení," Maggie started, appearing to perk up just a bit. "It's a rare, priceless jewel with a rich, contested history."

"Contested." Kevin looked up from the notes he'd been taking.

"Isle Bení is a small island off the coast of Greece. How exactly the jewel got into the hands of the British government is hotly debated to this day, but somewhere around the turn of the nineteenth century, the ruby went missing only to be 'found'—" Maggie made air quotes "—in the private collection of a British millionaire. I'm going to jump over a ton of history here. Let's just say the ruby changed hands multiple times, ultimately ending up property of the British government but the subject of multiple lawsuits arguing that it was stolen from the Bení people and is rightfully theirs. A number of lawsuits have been pending for years."

"Got it," Kevin said, making notes. The story didn't sound

all that unusual. He knew that a lot of cultural artifacts had contested ownership.

"Beyond the pricelessness of the piece, the ruby is also the subject of a legend," Maggie continued.

A legend. Well, that was interesting.

"Many of the citizens of the island believe that the jewel was the reason their land was prosperous and safe for many centuries before the British discovered it. Since the ruby was discovered in British hands, the island has contended with many of the issues other small islands have had to contend with. A struggling economy. Youth fleeing for greener pastures. Globalization."

"It doesn't seem fair to blame that on a ruby," Detective Francois said. "As you said, many places are dealing with the same issues."

Maggie shrugged. "Fair or not, that's what the legend holds."

"This is great background. Let's jump ahead a few hundred years or so to what happened here tonight," Kevin said with an encouraging smile.

Maggie let out a long, deep breath.

Kevin watched as the tension that had left her shoulders when she'd been talking about the ruby returned.

She crossed her arms over her torso. "I don't know where to start."

"Just start at the beginning," he said soothingly. "I understand you had some kind of party here at the museum tonight."

Maggie nodded. "Yes, a donors' open house. We have them before every big opening. We invite the big donors and those we hope will become big donors, the board, politicians, reporters and anyone else we can think of that could help us with funding and getting the word out about the museum and the work we do."

"How many people would you say were in attendance tonight?"

"Um…a hundred fifty. Maybe a little more. We are constrained by space limitations."

"Okay." Kevin nodded encouragingly. "When did the donors' open house end?"

"The last board member and Mr. Gustev left around nine thirty. The caterers were here for another forty-five minutes."

"But you stayed later? Why?"

A faint smile ticked her lips upward. "I wanted a moment to celebrate my success. The exhibit was my baby. Robert and the board had the ultimate sign-off on the loan of the Viperé ruby from the London Natural History Museum, but I was the one who broached the exchange and shepherded it through the thorny maze of contracts, permits and diplomacy that these kinds of trades require."

Kevin nodded. "That makes sense. So you were here in this room?" He jerked his chin in the direction of the shattered glass around the display case.

"Gallery, we call each of the rooms *galleries*. And yes, I was in the gallery that hosted the exhibit when I heard a thud. I stepped out into the hall to investigate, and a man in black just appeared out of the shadows." A small tremble went through her.

He had a sudden urge to wrap her in his arms.

"It all happened so fast. I know that's a cliché, but it really did happen so fast. The guy hit me, twice I think, maybe three times. I know I lost consciousness but not for too long." Her face scrunched. "At least, I don't think it was too long. The next thing I remember was waking up on the floor here in the hall. It took me a minute to stand without my head spinning, then I made my way to the security office where Carl usually sits. He was on the floor, blood around his head. I grabbed the office phone and called 911."

Kevin scribbled out everything she'd said in his notepad. "Can you describe the man?"

She shook her head, then stopped, wincing. "He was dressed in all black and had a mask over his face. I'm sorry that's all I can tell you."

"But you're sure it was a man?"

"Yes."

That was something, but not much.

"Did you, or maybe Carl, turn off the alarm after everyone left?" Tess said. "Maybe so you could take the jewel out of the case?"

Maggie's forehead furrowed. "Absolutely not. I mean I can't speak for Carl, but I don't know why he would. And I can say for a fact that I didn't turn it off. Why?"

"It looks like someone did," Detective Francois said.

Maggie's big hazel eyes widened even further. "Someone shut off the alarm?"

"Using an administrative code on site," Tess said. "I'd have to talk to Mr. Gustev to find out exactly who the code belonged to."

Maggie's arms tightened around her midsection, and her face blanched. "There's only one code. Mr. Gustev, Kim and I, we all used the same code." Tess's expression darkened. "But I showed Mr. Gustev how to create unique codes for each employee he wanted to have access to the system. That way, we could track who turns it on and off. I showed him how to do it."

"And Kim and I told him that we should all have our own

codes, but he didn't think that was necessary. Said it would mean changing codes every time someone left for a new job and that having more than one code meant there was more chances for a code to get into the wrong hands."

"But it's the exact opposite." Tess's voice rose. "One code makes it all the more likely that someone could get their hands on it!"

Maggie's expression was apologetic, even though it didn't appear she had anything to be sorry about. "I know, but Mr. Gustev has never been very accepting of new technology. We only got the upgraded security system because it was a condition in the loan of the Viperé ruby."

"I'm sorry. Who is Kim?" Kevin interjected.

"Kim Sumika," Detective Francois answered his question.

"The other assistant curator here," Maggie added. "She helped me set up, but she had a terrible migraine come on and had to miss the opening gala."

Detective Francois asked, "Were you, Ms. Sumika and Mr. Gustev the only three with the code to turn off the alarm?"

"And Carl and the day guards." Maggie's chin jerked up. "Wait. You can't possibly think that someone who works here had anything to do with stealing the Viperé ruby?"

No one spoke.

Maggie shook her head vehemently. "That's not possible. None of us would do this. We're like a family here. We've all had thorough background checks, and we've all worked for the Larimer for years."

Kevin had seen too much to discount anything. It was often the people closest that had the greatest power to betray the most.

The expression on Tess's and Detective Francois's faces said they were thinking along the same lines.

"Okay, let's set the alarm aside for now," he said, taking charge of the questioning again. "Was the man carrying anything? A hammer or some sort of baton?"

Maggie shook her head slowly this time, whether it was because she was thinking or to keep from wincing a second time, he wasn't sure. "No, nothing that I could see, but I was startled and terrified. He could have had something with him. I know he hit me with his hand. His fist actually, it is one thing I can remember very clearly."

Kevin's anger flared again. He hoped he found out who this guy was before the cops did. He'd make sure to get a few shots. Any man who hit a woman didn't deserve to be called a man in his book.

Maggie raised a shaky hand to the bandage on her forehead.

"I think that's enough for tonight," Detective Francois said.

Kevin nodded his agreement and closed his notebook. "Maggie, why don't you let me give you a lift home?"

"Thanks, but I have my car."

"You've been through a lot tonight. Let Kevin drive you home," Tess interjected. "If you give me your car keys and address, I'll make sure your car is in your driveway before you wake up tomorrow morning."

Maggie hesitated.

"Really, Maggie. It would be my pleasure to see you home safely." He gave her what he hoped was a reassuring smile. Tess was right. She'd been hit over the head hard enough to black out, and he wanted to make sure she got home safely.

She hesitated for a second longer. "Well, if you're sure. Yes, thank you, I'd love to go home now."

He waited for her to fall into step next to him, staying

on guard in case she needed a hand. Head wounds could be tricky, and the last thing he wanted was for her to get woozy and fall.

Chapter Three

Kevin drove them through the early morning traffic with ease. It was far too early for most commuters to be on the streets, thankfully.

Maggie sat in the passenger seat, her head resting against the side window. She'd answered with a soft "thank you" when Kevin held the passenger door open for her to get into the car but hadn't spoken otherwise. She could tell Kevin had more questions he wanted to ask her, but she was grateful when he didn't push.

It was a struggle to take in oxygen. She knew the Viperé ruby was gone, but she still struggled to process exactly what that meant. For her and for the Larimer.

Her throat constricted even further. Once word got out that the museum had let the priceless jewel be stolen, they'd never get another museum to agree to let them showcase their pieces. Not to mention the donors who would drop them, unwilling to be associated with a museum surrounded by scandal.

She would probably lose her job. Heck, the museum might close altogether.

Her head began to spin. She could feel a panic attack coming on. Great. That was just what she needed. To embarrass herself in front of the security specialist.

Breathe, breathe, she ordered herself. After several minutes, the spinning stopped, and she felt her pulse slowing to a normal speed.

She looked across the car to see if Kevin had noticed her near meltdown. His chiseled chin was still in profile, his dark brown eyes trained straight ahead at the windshield.

"Thank you for driving me home," she said, breaking the silence as they neared her street. "It's kind of you."

"I'm just doing my job."

Just doing his job. He was still painfully clear about where his priorities lay, and it wasn't with her.

"Of course. Your job."

His career was the reason he'd broken up with her in college. Or the career he'd planned on having as a wide receiver in the NFL. Unfortunately, a torn ACL during the preseason had ended his career before it really began. She was embarrassed to remember how she'd harbored a hope that he'd return and somehow they'd find their way back to each other. But he hadn't returned or reached out to her. He'd enlisted in the military. And she'd met and married Ellison, moved on with her life, but she'd never stopped thinking about him.

"I didn't mean it like that. I just meant West Security and Investigations was hired to provide security to the Larimer, and as far as I'm concerned that includes its employees. That's you. I'm sorry we failed you tonight."

They made the rest of the drive in a long awkward silence. Finally, he turned into the long driveway that led to her rental, a former carriage house situated behind Kim's much larger Tudor-style home. He stopped in front of the carriage home and put the car in Park.

He hit his seat belt release. "Let me help you into the house."

She unlatched her own seat belt and waited for Kevin to open the passenger door.

He offered his hand to help her out of the car. The skin-to-skin contact set off fireworks in her. Did he feel it too?

She gave herself a mental shake. It didn't matter. He couldn't have been clearer. Just doing his job. Heck, she'd seen his face when Detective Francois had implied she or someone from the Larimer might be involved in the theft. He wasn't attracted to her. He suspected she was involved in the Viperé's theft.

She pulled her hand back. "I think I've got it."

Kevin shut the car door, and they started for the cottage. "This is a nice place. How'd you find it?"

"Through my friend. Kimberly Sumika." She was moving slowly. Her entire body aching.

He frowned. "The other assistant curator?"

She nodded. "Yes. She owns the big house." She cocked her head toward the Tudor. "I rent the carriage house from her. She and I were friends in grad school, but lost touch after graduation. When Ellison died, she reached out."

Kevin shot a glance across the dark interior of the car. "Ellison. Your husband?"

"Ex-husband. We'd been divorced for a few months when he died. He'd...had some troubles at his job before his death. He had been charged with embezzling five hundred thousand dollars from his accounting firm." She shifted in the passenger seat. It was awkward telling Kevin about Ellison, but she'd rather he heard the story from her.

She cleared her throat and continued. "Even though Ellison was gone, the scandal that swirled around him wasn't. A lot of people in New York thought I was in on the theft or at least knew about it. It was horrible. I lost my job. No museum in New York would hire me. Kim got in touch and told me about an opening at the Larimer, where she worked. She put in a good word for me, and I got the job, so I moved back to California. She really went to bat for me to get the job."

"And she gave you a place to live. Sounds like a good friend." Kevin helped her up the two front steps.

She reached into the front pocket of her purse for her keys. "At a steep discount off market rates. She is a great friend." Worry niggled at her.

After dialing 911, she'd called both Robert and Kim, but Kim hadn't answered her phone. Maggie had left a message for her explaining the break-in. Kim loved the museum as much as she did. Why hadn't she at least returned the call?

She turned to look at the Tudor. The back door stood open.

She grasped his forearm. "Kevin. Something is wrong."

She felt his body tense beside her. He slipped in front of her, pinning her between the front door of the cottage and his large body.

"What is it?"

"Kim's back door is open." She pointed. "She'd never forget to lock her doors."

His body stiffened even more. "You go inside. I'll check it out."

He bounded off the porch stairs and moved like liquid across the lawn and up the Tudor's back porch staircase.

She was exhausted and injured, but there was no way she was going to cower in her house when Kim could need help. She followed Kevin across the backyard and into the Tudor.

The back door opened directly onto the kitchen. The Larimer didn't pay them anywhere near enough to afford a four-bedroom, three-bathroom detached home in the Los Angeles suburbs. Kim had inherited the house from her parents, and the mortgage-free home had allowed her the ability to use her salary to make extensive upgrades. The kitchen was modern, designed so that the appliances blended in with the cabinets.

The interior of the house was dark, and Kevin had disappeared somewhere inside.

Dread twisted in Maggie's stomach. She took a deep breath, attempting to calm her nerves, and made her way down the short hallway from the kitchen to the front of the house.

Kevin met her at the entrance to the living room. "You shouldn't go in there."

"Why? What's wrong? Where is Kim?"

Kevin tried to move her backward, but she skirted around him.

A sob caught in her throat.

Kevin wrapped his arm around her shoulders and turned her away from the living room. But not fast enough.

Kim was slumped on the sofa. She appeared to be asleep, but her skin was ashen and gray. Her eyes stared forward, empty, at nothing.

Kim wasn't asleep.

She was dead.

Chapter Four

Kevin took Maggie back to her cottage and got her settled before returning to the front porch of the Tudor to wait for the authorities. EMTs and officers responded quickly, as did Detective Francois. He pulled up right behind the ambulance although there was no need for anyone to hurry. Kim Sumika was beyond help.

The property around the house had been taped off with yellow crime scene tape, drawing neighbors out of their homes to gawk at the goings-on despite the early hour.

Francois paused on his way into the house only long enough to have Kevin recount how he and Maggie had found Kim's body and to ask him not to go anywhere. That had been thirty minutes ago, and Kevin was itching to go check on Maggie. He was just about to let the heavyset, young, uniformed officer with puffy eyes who manned the door know that he could be found in the cottage at the rear of the property when he heard Francois call out for him to come inside.

Kevin stepped into the house and found the detective standing in the entryway to the living room. The detective was alone in the room, the crime scene technicians having not yet arrived.

Francois turned his gray eyes on Kevin. "You're a former cop."

It wasn't a question, not really. He was sure the detective had checked him, Tess and West Investigations out. "San Jacinto PD. Seven years."

Francois nodded. "Tell me what you see."

Kevin looked at the scene. Kim's body sat on the sofa. She was in her late thirties or early forties and fit. It looked almost as if she'd been settling in for a relaxing night in front of the television. She wore loose-fitting pajama pants, a Clippers T-shirt and slippers that showed off electric blue toenails. An open bottle of wine and a mostly eaten bowl of popcorn sat on the coffee table. The television facing the sofa was off. An ordinary night except for the needle on the carpet at Kim's feet and the belt that was looped around the dead woman's right arm like a tourniquet. On the coffee table in front of the couch were various other indicators of drug use.

"Possible overdose."

Francois's bushy brows made a V over his nose. "Possible?"

Kevin shrugged. "I don't like making assumptions. It looks like an overdose based on the limited information in front of me. The television was off when I found her. You should check to see if it's one of those energy savers that turns itself off after a certain amount of time sitting idle."

Francois smiled slightly and made a note on his phone. "Would you like to take a closer look?" He waved for Kevin to come farther into the room.

He would. He stepped into the living room, careful to stay on the pathway that Francois had already marked off with police tape. The fact that Francois had made sure to delineate a confined pathway for the techs and any other required personnel marked him as a true professional. It was important to make sure that no one muddied the scene more than necessary.

Kevin scanned the room, turning slowly, marking the space on a mental grid and noting anything that seemed out of place or relevant. The first thing he noticed was that the carpet appeared to have been vacuumed recently. As in so recently that there were still lines in the material from the vacuum wheels.

He stepped closer to Kim's body. There were indications of track marks on both her arms, but they appeared to be old and scarred over. She had clearly been a drug user at some point in her life. Had she relapsed? It was possible. Relapse among former drug users was common even after years of sobriety. Many former users didn't realize that starting up with drugs again after years of being clean could have immediate and devastating effects on a body that had already been through so much.

Kevin turned back to Francois. "Can I take a look around the house?"

Francois nodded. "Certainly. We can look together."

They moved as carefully through the rest of the house as they had in the living room. There wasn't much to see. Four bedrooms and two bathrooms upstairs. A den, dining room, bathroom and kitchen on the main floor. The basement was unfinished, and it looked as if Kim used it as a gym and storage space.

No sign of anything amiss or disturbed anywhere except in the living room.

He and Francois stepped back into the foyer just as the crime scene technicians walked through the front door with their equipment.

"You should make sure they get photographs of everything in the living room, including shots of the carpet leading from the doorway to where Kim is sitting," Kevin said to Francois, hoping the detective didn't get piqued and decide he was overstepping.

Francois cocked his head to one side. "Why?"

"Look at it." Kevin, Francois and the crime scene tech turned toward the living room. "Doesn't it strike you as odd?"

"Odd?" Francois said.

"I see what you mean." The tech, a tall, easily six-foot-six, woman with vibrant green hair, nodded excitedly.

"Well, I don't." Francois frowned. "Can someone clue me in?"

"There are vacuum lines in the carpet but no footprint impressions," Kevin answered. "How could she have gotten to the sofa without mussing the vacuum lines or leaving footprints? Why would she even try? It's her house."

"She couldn't have." The tech shifted from foot to foot excitedly. "Someone vacuumed after this woman died. Probably trying to get rid of any evidence he or she might have left." The tech snorted. "As if." She looked to Detective Francois. "Can I get started?"

"Yes, and you heard the man." Francois sighed. "Lots of photos and be careful. This is shaping up to be a homicide."

MAGGIE OPENED THE front door and let Kevin and Detective Francois into her small home. She'd fallen in love with the cottage the moment she'd stepped into the house. The gleaming hardwood floors, soaring ceiling and wall of windows looking out of the back onto a sea of green grass had sold her on the place. Kim had helped her make a fresh start when she'd been convinced her life was over.

And now her friend was gone. Maggie beat back another crying jag. She'd already indulged in a good one while waiting for Kevin and Detective Francois to come for her.

She waved the men to the sofa. "I've made coffee. Can I get either of you a cup?"

"Please." Detective Francois smiled.

"None for me," Kevin answered.

"Still not a coffee drinker, I see." A faint smile crossed her lips. He'd always said it tasted like liquified mud when they were in college.

"Never acquired a taste for it." Kevin smiled back.

It only took a moment to pour two cups of coffee, one for the detective and another for herself. She arranged the cups, a small carafe of cream and a sugar bowl on a tray and carried it into the living room. She settled the coffee on the table beside the sofa and took her cup to the only other seat in the room, a blue easy chair she'd found at the Salvation Army that had still been in good shape. Or at least good enough shape.

Detective Francois took a long sip of coffee.

Maggie held the cup in her hand, staring at the dark liquid inside but not drinking. "Kim is dead." She didn't need confirmation of that. "How?"

"We are very much still in the preliminary stages of the investigation." The detective set the mug aside and pulled out his cell phone. "Can you take me through what happened from the time you and Mr. Lombard left the museum?"

Maggie let out a shuddering breath and began. Kevin remained quiet while she recounted their steps from the museum to finding Kim, but she could tell he'd already gone through the story with Detective Francois.

"Did Ms. Sumika do drugs?" Detective Francois asked.

Maggie jolted at the detective's question. How could he know? She shook her head. "No. Not anymore. She'd been clean for years. A decade."

Francois pinned Maggie in his gaze. "But she used to do drugs."

Maggie hesitated.

"I know you might not want to say something that could paint Kim in a bad light," Kevin said, "but anything you can tell the detective could help to figure out exactly what happened here."

"Kim didn't do drugs." Maggie believed that despite what she'd seen when they'd found her friend's body. "Not anymore. She had a problem when she was an undergraduate. Before we met. She dropped out of college for a while, but she went into rehab, and she was clean by the time we met in grad school, although she was up-front about her addiction."

"I believe you," Kevin said.

She searched his face and found nothing, but he seemed sincere. Unfortunately, she couldn't say the same about Detective Francois's expression. To say he appeared skeptical was an understatement.

"Do you know where or from whom she got her drugs?" Detective Francois asked.

She gritted her teeth. "I don't. I told you that was before we met. I wouldn't have moved in here if I didn't believe that she'd conquered that demon."

Detective Francois stopped typing the note he'd been putting in his phone. "What do you think happened then?"

Maggie stayed silent. That was the question, wasn't it?

She thought Kim had beat her addiction, but relapses among addicts weren't uncommon. She'd been busy planning for the opening and the Viperé exhibit. Maybe she'd missed the signs. Maybe she'd failed her friend. Or maybe there hadn't been any signs because Kim hadn't relapsed. Maybe her overdose wasn't an accident. Maybe it was murder. But that was just too hard to comprehend.

"I don't know." It wasn't satisfactory for anyone, but it was the only answer she could give the detective.

"We'll have to wait for the medical examiner's report to be sure, but the scene has all the signs of an overdose, and at the moment, we are proceeding as if it is such. We will of course explore every avenue and go wherever the evidence takes us," Detective Francois said.

He moved on. "Did Ms. Sumika do her own housework?"

The sudden change in subject threw Maggie. "Housework?"

"Yes, you know." The detective waved the phone as he spoke. "Laundry. Cooking. Doing the dishes. Cleaning. Vacuuming."

She had no idea why that information would be relevant to Kim's death but wanted to do anything she could to help the detective. "No. She had a service come in twice a week."

"Huh. Sounds expensive," Francois remarked. "I don't expect that she would have made the kind of money to afford the house, a twice-a-week cleaning service, and I saw a very nice Audi Sport in the garage."

Maggie let out a frustrated breath. Kim shouldn't be the one on trial. She was a victim. "Kim came from money. The house was her childhood home. She inherited it when her parents died a couple years ago within months of each other. A real love story."

Maggie had been almost as devastated as Kim when, first, Kim's mother had passed then, two months later, her father, both from heart attacks, although Kim believed her father's had been brought on from the devastating loss of his soulmate.

"Ah, well that makes sense then."

Kevin cleared his throat, drawing the attention in the room to him. "Was Kim right-or left-handed?"

"Oh…" Another question out of left field. "She was right-handed. Why?"

The men shared a look, but neither answered her.

That wasn't going to do for her. She stood. "Look, I want to help. I want to know what happened to Kim, and if someone…" She swallowed the sob that bubbled in her throat. "And if someone hurt her, I want them brought to justice more than anyone. I can help you."

Both men stood.

"You are helping," Detective Francois said. "By answering my questions."

She shot a glance at Kevin and then back at Francois. "You're letting him into the investigation. Why not me?"

"Mr. Lombard is a former police officer and trained security specialist."

And Kevin wasn't a suspect in a major jewel theft. The detective didn't say that, but Maggie had no problem hearing it in the silence that fell. She had a feeling she was going to get good at hearing the things Francois didn't say.

Detective Francois tucked his phone into his suit pocket. "It's been a long night. We'll go and let you get some sleep, but I'll likely have more questions for you in the coming days. About the theft and Ms. Sumika."

She crossed her arms over her torso and followed the men to the front door.

Detective Francois stepped into the night, headed to the Tudor without a glance back.

Kevin stopped on her small front stoop. "Hey, he's right about one thing. You've been through more than any one person should have to deal with in one night. Try to get some rest. Maybe call a friend to come stay with you."

Maggie shook her head and finally let the tears she'd been holding back fall. She met his gaze, surprised to find sympathy there. "Rest isn't what's going to help me get through this. Helping to find Kim's killer will."

Chapter Five

Kevin arrived at police headquarters just after ten the next morning. Tess had set up a status meeting for them with Detective Francois. His boss had been busy in the hours since he'd seen her last. The Larimer Museum's insurance company had agreed to employ West Investigations to find the Viperé jewel, although Tess had stressed that the working relationship was tenuous. West's reputation had taken a hit with the theft, but they had a longstanding relationship with this particular insurance company, and that had gone a long way in convincing them to allow West to take the first crack at the case.

The Los Angeles Police Department had also agreed to let West work with them. They had more than enough to deal with without adding a jewel heist to their ever-growing list of investigations. They'd still take the lead with respect to Kim Sumika's possible homicide, but Kevin would work with Detective Francois on the jewel theft and have full access to the detective. Kevin was surprised Tess had been able to pull off such access, and she'd admitted that his prior experience as a police officer had helped her convince the powers that be in the LAPD to let him help. Despite the show of faith from the insurance company and the police departments, both he and Tess knew that the reputation of West's new West Coast office was on the line.

He gave his name to the young officer who sidled up to the bulletproof glass separating the clerk's desk from the public. After showing his identification and going through the metal detectors, he took a precarious ride on a rickety elevator to the fourth floor.

The elevator doors opened onto a depressingly gray hallway where Detective Francois and Tess waited.

"Sorry. Am I late?" Kevin said, stepping out of the elevator.

"Not at all," Detective Francois answered. He held a black leather folio in one hand. "Tess was on her way up when I got the call that you were right behind her, so we figured we'd just wait and take the walk to the conference room together."

Detective Francois started off down the hallway. Kevin and Tess followed closely behind. The detective waved them into a small conference room at the end of the hall. He offered water and coffee, which Kevin and Tess declined. They settled in around the conference table, Francois pulling out his phone while Tess pulled out a tablet. Kevin went old school with his trusty lined notebook.

"The lab is still running tests on the evidence collected from the Sumika scene, but the medical examiner was able to give me a preliminary time of death, 10:04 p.m."

Tess wore a questioning expression. "That's unusually specific for a time of death."

Francois read from his phone. "We lucked out there. Ms. Sumika's watch was also one of those heartbeat, pulse thingies. We were able to get the exact time her pulse and heartbeat went to zero."

"Lucky for us. Not so lucky for Kim Sumika," Tess said.

Kevin noted the timing. "That is about forty minutes before Maggie Scott and the guard at the Larimer were attacked."

Francois nodded. "Give or take."

Tess's gaze bounced between the two men. "Just so we are all on the same page, everyone here is suspicious of the timing of the theft and Ms. Sumika's death. I mean, I know we don't have a definitive ruling of homicide—"

"Yet—" Kevin said because he wasn't just suspicious. He'd thought about it all last night, and it was too convenient to believe that the assistant curator just happened to overdose on the very night a priceless jewel was stolen from the museum where she worked.

"It's hard to believe they are unrelated," Tess continued.

Francois shifted in his chair. "It seemed unlikely, but we have to keep an open mind and explore all possibilities."

"Of course," Tess said without conviction.

"I pulled background and credit checks on Kimberly Sumika, Maggie Scott, Carl Downy and Robert Gustev." Francois pulled several sheets of paper from his folio and slid them across the table to Tess and Kevin.

"Did you go home at all last night?" Tess joked.

"No," Francois answered seriously.

The detective was dedicated. Kevin respected that.

"Scott, Downy and Gustev all look clean, but Sumika has run up quite a bit of debt."

Kevin flipped to Kim's financials. Francois wasn't joking about the amount of debt. Nearly three hundred fifty thousand dollars' worth.

"Maggie said that Kim had an inheritance from her parents. How did she get into so much debt?" Kevin asked.

"It looks like the inheritance was limited to the house,

which to be fair, in this market isn't paltry," Tess said, reading through the packet Francois had given them.

She cocked her head to the side, thinking. "But a house isn't liquid. Getting cash out would require taking a mortgage or selling."

"Exactly." Francois nodded. "It looks like Sumika maxed out her credit cards and a home equity line of credit."

Kevin frowned. That didn't make sense. "The house is worth a lot, but Kim didn't make the kind of money to pay that loan back. But why did she need that much money in the first place?"

Francois pointed a finger. "That's the three-hundred-fifty-thousand-dollar question."

"Maggie might know the answer," Kevin offered.

His thoughts had strayed to Maggie more than once during the night. She really should have gone to the hospital to have her head wound checked out. If she had a concussion, they could be tricky, and it didn't seem as if she had anyone to check up on her. His thoughts hadn't been exclusive to her health. He'd also wondered if she could have had anything to do with the theft of the Viperé ruby. At least, she couldn't have been involved with Sumika's death, not directly anyway. The time of death made that impossible.

"I plan on questioning her again today. Maybe she'll remember something helpful," Francois said.

"Do we think that Ms. Scott or the guard had a hand in the theft?" Tess asked.

Even though he'd been entertaining the idea himself, the knowledge that Tess and Detective Francois might also be considering it didn't sit well in Kevin's gut.

"I mean, we have to consider it," Tess added, though she couldn't have known how he was feeling.

"I'm definitely considering it." Francois frowned. "Ms. Scott's financials don't throw up any flags, but I find it strange that she works with and lives on the same property as our victim. Not to mention she also knew the code for the security system and knows how valuable the Viperé ruby is."

Tess propped her tablet up. "I downloaded the security footage from our server. We can see what happened up until the time the cameras were shut off."

Tess cued up the video, and the screen sprang to life. They watched Maggie enter the empty gallery and have a drink in front of the Viperé ruby. After a couple of minutes, she suddenly jerked as if something startled her then walked toward the hallway. The screen went black after that.

"Any footage of the guard's attack?" Francois asked.

Tess shook her head. "No cameras in the area where the security office is. None of the other cameras picked up anything or appeared to have been tampered with."

"So someone gets into the museum without being seen—"

"That might not have been difficult. The intruder could have come in during the donors' open house and hidden himself or herself until the party was over."

"It's as good a theory as any," Francois concurred. "But the intruder had to know that there weren't cameras in the hall leading to the security office and to hide there."

Kevin frowned. "If you're thinking about Maggie Scott, the timing doesn't work. The video we do have clearly shows her in the gallery with the ruby when the camera shuts off."

Francois's shoulders rose then fell. "Maybe she figured out a way to shut the camera off remotely. Or maybe she had help."

"Kim Sumika." Tess said what Francois had left unspoken.

Francois's shoulder went up and down again.

A protective instinct flared in Kevin's chest. That would not do. Francois was right to explore the possibility that Maggie Scott had something to do with the theft. The detective wouldn't be doing his job if he didn't. And neither would he if he ignored the possibility because he had a misplaced attraction to the pretty assistant curator.

"Maggie and Kim working together doesn't get around the timing issue," Kevin said, hoping his voice sounded nothing but professional. "Maggie couldn't have killed Kim, and if Kim was somehow involved with the theft, where is the ruby?"

"There could be a third player," Tess offered. "In fact, there is likely at least one other person involved whether or not Maggie Scott or Kim Sumika was. Whoever stole the ruby would need a fence to sell it."

"Maggie Scott probably knows a lot of people in the antiquities world, including dealers." Francois rubbed his chin.

"Everyone involved in this case probably knows art dealers. They are all involved in the art world," Kevin growled.

"Point taken." If Francois noticed the tone in his voice, he kept it to himself. "Still, I think that reaching out to the local dealers is a good idea."

"Me too," Tess said.

"Agreed," Kevin rumbled. "We also have to consider that the jewel wasn't stolen in order to be sold."

Francois tapped his phone screen. "That someone stole it because of the legend and dispute surrounding it."

"Exactly," Kevin said. "I did a little research of my own last night after leaving Maggie Scott's place, and there are very passionate groups on both sides of the issue. The government of Isle Bení has been in litigation with the British government for decades arguing that the jewel should be returned to the people of the island. So far, they've been unsuccessful."

"Someone could have gotten tired of waiting and decided to take matters into their own hands." Tess spun the tablet around and closed its cover. "But it's not as if they could just give the ruby back to the Bení government."

"No," Kevin agreed, "but it wouldn't stop them from returning the jewel to the island. The general public might not know it was there, but if the thief is a true believer, they may not care. The ruby being back on the island may be the goal, not public acknowledgment that it is there."

"So, we have two possible theories right now," Francois summed up. "One, the ruby could have been stolen to sell it."

"Or two," Tess picked up the detective's line of thought, "it could have been stolen by someone who believes in the legend and wants to return it to what they believe is its proper place on the island."

"We still have more questions than answers," Kevin said, looking from Francois to Tess, "but one thing that seems to be clear is that Maggie Scott is in the middle of whatever this thing is."

Chapter Six

The next day dawned bright and clear, and if she didn't look out of the cottage's front windows, Maggie could pretend that it was just another ordinary day. But when she inevitably did look, she could see the yellow crime scene tape still strung around the perimeter of Kim's Tudor, and the events of the night before washed out any fantasy she might have had.

The Viperé ruby was still missing, and Kim was dead. And she was a suspect in both crimes if she'd read Detective Francois and Kevin correctly.

That was more than enough to make anyone want to hide in bed indefinitely, but she couldn't. She wasn't sure whether the police would allow them back into the Larimer so soon, but Colin Rycroft, director of the London Natural History Museum, the museum that had loaned the Viperé ruby to the Larimer, would be in town that afternoon for a private tour of the exhibit. She hadn't spoken to Mr. Gustev since the night before, but surely he would have notified Rycroft and the London Natural History Museum of the theft by now.

She had switched on the television as soon as she'd awoken that morning, and there'd been a short segment on the break-in, although thankfully no mention of exactly what had been stolen. Rycroft was sure to be apoplectic about the missing Viperé, and the Larimer's reputation in the community would be ruined. They might never convince another museum to agree to an exchange again.

She'd just finished showering and dressing when her phone rang. Boyd Scott's gruff, smiling face filled the screen.

It had been several weeks since she'd spoken to her father. She knew her father loved her. He'd been a single parent since his beloved wife, her mother, died when she was ten. It had been a crushing blow to father and daughter. Boyd had dealt with losing his wife by entering into a series of short-term, ill-fated marriages that had led to them moving around the country a lot. In her sophomore year of high school, they'd moved to Los Angeles, Boyd's sixth wife's hometown. The marriage was over by the start of her senior year, but she convinced her father to stick it out in the city until she graduated. He'd made it a whole week after her graduation before taking off. These days, her father generally only called when he needed something from her, usually money. Her father's itinerant lifestyle hadn't exactly laid the foundation for a stable, well-funded retirement.

But she couldn't help hoping that this time was different. That her father had heard about the robbery at the Larimer and that he was calling now for no other reason than to make sure his only daughter was safe.

She answered the call.

"Hi, sweetheart," her father said cheerfully. "How's my favorite girl?"

"Tired. I didn't get much sleep last night, and today isn't likely to be any better."

"Oh?" A note of surprise sounded in her father's voice. "That's too bad. It's important to get the proper amount of sleep."

So this call wasn't to check on her. Her father had no idea about her assault at the Larimer or the stolen ruby.

She sighed. "I do my best, Dad. So what can I do for you?"

"Nothing. Why do you always assume I'm calling you for something? Can't a father call his daughter just to check in on her?"

A father could, but her father didn't. But she kept that thought to herself. She was in no mood for an argument.

"Sorry, Dad. Like I said, I didn't get a lot of sleep."

"It's okay, sweetie. I won't keep you. I did have a little favor I wanted to ask you."

And there it was.

She loved her father. She really did. She wouldn't say her childhood was stable or financially secure, but she'd never worried about having a roof over her head or food on the table. Her father had always been there for her, helping her with homework, showing up at every performance the semester she was in the school play, and coming home every night even when she might have wished he'd pull an extra shift or two just to have a bit of savings in the bank.

But that was just it. Boyd Scott didn't believe in saving. "You can't take it with you" was his favorite saying. And to her father that saying was a license to spend, spend, spend. He spent money as fast as he made it, which often led to the need to borrow money from his daughter in order to deal with those pesky obligations like rent, electricity and car insurance, to name a few bills she'd forked over money to cover in the last year. She knew she should refuse. As long as her father knew she'd be there as a safety net, he'd never get his own financial house in order, but it was hard to say no to Boyd Scott. As evidenced by his six wives.

"How much do you need?" she asked, resigned to their respective roles in this scene.

"Nothing," he said with a touch of indignation in his voice that almost made her laugh. "I don't need any money." He took a pregnant pause. "I got engaged."

Maggie sat down hard in the chair at her kitchen table. She'd figured her father's days of getting hitched were over. It had been sixteen years since his divorce from wife number six, and while he'd had a few serious-for-him relationships since then, they hadn't ended in marriage. She knew it was immature; her father was only fifty-nine, hardly an old man, but...*ewww.*

She stifled her first reaction and instead said, "Engaged?"

"I know it's a shock. It was a surprise to me too. Well, not a surprise, I've been seeing Julie for nine months now."

She vaguely remembered her father mentioning a girlfriend in one of their prior calls, but honestly, she'd stopped attempting to remember his girlfriends' names long ago. *Julie.* It didn't ring a bell.

"We took a weekend getaway to Vegas, and one thing led to another, bing bang boom, I'm going to be a married man. Again."

Again.

"I..." Maggie wasn't sure what to say. Her father married again on top of everything else was too much to process, so her mind just didn't. "Congratulations, Dad."

"Thanks, baby. Now about that favor I mentioned. I want you and Julie to meet."

"Dad, now is not a good time. I..."

"Maggie, it doesn't have to be today, but soon. I want my two best girls to get to know each other. I know you and Julie are going to love each other. As much as I love you both."

The doorbell rang, saving her from having to come up with an answer right away.

"Dad, there's someone at my door. I'll call you back."

"Okay." She noted the hint of disappointment in her father's voice, guilt flooding through her. "Hey, sweetie. I love you."

"I love you too, Dad. I'll call soon, and we'll set something up."

She ended the call and went to the door.

Lisa stood on the stoop with a to-go cup in each hand. "Open up!"

Maggie swung the door open. "What are you doing here?"

Lisa pushed her way into the house and threw her arms around Maggie, careful not to spill as she did. "What am I doing here?" she said, pulling back. "I wake up to a text that says, 'Theft at the museum. I'm banged up but fine. Call you later,' and you think I'm not going to come and check on you? What kind of bestie do you think I am?"

Maggie grinned. "You are the best bestie there is."

She and Lisa had met not long after Lisa moved to Los Angeles at an event at the Getty. Maggie had never found it particularly easy to make friends, especially as she'd gotten older, but Lisa Eberhard was a force to be reckoned with. She'd been admiring the painting *Portrait of a Woman* when Lisa had walked up and begun rattling off the history of the painting and the Dutch artist who'd painted it, Jan Mytens. She'd learned that Lisa was a writer, a ghostwriter to be exact, and that she had the same love and appreciation of art that Maggie recognized in herself. She'd walked the rest of the exhibit with Lisa then they'd gone for coffee. It had been an instant connection, and they'd been friends ever since.

"Damned straight." Lisa thrust one of the to-go cups at Maggie. "Dark roast. Figured you'd need strong stuff today."

Maggie took the cup and sipped. "You figured right."

"What's with the caution tape around Kim's house? Is she doing renovations again?" Lisa asked, settled in on the sofa in her usual spot.

Maggie sat. Kim and Lisa were cordial, but they'd never really taken a liking to each other. Still, it hadn't seemed right to mention Kim's death in the text she'd sent to Lisa last night. She'd planned to call her friend and catch her up on everything that had happened later that day.

"Lisa, Kim overdosed last night. She's…gone."

Lisa sat stunned for a moment. "Overdosed? But I thought she'd kicked her habit a long time ago."

"I don't know what happened." She felt tears welling in her eyes.

"Oh, honey." Lisa set her cup on the coffee table and scooted forward on the sofa so she could wrap Maggie in a hug. "I'm so sorry."

Maggie let herself cry on her friend's shoulder for a minute before straightening. "It doesn't make any sense. Kim was clean. I know she was. This whole thing, the theft, Kim's death, it's like the world has gone crazy. None of it makes sense."

Lisa studied Maggie while she sipped her coffee. "Maggie, are you really okay? You know you can come and stay with me for a while. Or I can stay with you."

"I love you for offering, but we're going to be all hands on deck at the museum dealing with the fallout of the theft and Kim's death."

"You can't possibly be thinking about going into work today?"

"I have to. At least, if the museum is open. The director

of the museum who loaned us the Viperé is scheduled for a private walk-through of the exhibit."

Lisa made a face. "Yikes."

"Exactly. I'd planned to call Mr. Gustev at nine thirty to find out what he wanted to do."

"If you are going to work, what are you planning to do with that black eye?"

Maggie touched two fingers to her eye. It was still tender. "I tried to cover it."

Lisa made another face. "You did not succeed."

"It looks worse than it is."

"It looks pretty bad."

It did. She'd tried to cover the worst of it with makeup, but that had only seemed to make the purplish bruise stand out more.

Lisa stood abruptly. Everything Lisa did had an abrupt quality about it. She was one of those people who vibrated with energy even when she was standing still. "Where's your makeup kit? I'll see what I can do with it."

Maggie did all right with her day-to-day makeup, but Lisa was a wiz at makeup. She had the patience for layering, blending and whatever else professional makeup artists did that made a face full of products look barely there.

She followed her friend into the bathroom and sat down on the closed toilet seat while Lisa rifled around in her makeup bag, lamenting the slim pickings.

"Ah-ha." Lisa turned with concealer in one hand and foundation in the other. "Now tell me all about last night."

Maggie did as Lisa asked while she did her best to cover her black eye. As a ghostwriter, Lisa had penned books for a handful of celebrities as well as a few politicians. She was good at what she did, and one of the many skills she'd developed from working with recalcitrant rich people was a knack for interrogation without seeming to be prying. By the time she'd finished covering the worst of the shiner, she'd pulled the whole story, detail by excruciating detail, from Maggie. By the end of the tale, though, Maggie felt marginally better.

"Ta-da." Lisa pulled Maggie to her feet and over to the bathroom mirror.

She could see a dark ring around her eye, but it looked more like she'd had a rough night and less like she'd been in a cage match.

"Thank you."

The doorbell rang.

Lisa's brow arched. "Expecting someone?"

She wasn't. She and Lisa walked to the front door together. Maggie looked out the peephole while Lisa went to the front widow and pulled back the curtain.

Kevin Lombard stood on the front stoop, a to-go cup and white paper bag in one hand.

Lisa let the curtain drop and shot her friend a crooked grin. "Girlfriend, have you been holding out on me?"

MAGGIE OPENED THE door to Kevin. "What are you doing here?"

He held up the coffee and bag. "I came to check on you. And I brought breakfast. Can I come in?"

Maggie hesitated for a moment before moving aside to let him cross the threshold.

Lisa cleared her throat, still standing by the window. Kevin spun in her direction.

"Hello, I'm Lisa, Maggie's best friend. And you are?"

Kevin quirked a brow. "Kevin Lombard."

"He's the security expert I told you about. With the firm that provides security for the Viperé ruby."

Lisa tsked. "You guys are in a spot of trouble then." She ambled to the sofa and slung her purse over her shoulder. "I have to go. I have a meeting with a prospective client that I can't reschedule, but if you need me to, I can come back this evening. Stay the night. We can have an old-fashioned sleepover."

Maggie wrapped her arms around her friend and pulled her into a tight hug. "I'll be fine. I'll call you tonight."

"You better," Lisa said, stepping back and heading for the door. "Bye, Kevin Lombard."

"I'm glad to see you asked a friend to stay with you," Kevin said after the door closed behind Lisa.

"I didn't actually call." Maggie turned and walked to her small kitchen, sitting at the table. "Lisa just showed up."

"The sign of a true friend," Kevin said, sitting across the table from her. He slid the coffee and bag to her. "It's a blueberry muffin. I don't know what you like, but who doesn't like blueberry muffins?"

"Thank you." She pushed the coffee to the side, it was too soon for a second cup, but she did like blueberry muffins. She pulled the muffin from the bag. "You didn't get yourself anything."

"I had a muffin on my way here."

"So—" she swiped her hands together, dusting off crumbs "—why are you here?"

"I have a few more questions I'm hoping you can answer."

"Why isn't Detective Francois asking the questions?"

Kevin frowned. "The LAPD has agreed to allow West Investigations to work with them on this case. Specifically, looking into the jewel theft. Detective Francois has enough on his plate looking into your friend's death."

Despite feeling more exhausted than she'd ever been in her life, she'd barely slept all night, thinking about the ruby and Kim. The two situations had to be connected. Had the thieves killed Kim? But if so, why?

"I can call Detective Francois if you'd be more comfortable speaking to him?" Kevin said, pulling her attention back to the present.

"No, it's fine. What did you want to ask me?"

"I'm sure Detective Francois asked you this last night, but can you think of anyone who had a grudge against the Larimer or anyone who took an unusual interest in the ruby?"

"Actually, Detective Francois did ask me that question already, but I was in such a daze last night—"

"Shock," he offered. "You'd just been through a scary and traumatizing experience."

She hugged her arms around her middle. "That's for sure. I told Detective Francois that I couldn't think of anyone who'd steal the ruby, but that's not true. At least, I don't think they would go so far as to steal the ruby, but…"

Kevin pulled a small notebook from his pocket. "Who are they?"

"The Art and Antiquities Repatriation Project."

Kevin laughed. "AARP? Really?"

Maggie held her hands up, palms out, a smile tipping her lips. "Hey, I didn't name the group. They're a non-profit that works to return art and other cultural artifacts back to their countries of origin."

"And they had a problem with the Larimer Museum?"

She nodded. "They have a problem with a lot of museums. They were upset that we were hosting the Viperé exhibit.

They staged a protest outside the museum a few weeks ago. But, like I said, they're a passionate group but reputable. I don't think they'd break the law. At least, not this way."

Kevin jotted something in his notebook. "You never know how far people will go if they feel they don't have any other choice. I'll check them out. Let's change focus for a moment. Assume that the thief doesn't want to repatriate the ruby but wants to sell it instead. How would they go about doing that?"

Maggie shook her head. "That wouldn't be easy. You can't just take a well-known, stolen gem to a pawnshop and trade it in for cash."

"Of course not, but these things can be sold on the black market. We both know that."

"Are you asking me if I know any shady antiquities dealers who'd be willing to offload the Viperé ruby on the black market?"

"I'm sure you and the Larimer only do business with reputable dealers, but you are in this industry. At this point, any lead would be helpful. Rumor. Speculation. Can you think of anyone who'd be willing to resort to theft to get the ruby?"

She shook her head again. "That might be a better question for Colin Rycroft."

She watched Kevin write the name in his notebook. "Colin Rycroft. Who is he?"

"He's the director of the London Natural History Museum. They loaned the ruby to the Larimer for the exhibit. Mr. Rycroft will be in town this afternoon. I can ask him if he'd be willing to speak with you."

Although, she was sure Colin Rycroft would be in no mood to do her or anyone affiliated with the Larimer any favors. But maybe in the interest of getting the Viperé back quickly, he'd agree to speak to Kevin. He'd almost certainly have to speak to Detective Francois.

"That would be helpful. Back to the dealers."

Maggie held up a hand. "I don't know any dealers who would risk their reputations, not to mention a lengthy jail sentence, to fence the ruby, but I will ask around. Maybe someone has heard something."

"Thank you again. You mentioned that the ruby is the subject of several lawsuits over ownership. Have any of the parties involved in the lawsuits contacted you? Maybe someone was upset enough about the exhibit to go to extremes."

"We had a few emails and phone calls from people expressing disagreement with the museum's decision to feature the ruby in an exhibit given the disputes over provenance and expatriation."

"Did you keep a list of those names?"

She shook her head. "I didn't, but I could probably generate one."

"That would be very helpful."

Maggie chewed her bottom lip. "Can I ask you something?"

"Sure."

"Why were you and Detective Francois asking all those questions about Kim's cleaning habits and whether she was right-or left-handed?"

Kevin hesitated.

"Kim was my friend," Maggie pressed. "I deserve answers."

"There are some indications that Ms. Sumika may not have voluntarily overdosed."

Her mouth went dry. "Are you saying Kim was—"

"I'm not saying anything other than that Detective

Francois's investigation is ongoing and he's investigating all possibilities."

She wasn't sure what to do with the information he'd just dropped on her. It was clear that he and Detective Francois at least suspected Kim's death might not be an accidental overdose, but if it wasn't... She wasn't sure she could deal with that blow on top of everything else.

Maggie balled up the now empty muffin wrapper. "Is there anything else?"

She still needed to call her boss and find out if going into the museum was possible, but Kevin didn't need to know that.

"Just one more thing," he said, looking up from his notebook. "Detective Francois pulled Ms. Sumika's finances, and it appears that she was in serious debt."

"No." He had to be wrong. "Kim never mentioned anything about being in debt. Her parents passed, so I don't know the particulars about her inheritance, but I got the feeling her parents left her a substantial amount."

"It appears she inherited the house free and clear, but there was very little money. She took out a mortgage on the house, and combined with her credit card debt, she owed more than three hundred thousand dollars."

"Three hundred—" she sputtered "—thousand?"

"It looks that way. You don't have any idea what the money was for or where it went?"

She had an idea of where the money could have gone, but it was just speculation, and she wasn't sure she wanted to share it with him, not yet at least. "She did some renovations to the house."

Kevin's eyes narrowed on her. He was shrewd. A former cop? She could see him in a uniform. Warmth flowed through her. Even with everything that had happened the night before, it hadn't escaped her notice how attractive he was. His penetrating dark gaze, athletic body and full beard was hard not to notice.

"Maggie," Kevin said, pulling her from her thoughts of him. "Holding back is only going to make it that much more difficult to find the ruby."

And possibly Kim's killer, although Kevin stopped short of saying that. But she was sure he didn't believe the ruby's theft and Kim's death were unconnected.

She sighed, reluctant to share her friend's confidences with Kevin if it would help them find Kim's killer. "Kim had a problem with gambling."

. "Gambling."

"Kim was a good woman, but everyone has their troubles. Kim had an addictive personality. She kicked the drugs, but she replaced that habit with online gambling." Maggie rose, gathering the trash from the breakfast Kevin had bought her and tossing it into the trash can. Even though Kim was gone, it felt too much like she was betraying her friend.

"It started off small, just some online stuff." She leaned against the kitchen counter, wrapping her arms around herself. "I know Kim's parents helped her pay off an earlier debt about a year before they passed away. I had no idea she'd fallen back into that vice again."

It seemed there was a lot she didn't know about Kim even though they'd been living only footsteps apart for the last two years. How had she been so blind? Guilt swam in her chest. She hadn't been a good friend.

Kevin's pen scratched over the paper. "Three hundred thousand is a lot to spend online. Did she gamble anywhere else?"

She felt her face twist into a scowl. "She had a bookie. I haven't seen him around in years, so I don't know if they still communicated but…"

"It's a place to start. Do you remember the bookie's name?"

Maggie pushed away from the counter and stepped back to the table. "I do."

Kevin's eyebrow quirked up. "Will you share it with me?"

She shook her head. "No." She owed Kim more than that. She'd been her friend, and when she'd needed her, Maggie had failed her. She wanted to have a hand in bringing the person who'd hurt Kim to justice.

"No?"

"No, I won't tell you Kim's bookie's name, but I will take you to him."

Chapter Seven

Kevin did his best to get Maggie to let him talk to Kim's bookie on his own, but she wouldn't budge. He'd finally given in, and now he was following the directions barked out by his GPS system to the address Maggie had given him. At least the address was in the NoHo Arts District, a North Hollywood neighborhood, and not in a seedier area of town where Kevin would have assumed a bookie would reside.

Maggie called her boss as he drove them across town. The call wasn't on speaker phone, but he could hear both sides of the conversation easily. The police were planning to release the crime scene at noon, and although the museum wouldn't open to the public for at least several more days, Robert Gustev wanted to meet with the staff that afternoon. Colin Rycroft's tour of the exhibit was still on. Apparently, the director of the museum that lent the Viperé ruby to the Larimer was insisting on seeing the scene of the crime with his own eyes.

Miraculously, he found a parking spot on the street a half a block from the address Maggie had given him just as she ended her call.

This area of Los Angeles had undergone a renaissance in the last couple of decades. New shops and businesses had sprung up almost as fast as the rehabbed condos and apartments that had been bought and rented by hip millennials and Gen Zers.

Maggie strode ahead of him on the sidewalk, reaching for the door of a redbrick building in the middle of the block of buildings that housed various shops and businesses.

Kevin pulled up short. "Are you sure this is the right place?"

The sign above the door Maggie reached for read The Cupcake Bar.

She shot a grin at him over her shoulder. "Trust me. This is it."

He followed her through the doors. It was obvious that at some point this place had actually been a bar. The space was a mixture of light and dark: wide pine plank floors, dark red exposed brick walls and a long oak bar that ran the length of one side. The front of the bar had been retrofitted into a glass-fronted display case for the cupcakes inside. Behind the bar was a mirrored wall, but instead of the expected shelves of various and sundry liquors, the shelves were also lined with cupcakes.

The shop was empty, but the bell tinkling as they walked in brought a man in a pink apron with Cupcake Bar emblazoned on it through the swinging doors behind the bar.

"Good morning. Welcome to the Cupcake Bar. How may I help—" The clerk's gaze moved from Kevin to Maggie. "Oh, Maggie, it's you."

"Anthony, we need to talk to you," Maggie said.

Anthony's eyes moved back to Kevin, sliding over him appraisingly. "Who is *we*?"

Kevin stuck his hand out. "Kevin Lombard. My firm has

been hired to provide security at the Larimer Museum. Maggie and I have a few questions for you about Kim Sumika."

Anthony gave his hand a brief shake and sighed. "Maggie, you know I can't talk to you about my business with Kim."

"Anthony, Kim is dead."

Anthony's eyes went wide, and his mouth fell open. "What? How?"

"She was found last night, or this morning I guess. It looks like she accidentally overdosed, but—" Maggie shot a questioning glance at Kevin, her eyes asking how much she could tell Anthony.

He should have briefed her on what to say and not to say before they'd entered. Interviewing a witness could be a tricky business. Asking the right questions but doing so without leading the person in any particular direction was a learned skill. It was too late now.

He jumped into the conversation before Maggie said too much. "The police are still investigating. Maggie says you and Kim were...friends. We were wondering if you'd seen any signs that she was using again?"

Anthony looked confused. "If you work security for the Larimer, why are you asking me questions about Kim's death?"

"Because the Larimer was also robbed yesterday," Maggie answered.

"Damn." Anthony walked around the bar to one of the tables and sat.

Kevin and Maggie took seats across from him.

"A very precious ruby was stolen, and a guard and I were attacked," Maggie continued.

"Damn. I'm sorry to hear that. So you think Kim's death

is connected to the theft? It would be quite a coincidence if it wasn't, I guess." Anthony answered his own question.

"As I said, the police are exploring every possibility. My firm, West Investigations, is helping with the investigation into the theft," Kevin said. "So, about Kim's possible drug use."

Anthony gave a wan smile. "If Maggie brought you here, I'm sure she would have told you about my relationship with Kim. We weren't friends, not in the traditional sense."

"She told me you are Kim's bookie."

Anthony's shoulders went back, and he stayed silent.

"Okay." Kevin held up his hand. "During your nontraditional friendship, did you notice any signs that Kim might be using again?"

Anthony cocked his head to the side and thought for a moment. "I can't say I did, but I only saw Kim for short stretches of time. She'd come in, grab a cupcake, maybe a little something else—" he looked away guiltily "—and leave."

Kevin sighed. The whole baker-bookie thing was cute, an innovative way to stay under the radar, but he was investigating a theft and possible murder. He didn't have time for cuteness. "Look, man. I'm not a cop. I don't care about your bookmaking business unless it led to Kim Sumika's death. I just want some answers."

Anthony's expression hardened.

Maggie reached across the table for the clerk's hand. "Anthony, I know we haven't always seen eye to eye. I don't like your side hustle. I don't like what it did to Kim, but this is bigger than all that. There's a chance…" She shot a glance at Kevin, and he gave a slight nod. Sometimes giving a little led to getting a lot. He suspected this was one of those times. "A good chance Kim didn't accidentally overdose. That someone set it up to look like she did."

Anthony pulled his hand from Maggie's grasp, his expression incredulous. "You can't possibly be suggesting it was me?"

"Was it?" Kevin pressed.

"No. Of course not!"

Maggie straightened in her seat. "Kim was in a lot of debt."

"She'd been placing a lot of bets lately that didn't pan out, sure, but I wouldn't kill anyone over that. Most of my clients aren't good gamblers. It's how I stay in business."

"People have been killed for a lot less than three hundred thousand dollars."

"What?" Anthony stood so quickly his chair fell over backward. "Three hundred thousand. Uh, uh. No way. Kim didn't owe me anywhere near that amount of money."

"Sit," Kevin directed. He waited for Anthony to right his chair and reclaim his seat. "How much did she owe you?"

"A couple thousand. Look around, man. You think I'd be slinging cupcakes if I had three hundred thousand dollars to front one person? I'd be in Tahiti or something."

Kevin believed him. Three hundred thousand was a lot of cupcakes. "Do you have any idea why Kim would be in that kind of debt?"

Anthony's eyes darted to the ceiling.

"Anthony, please," Maggie said.

Anthony sighed. "I'm small-time, okay? I did the bookmaking thing to earn enough money to open the shop, and I continued taking bets from a select number of clients after I opened, but it's not my main source of income, you know."

"Okay." Kevin wished the man would just come out and say whatever it was.

"She was obsessed, addicted to gambling. I've seen it before, and I tried to steer her away from getting in too deep but..." He shrugged.

"She started placing bets with another bookie," Kevin said, seeing where this was going.

Anthony nodded. "Yeah."

"Do you know who?"

Anthony's gaze strayed again. "I don't know for sure..."

"You have an idea," Maggie said. "Tell us."

"Look, like I said, I don't know for sure, but she did ask me about Ivan Kovalev."

"Russian mob?" Kevin didn't know the name. He hadn't been in Los Angeles long enough to get to know who the major players in the local underworld were, but the Russian mob had long tentacles in the US. And they weren't the kind of men you wanted to owe money.

Anthony shrugged then nodded. "When Kim asked me about Ivan, I warned her to steer clear."

Maggie was chewing her bottom lip again. "What exactly did Kim want with this Ivan person?"

"She wanted to know if I knew him. Could I make an introduction." Anthony twisted his hands in his apron. "To be clear, I don't. I stick to my small-time hustle and don't mess with those guys."

"Smart," Kevin said.

The bell on the door tinkled, and four women walked in, chatting.

Anthony stood. "Listen, I have to go. I don't know anything else that can help you. I hope you figure out what happened to Kim. She had her issues, but she was a nice woman."

Anthony headed for the bar display case to help the new customers.

Neither Kevin nor Maggie spoke until they were back in his car.

"Do you think Kim got involved with this Ivan person? Could he have killed her? Or had her killed?"

It was definitely a possibility, but he could see the idea was already weighing on Maggie.

He reached across the car and squeezed her hand. The electric currents that he'd felt the first time he'd touched her were back, even stronger.

"I think our talk with Anthony the baker slash bookmaker raised more questions than answers."

Chapter Eight

Kevin called Tess from the car as he drove toward the museum and updated her on what they'd learned from Anthony.

"Ivan has his hands in a number of pies in Los Angeles and beyond. He owns several seemingly legit businesses, including a bar in downtown Los Angeles. Nightingale's. Conducts his shadier business at night out of the party room."

"Think you can get a meeting with him?" Kevin asked.

"I'll see what I can do," Tess answered before ending the call.

"If we know this Ivan guy hangs out at Nightingale's, why don't we just go there tonight and ask to speak to him?"

"Because, *a*, you don't just drop in on a mobster. And, *b*, we are not going to talk to him." Kevin glanced across the car. "He's someone you should stay away from."

She rolled her eyes. "Are you planning to go to talk to him? Find out if he knew Kim and lent her money?"

"Maggie, listen to me. Ivan Kovalev, the people he probably works for, these are not men you want knowing you even exist. I'm not going to let you anywhere near them, do you understand?"

"Let me?"

He sucked in a deep breath then let it out slowly, which only infuriated her more.

"I didn't mean it that way. I'm just trying to protect you. We don't know what Kim got herself into, but it is starting to look very dangerous."

As if it hadn't been dangerous before now. She'd been clocked in the head, her friend was dead, likely murdered, and a precious historical jewel was missing. She hadn't exactly been living in Shangri-la.

They made the rest of the ride in silence. He pulled to a stop in front of the museum a few minutes after twelve thirty.

"I can come back and pick you up at the end of your workday if you'd like," he offered, stiffly.

"That's nice of you," she responded, already reaching for the door, "but I'll get a ride from a colleague or call an Uber."

She hopped out of the car and headed for the museum. It actually wasn't that far of a walk from the museum to her cottage. She'd made the walk before.

The police tape was gone from the front of the museum, and her employee identification, which doubled as a key card, opened the door to the employee entrance without any trouble.

Her head was still swirling with news that Kim might have gotten herself involved with mobsters. She was so caught up in her thoughts that she gave a startled scream when the door to the ladies' room swung open as she passed and Diyana Shelton stepped out.

"Oh my gosh, Maggie. I'm so sorry. I didn't mean to frighten you," Diyana said, a flush pinking her pale cheeks. Diyana was in the UCLA graduate art history program and interning at the Larimer for the semester.

"No, it was my fault," Maggie said, her hand still pressed to her racing heart. "I wasn't paying attention."

"How are you?" Diyana cocked her head to the side, her expression one of concern. The graduate student was pretty in a somewhat unconventional way. Dark brown eyes were set a little wide and her lips were thin lines, but her olive-colored skin was smooth as silk, and somehow the individual features worked together. "I heard you and Carl were here when the ruby was stolen and that the thief attacked you both." Her eyes strayed to Maggie's injuries. This close, Maggie had no doubt Diyana could see the results of her encounter with the thief clearly enough.

"I'm okay and, thank goodness, so is Carl. It's the museum I'm worried about." Maggie started walking again toward her office.

Diyana fell in step next to her. "You're right to be. The theft is huge. I mean, I'm not sure what Robert is going to do. I heard him talking to Colin Rycroft on the phone earlier, and it did not sound like a friendly conversation. How could this have happened?"

Maggie stopped in front of her office. She didn't usually mind Diyana's curiosity, but she was simply in no mood for it today.

"I don't know, but I'm sure the police will find out. I can't chat right now, Diyana. I have to get ready for the staff meeting. I'll see you there." She slid into her office, closing the door behind her firmly before a wave of guilt hit.

She'd been a little abrupt, possibly bordering on rude. Diyana didn't deserve that. She'd apologize after the meeting.

Remembering her promise to Kevin to reach out to the dealers she knew about the stolen Viperé ruby, she put a call in to several dealers, including her friend Apollo Bouras. She left him a message asking him to call her back as soon as he could. No doubt he and every other dealer in the Los Angeles area had already heard about the theft of the Viperé ruby, and they'd either want to stay as far away from her and the Larimer as possible given the situation or they'd call back quickly, eager to snatch up any crumb of gossip to spread.

Messages left, she got busy wading through the hundreds of emails she'd received overnight. Several were from colleagues at other museums asking if she was okay and wanting the skinny on the break-in. She'd respond to those later. More than a dozen were from news organizations, several from the same reporters. Interview requests. She deleted those without opening most of them. All too soon, it was time for the staff meeting.

She was surprised to find Carter Tutwilder, chairman of the Larimer's board of directors, standing in front of the room next to Robert.

"Come in, come in. Find a seat. Quickly please," Robert said, waving her inside.

Maggie grabbed the empty seat next to Diyana and shot the young woman what she hoped was an apologetic smile. Diyana smiled back wanly.

"Okay, before we get started with the meeting, Mr. Tutwilder wanted to say a few words."

"Thank you, Robert." Mr. Tutwilder buttoned his suit jacket. "I won't impose for long. I just wanted to acknowledge the heinous crime that has been perpetrated against the Larimer and those of us who love the museum. Of course, no one more than Maggie and Carl." Mr. Tutwilder extended a hand in her direction. "Maggie, the Larimer and the board stand behind you one hundred percent. Whatever you need, we're here for you."

"Thank you," she said, touched by the show of concern.

"As soon as things settle down, we'll also be planning a memorial for our colleague Kim Sumika. The board has made grief counselors available to anyone who feels they need to talk." Mr. Tutwilder turned back to Robert. "I'll hand things back over to you, Robert."

"Thank you, Carter."

A polite smattering of applause broke out as Mr. Tutwilder left the room.

"Okay," Robert said. "Let's get started."

Robert began the meeting with an update on Carl's condition. He was admitted to the hospital with a serious concussion, but the doctors expected him to make a full recovery. The doctors planned to release him from the hospital in a few days, but it might be a couple weeks before he was up to returning to the job. Then Robert turned to the theft of the Viperé ruby and did his best to set everyone's concerns at ease, although Maggie wasn't sure how much he accomplished. They all knew that the longer it took for the police to find the ruby, the worse things would get for the Larimer. And there was a fair chance that the ruby would never be found. It would be a coveted possession amongst the sordid world of private collectors, a notoriously secretive bunch of people who collected treasures that should rightly be seen by the masses. A lot of these extremely wealthy collectors didn't much care how they came into possession of items, just that they obtained them.

It was a short meeting. Maggie pulled Diyana aside before she left and apologized for her abrupt dismissal earlier.

"It's okay." Diyana smiled sweetly. "We're all under a huge amount of pressure right now."

Maggie returned the intern's smile. "Thank you for understanding."

"Maggie." Robert stepped up next to Maggie and Diyana. "I'd like to speak to you for a moment, please."

Diyana nodded and scurried from the conference room. All the other staff members had already left the room.

Robert gestured for her to sit and she did. He sat across from her, folding his hands on the table in front of him. She felt like a child being admonished by the principal. She smoothed the front of her slacks nervously. Was he going to fire her? He wouldn't. She wasn't responsible for the theft. She was a victim as much as the Larimer.

She sat silently, waiting for him to start.

"I'm glad to see you weren't hurt badly."

She tried for a smile and failed. "No. I'm fine."

"Good, I'm happy to hear that, although I have been thinking that it might be a good idea if you took a leave of absence."

"A leave of absence?"

So he wasn't firing her. At least, not yet. But a leave of absence was no consolation.

"Well, some time off, really. Vacation time."

"Vacation time? Now?" She was confused. It was quite possibly the worst time for her to take a vacation. With Kim…and the media storm around the theft. "Robert, what is this about?"

He sighed heavily. He looked as if he'd aged two decades in the last twelve hours. "The Larimer is under a tremendous amount of pressure at the moment. All eyes are on us with the theft and Ms. Sumika's untimely death. And well, there are already rumblings that Kim might have had something to do with the theft, and that's what led her to do—" Robert rolled his wrist "—what she did."

"You can't believe that! You worked with Kim for years. You know as well as I do how much she loved the Larimer."

Robert avoided meeting her gaze. "I have a hard time believing anyone associated with the Larimer would have committed such a heinous act, but the fact is someone did. And your relationship with Ms. Sumika—"

Maggie felt her back stiffen. "My relationship with Kim was that we were friends and coworkers."

His lips thinned. "Be that as it may, I have an obligation to look out for the best interests of the museum, and we simply cannot afford to have even a hint of impropriety at the moment."

"Impropriety—"

"I believe that it would be best for you to separate yourself from the Larimer, at least for a time." He stood as if that put an end to the conversation.

Maggie got to her feet as well. "Well, I have a contract, and I expect it to be honored. And if you try to fire me or force me to take vacation time, I have no problem taking my grievances up with the board of directors."

"Now, just a moment—" Robert held his hands out as if they might stop the onslaught of words coming his way.

Her heart pounded wildly. She'd been through this before when Ellison was charged with embezzling from his accounting firm. Guilty by association. She couldn't go through it again. "No, no moments. I will not let you suggest that I am somehow involved in the theft of the Viperé ruby."

"I never said—" he spoke quickly.

"You came close enough. And if I'm suddenly placed on

leave or taking a vacation, those same people who are rumbling about Kim maybe being involved with the theft will be rumbling about me next. I will not have my reputation impugned when I did nothing wrong."

"No one is saying you did anything wrong."

"Great." She flashed a smile at him that she was pretty sure looked more feral than friendly by the way he took three quick steps backward. "Good. Then I'll head back to my office. Mr. Rycroft should be here any minute, and I'm sure we both want to be prepared for that meeting. I'll see you soon."

She stepped out of the room and marched back to her office. Inside, she rested her back against the closed door, shaking from a combination of anger and adrenaline. It had felt good standing up for herself, but she knew if Robert really wanted her out, there wasn't much she could do to stop him. He had far more sway with the board members than she had, and they'd likely do whatever he suggested if it meant a chance at saving the Larimer's reputation. Even if it ruined hers.

She pulled herself together moments before the security guard on duty buzzed to say that Colin Rycroft had arrived. She let Robert know then picked Rycroft up from the reception desk.

The Brit was not happy.

She and Robert spent the next two hours walking Rycroft through the exhibit and explaining how the Viperé ruby's theft couldn't have been foreseen. Rycroft made them walk through the security measures they'd had in place three times, and he read them the riot act for the failure of the cameras. It would have been nice to have Tess or Kevin there to explain the security system in more detail, but neither she nor Robert had thought of it in time. And given Tess's disgust at the museum's decision not to go with her original plan for securing the ruby, they might have been better off without a representative from West Investigations. Rycroft insisted that they set up a meeting with the insurance company and West Security and Investigations to go over the steps that were being taken to recover the ruby. Of course, the Larimer had obtained an insurance policy on the Viperé, but Rycroft wasn't incorrect that money was poor consolation for a piece as rare as the Viperé.

Maggie promised to set up a meeting between the parties in the coming days and hoped that Kevin's and Tess's obvious experience and expertise might work to mollify the Brit at least a little.

By the time Rycroft finally left the museum and headed back to his hotel—he planned to be in town for the next several days—she was wiped. It wasn't quite five thirty, officially quitting time, so she headed back to her office with every intention of going home. All she wanted was a big glass of wine.

She knew the moment she entered her office that someone had been there. The air felt different. There was a slight chill to it. Maybe that was why she'd shivered as she'd stepped over the threshold.

Or maybe it was the blood-red envelope that lay, center stage, on her desk.

A get-well card probably. She was overreacting to a colleague's caring gesture.

She grabbed the envelope and slipped the piece of paper from it.

Her heart stuttered to a stop as she read then reread the words on the card.

Beware the Viperé curse. You are next to die.

Chapter Nine

Kevin stepped into his apartment, dropping his keys on the table next to the door. He still had a lot of work to do, but luckily West Investigations equipped each of their employees with a fully secure laptop so they were able to work from practically anywhere in the world.

But it didn't seem likely that he was going to get a lot of work done at the moment. The television in his living room blared.

"Tanya," he called from the doorway. He couldn't see his sister from the entrance, but this wasn't the first time he'd come home to find her camped out on his sofa, the television loud enough to wake the dead.

He slipped out of his shoes and padded into the living room. "Tanya," he yelled at the back of his sister's head.

Tanya turned and grinned at him over the back of the sofa. "Hey, bro."

People were always surprised when they found out he and Tanya were brother and sister and outright shocked when they found out they were twins. He was tall, six two and dark—dark brown hair, eyes and skin. Tanya, in contrast, was petite at five foot one, with skin the color of café latte, piercing hazel eyes and light brown hair streaked with blond.

Two sides of the same coin their mother liked to call them, pointing out that where it really mattered they were very much alike. They were both driven, bossy, stubborn and thought they knew best. Kevin couldn't really dispute their mother's assessment. He and Tanya were very much alike, which tended to both draw them close and lead to a fair amount of arguing. But there was no one more loyal than Tanya, and he would do anything to protect his younger-by-seven-minutes sister.

Kevin dropped down on the sofa next to his sister. He didn't bother asking her what she was doing there. The red beans and rice she was shoveling into her mouth was all the answer he needed.

Tanya was an emergency room doctor at the nearby hospital, and given that she was still in her scrubs, her crocs lined up neatly by his front door, he inferred she'd come over directly at the end of her shift. When he'd announced he was leaving the Idyllwild Police Department and accepting a job with West Security and Investigations that would put him in Los Angeles and closer to her, Tanya had conveniently found him the perfect rental just minutes away from the hospital. Since the place had two bedrooms, he'd offered to let her move in with him, but she'd declined, saying that they needed their space. That hadn't stopped her from accepting the spare key he'd offered her and stopping in whenever she wanted, most often to bum leftovers off of him. He chided her about her visits, but the truth was he loved spending time with her. She was more than just his sister, she was his best friend.

"You look tired," she said, peeling her gaze away from the rerun of *The Office* playing on the television screen.

He put a hand to his ear and leaned toward her. "I'm sorry,

I can't hear you. What did you say?" he yelled over the sound of the television.

She rolled her eyes but reached for the remote tucked under her legs and turned the volume down to something reasonable. "Better?"

"Yes, thank you. You know turning the sound up that loud isn't good for you."

"I wanted to hear the show while I was in the kitchen heating up dinner. You really outdid yourself, by the way. This is good." She shoveled more beans and rice into her mouth.

"You know, I seem to recall giving you the recipe for this dish. And showing you how to make it. And a few others. I know you are far more skilled in the emergency room than the kitchen, but for a smarty-pants doctor like you, red beans and rice can't be that hard to master," he teased.

"It's not hard to master," she said around a bite of food. "But you know what is easier? Coming over here and eating your food." She grinned at him again. "Anyway, you cook enough for a small army."

"I wonder why." He pulled the throw pillow from behind his back and tossed it at her before slouching down until his head rested against the back of the sofa.

Tanya shifted, crossing her legs on the sofa and facing him. "New job putting you through your paces?"

"I caught a particularly thorny case."

Tanya had gone to CalSci University with him and Maggie. Although they'd tried to give each other space to explore who they were outside of being Kevin's twin sister and Tanya's twin brother, Tanya had been there throughout his relationship with Maggie and had been there for him when he'd decided to end things with her. She'd even tried to talk him out of ending things, arguing that she could take out loans and work her way through medical school. But he hadn't wanted her to be burdened with the kind of debt that most medical students graduated with. He'd spent three years playing college football, making who knew how much money for the university, and he figured it was time that some of those big bucks benefited his mother and sister. Professional athletes were always on borrowed time, and he didn't want to waste any of his. So he'd left school after his junior year and directed his entire focus toward his NFL career. A career that, unbeknownst to him at the time, would only last for two years.

"Can you tell me about it?" Tanya asked.

"Some things. Have you heard about the theft at the Larimer Museum?"

Tanya squinted, the sign that she was thinking. "Yeah, I think I saw a post about it while I was scrolling through social media during my break."

"Well, that's my case. West Investigations provided the security for the exhibit."

Tanya sucked her teeth. "Not good."

"Definitely not good." He hesitated for a moment, but knew it was better that she heard it from him than stumble on the information somewhere else. "Maggie Scott is one of the curators at the Larimer. She's actually the curator responsible for the exhibit. She was hurt during the commission of the theft, not badly, but the police are also very suspicious of her at the moment."

"Kevin." Tanya closed her eyes and let her head fall to her chest.

"I know what you are going to say."

She opened one eye. "Do you?"

"Okay, what are you going to say?"

She lifted her head, both eyes open and pinned on him now. "I'm going to say that you should recuse yourself from this case. You and Maggie have a fraught history, and that is putting it mildly. I saw how torn up you were after you broke up with her. It took you years to get over her. This can come to no good for either of you."

"I wasn't torn up. I broke up with her."

Tanya snorted. "That may be, but you were broken-hearted." She held her hand up in a stop motion. "Save it. You threw yourself into football, but I know you. Heart. Broken."

"Whatever. That was a long time ago. We're both different people now."

"Yeah, that's why you haven't had a serious relationship since that relationship ended," his sister said pointedly.

"I've had relationships."

She rolled her eyes at him. "I said a serious relationship. One where you bring the woman home to meet Ma."

"This is a pointless conversation. This is my job. The other assistant curator, Maggie's friend, was found having apparently accidentally overdosed the same night as the theft, and Maggie insists on being involved in the investigation. There's nothing I can do."

Tanya set her now empty bowl aside. "Kevin, there's something you don't know."

He watched something flicker behind his sister's eyes. "What?"

She studied him for a long moment. He knew her well enough to see she was struggling with whatever it was she wanted to tell him.

He took her hands in his. "Hey, you know you can tell me anything, right? I'm your big bro. There are no secrets between us."

Tanya gave him a faint smile, slipping her hands from his. "I know. I was just going to say that Maggie was really hurt when you left her."

His twin instinct told him that she was holding something back, but she spoke again before he could press her on what it was.

"I don't say that to make you feel bad or guilty. It is just a fact. I saw her a few times after you left, and she was devastated. Just be careful. Be sure. I know you don't want to hurt her again."

She unfolded from the sofa and carried her bowl into the kitchen.

Be careful. Be sure.

He wasn't sure about anything at the moment except that Maggie wouldn't hurt anyone, especially not someone she considered a friend. And she wouldn't be involved in theft.

The Office's distinctive theme song began playing, the credits rolling on the television screen, just as his cell phone rang. He groaned when he saw Tess's name.

"What's up, Tess?"

"You need to get to the Larimer right away. We have a problem."

It felt like the situation had just taken a darker, more sinister turn. Stealing a priceless ruby was one thing, and they couldn't be sure yet if Kim's death was in any way connected. But coming after Maggie now? When the thief should be concerned about getting away with the gem without getting caught, that meant they weren't dealing with a run-of-the-mill criminal.

"Do you know anything about the curse that's mentioned in the note?" Francois had directed the question to Maggie.

She looked shell-shocked, which made Kevin ache to wrap his arms around her. Tess eyed him. He kept his hands down by his sides.

The four of them stood in Maggie's office. After finding the letter, Maggie called Tess and the detective. She'd explained that Robert Gustev had held a staff meeting and kept her after for a brief discussion. He got the feeling that it hadn't been a positive discussion, but Francois didn't ask what it was about and Kevin hadn't wanted to step on the detective's toes. She'd found the envelope when she'd returned to her office.

Kevin assessed the space. It was neat and orderly. A handful of files were stacked on the corner of the desk, pens, a stapler and tape dispenser lined up in a row across the top edge. The books on the bookshelf behind the desk had been organized alphabetically by the author's last name. A printer sat on a credenza to the right of the door. There were no personal items at all. No photos of Maggie or a pet. No artwork on the wall, which he found surprising. But according to Maggie there was also nothing out of place or missing. Whoever had left the note had come in, dropped it on her desk and walked out. Their mystery person had likely touched nothing and spent less than twenty seconds inside the office.

Which meant there wouldn't be much to go on.

Maggie's voice pulled him out of his thoughts. "I have no idea what it means. I told you about the legend associated with the ruby, but I don't know anything about a curse."

Francois rubbed his chin. "Maybe the note writer meant the legend."

"The legend doesn't mention anything about people dying," Kevin pointed out.

"Yes, well…" Francois shrugged and slid the note into a plastic evidence bag.

Kevin could tell that Francois didn't think much of the threat, but it put him on edge. Even more on edge. Someone had come into Maggie's private space and lobbed a direct threat of violence. He couldn't just dismiss it as idle. The fact that there were no cameras in the areas only accessible by staff meant that any one of a number of people could have left the note, including someone who worked with Maggie.

Kevin had spent the last hour shadowing Francois while he'd questioned the staff members, but no one had admitted to seeing a stranger or anyone enter Maggie's office. He wasn't surprised by that. One thing he and Francois would probably agree on was that it seemed more and more likely that the person behind the theft, and now the threat against Maggie, was someone well known by Maggie and the employees of the Larimer. Someone who was pretty confident their presence in the areas of the museum restricted to employees wouldn't be notable if they were seen.

"I'll take the note in to be fingerprinted," Francois said.

"That's it?" Maggie shot back.

"There's not much more we can do, Ms. Scott. I'd urge the museum to increase its security measures. It wouldn't be a bad idea to install cameras in the employee work areas, at least the hallways here."

"Francois, this is a direct threat aimed at Maggie," Kevin said.

Francois darted a look between Kevin and Maggie, assessing.

Okay, so maybe he'd come on a bit too strong, but he didn't think the detective was taking this situation seriously enough. "And the LAPD is doing what it can to address the threat, but you know how these things go. Without more, my hands are tied." Francois looked at Maggie again. "Ms. Scott, you should remain vigilant about your surroundings. If you see or are approached by anyone suspicious, call me immediately." He handed Maggie his business card and shot a glance at Kevin. "Or I'm sure you can also call Mr. Lombard if you're feeling unsafe."

Kevin fought back the urge to punch the man.

"Kevin, a word please." Francois stepped out of Maggie's office and moved away down the hall where they wouldn't be overheard.

"Don't you think you might be getting too emotionally involved with this case?" Francois said, shooting a pointed glance at the door to Maggie's office.

"No, I don't." The lie hung between them. "Have you considered that your suspicion of Mag—Ms. Scott," Kevin corrected himself but not before Francois's brow cocked, "might be leading you to dismiss the danger she could be in?"

Francois scowled. "I'm not dismissing anything, including the possibility that Ms. Scott left this threatening letter for herself."

"Oh, come on." Francois was exasperating. "Why would she do that?"

"To take suspicion off herself." Francois held up a hand. "Look, I'll keep an open mind if you will. I think we can agree that whatever we're dealing, with Ms. Scott is at the center of it whether she wants to be or not."

"At the center, how?"

"Well, just look at the situation." Francois began ticking off his points using his fingers. "Ms. Scott advocated for bringing the ruby to the Larimer. She designed the exhibit and knew all about the security measures."

"She was one of several people who knew about the security measures for the Viperé."

"I'll give you that. She was at the museum the night the ruby was stolen."

"She was also attacked that night."

"True. She lives on the property where another museum employee was found dead, possibly murdered." Francois continued his list. "She was married to a man charged with embezzlement, who subsequently died, and no one can find the money. And now she has received a mysterious threat citing a curse no one seems to have heard of."

"None of that proves she had anything to do with the things that have happened."

Francois's scowl deepened. "I'm not a man who believes in coincidence. I'd think as a former law enforcement professional, you'd appreciate that."

"I think you're wrong about Maggie," Kevin said. "I think she's in real danger, and the reference in this threat to a curse might explain why."

"You think we might be dealing with some sort of conspiracy nut? A fanatic who's heard of or even made up some curse and associated it with the Viperé ruby?"

"I think it's possible. The internet can put all sorts of questionable ideas in people's heads, especially when there is already the hook of the so-called Viperé legends. I think it's definitely worth looking into."

Francois shook his head, but he was also rubbing his chin, a sign Kevin now knew that the detective was considering the point he'd made. "I have enough on my plate. I can't start chasing down curses. And—" he shot Kevin a pointed look "—I think you might be stretching here."

"Then I'll do it, but if I bring you something concrete, you have to promise you'll give it real consideration."

Francois considered for a moment longer before nodding. "Okay, but no cowboy stuff. If you find something, you bring it to me right away."

They shook on the deal.

Francois started to walk away then stopped and turned back. "Lombard, a word of advice. I know you think you can handle it, but it's very easy to lose your objectivity around a woman like Ms. Scott. I'd be careful if I were you."

Maggie was still standing exactly where she'd been when he'd left her office with Detective Francois. She looked scared and unsure. The urge to take her in his arms hit him again, even stronger this time.

"Come on. I'll take you home."

"Detective Francois thinks I left the note for myself, doesn't he? He thinks I was involved in the theft and that this is all just some big game I'm playing with everyone." Her voice was edging toward hysteria. "He probably thinks I killed Kim."

"Hey." Kevin reached out to her, and despite knowing what Detective Francois would say if he walked by and saw them, he pulled Maggie to his chest. "Francois is just doing his job. He'll come to see you had nothing to do with any of this."

Maggie pulled back just enough to look up at him with teary eyes. "You believe me though, don't you? You believe that I had nothing to do with any of this?"

He held her gaze. "I believe you."

Chapter Ten

I believe you.

Kevin's words bounced around in Maggie's mind during the drive from the Larimer to her house. She knew he'd been suspicious of her at first, but a good part of the weight, the fear, that she'd been carrying inside since she'd been attacked was alleviated by those three words.

I believe you.

She'd never developed such strong feelings so quickly for a man, but her attraction to Kevin was palpable and intense. She needed to keep it in check though. He seemed like a good investigator, as good a man as he was all those years ago, but it would be folly to trust him with her heart again.

He pulled to a stop in front of her cottage, and she exited the car, careful to avoid looking over at Kim's house. She didn't know how long she could keep living in the cottage, because of her feelings about Kim's death occurring only steps away and because she wasn't sure whether whatever relative of Kim's who inherited it would allow her to stay on the property. Just the idea of having to find a new place to live and move was too much to deal with, so she put the thought out of her mind. She just wanted to go inside and block out everything and everyone for a while.

She opened the door and turned back to Kevin. "Thank you for the ride."

"You're welcome. I'll be back in the morning to take you to work."

She jolted with surprise. "You don't have to do that."

"I know I don't have to, but in light of the assault against you and the threat today, I think it's best to err on the side of caution."

"I—"

She was cut off by the sound of her ringing phone. It was Apollo Bouras, the dealer she'd called earlier.

"It's one of the dealers I reached out to earlier today. I have to take this." She accepted the call.

Apollo was about twenty years older than Maggie, a Greek immigrant who knew everything there was to know about Southern European antiquities. He also did a fair amount of business as a go-between for sellers and buyers of rare gems.

"I'm sure you've heard about the theft of the Viperé ruby," Maggie said, jumping right into the heart of the call.

"Yes. Shocking," Apollo answered.

"Well, the museum is working with an investigator, and we'd like to pick your brain."

"Of course, of course. I will do anything I can to help you. You know that. Why don't you stop by the shop tomorrow? I'll be in all day as usual."

"Wonderful. Say tomorrow morning around nine thirty?" She looked at Kevin and got a nod from him confirming the time worked.

"Nine thirty is perfect," Apollo answered. "See you then."

She ended the call and turned back to Kevin.

"So I guess you will need that escort after all." The full-wattage smile he gave her sent her heart fluttering.

She returned the smile. "We could meet there." She was flirting, and it felt, well, it felt a little strange under the circumstances, but also exciting.

His gaze lowered to her mouth, and she noticed a subtle change in his expression. When his eyes met hers again there was a spark of desire there. The cool evening air warmed. She took a small step toward him, and he did the same, slipping his hand behind her head and lowering his mouth to hers.

The kiss was better than anything she had imagined, and she had to admit that she'd imagined kissing Kevin again several times over the years. She'd never forgotten what it felt like to be in his arms. The warm sensation quickly intensified into something fiery. She slid her hands up his chest and around his neck, pulling him closer and melding her body to his.

She'd forgotten how good a kisser he was. Extraordinary really. Need boiled inside of her. This couldn't be normal. The smoldering desire between them had to be some sort of response to the intensity of the situation they found themselves in.

She pulled back from the kiss. "I should go in."

He stepped back, his eyes shrouded. "I'll pick you up in the morning."

"Good night, Kevin."

His dark brown eyes were piercing. "Sleep tight, Maggie."

MAGGIE SPENT A fitful night tossing and turning. The few snatches of sleep she was able to get alternated between grief-riddled dreams of Kim and memories of her past relationship with Kevin. Her past and present were colliding in an emotional tumult that felt like it had the potential to spin out of control. She awoke more exhausted than she'd been when she fell asleep.

She was working on her second mug of coffee when Kevin rang her doorbell, and she let him in.

He held out the to-go cup in his hand. "Looks like you don't need this," he said, handing her the cup.

She smiled and took the cup. "Not right now, but probably later."

He cocked his head to the side. "Didn't get much sleep last night?"

Heat crept up her neck as she recalled the dreams she'd had about him. "Not much, no." She turned away from him, carrying her empty coffee mug to the sink. "We should get going."

Even with her back to him, she could feel Kevin's frown. After a moment, he rose and tossed his trash in the garbage bin.

She grabbed her purse from the sofa as they passed through the living room and headed for the front door.

A police cruiser and an unmarked black sedan pulled into the driveway as she locked up.

Detective Francois stepped out of the sedan and walked toward her and Kevin. He stopped at the bottom of her stoop.

"Ms. Scott." He held a piece of paper out to her. "I have a warrant to search these premises."

As a former police officer, Kevin was used to search warrants, but he wasn't usually on this side of the execution.

"Can I see that?" He gestured to the warrant in Maggie's shaking hand. She was looking at it, but he could tell she wasn't seeing the words. She handed him the papers.

He skimmed them, looking for the most important piece

of information. The suspected crime that Francois listed to justify the search. Felony theft. Second-degree murder.

Murder.

That must mean the police had determined that Kim Sumika hadn't accidentally overdosed.

He skimmed the rest of the warrant, noting the items the officers were allowed to seize. It was pretty typical. Electronics. Diaries. Writings. Receipts. Medications. Disposable gloves. Cleaning products. Vacuums. The warrant also gave Francois the right to search Maggie's car and phone.

So Francois thought Maggie could have killed her best friend, cleaned up after herself then pulled off the theft of a priceless ruby.

He caught Francois's eyes, but the man was good. He saw nothing there.

"I don't understand. I didn't do anything," Maggie pleaded.

Francois turned to her. "Ms. Scott, I understand this has to be upsetting for you. You are welcome to stay as long as you do nothing to interfere with the search in any way. We should only be an hour or two since your residence isn't terribly large."

"Should I have a lawyer present?" Maggie's gaze darted to him.

The knot in his stomach grew. He wished he could do or say something to help her in that instant, but he knew there was nothing. Francois had a warrant, and that gave him the power to be there. They could only make the situation worse. "You could," he started to say.

"But we do not have to wait for your attorney to arrive before beginning our search," Francois declared, correctly.

Kevin worked to check the anger he felt toward the detective at the moment. "Detective Francois, could I speak with you for a moment. Please," he added when the detective looked ready to refuse.

Francois hesitated for a moment then nodded.

They walked to the end of the driveway, away from the two officers who had shown up with Francois.

"It's not personal," Francois said. "I'm just doing my job. Maggie Scott had the means and opportunity to carry out the theft of the ruby and the murder of Kim Sumika."

"Let's slow down for a minute. You know for sure Kim Sumika's death was a homicide?"

Francois looked as if he was kicking himself for having said too much. He pressed his lips together tightly.

"Francois. Detective, please. I would really appreciate it if you could tell me what you can."

Francois sighed heavily. "The coroner found heroin and Rohypnol in Kim Sumika's system. The killer may have thought we wouldn't check, but Dr. Brown is thorough."

"So the killer sedates Kim with the Rohypnol then injects her with the heroin, making it look like she overdosed."

"That's the working theory at the moment."

"You still have a timing issue. Maggie was at the museum when Kim Sumika was killed."

"Sumika's house is only ten minutes from the museum. That gives Maggie plenty of time to get to Kim's place, slip her the overdose and get back to the museum in time to be 'assaulted'—" Francois made air quotes "—giving her a pretty good alibi for the theft and murder."

"Come on!" Kevin shook his head, accentuating the absurdity of the idea.

"You know how this goes, Lombard. If she's innocent, we'll find nothing and move on, but you know I have to do this."

He understood where Francois was coming from. He'd stood in his exact spot hundreds of times and not that long ago. That didn't mean he liked it now.

"I'm going to take Maggie out of here."

"That's fine. You'll have to take your car though. We'll need hers for searching and processing. It's included in the warrant. And, Ms. Scott, we'll need your phone before you leave. If you give me a minute, I can have a tech copy the hard drive now, and I can give it right back."

Kevin appreciated the gesture.

He started back toward Maggie, but Francois's hand on his arm stopped him.

"Lombard, I am keeping an open mind here, I assure you," Francois said with a seriousness that hardened his jaw. His gaze darted to Maggie then back to Kevin's face. "You would do well to do the same."

Chapter Eleven

The sky was cloudless, the day already warm even though it was only midmorning. Maggie stared out of the car window as Kevin drove. They stopped at a red light, and she watched a group of kids, about middle school age, amble down the sidewalk, chatting and laughing, backpacks strapped to their backs. It was a picture-perfect day, and yet Maggie felt like she was in purgatory. She hadn't understood most of what was written in the search warrant, but several words had stood out.

Theft.

Second-degree murder.

Detective Francois thought she'd killed Kim.

She was a murder suspect.

Despite her question about having a lawyer present at the search, the reality was she didn't have the money for a lawyer. She was barely getting by. If not for Kim offering her a cut-rate rent far below the going market, she wouldn't have been able to afford to live in such a nice neighborhood so close to the Larimer.

A lump grew in her throat, but she was determined not to cry. He'd suggested they head out to meet with her dealer friend as they'd planned, and she'd agreed. The last thing she wanted to do was stand around while strangers pawed through her belongings.

Her phone dinged, indicating she'd received a text message. Her father had made a 1:15 p.m. lunch reservation at a restaurant she wasn't familiar with in Chinatown.

She couldn't hold back the groan that escaped as she read it.

"What is it? Is everything okay?" Kevin darted a look at her from the driver's side of the car.

"No, but yes. Nothing for you to worry about. It's just my father."

Kevin grinned. "How is Boyd?"

"Getting married."

Kevin's grin widened. "I guess he's pretty good then."

She groaned. "He wants me to meet his fiancée today over lunch. What kind of woman willingly becomes a man's seventh wife? The man is clearly incapable of making a real commitment to anyone."

"I know Boyd was a nontraditional father, but he's a good guy. A bit impulsive, but he embraces life."

"Of course you'd take his side. He always liked you, probably because he saw so much of himself in you."

A heavy silence fell over the car.

"I'm sorry. I shouldn't have said that."

"You don't have to be sorry for how you feel. I hurt you. From your perspective, I can see how you view me and your father as alike. But, Maggie, I was a twenty-year-old idiot when I walked away from you. I didn't realize what I had until it was too late. And I was even stupider for not crawling back to you on my hands and knees once I realized what a fool I'd been. But I want a second chance."

"Kevin, I can't do this right now."

"No, I know. It's terrible timing, but let me do one thing. Let me go to lunch with you."

She was surprised. "You want to be my date to lunch to meet my father's fiancée?"

"Yes, you said it yourself, your dad and I get along well. I can help keep the conversation going, smooth over any awkward bumps and be a sounding board for your inevitable meltdown afterward."

She slid a sidelong glance at him. "I'm not going to melt down."

"Of course you won't. So what do you say?"

It wasn't a bad idea. He could be a buffer if she needed one.

"Okay." She hesitated. "But about this second chance."

He reached for her hand. "I meant it. I'm not going to run away this time. I know that I want a second chance with you. You may not want the same, and I'll have to live with that if you don't, but I'm putting it out there. Just think about it, okay?"

She nodded. It was going to be hard not to think about it, but there was a more pressing situation facing them at the moment. She forced herself to focus on it.

Kevin parked in the lot behind the store, and they made their way to Xanthe's Treasures. The chime from the security system rang out as they stepped through the doors.

Antiques filled every shelf and cabinet, and Maggie knew each item had been carefully curated by Apollo Bouras. The items that were worth substantial amounts were locked in glass cases strategically placed in the space.

Apollo flashed a quick smile as she and Kevin entered, before turning back to the customer he'd been working with, an older woman who reeked of money in a black-and-white-checked Chanel suit, string pearls and low-heeled pumps.

They milled around the store while Apollo finished with his client.

It took close to fifteen minutes for Apollo's customer to finally settle on her purchases and pay. Apollo kept a cheery smile on his face until the woman had left the store and disappeared from sight.

"Finally. Mrs. Lowell is richer than a sultan, but the woman is just so indecisive."

"It's fine. We didn't have a problem waiting." She exchanged air kisses with Apollo.

"Maggie, my God! How could something like this have happened?" Apollo said, holding her at arm's length. "I can't believe it."

"Me either, but I'm hoping you can help. Oh, excuse my rudeness. This is Kevin Lombard. His firm has been hired by the board of directors of the museum to try and locate the Viperé ruby."

The two men shook hands.

Apollo focused on Maggie again, confusion wrinkling his brow. "And you're here because of the Viperé?"

"Well, we think it's possible the thief has plans to sell the Viperé on the black market."

Apollo looked thoughtful. "That would make some sense. It's quite valuable. Even more so if the thief is able to find someone who will cut it for him."

Maggie brought a hand to her throat, a small gasp escaping.

Apollo chuckled. "Don't stroke out on me. It's just speculation."

"I honestly hadn't thought about the thief cutting the ruby," she answered.

"Why would it be more valuable cut?" Kevin asked.

"It would be easier to conceal and move for one thing. The authorities are on the lookout for a large ruby, not several small rubies," Maggie answered.

"And the thief could likely get more money overall as long as he finds someone who knows what they are doing when they cut the stone. It's like those investors who buy a company, chop it up and sell it for parts. Sometimes the parts are worth more than the whole. In this case, smaller stones can be set in several different settings, obscuring the origin of the whole."

Kevin nodded his head in understanding, but Maggie was still dealing with the shock of realizing the Viperé stone might not even exist any longer. At least, not in its original form.

"We're actually here looking for your help," Kevin said, giving her a look.

"Yes." She shook the shock away. Until she knew otherwise, she was going to assume the ruby was intact. And pray it stayed that way. "I know you have handled transactions involving jewelry and gems of a certain significance. Have you or any other dealer you know of had an inquiry from someone asking about the Viperé ruby?"

Apollo looked uncomfortable. "You know I keep my clients' information in the strictest of confidences."

Kevin's mouth tightened. "We could have the police visit."

Apollo frowned.

Maggie placed a hand on his forearm. Apollo required honey, not vinegar. "Apollo, I know you have the utmost integrity. We're not asking for confidential information. Just whether there's been anyone asking about the Viperé."

Apollo still did not look happy. "No. Not asking about the Viperé."

"But someone was asking about rubies?" she pressed.

"Not rubies per se, but whether I knew about any large, precious gemstones that might be on the market, or coming onto the market soon. I didn't have, or know of, a current seller, so I couldn't help the potential buyer."

"And who was this potential buyer?" Kevin said.

Apollo hesitated again.

"Please, Apollo," Maggie said.

Apollo gave a resigned sigh. "I can't imagine he'd have anything to do with the theft anyway. The Larimer is his museum, after all."

Maggie felt herself leaning in. "His museum?"

Apollo nodded. "Carter Tutwilder. He's the potential buyer who made the inquiry."

CARTER TUTWILDER'S OFFICE was in Los Angeles's financial district. Maggie called ahead to Tutwilder Industries, explaining who she was and that she'd like to speak to Mr. Tutwilder at his earliest convenience, that day if it was at all possible. Tutwilder had agreed to give them ten minutes.

The Tutwilder family had a long and storied history on the West Coast and in the Midwest. The family had built their fortune in agribusiness. They had their hands in farming, fuel, fisheries, grain and other commodities, as well as biotechnology, to name just a few industries that had contributed to their multibillion dollar fortune. Still, the family somehow managed to remain under the radar and out of the public eye.

Kevin pulled into a garage two blocks from the Wilshire Grand Center, and he and Maggie walked to the building.

Office space in the Wilshire went for thousands of dollars per square foot, and Kevin had no doubt that Tutwilder's offices would be among the grandest. He wasn't disappointed. Tutwilder Industries' offices comprised floors twenty-five through twenty-nine.

He and Maggie signed in with security in the lobby then took the elevator to the twenty-ninth floor.

The office suite was decorated in rich, dark colors of walnut and burgundy that gave the space an elegant and expensive feel.

An attractive young brunette looked up from her computer monitor as they made their way to her desk.

"Good afternoon and welcome to Tutwilder Industries. How may I help you today?" She smiled.

"We have an appointment with Mr. Tutwilder," Maggie said.

"And your names?"

Maggie gave their names, and the receptionist clicked a few keys on the computer. "Yes, of course. One moment, please."

The receptionist reached for the phone. She spoke softly into the receiver before hanging up and standing.

"Mr. Tutwilder is ready for you now. If you'll follow me, please."

Kevin looked at Maggie with raised eyebrows. He hadn't expected it to be so easy to get in to see a man like Tutwilder, but he'd been impressed when Maggie had convincingly argued to whichever gatekeeper she'd spoken to about arranging this meeting that Mr. Tutwilder would want to do whatever he could to help them find the Viperé ruby. And from all appearances, it had worked.

The receptionist led them down a long corridor full of large offices and busy-looking people in them. They stopped at the only office with a frosted-glass door and no nameplate.

The receptionist rapped on the door and waited until a brisk "come in" came from the other side.

She pushed open the door, and he and Maggie stepped around her and inside a spacious office outfitted with buttery black leather furniture and a massive glass-topped desk. But the showstopper was the view. A glass wall of windows overlooked downtown Los Angeles.

Carter Tutwilder rose from behind his desk.

"Ms. Scott," he said, circling the desk and offering his hand. "And you must be Kevin Lombard. Tess Stenning had said wonderful things about you. I trust you are getting close to finding the criminals who have absconded with the Viperé ruby."

"I am doing everything in my power along with the police," he said, shaking the man's hand.

The receptionist slipped from the room, shutting the door behind her.

Tutwilder made his way back behind the desk, and Kevin took the opportunity to really study the man.

He had the presence and confidence of someone who'd been born into wealth and privilege. He stood tall in a black suit that looked like it had been made specifically for him, which it probably had. The tailoring was impeccable, but it didn't quite mask the soft upper body. His face showed the beginnings of a double chin, and his hair had been combed over to hide a bald spot at his crown, again expertly, but there was only so much that could be done to fight a receding hairline.

Tutwilder sat, waving them into the chairs across from his desk. "So, how can I help you?"

"You are the chairman of the board of the Larimer Museum," Kevin started them off.

"Correct. And one of the museum's largest donors."

Maggie smiled. "You and the members of your family are very generous, and the museum appreciates it more than I can say."

Tutwilder relaxed, leaning back in his chair. "I'm happy to do it. The arts are so important and artists so under-appreciated by society. There never seems to be enough funding."

"As one of the biggest donors, you received an invitation to the open house two nights ago, correct?"

Tutwilder smiled, but it wasn't as bright as the smile he'd given them when they'd entered. "I see where you're going with this. I did receive an invitation to the opening, of course, but unfortunately I had a prior commitment and could not make it."

"But you have an extensive art collection—" Kevin paused with intention "—that includes a collection of rare gems, I understand."

Tutwilder's eyes narrowed. "I do, although it's not common knowledge. I'd sure like to know how you came across that information."

He returned Tutwilder's narrow gaze. "I am an investigator."

"A very good one it would seem," Tutwilder said in a clipped tone.

"Mr. Tutwilder—"

"Ah, now, Ms. Scott. Please call me Carter."

"And I'm Maggie. Carter, please know that we mean no

offense. Kevin and I thought that with your knowledge of gems you might be able to help point us in a few directions that we might not otherwise think of."

Kevin studied Tutwilder and saw that he wasn't buying Maggie's buttering him up. You didn't run a multibillion dollar corporation and not develop well-honed instincts for when someone was attempting to pull one over on you. He'd conducted enough suspect interviews to know that the best way to get information out of Tutwilder would be to go directly at him. He'd definitely anger the man, but it would be that anger that tripped him up.

"Where do you keep your collections?"

"That is need-to-know information, Mr. Lombard."

"I'm sure the LAPD will feel they need to know. I can call Detective Francois."

"Carter—" Maggie started then stopped abruptly when Tutwilder held up a hand.

"What are you suggesting? That I had something to do with the theft of the Viperé ruby?"

"I'm not suggesting anything," Kevin shot back. "I'm asking questions and seeking answers."

"Well, I don't like your questions."

"And I don't like your answers. We have it on good authority that you were asking about the purchase of rare jewels just a few weeks ago."

"We?" Tutwilder's angry gaze slid to Maggie's face.

Maggie wrapped her hand around his forearm and squeezed. "Carter—" she tried again.

And again Tutwilder cut her off. "I don't know where you are getting your information, but it appears you aren't as good an investigator as I first thought."

"So you haven't been looking to acquire more jewels for your private collection?"

"Mr. Lombard, what I am or am not looking to acquire is none of your concern." Tutwilder looked at Maggie. "Or yours, Ms. Scott. Now, I squeezed you into my schedule because I thought I might be of some help. I can see that I was mistaken. I really don't have any more time for you today."

Tutwilder slid on the glasses lying on his desk, an obvious dismissal.

Maggie gripped his arm tighter, goading him to stand.

Tutwilder could kick them out of his office, but he couldn't stop them from looking for more information on his collection.

"What the hell were you thinking?" Maggie whirled on him the moment they stepped into the elevator. "That man is my boss's boss, kind of. He's basically the head of the museum, and I'm already on thin ice. I can't afford to lose my job."

He didn't break eye contact. "Your job is the last thing you should be worried about right now. You could be on the verge of losing your freedom if we don't give Detective Francois someone else to focus on quickly."

Maggie stalled hard then focused on the closed elevator doors.

He sighed internally. This had not gone the way he'd hoped. "Look, I'm sorry if I came on strong in there, but Carter Tutwilder is lying."

Maggie didn't answer. They made the walk back to the car silently. She didn't speak until he'd paid the parking fee and they were headed out of the garage. "Even if he is lying, how are we going to prove it?"

His stomach churned because that was the million-dollar question and one he didn't have an answer to. "I don't know, but I will."

Chapter Twelve

Maggie would have liked to continue pushing ahead on the case, but it was 12:40 p.m. They were meeting her father and his fiancée at 1:15 p.m. Of course, when it came to her father, 1:15 p.m. more likely meant 1:30 p.m. or even 2:00 p.m., but she didn't want to be the one who was late to the party, so to speak.

"Do you need to stop by the museum before we head to the restaurant?" Kevin asked.

"No. There's no time and no point."

She really should call Robert and let him know she wouldn't be in until later in the afternoon. They didn't punch timecards at the museum. There were times when they were expected to stay late or come in early, so everyone just kept their own schedule. It wasn't unusual for any of them to take a half day for personal reasons, so it shouldn't be a problem that she hadn't gotten to work yet. *Shouldn't*, though, was the operative word. It still hurt that Robert had tried to sideline her. She skipped the call and shot Robert a text telling him she'd be in after lunch.

The restaurant was in Chinatown.

She and Kevin were the first to arrive, but they were seated immediately. The hostess had just walked away from the table when the door to the restaurant opened and Boyd Scott entered.

Her father and a woman who could only be Julie walked into the restaurant holding hands, and Maggie was instantly thankful that Kevin had invited himself to come along.

The panic must have shown on her face because Kevin leaned over from where he sat by her side and said, "You doing okay?"

She couldn't form words at the moment, but she smiled and nodded.

Just be polite and keep it together for one lunch. That was all she had to do. That wasn't hard. She was an adult, after all.

"Maggie," her father said, coming to a stop beside the table. He wore a sports jacket and khaki pants. The dark brown skin on the top of his head hadn't seen hair for more than two decades, but he still wore a neatly trimmed mustache above his top lip.

Maggie stood and let him pull her into a bear hug. He smelled as he usually did, like cigars. The familiarity of it put her more at ease. This was her father, Boyd, a new woman on his arm, but he was the same as always.

"This," her father said, reaching behind him for the hand of the woman he'd come into the restaurant with, "is Julie." He pulled Julie to his side.

Julie wore a ruffled white shirt, a peasant skirt with colorful flowers all over it and gold goddess sandals that laced up her legs. Her makeup was as colorful as her outfit—bursts of pink on her lips, her eyelids and her cheeks. Her blond hair was streaked with gray and piled atop her head in a messy updo. The thing that surprised Maggie most though was her age. Her father's girlfriends had trended down in age for the last decade and a half. Based on that, Maggie had been expecting a woman in her mid to early thirties. She had to be at least a decade older than thirty, which still made her more than a decade younger than her father, but at least she wasn't younger than Maggie like the last woman her father had insisted she meet. She knew it wasn't forward-thinking or liberated to care about the age difference between two consenting adults, and usually she didn't, but this was her father. Maybe it was childish and immature, but it was weird to think about her father dating someone younger than she was.

A wave of sickly sweet perfume came at Maggie as Julie threw her arms around her. "It's so nice to finally meet you."

"Oh! It's, ah, it's nice to meet you too."

"I'm sorry," Julie said, taking two steps back. "I'm a hugger. Especially when I'm nervous. I just want us to get along."

"Honey, now don't you worry about that. I know you and Maggie are going to get along swimmingly. Just you wait and see. Kevin!"

Several heads at the tables around them turned. Boyd Scott was a man with a personality that grabbed attention even when he didn't mean to.

Kevin stood. "Mr. Scott." Kevin extended a hand.

Body shook it heartily. "It's been a long time. I'm glad to see you and Maggie are spending time together again. Maybe you two will finally get your acts together then."

"Dad."

"Boyd, darling. Let's sit," Julie said, seeming to catch on quicker than her fiancé to Maggie's distress at his comments. "We have all lunch to catch up with the kids."

Maggie frowned. Now she was one of the kids. This woman barely knew her.

Kevin squeezed her hand. "You can do this," he mouthed.

She sucked in a deep breath and let it out slowly as they settled in at the table.

Maggie reached for the wine list. There was no way she was getting through this lunch without liquid help.

"Let's have champagne," her father said. "After all, we are celebrating. And it's on me."

Maggie's eyebrows arched. The restaurant her father had chosen wasn't going to be getting any spreads in a magazine, but it wasn't cheap either.

Her father laughed. "I know. I know. But I got a job."

Maggie's brow climbed higher.

"I didn't want to tell you until I got through the probationary period, but I've been working for a nonprofit for older adults. The organization provides classes—computer, horticultural, painting—and social activities like dances and cocktail hours. It's like summer camp for us mature individuals, but since most of the people who sign up are retired, we can do it all year round."

Maggie set the wine list down. "Wow, Dad, that's great. Congratulations."

Her father beamed. "Thank you, baby. That's actually how Julie and I met. She teaches the gardening and horticulture classes at the center."

"My husband and I used to own our own landscaping business," Julie added.

"Oh, that's great." What she knew about gardening could fit on a Post-it. She didn't even have plants in her house, couldn't keep them alive. But if Julie had owned a business, she wasn't under the illusion that marrying her father would be some sort of financial windfall.

"I started going to the center to have something to fill my days with," Boyd continued telling the story of how he and

Julie met, "and when the office assistant moved to Phoenix to be with her children, the manager offered me the job."

Their waiter arrived. Her father ordered champagne for the table, and they each placed their orders. The restaurant had pretty standard American fare. Her father and Kevin ordered burgers and fries, Julie got the salmon and Maggie ordered the chicken salad.

"So, how long have you two been dating?" Kevin asked once the waiter had hurried off the put in their orders.

Boyd's brow arched. "I could ask the same question of you two."

"We're not dating, Dad."

"No? Then what is he doing here? No offense there, Kevin, but it's been a minute since I've seen you and my daughter together. Always liked you, though. I figured when you disappeared and Maggie stopped talking about you that she'd thrown you back into the ocean, so to speak."

"We're friends, Dad. I thought we were here to get to know Julie," she said, attempting to divert her father's attention from her love life to his own.

Kevin's shoulders shook with suppressed laughter.

"We are, we are. I want my two favorite ladies in the whole wide world to get to love each other as much as I love you both. But—" her father held his hand out palm up "—you can't just show up with your long-lost first love and expect me not to ask questions. I am your father."

Maggie massaged her temples.

"Boyd, darling, I think you're embarrassing Maggie. She is your daughter, but she's a grown woman who may not want to talk about her love life with her father."

Maggie shot Julie a look of gratitude. Maybe she wasn't so terrible.

"So, Julie, why horticulture?" Kevin said, finally doing what she'd brought him along to do—keep the situation from going off the rails.

Julie explained that her husband had started the business before they'd met, and after they married she'd joined him. He'd passed away from a heart attack four years earlier. Their three children were scattered across the country, and none of them had the green thumb their parents had, so she'd sold the company after her husband's death.

The waiter came back with the champagne as she'd talked, and they toasted to the engagement.

Maggie had to admit, Julie wasn't what she'd expected and her father seemed genuinely happy. Not that he hadn't seemed happy at the beginning of the relationships with his other wives, but he did seem different with Julie. More grounded. The woman was an expert at rooting things. Maybe she'd found a way to give her father roots.

They ate and chatted, and Maggie found herself genuinely liking Julie. In addition to her job at the center, Julie liked to sew and paint and to visit with her grandchildren. Maggie was reeling a bit from the realization that once her father and Julie married, she'd have stepsiblings. At the age of thirty-six, she was finally going to have a sister and two brothers. And five step nieces and nephews. As much as she'd always wished she'd had more family, it was all suddenly a bit much to take in.

More than anything, she was thankful that the theft at the museum didn't come up. She was not surprised her father didn't know about the theft or Kim's death. He wasn't much of a paper reader and didn't particularly care for art. She didn't want to worry him nor did she want to hash through the mess that was her life at the moment.

Her head spun, and she felt sick to her stomach. She pushed her chair back from the table abruptly. "Excuse me for a moment."

She rose and made her way toward the restrooms.

"Maggie." Julie rushed to catch up to her at the door to the ladies' room. "Your father wanted me to check on you and make sure you were okay."

"I'm fine." She tried for a smile. "I think I might have had a little too much champagne."

Julie laid a light hand on Maggie's forearm. "I just wanted to let you know that I love your father and I plan to do my very best to make him happy. And I hope that we can forge our own relationship."

Maggie didn't have to force a smile this time. "I hope so too."

Maggie's phone rang.

"I should be getting back to the table. I'm sure the guys are eager to know you're okay."

The call was from Robert. "I'll be there in a moment. This is my boss. Probably wanting to know when I'm coming in today."

Maggie accepted the call as Julie made her way back to the table.

"Hi, Robert. I know I should have called you and let you know that I was going to be in late today, but this morning has been hectic."

"That's one way to put it. I just got off the phone with Carter Tutwilder."

Crap.

"I know I should have called you first—"

"It wouldn't have made a difference. Carter was not pleased to hear that the police searched your home this morning."

"How did Carter even know about that?"

"Are you saying it's not true?" Robert shot back.

"No. The police did search my home this morning, but I had nothing to do with that. They are investigating—"

"Yes, they are. And in order for them to have gotten a search warrant for your home, they'd have to have some sort of evidence that you could be involved in a crime. I'm sorry, Maggie, we just can't have that kind of rumor and supposition associated with the Larimer."

Her jaw clenched. "Robert, we've discussed this."

"That was before. Carter and the board agree. Until this matter is resolved, you are being placed on administrative leave."

She was sure Carter had agreed. She didn't know how he found out about the search of her house, but she had no doubt that his decision to have the board put her on administrative leave was motivated by the meeting they'd just had.

"Until the matter is over. Robert, police investigations can take months. Even years."

Administrative leave meant no paycheck. They may as well have fired her. They probably would. They just wanted to get their ducks in a row before they did.

"I'm sorry, Maggie. I'll have the personal effects from your office shipped to your house."

The line went dead.

"Maggie?"

She turned to find Kevin behind her.

"You okay?" he asked, concern crinkling the skin around his eyes.

She shook her head. "No, no, I'm not." It was happening again. Losing her job. Being suspected of having committed a crime. Being ostracized. Just like it had in New York with Ellison.

She swallowed and said the words that sent panic streaking through her. "I just got fired."

Chapter Thirteen

Maggie went back to the table and pleaded sickness to her father and Julie, promising that they'd get together again soon. Now she and Kevin stood outside in front of the restaurant.

She turned angry eyes on him. "I just lost my job. The board has voted to put me on administrative leave until the police case is over." The words burned their way out of her throat.

"I'm sorry. I—" Kevin reached out to her, but she stepped back, away from his touch.

"You went into Tutwilder's office like a bull in a china shop and basically accused the chairman of the board of the museum of what? Stealing a priceless artifact." She shook with anger.

Kevin held his hands out. "Look, I could have been more diplomatic. I wasn't thinking."

"That's just it. You never think about me. When we were together in college, it was all about you."

Kevin's face hardened. "It was never about me. It was about making money so my mom didn't have to struggle anymore and so Tanya wouldn't have to worry about paying for medical school."

"Was it?" she shot back at him. "That's why you played

football. Why you went into the NFL. But it doesn't explain why you dumped me." Her voice dropped low. "We were planning a life together after graduation. A family. And then, just like that—" she snapped her fingers "—you were out. Gone." She looked at him and all the hurt she'd felt the moment he told her it was over welled up again. "And what? Now you want a second chance?"

"Walking away from you was the biggest mistake of my life. I have and will always regret it and I am more sorry than I can ever express. I know I hurt you—"

"You have no idea," she hissed. Hot tears rolled down her cheeks. She wished she could stop them, but she was well past controlling her emotions. Or the words that were tumbling from her mouth. "I was pregnant."

Kevin stilled, the color fleeing from his face.

"I found out a week after you broke up with me," she continued. "And the next week, I miscarried."

"You were pregnant?" His voice was barely audible. "Why didn't you tell me?"

"Because you weren't there." The accusation whipped from her lips.

He flinched.

"And then it didn't matter."

Anger flashed in his eyes. "It mattered. You should have told me."

"No." She pointed at him. "I was nineteen, pregnant, and the man I thought was going to love me forever had just walked out on me. You of all people do not get to judge my choices."

His jaw clenched. "I had a right to know."

She stepped forward, holding his gaze. "Then you should have been there."

A long moment passed.

"Is that why you married Ellison after we broke up? Because I wasn't there?"

She shook her head, some of the anger she felt toward him dissipating. It was useless being angry. It wouldn't get her job back, and it wouldn't change anything. "I'm not doing this with you. The past is in the past, and that's where I'm leaving it."

She turned and started away from him.

"Where are you going?" He jogged to catch up with her.

"Home." She pulled out her phone and called up the rideshare app. "I'll get there myself."

"Maggie—"

"No." She turned to him, looking him in the eye. "I don't want to be around you right now, Kevin."

KEVIN CAUGHT TANYA at her apartment the next morning before she left for her shift at the hospital. Tanya already had her coat on, thermos of hot coffee in hand, when she opened the door to him.

"Kevin? Hi, what's up? Are you okay?" she asked, stepping back so he could enter the apartment.

He didn't waste time or mince words. "You knew about Maggie's miscarriage? About the baby, didn't you?"

"How did you—"

"Maggie told me. That's what you were going to tell me the other day before you stopped yourself."

Tanya sighed and set her thermos down on the side table next to her purse. "I knew."

"Why didn't you tell me?" Fury rose in his tone.

"Because I couldn't. Maggie came into the student health center once she realized she might be pregnant. You know I held a work-study job there while we were in school. I was on duty. Patient confidentiality laws prohibited me from saying anything to you or anyone about a patient's medical history."

He glowered at her. "You're my sister. It's been years."

She shook her head. "It doesn't matter who I am or how many years it's been. Confidentiality still applies. And, to be honest with you, I'm not sure I would have told you if I could have."

He threw up his hands. "Is everybody losing their minds?" he yelled.

"Kevin, there was nothing you could have done. Miscarriages are common, much more common than most people even realize. Telling you would have only left you feeling guilty for something that you had no control over." She reached out, placing a hand on his arm. "Something that was not in any way your fault, do you understand me?"

He understood her just like she understood where his anger emanated from. Fear. Fear that his decision to break up with Maggie had upset her enough to cause a miscarriage.

"If I hadn't left—" he said softly.

"She would have still lost the baby," Tanya said firmly.

"I should have been there for her."

"What is it Mom always says, 'the shoulda, woulda, coulbdas will drive you up a wall if you let them'?" She gave him a small smile. "You can't change the choices you made, and you shouldn't want to. Right or wrong, they made you, and to some extent Maggie, who you are now. And you're not that bad." She gave a little sister shrug he knew was intended to draw a smile from him.

He wasn't ready to smile, but talking to his sister did make him feel a little better. It didn't alleviate all his guilt. He wasn't sure anything could do that, but he felt a little lighter than he had when he'd walked into her apartment. He pulled his sister into a tight hug.

"So Maggie finally told you," Tanya said after they pulled apart. "Interesting."

"What's interesting about it? She was mad at me for getting her fired, and she shot it at me like a bullet."

Tanya's mouth fell open. "You got her fired?"

He ran a hand over his head. His life felt as if it was spinning out of control, and he didn't like it. "Not on purpose. I came on a little strong when questioning her boss's boss, and he's taking it out on her."

"You remember what I said about you. Maggie. This case." She threw her hands up in a gesture simulating an explosion. "Kaboom."

"I know, I—"

"Should have listened to your younger, but wiser, sister." She pressed her palms to her chest. "Yes, you should have."

"Didn't you just say something about 'shoulda, woulda, couldas'? I'm trying to remember what that was."

"Point taken. So what are you going to do now?"

"I have to get my head on straight and focus. West Investigations has been hired to find the ruby, and I'm convinced its theft is somehow tied to Maggie's friend's murder."

"And Maggie is intent on helping solve said friend's murder." Tanya looped her purse over her shoulder and picked up her thermos. "Well, maybe you'll have the rarest of opportunities, big brother. You might be able to rectify some of your 'shoulda, woulda, couldas.'"

Chapter Fourteen

"Thanks for coming in," Detective Francois said, settling into the chair on the opposite side of the table from Maggie.

Maggie had spent the first morning of her forced leave giving her house a deep clean and chastising herself for letting her anger get the better of her the day before with Kevin. Detective Francois had shown up on her doorstep around noon, requesting her presence down at the station for a formal interview. He'd posed it as a question, but she'd gotten the distinct impression she didn't have a choice.

She'd hesitated a moment, wondering if she should have a lawyer present, but had dismissed the idea quickly. She had nothing to hide. The faster Detective Francois saw that she'd had nothing to do with the theft or Kim's murder, the quicker he could turn his attention to viable suspects.

So she'd ridden to the police station beside him in his unmarked police sedan.

He'd shown her into an interrogation room and offered her coffee and water, which she'd declined. She considered a lawyer a second time when Detective Francois read her Miranda rights, but she again rejected the idea. She didn't have the money, and she didn't have anything to hide.

"There are just a few things I want to clarify." He looked

up from the notepad in front of him and gave her a smile she guessed was meant to be disarming. To her, it looked a little more predatory. No matter how polite Detective Francois was, she wasn't going to make the mistake of thinking that he was her friend. He was looking for a thief and a murderer, and right now she knew she was his best suspect.

She flashed him a quick smile. "Anything I can do to help, Detective. Have you made any headway with Kim's case?"

His smile tightened. "I assure you we are doing everything we can."

"I'm sure you are," she lied.

"Just so I'm sure I have things correct, can you go over the night of the theft and finding Ms. Sumika's body again?"

Maggie bit back her frustration and walked the detective through the worst night of her life once again.

"And when was the last time, before you found Ms. Sumika, that you were in her house?"

Maggie thought for a moment. "Two evenings before. Kim invited me over for dinner. She did that on occasion. She did seem a little distracted."

Detective Francois perked up. "Distracted? How?"

"Like she had something on her mind. I asked her about it, and she said it was nothing." Guilt hung heavy on her heart. "I wish I'd pressed her on it."

"You have no idea what might have been worrying her?"

"No. I was assigned to take the lead on designing the Viperé exhibit, but we were all under a bit of stress with the donors' open house coming up and making sure everything went as scheduled. I remember thinking that it could just be that."

"Huh." He wrote something she couldn't read on the notepad.

Detective Francois's eyes narrowed to slits. "So, two

days before. That was the last time you were in Ms. Sumi-ka's house."

"Yes, that's what I said."

"And the last time you saw her was the day of the donors' open house?"

"That's right. Right before the event, Kim complained of a migraine. I had everything under control, so I told her to go home and rest."

Detective Francois cocked his head to the side and gave her a contemplative look. "That didn't seem odd to you? I mean, this donors' open house is a big deal, right?" Maggie nodded. "So suddenly Ms. Sumika is too sick to attend, and neither you nor Mr. Gustev thought that was odd?"

Maggie fought to keep her annoyance in check. Detective Francois hadn't known Kim or how devoted she was to the museum. Then again, it seemed like there was a lot she hadn't known about Kim either. She hadn't thought it was suspicious for Kim to miss the event at the time, but now... Maybe she should have paid a little more attention to Kim in the last days of her life.

"Kim suffered from migraines," she answered. "I didn't think it was suspicious that the stress of the new exhibit and the party got to her."

Detective Francois frowned. "What do you know about Ms. Sumika's finances?"

Maggie shrugged. "Nothing, really. I mean, I knew she'd inherited the house from her parents. I know how much a place like that would go for, so I assumed Kim wasn't financially strapped, even with the gambling. At least, not on paper."

The detective leaned forward. "What do you mean 'at least, not on paper'?"

Maggie found herself instinctively leaning away from the detective. She could see why he'd insisted on having this conversation in an interrogation room. It was effectively intimidating.

"I didn't mean anything. Just that houses like Kim's sell for quite a bit these days. Neither of us made a fortune working for the Larimer, but I figured Kim at least had the house as an asset."

"And your rental income."

"Yes, although she wasn't charging me anywhere near market rate."

"Right." He pulled stapled sheets of paper from between the pages of his notebook. "Have you seen this before?" He passed the pages across the table to her.

Last Will and Testament. The first paragraph looked to be standard boilerplate language with Kim's name typed onto a thick black line.

"I've never seen this before this moment, no."

Detective Francois reached for the papers and flipped the pages until he got to a section highlighted in yellow. "Please read this paragraph for me."

Maggie read, her heart picking up its pace until it was thundering as she read the last words.

Kim had left her house and all personal possessions to Maggie.

She met Detective Francois's gaze. "I didn't know."

"You had no idea you were the sole benefactor, save for a few charitable bequests, of Kim Sumika's will?"

"I had no idea, Detective. You have to believe me."

Detective Francois studied her.

She couldn't tell if he did, in fact, believe her, but she was stunned. Kim hadn't even hinted about the arrangements she'd made. Maggie knew she'd been an only child, but she recalled Kim speaking about a cousin in Indiana. Heck, she was surprised her friend even had a will. She'd only had one drawn up after Ellison had died without any instructions regarding his final wishes. Since they were divorced by then, she hadn't had any say in how his property was distributed. She'd heard his sister got everything, but it hadn't been her place to inquire.

Detective Francois took the will from her and slid it back between the pages of his notebook. "One of your other colleagues mentioned that there was a group that wasn't happy with the Larimer exhibiting the Viperé ruby. They staged a protest in front of the museum several weeks ago."

The sudden change in topic was jarring. She just looked at the detective for a moment.

"Yes," she answered finally. "Ah, the Art and Antiquities Repatriation Project people. They've staged protests at various museums in California and elsewhere against exhibits that show items that are the subject of cultural or repatriation claims."

"Are you a member of this organization or any similar organization?"

Maggie frowned. "No."

"Several of the board members I spoke with mentioned that you'd made an impassioned argument against the Larimer mounting this exhibit. Why is that?"

She didn't try to hide her irritation this time. "I wasn't arguing against the exhibit. I just thought that the board should be aware of and prepared for the fact that not everyone was going to agree with a decision to exhibit the Viperé."

"Huh." He tapped his pen against the notepad. "And did you agree with the board's decision to move forward?"

"I didn't disagree. It's a complex issue, as evidenced by the various lawsuits."

The detective leaned forward in his seat. "So you sympathize with the plaintiffs in these lawsuits and organizations like the one that was protesting your museum."

"I do," she gritted out, regretting her decision to speak with the detective without a lawyer.

It was clear that Detective Francois wasn't broadening the scope of the investigation. He was narrowing it. On her.

She reached for her purse at her feet. "Detective, I don't think I wish to answer any more questions without an attorney."

Detective Francois spread his hands out. "Ms. Scott, I'm just trying to get to the bottom of the crimes that seem to be swirling around you."

She stood, her chair scraping against the linoleum flooring. "And I hope you do get to the bottom of these crimes. For Kim's sake. But I promise you, when you do, I won't be the person you find there."

His expression clearly said he didn't believe that, but he stood and opened the door for her.

She marched down the short hallway leading away from the interrogation rooms and toward the front exit. She came to a stop just past the front reception area.

Kevin was leaning against the side wall, his arms crossed over his chest.

He straightened when he saw her.

"What are you doing here?" she asked, approaching warily. Guilt gnawed at her. She didn't regret the choice she'd made in not telling him about her miscarriage when it happened, but it had been unkind to drop it on him like she had.

"I heard Detective Francois brought you in for questioning." He took a step closer to her.

"Do I want to know how you knew that?"

"I have my spies." He gave her a tepid smile. "Are you ready to get out of here?"

She definitely was, but they had so much they needed to talk about, and she wasn't in the right headspace to tackle it at the moment.

"It might be best if I get an Uber. I know we have things we need to talk about, and we will, but I just can't right now."

Kevin held his hands up. "I'm just offering you a ride home. We don't have to speak at all if you don't want."

She hesitated for a moment more before her shoulders relaxed and she returned his tepid smile with one of her own. "Okay then, thank you. A ride would be great."

He led her out the front doors of the police station and to the parking lot. The farther they got from the station, the more she relaxed.

"Do you mind if I ask you what Detective Francois asked you in there?"

She looked up at him, her throat constricting with fear. "He thinks I killed Kim. He pretty much said as much." She stopped walking, and Kevin paused alongside her. The man walking behind them shot them a dirty look and veered around them. "Kevin, Detective Francois had Kim's will, and she left me everything."

Kevin stroked his chin. "And I take it you had no idea she was going to do this."

"None at all." She pulled him to the side, out of the path of another pedestrian heading their way. "I mean, I knew Kim didn't have much family to speak of, but I never expected her to name me in her will."

Kevin's eyes darkened. "And because she did, it now looks like you had a motive for wanting her dead."

She nodded. "That seems to be what the detective is thinking. Kevin, I'm scared. Detective Francois isn't looking at anyone else. He thinks I did this. The theft and killing Kim."

He pulled her into his arms and dropped a kiss on the top of her head. "We're going to get to the bottom of this. I promise you."

Maggie wrapped her arms around him. Let his warmth seep through her. And tried to believe that he was right and that they'd find the real culprit.

Chapter Fifteen

Kevin led Maggie toward his Mustang. Tess had called him less than an hour earlier with the contact information for Josh Huber, head of the organization that had staged the protest against the Larimer Museum. She'd also informed him that Detective Francois had brought Maggie in for another round of questioning. He'd asked Tess to give Huber a call and set up a meeting for that afternoon and hopped in the car, headed for the police station.

Of course, the cops wouldn't let him into the interrogation room with Maggie, but he'd refused to leave. Detective Francois seemed to have homed in on Maggie as his prime suspect, and he wanted to be there if she needed support or, worse, needed someone to get her a lawyer. He'd breathed a sigh of relief when she'd walked out of the back of the police station.

But now he wasn't sure what he wanted to say to her. He was still upset with her for having kept her pregnancy from him, even if he was beginning to understand why she'd done so. More than anything, what he felt was remorse. Remorse for having not been there for her when she'd needed him. Guilt at having broken up with her at all. As much as he'd tried to convince himself that he'd had to leave everything behind and focus all his efforts and attention on football, he knew now that he'd just been scared. Scared of the intensity of his feelings for her. So he'd pushed her away. Ran away from her, actually.

But it hadn't worked. He'd never stopped thinking about her.

And now? Now that she was back in his life, he wasn't willing to let her go.

They both got in his car, but he made no move to start the engine.

"Maggie, about yesterday—"

She reached across the console for his hand. "Kevin, I'm sorry. I shouldn't have sprung the miscarriage on you like that," she interrupted.

"No, you have nothing to apologize for." He turned her hand palm up and ran his index finger along her wrist.

"I do. I was angry about losing my job and frustrated with everything that's going on right now, and I lashed out at you. I wanted to hurt you, and that was wrong."

He entwined his fingers with hers. "There are a lot of things I want to say, but I'm not sure how to say them at the moment."

"We do need to talk, but maybe right now isn't the best time. We both need time to process, and then there's this." She gestured toward the police station.

"So let's make a deal. After this—" he made the same gesture that she had toward the police station "—is all over, we'll talk. Really talk. Deal?"

She smiled at him, and his heart turned over.

"Deal," she said.

He wanted to kiss her. He always had loved kissing Maggie.

His phone beeped and he groaned inside. He pulled it

from his pocket and looked at the screen. "It's a text from Tess. She's set up a meeting for me with Josh Huber. He's the director of the Art and Antiquities Repatriation Project. The group that protested the Viperé exhibit at the Larimer. He has time to speak with me now." He looked at her with a question in his eye. "To see us now?"

"What are you waiting for?"

The Art and Antiquities Repatriation Project was housed in a rundown slip of a building that had seen better days. In fact, the entire block looked as if it had seen better days. There was a hotel on one corner, its front window so filthy the Vacancies Available sign was nearly obscured, and a corner store on the other. Several of the storefronts had signs proclaiming them For Rent, but a handful of businesses seemed to be holding on. A tarot card reader, a yoga studio and a fabric store were among them. Seeing this area, Kevin regretted bringing Maggie with him and even considered blowing the meeting off and rescheduling. But Maggie wasn't wrong about one thing: the pressure was building to give Francois anyone other than her to focus on as a suspect. And he hoped he could find that someone among the workers and volunteers at the Art and Antiquities Repatriation Project.

He parked at the curb in front of the address he had for the AARP. It took a minute for a voice to come over the intercom after he pressed the buzzer, but the door unlocked as soon as he identified himself and Maggie.

The space was uncomfortably warm bordering on sweltering, but it was clear that someone had done their best to do what they could with the AARP offices. The walls were a bright white made brighter by the recessed lighting illuminating the space. Fresh flowers sat in a vase on the desk just inside the doorway. The space was empty, save for several mismatched desks, some wood, some metal, in what was clearly a shared workspace. A number of file cabinets lined one wall, and a table in the back held a coffee maker, paper cups and other assorted items.

A man stepped out of the office at the back of the workspace. He was short, no more than five foot five or six, middle-aged and bald.

"Kevin Lombard?" The man approached them warily.

Kevin held out his hand. "Yes. And this is Maggie Scott. Thank you for meeting with us, Mr. Huber."

Josh Huber was the director of the Art and Antiquities Repatriation Project. Since he'd done his homework, Kevin knew that Huber had a degree in art history and that he'd spent more than a decade lecturing at a local college before taking on the position at the AARP. The protest at the Larimer was one of many the group had staged over the past several years. They'd seemingly had a few successes, getting a couple of museums and private collectors to donate smaller pieces to museums in the countries from which the pieces originated. But through his research into the group, he'd learned that repatriation was a tricky, costly and sometimes politically fraught endeavor.

Huber led them into his office. The space was cramped and stuffy.

"Sorry about the heat in here. Seems like no matter what I do, this office is always too hot." Huber dropped down into his office chair.

There was only one visitor's chair. He let Maggie take it and stood next to her.

"It's fine," Kevin said. "We don't want to take up too much

of your time. We're hoping you can answer some questions for us."

"About our protest at the Larimer." Huber leaned back in his chair, pen in hand.

"Well, yes. I'm sure you're aware the Viperé ruby was stolen the night before last."

Huber frowned. "And you think that the Art and Antiquities Repatriation Project had something to do with that? Sorry to deprive you of an easy answer, but no way."

Maggie leaned forward in the chair. "We're not looking for an easy answer, Mr. Huber. We just want to get the ruby back."

Huber spun the pen in his hands. "I'm afraid I still can't help you. I'm not even sure I would if I could, but I can't."

"We know your organization believes that these types of items belong to the people of the countries from which they came," Kevin said.

"They do." Huber straightened. "They were stolen during periods of colonization." He pounded a fist on his desk.

Kevin caught the glance Maggie sent him. "Mr. Huber, we really aren't here to debate you on your views."

"I work at the Larimer," Maggie cut in. "I think you make some very good points, and I did articulate them to the board when they were considering whether or not to go forward with the exhibit."

Huber looked surprised. "Didn't seem to do much good though."

"From your point of view, no, I guess it didn't," Maggie conceded.

"Mr. Huber, was there anyone in your group who was particularly upset that the protest didn't have the desired effect of getting the museum to cancel the exhibit?"

Huber sighed. "Now why would I tell you that? You'll just use it to paint a target on the back of our volunteers."

"I promise you that's not what we intend to do," Maggie spoke up. "If you're aware of the ruby's theft, I'm sure you also know that one of my coworkers was found later that night having died of an overdose. I don't think it was an accident."

"You think your coworker was killed by whoever stole the ruby." Huber shook his head. "There's no way anyone associated with our group would be involved in what you're suggesting. No way."

"If that's true, then there's no harm in helping us," Kevin responded.

"Please," Maggie added when Huber continued to hesitate.

Huber sighed again. "Look, like I said, no one in this group would be involved in a theft. That would make them no better than the people who took these artifacts from their countries in the first place."

They weren't going to get names of members from this guy. Kevin wasn't surprised about that. Maybe Francois would have better luck. Still, he needed to get what he could from Huber. "What about people not associated with the Repatriation Project? There are always people who think that lawful protest simply isn't enough. Has anyone like that expressed an interest in the ruby lately?"

"You are right. There are always people who think that more…aggressive measures should be taken to address wrongs." Huber paused, thinking. "I can't think of anyone though who expressed an interest in the ruby per se."

Kevin's ears perked up at the hedge. "But you can think of someone who fits the description of the kind of person we're talking about generally."

"There was a girl, a woman, early twenties. Just out of college. Idealistic, you know the type." Huber was back spinning the pen between his fingers. "I don't know her name. She came to one of the protests we held, oh, maybe a month or two ago. Really aggressive. Said talk wasn't enough. We needed to get our hands dirty in the fight if we wanted to affect real change." Huber scoffed. "I've been doing this kind of work for more than twenty years. Maybe longer than this woman had been alive. I think my hands are plenty dirty."

"Do you know her name?" Kevin asked.

Huber shook his head. "No. She only came to the one protest. She made such a scene I had to ask her to leave. Never saw her again."

"Can you describe her?"

Huber shrugged. "Brunette, shortish hair. Not too tall."

That probably described thousands of women in the Los Angeles area, and they weren't even sure the woman was from here.

He and Maggie thanked Huber for his time and left.

"What do you think?" Maggie asked when they were back in the car.

"I think Francois will get the names of the members of the organization, but I don't think this group has the know-how to pull something like this off."

"So where does that leave us?"

Continuing to spin their wheels looking for a suspect that wasn't her. Since that was an answer he wasn't willing to give her, he started the engine and pulled away from the curb without a word.

Chapter Sixteen

Kevin glanced at the clock on his bedside table: 11:10 p.m. He sighed and climbed out of bed. Maybe some calming mint tea would help him finally get some sleep.

He couldn't stop thinking about Maggie.

He hoped she was getting more rest than he was, although he doubted it. Even though she insisted she wasn't going to be run out of her home, he'd seen the fear in her eyes. Everything inside of him wanted to make her feel safe.

He'd crossed the line from professional to personal the moment he'd kissed her on her front porch. Scratch that. He'd crossed that line the moment he'd realized she was the curator who had been attacked during the theft of the Viperé ruby. From that moment on, he'd wanted nothing more than to catch the man who'd put his hands on his Maggie and make him pay.

His Maggie.

That was how he used to think about her all the time. He wasn't sure when he started thinking about her like that again, but sometime in the last several days, he had. And he realized something else. He wanted another chance with her. Now he just had to figure out a way to convince her to give him one.

He glanced at the phone, wondering if it was too late to

call. Of course it was. But he wasn't sure he could wait until the more socially acceptable time the next morning.

It wasn't just the nearly uncontrollable desire to at least hear her voice. This case, everything about it, bothered him.

The theft, Maggie being attacked and the threat against her, Kim Sumika's murder and now Carter Tutwilder's possible inquiries into buying a gem like the Viperé only weeks before it was stolen. None of it made sense. Especially not the attacks on Maggie. If the thief was the same person who'd made the threat against her, why had he hung around to do so? And if the thief and the person threatening Maggie weren't the same person? He wasn't sure what that would mean, and he didn't like not having answers. Not when it came to Maggie's safety.

There were simultaneously too many clues and not enough. Carter Tutwilder had been keeping something from them, he was sure of that, but was his secret relevant or just something the billionaire didn't want to see in the papers? Kim Sumika had a gambling problem, but so did thousands of other Los Angelenos. It might not have anything to do with the theft or her murder. And if Kim had reached out to Kovalev to be her new bookie, Kim would have brought real trouble down on her head by not paying up. But the timing was just too coincidental for him to shake off.

The tea kettle whistled. He poured the tea into a travel mug and carried it to his bedroom to change.

Midnight might be too late for a phone call, but nothing was stopping him from taking a drive by Maggie's house to make sure all was quiet there.

MOONLIGHT WAS STILL peeking around the edges of the blinds when she opened her eyes. She'd gone to bed at ten, exhausted. The dream she'd been having involved her and Kevin walking hand in hand on a beach, which had led to a romantic dinner, which had led to the two of them in bed. It had felt so real she almost expected to see Kevin lying in bed beside her, but of course he wasn't there. She touched the cold spot next to her with longing before chiding herself. She couldn't fall back into things with Kevin.

A shadow shifted outside her window. She stilled, her heart in her throat. A long minute passed and she relaxed. Just shadows.

The last several days had put her on edge, and she hated it. Hated looking over her shoulder all the time. Hated feeling unsafe in her own home. And it didn't feel like she and Kevin were getting any closer to discovering who was behind the theft of the ruby, Kim's death or the terror campaign against her.

Something caught her eye outside the window. It wasn't just a shadow. There was someone out there. A glance at the clock showed that it was 11:25 p.m. No one with good intentions would be lurking around her house at this time of the night.

She slid from her bed as quietly as she could, her heart in her throat.

Grabbing her cell phone, she moved into the living room, not turning on any lights. As long as the person outside thought she was still asleep, she had the element of surprise.

She waited impatiently, her eyes moving from the windows at the front of the house to the ones in the back, looking for any movement, as Kevin's phone rang. After what seemed like hours, he picked up.

"There's someone here," she whispered frantically as soon as the call connected.

"I'm two minutes away." She wondered how he could already be so close, but any thought of asking the question was cut off by the sound of the glass pane in her back door shattering.

She dropped the phone and lunged for the end table in the living room where she kept a Maglite flashlight.

"Maggie? Maggie, are you there? Answer me, Maggie."

She grabbed the flashlight, which was heavy enough to double as a weapon if it came to that, and clicked it on. She turned the light toward the back door just as the hand jutting into the house through the broken pane found the lock and turned it. She jerked the beam toward the intruder's face.

He wore a mask, but this one was different from the one the thief at the Larimer wore. It covered the top of the intruder's head and his neck and came up to his nose, but left his forehead and eye area uncovered. Something tugged at the back of her mind for a fleeting moment, but the intruder's startled jerk chased it away.

"The cops are on their way, and I have a gun. If you come any closer, I will shoot." She could only hope the intruder couldn't hear the lie in her voice.

Luck was on her side. A pounding sounded on the front door as the last words left her mouth.

"Maggie!" Kevin yelled.

"I'm okay," she shouted back. "He's at the back door."

The intruder's eyes went wide. He pulled his hand out of the door and lurched away.

She waited several seconds before going to the door and peering out of what was left of the window.

The intruder hoisted himself over the back fence and disappeared into the darkness of the neighbor's lawn.

Kevin rounded the side of the cottage.

She jerked the damaged door open and pointed at the house behind the cottage. "He went over the fence."

Kevin looked her up and down quickly.

"I'm fine. He didn't make it inside."

"Call 911, tell them you had an intruder and ask them to call Detective Francois," he said before taking off after the intruder.

Into the darkness.

KEVIN WAITED UNTIL he saw Maggie slip back into the house and the door close. Then he headed for the back fence, vaulting over it with one hand, his gun in the other. The neighbor's yard was shrouded in darkness. The little bit of illumination came from the bulb over the neighbor's back door and created eerie shadows and shapes. He froze, listening for the sound of an animal bigger than the usual night creatures moving about. For several long moments, all he heard were the chirps of crickets. Then, almost as if they were warning him of impending danger, the chirping to his right fell silent.

He turned in that direction and saw the shadow moving quickly along the side of the porch toward the front of the house. He started for it, but the man must have seen or heard him coming.

The intruder took off running.

Kevin gave chase.

The intruder didn't seem to be worried about being quiet or stealthy anymore. He just wanted to get away now. And he was fast. In a matter of seconds, he'd managed to put a good distance between them.

It struck him that the intruder seemed familiar with the neighborhood. Was that because he'd been staking out Maggie's home or could there be another reason? He'd be sure to ask, as soon as he had the man in custody.

He picked up his pace, trying to close the distance. Even though the sun had long since set, the night was warm, leaving him sweaty even though he'd only run two blocks. He kept in shape, running several miles every week. But his heart was pounding, and the adrenaline rushing through his body wasn't helping him pace himself. And he was worried about Maggie. What if the intruder was leading him on a wild-goose chase just to get him away from her house? He could have a partner or double back. Maggie was all alone. Where the hell was the patrol that was supposed to be keeping an eye on her house?

Coming to the corner, Kevin turned in the direction he'd seen the intruder flee. The street and sidewalk were empty.

"Damnit." The intruder couldn't have disappeared.

He hadn't heard the sound of an engine turning, so he doubted the person had escaped in a car. He scanned the street.

A thick hedge ran along the property line of a nearby house.

Kevin crossed to it; it was dark, but it only took him seconds to find the narrow path leading between two neighboring houses. The shadow at the end of the path turned in time for Kevin to catch the whites of the man's eyes before he darted away again.

Propelled by a new surge of adrenaline, he raced down the path after the man. He had to catch the intruder and put an end to him terrorizing Maggie.

He got to the end of the path and found himself surrounded by trees. The path had ended at what appeared to be the beginning of a wooded area behind the homes. Maggie's intruder could be anywhere. Hiding among the trees. It wouldn't be safe for him to plunge into the thicket.

A moment too late, he sensed someone behind him.

Before he could turn, something hit him hard over the back of his head.

He went down to his knees, dizzy, stars flashing behind his eyes. Thankfully, he didn't lose consciousness. He could hear footfalls heading back down the path. He struggled to his feet, disoriented and woozy.

The footsteps faded into silence.

Chapter Seventeen

When he arrived back at Maggie's house, she was already
speaking to one of the police officers that had responded to
her call while the other officer searched around the perimeter of the house. Detective Francois arrived minutes later,
and Maggie described the attempted break-in, with Kevin
taking over the tale once the foot chase began. Francois
sent the officers out to scour the neighborhood, but Kevin
wasn't surprised when they returned without having spotted the intruder.

"Do you need to get checked out at the hospital, Lombard?" Francois asked.

Kevin rubbed the back of his head where he'd been hit.
There was a little bump there, but he'd had worse. "I'll be
fine."

Francois gave him a look that said he disagreed with his
decision, but he didn't push. "Ms. Scott, the police department is doing everything it can to get to the bottom of the
current situation, but it appears we are dealing with someone who wants to hurt you and who may have already killed
Kim Sumika. I'd strongly advise you to stay with a friend for
a while. Just until we have a better handle on the situation."

Maggie made a face. "I could ask my friend Lisa, but her

place is an hour away and small. And she has a cat that hates me." She shook her head, seemingly rejecting the idea even as she mentioned it.

"You can stay with me." Warning bells went off in his head immediately. Having her only feet away from his bed was probably not the best idea he'd ever had. Not when he couldn't have her in his bed. But he could see she was afraid, and he could keep his libido in check if that was what it took to make her feel safe.

"I don't know," she said hesitantly.

"I do. I have a guest room. It's yours for as long as you want it."

She gave him a grateful smile. "Thank you."

He waited while Maggie packed a bag and locked up the cottage. She didn't want to be stranded without a car, so she followed him to his place in her own car. When they got there, he ran inside the apartment building to get her a visitor's parking permit, then called Tess and updated her on the night's events as Maggie pulled into one of the reserved spaces while he kept an eye out.

"None of this is making a whole lot of sense," Tess said when he'd finished his update.

"On that, we agree."

"Well, I do have some news that's good. My source was able to get a location on Ivan Kovalev. He's partying at the bar he owns, Nightingale's. My source says the way the booze and recreational drugs are flowing, Ivan is likely to be there until closing at four. The source can get you into the club, but he can't guarantee Ivan will meet with you."

"But Ivan knows I want to speak with him?"

"Oh, he knows. There isn't much Ivan doesn't know. Once

you're in the club, if Ivan is open to talking to you, he'll find you."

Kevin watched as Maggie got out of her car and went to the trunk for her overnight bag. "The timing sucks. Maggie is going to stay with me for a while. I want to get her settled, and I'm not sure about leaving her alone."

"We know where Ivan is going to be tonight. I can send someone else if you really can't make it, but you know the details of this case back and forth."

And he didn't want to leave Ivan's questioning to anyone else. Finding out what he knew might be the key to figuring out what was going on and stopping it. Maggie was heading for him now. He glanced at his watch: 12:18 a.m. That gave him time to get Maggie settled, wait till she fell asleep and head to the club.

"And you're sure he's going to be at Nightingale's?" Kevin asked.

Maggie stopped in front of him and waited.

"That's what the source said."

"Okay, got it. Maggie is here. I've got to go." He ended the call.

"Who was that?" Maggie asked.

"Tess." He slid her bag from her shoulder and tossed it over his own. "I was filling her in on the attempted break-in at your house and you staying with me for a while."

"I don't know if it will be awhile. Let's just take it one day at a time."

"Whatever you want. You ready to go up?" He led her to the elevators into the building.

"I heard you and Tess talking about Nightingale's. That's that trendy club in Hollywood where all the celebrities hang out right? Who is going to be there tonight? Clooney? Pitt?

One of the many, many Chrises?" Maggie asked jokingly after the elevator doors closed and they'd started their ascent.

"Tess's informant got a location on Ivan Kovalev. He owns Nightingale's, a club in Hollywood."

"Are we going to talk to him?"

Kevin raised his hands. "Ivan Kovalev is a dangerous man. I don't want you anywhere near him."

Maggie frowned. "He may have answers to who killed Kim and is trying to destroy my life."

"I get it, but we have to be careful. Your safety is my number one priority."

"Kevin—"

The elevator stopped on the twelfth floor, and the doors slid open.

"We don't have to speak to Ivan tonight. Tess said he's at the club nearly every night." He felt a moment of guilt about the white lie then shook it off, remembering that, while she may not have lied to him, she'd kept a pretty major piece of information from him. At least he was doing it to protect her.

He could tell from her deepening frown that she didn't like that answer, but she nodded.

They got off the elevator, and he led her to a door at the end of the hallway.

He opened the door, flicked on the light and led her into the space.

"You have a nice place," Maggie said, her eyes roaming over the space.

"Tanya found it for me. It's five minutes from the hospital, which is its best feature. At least, in her opinion."

Maggie shot him a wan smile.

"You have to be exhausted. The guest room is just down

this way." He led her down the short hallway to the left of the front door.

His guest bedroom wasn't much, just a bed, dresser and nightstand, but it was warm and comfortable, and she'd be safe in his place.

He set her bag down at the foot of the bed and stepped back into the hall.

Maggie touched his arm as he passed by her, sending sparks of electric desire through him.

"Thank you," she said softly.

He pressed a kiss to her forehead then stepped back. He'd wanted to do much more, but she needed to rest. "You don't ever have to thank me. I'll always be there when you need me."

He retreated to his own room but didn't change into pajamas. He knew she'd be angry with him, but there was no way he was going to take her to Ivan's club. Especially when he wasn't sure Ivan wasn't behind everything that had been happening. He just had to wait for her to go to sleep, and then he could slip out of the apartment.

He heard Maggie's bedroom door open and her footsteps as she headed for the single bathroom in the apartment. She took a long shower then he heard the bathroom door open and the floor creak as she headed back to her room.

The bedroom door snapped shut, and the apartment fell quiet.

He lay back on his bed, planning to wait a few minutes for her to fall asleep before he left. While he waited, he ran through the events of the night in his head. The attempt to break into Maggie's home was bold, and it had terrified him. Whoever was behind everything that was happening seemed to be obsessed with Maggie. And obsessions only ended one of two ways. The person was caught or the object of the obsession was eliminated.

Fear and fury burned in his chest.

He would not let anything happen to Maggie.

The sound of the guest room door creaking open sent him on instant alert. Light spilled out of the guest bedroom. He sat up in bed, watching as Maggie's shadow moved closer and closer to his room.

She crept forward, headed for the bathroom, he guessed.

Maggie continued to creep forward, but not to the bathroom. She stopped at his bedroom door. "Kevin?"

"You okay?"

"I can't sleep."

He swung his bare feet to the floor. "I can make you some tea. Something soothing that might help you fall asleep."

She came into the room, and he got a good look at her. She was wearing a satin nightie that hugged her plump breasts and showed miles of long silky leg.

His lower body sprung to attention.

She stepped up to the side of the bed, her thigh brushing against him. "I was thinking about something else that might help me sleep."

"Maggie." His voice came out low and rough. He was surprised he was able to form words with her standing so close. So nearly naked. "This might not be a good idea."

But even as he spoke, he couldn't help reaching out and drawing his hand lightly over Maggie's hip.

"I don't want to think about rubies or death or tomorrow. I just want right now. With you."

She lowered her mouth to his, and his control snapped.

The years, the fears, the secrets, they all melted away with that kiss. All that was left was desire.

With those words, he closed the remaining distance between them, capturing her lips in a fervent kiss.

It was as if time hadn't passed at all. Her mouth claimed his, her tongue exploring with hunger. She kissed him like a woman desperate.

He knew the feeling because he felt it too.

Her hands rose and pressed against his chest, coaxing him back on the bed. He let her take the lead. She straddled him, and it was a fight not to lose control.

How many nights had he dreamed of this? Too many to count.

He wrapped his hands around her hips, pulling her against the hardness and heat between his thighs. He wanted her to feel how much he wanted her. To feel the weight of his arousal.

Her mouth left his, but her hold on him remained firm. She began a sensual exploration down his neck, her tongue caressing and igniting a thunderous beat in his chest and ears.

There were countless reasons why he should pull away. But he curled around her hips, fitting her tightly against him.

As if she sensed his hesitation, she whispered in his ear, "I want this. I need you."

What little control he had left shattered. Kevin flipped them so she was under him. He kissed her with raw desire, unchecked by any more reservations.

Already shirtless, he removed his pants, letting them fall to the floor.

A soft gasp escaped her lips.

He tugged on the hem of her nightie, pulling it over her head.

It joined his pants on the floor.

He took her breast into his mouth, tasting her. As his tongue caressed her, she arched toward him, eager.

The events of the past and the last several days vanished, leaving only desire.

He kissed a scorching trail down her stomach, causing her breath to catch.

He reached for the nightstand next to his bed, where he kept protection. The next time, and there would be a next time, they'd go slow, but right now…right now he had to sink into her or he felt like he might explode from pent-up need.

After sheathing himself, he settled between her thighs, entering her slowly so she had time to adjust to every inch of him.

Seated fully, he gazed down at the woman beneath him.

Her eyes burned with passion.

"You are so beautiful," he said huskily.

"Kevin," she moaned.

Their eyes locked.

He withdrew and thrust into her, hard and fast. He withdrew again and plunged again, the rhythm desperate, greedy. The need had swelled too rapidly for him to hold back.

Her legs wrapped around him, her nails digging into his shoulders as their pleasure surged and intensified.

Their bodies met again and again.

He kissed her, caressed her, driving her to the precipice of desire—

And then her release crashed over her, and she gasped his name, her release unleashing his own.

He had expected pleasure. But this…this was something beyond his wildest imagination.

The world spun away as her body quivered under him, waves of ecstasy rippling through her. He was there with her, growling out her name, holding her just as tightly as she held him as pleasure consumed him.

He lifted his body, supporting his weight, and gazed down at her. "Are you okay?"

She leaned up, and he was amazed that his arousal surged again. She swept her lips over his and said, "No thinking. Tonight, there is only this."

Chapter Eighteen

Maggie woke up alone in Kevin's bed.

"Kevin?"

Only silence answered her.

She rose and padded from the bedroom. The kitchen and living room were empty. She glanced out of the front window of the house, her suspicions rising. Kevin's car wasn't in the driveway where he'd parked it.

Then she remembered the earlier call from Tess. Her ire peaked. She had a pretty good idea where Kevin had gone. She was happy she'd followed him to his place in her own car.

She pulled up the address for Nightingale's on her phone and got dressed. The club looked nice, upscale, not the kind of place where she could wear the jeans and sweater she'd arrived at Kevin's house in. Luckily, she'd had the foresight to pack a dress that was nice enough for a night out.

Foresight or wishful thinking? She'd seen the dress, one of her favorites because it hugged and gave in all the right places, while packing, and a thought had flashed through her mind. Her in the dress sitting across from Kevin at a candlelit table. Ridiculous under the circumstances, but she'd thrown the dress in her bag just in case.

She put it on then hopped into her car. She didn't know exactly how much of a head start Kevin had on her, but the restaurant wasn't far from his house.

She made a right turn and noticed that the dark SUV behind her did the same.

She told herself to relax, that it didn't mean anything. The driver could be going in the same direction.

She made a left at the light, and the SUV did the same. She made another left and the next immediate left. The SUV followed.

Okay, that wasn't a coincidence. There was no reason for the SUV to circle the block unless it was following her.

Her phone rang and she started, tapping the break. The SUV fell back but continued to follow her as she drove. She reached for the phone with one hand, the other still on the wheel.

"What do you think you're doing?" Kevin's voice boomed from the phone.

"What are you—"

"You didn't think I'd leave you without protection, did you? One of the other operatives from West Investigations was watching the house. He said you took off in your car before he could stop you."

She glanced at the rearview mirror. "Is that who's following me?"

"Yes. Pull over," he demanded. "I'm a block away."

She pulled to a stop at the curb, as did the SUV. It was less than a minute before Kevin's black Mustang rolled to a stop behind the SUV.

He stopped at the driver's side of the SUV and said a few words to the driver before heading for her car.

Maggie stepped out, slamming the door behind her. "Who

do you think you are? Sending me off to bed like a child and then sneaking out of the house like some sneaky sneak."

Okay, so it wasn't the strongest admonition, but she was a novice at telling someone off.

Kevin looked angry, but she thought she saw the ends of his mouth tip up slightly, which only stoked her ire.

She poked him in the chest. "I am not a child. Kim was my friend, and the Viperé ruby was my responsibility. I am a part of this whether you want me to be or not. I'm not going to hide from this maniac, no matter how much—"

The rest of her rant was cut off by Kevin's lips crushing against her mouth.

For several long moments, she was lost in his kiss. Finally, Kevin stepped back.

She shook the fog of his kiss from her head. "If you think that's going to stop me from going—"

Kevin held up his hand. "I know nothing is going to stop you." He caressed her cheek with the pad of his thumb. "Nothing ever stops you from doing what you think is right. It's one of the things I lo—"

This time it was she who pressed her mouth to his. She wasn't ready to hear what he was about to say.

She pulled back after a moment. "So, Nightingale's."

He took her hand. "I'll drive. I've already got someone coming to take your car back to my house. Miller will stay with your car until he gets here."

Heat crept up her neck at the realization that Miller had seen them kissing. She left the keys to her car with Miller and got into the Mustang beside Kevin.

Nightingale's looked like a typical bar. A long bar ran along one side of the space and white tableclothed tables filled in the rest in a seemingly random pattern.

Kevin led her toward the bar. They slid onto stools and ordered drinks, tonic water for him and white wine for her.

"Shouldn't we tell someone that we're here?"

"Ivan Kovalev knows when each and every person walks through his doors. Trust me, he knows we are here, and if he doesn't know already, if we give him a few minutes, he'll know who we are."

They continued to sip their drinks at the bar, exchanging a few words but mostly waiting. It seemed like forever, but it had probably only been ten or fifteen minutes when a large man with biceps the size of tree stumps and a raised scar running along the right side of his jaw appeared beside Kevin.

"Sir. Mr. Kovalev is ready to see you now."

The man turned and started away, clearly intending for Maggie and Kevin to follow him.

She slid from the barstool. Kevin palmed her elbow, angling his body between her and the man they followed.

The man led them through the bar's main area and down a narrow hallway toward the back of the building. They passed the kitchen and heard the clank of dishes and the sound of raised voices on the other side of the swinging door. Finally, the man stopped in front of a door. A private dining room.

There were no windows and the walls were dark wood paneling. With the dim lighting, the overall feel was menacing, which Maggie was sure was the point.

A circular table dominated the space, and in the seat facing the door sat a man who Maggie had no doubt was Ivan Kovalev.

He waved them into the room and toward the table without rising. "Mr. Lombard. Ms. Scott. So good of you to join me," Kovalev said as if he'd invited them to dine with him.

Kevin squeezed her elbow, in caution or as a soothing gesture, she wasn't sure.

He pulled out a chair on the opposite side of the table for her and waited until she was seated before taking the seat next to her.

Ivan Kovalev looked to be in his early sixties, maybe a little older, lean with hair that had gone more white than gray and eyes that were shrewd. If she'd passed him on the street, not knowing that he was part of the Russian mob, she would have still given him a wide berth. Everything about the man screamed he was dangerous.

A waiter hurried in with glasses of wine and a breadbasket. He set the glasses of wine in front of Maggie and Kevin—Kovalev already had a full glass—and left the breadbasket in the middle of the table before slipping back out of the room.

"Thank you for seeing us," Kevin said.

Kovalev waved a hand in dismissal. "It is nothing. I'm sure we were destined to meet at some point with you being the new head of West Security and Investigations' corporate accounts."

It was a show of power. Kovalev knew exactly who they were.

"I've been thinking about upgrading the security at my various buildings. Maybe I should give you a call."

"West would be glad to help," Kevin responded.

Kovalev smiled. "I'm sure you would. But am I incorrect in thinking you are not here to solicit my business?"

Kovalev's gaze swung to Maggie. She was used to men assessing her, but the look Kovalev swept over her was more than just a man appreciating a woman; it was predatory, and it left her feeling as if she needed a shower. Immediately. She shook off the feeling.

Out of the side of her eye, she saw Kevin's jaw tighten. He hadn't missed the way Kovalev had looked at her.

"We're here to ask about Kim Sumika," Kevin gritted out.

Kovalev shot Kevin a smile, taking pleasure over having gotten under his skin, no doubt. "Such a shame. I'm sorry for your loss." Kovalev tipped his head at Maggie.

"Thank you," she said. "It's come to our attention that Kim may have borrowed a sum of money from you. I'm hoping you can tell us more about that."

Kovalev frowned. "I'm not sure that's any of your business."

"We've made it our business," Kevin shot back.

Kovalev's frown turned into a hard scowl.

"Mr. Kovalev, please," Maggie jumped in, hoping to dispel some of the tension. "Kim was my friend. She wasn't close to the little family she had left. I'm all she had, and I feel an obligation to find out what happened to her."

Kovalev's gaze lingered on Kevin for several seconds longer then shifted to her. His face softened, but only a fraction. "Your loyalty is admirable, but maybe misguided. You should allow the police to look into these sorts of things."

Maggie shifted her gaze to the table and said softly, "Would you? If you were in my situation?"

Her words hung there for a moment, silently. She looked at Kovalev through her lashes and waited.

Finally, he spoke. "Point well taken, my dear. What would you like to know?"

Since Kovalev seemed more willing to share with her than with Kevin, she took over the questioning. "We know Kim had a gambling problem. She'd maxed out her credit cards and a home equity line of credit, and we were told she might have borrowed money from you."

"It appears that Anthony Cauley knows more than just wine and cupcakes. Seems to know more than I've given him credit for."

Maggie sucked in a breath. The last thing she wanted to do was to get Anthony in trouble with Ivan Kovalev. She started to speak.

Kovalev waved her off. "It's nothing. People talk. Mr. Cauley is of no concern to me." He took a sip of wine before he spoke again. "Yes, Ms. Sumika owed me money. Or she did. She paid off her debt, in full, with interest, about a week before her untimely death."

Maggie shot a surprised look at Kevin. For his part, his expression remained unchanged.

"Would you mind telling us how much that was?"

Kovalev's frown returned. He was silent for a beat. "Fifty thousand dollars, give or take."

Maggie swallowed hard. That was, she knew, nearly Kim's entire salary for a year. Where did she get that kind of money?

The Viperé ruby. If she was involved, maybe the fifty thousand was her cut. Or part of it. The ruby was worth multiples of fifty thousand dollars.

"Is there anything else you'd like to know? I'm sorry but I have a busy evening ahead of me." Kovalev downed the remainder of his wine. He'd clearly lost interest in them. It was time to go.

But there was one question she wanted to ask. Something she needed to know.

She started to speak, but Kevin reached for her hand. This time, it was clear what he intended to convey.

He stood, pulling her with him. "Mr. Kovalev, thank you for your time."

Kovalev waved at them again, a clear dismissal.

Big biceps waited for them outside of the room. He led them in a reverse trek down the hall and through the bar's dining area to the door.

She guessed Kovalev didn't want them to stay for a nightcap.

The door to the bar banged closed after them.

"Why didn't you let me ask him if he'd killed Kim?"

"Because he wouldn't have told you the truth," Kevin said, his arm around her, leading her to the car. "And I already know he didn't kill Kim."

She stopped walking. "You do? How?"

"Kovalev knew who we were before we stepped foot in the bar. He knew who you were. That tells me he's done his homework, and I have no doubt that he knows you inherit Kim's estate."

She wasn't following. "So?"

"So, if Kim hadn't paid him the money she owed him, he'd have made it clear that he expected you to pay out of the money she left you. Men like Kovalev don't just let a debt die when the person who owes the debt dies, not if they can help it."

"So you think he was telling us the truth about Kim paying off her debt." Maggie let out a breath of frustration. Her prior thought about where Kim had gotten the money to pay off that debt came swimming back to her. "Which means he didn't have a motive to kill Kim or steal the ruby."

"Exactly," Kevin said, walking them to the car.

"So what now?"

Kevin pulled open the passenger-side door for her, but she made no move to get into the car.

He looked her in the eye. "Now we keep pulling threads until we find the one that unravels this whole mess."

Chapter Nineteen

Two hours after leaving Ivan Kovalev, Maggie lay in Kevin's bed, one leg slung over his, her head resting on his chest. He snored lightly, but she hadn't been able to fall asleep after they'd made love. She knew that the more time she spent in his arms, in his bed, the harder it would be to walk away from him when the time came. And it would come. No matter how electric their lovemaking or how safe she felt with him, she wasn't willing to risk her heart again. She'd tried love twice and failed both times. That was enough for her.

Repressing a sigh, she eased herself out of Kevin's arms, slipping from the bed. She wrapped herself in the quilt from the bottom of the bed and padded from the room, closing the door behind her. After a quick stop in the guest bedroom where she was supposed to be sleeping to grab her laptop, she settled onto the living room sofa.

She opened the laptop and logged on to Facebook. She'd tried to avoid the news about the Larimer, but curiosity was finally getting to her. She went to the museum's Facebook page and scanned the comments. Most of them were sympathetic, dismay and disgust about the theft the chief responses. But a few almost seemed to celebrate the ruby going missing. She scanned the thumbnail photos of the commenters, wondering if one of the posters was the aggressive brunette that Josh Huber had told them about. None of the photos jumped out at her.

She navigated to the AARP page. There were several posts about exhibits that the group was against and pictures from the many protests that they'd held. She scrolled through the posts, not sure what she was looking for. Probably nothing, but maybe mindlessly scrolling would slow her racing thoughts enough that she'd be able to go to sleep.

The last several days of her life had been nothing but chaos. One of her coworkers and closest friends was dead, quite possibly because she'd been involved in stealing the Viperé. Why hadn't Kim come to her if she was in trouble? After everything Kim had done for her since the scandal in New York, Maggie would have lent her money to get out of debt if she'd needed it. It might not have been enough, but it had to be better than borrowing from a mobster or, worse, getting involved in a major jewel theft.

If that was what Kim had done. Maggie still didn't want to believe it. She wasn't sure she would believe it until there was incontrovertible proof.

She scrolled past a photo of a protest then paused, swiping down so the photo came back onto the screen. The picture was of two young women and a young male holding protest signs. The man and one of the women were blond, but the brunette with them, she looked familiar.

Maggie clicked on the photo, and it popped up in its own browser window, filling her computer screen. The bigger picture was sharper, the faces in it clearer.

Clear enough that there was no doubt.

The brunette woman in the photo was Diyana Shelton.

MAGGIE HAD AWAKENED him at four in the morning with the photo of Diyana Shelton, the intern at the Larimer, at an AARP protest. He had to admit that she did fit the description of the young brunette that Josh Huber had given them, but he'd cautioned Maggie against jumping to any conclusions. Maggie had been ready to drive to Diyana's apartment and confront the woman before dawn. He'd convinced her to wait until a more reasonable time that morning, but just barely. At seven thirty, they headed to Diyana's apartment, hoping to catch her before she left for the day.

Maggie had given the intern a ride home several times when they'd both had to stay late working on the exhibit, so he hadn't had to tap into West Investigations' vast resources to find an address for the young woman. Diyana lived in a nondescript garden-style apartment. Each of the apartments had a balcony, and the grounds seemed to be fairly well kept. He wasn't sure how much interns made, but it must be a decent amount if Diyana was able to foot the rent here. Residents had to buzz the front door open for their guests, so their appearance at her apartment couldn't come as a complete surprise to Diyana.

Kevin pressed the button for apartment 303, the top floor of the three-floor building, and they waited. It was just after eight, and Maggie had been pretty sure that Diyana would still be at home since the intern didn't usually arrive at the museum until nine thirty.

He was about to press the buzzer again when a voice came over the intercom mounted on the outside wall.

"Yes?"

"Diyana, it's Maggie Scott and Kevin Lombard. I'm sorry to drop in on you so early in the morning, but there's something important we need to discuss with you. Can we come up?"

Diyana didn't respond, but static crackled on her end, so he knew the line was still open.

Maggie shot him a look then said, "Diyana, please."

"Okay."

The line went dead, and a moment later there was a buzz then the door unlocked.

He and Maggie took the stairs to the third floor.

Diyana waited for them outside of apartment 303, barelegged in fuzzy pink slippers, an oversized sweater wrapped around her. "What is it?"

He couldn't blame her for the irritation he heard in her voice. He wouldn't have been happy at having people drop in on him at eight in the morning on a workday. And, if Diyana had a hand in the theft of the Viperé ruby, it was likely him and Maggie showing up at her apartment at this time of the morning had spiked a bit of fear in her.

Good.

He didn't take Diyana for a criminal mastermind, which meant that fear was likely to drive her to make mistakes. And mistakes were good for him and Maggie.

"Again, I'm sorry for dropping in on you, but you know I'm not allowed at the museum, and we really do need to speak with you," Maggie said again without smiling.

Diyana shrugged, but the movement made her appear scared more than nonchalant. "Okay, so what is so urgent?"

"We might want to have this conversation inside," Kevin said.

Diyana hesitated for a moment then stepped back and let them pass into the apartment.

Maggie had printed out a copy of the photo she'd found

on Facebook. She pulled it from her purse now. "This." She handed the piece of paper over to Diyana. "That's you at a protest organized by the Arts and Antiquities Repatriation Project."

Diyana's eyes widened. She licked her lips, panic in her eyes. "So?"

"So what were you doing there?" he snapped.

She shifted her weight from one leg to the other, chewing her bottom lip. "It was a protest. Like some museum was profiting off of the stolen artifacts from Mexico."

"AARP is the group that staged the protest against us a few weeks ago."

"So?" Diyana repeated, her gaze skittering away from Maggie's.

The girl was a terrible liar.

"Look, you can tell us what you know, or I can call Detective Larimer and tell him what we know about you. I'm sure he will have no problem hauling you down to the police station."

"But I didn't do anything!"

"Then you have nothing to worry about," Maggie said.

Diyana pressed her lips together.

"Fine." The intern was working his patience. He pulled his phone from his pocket. "I'm calling Detective Francois."

"No. Don't do that." Diyana reached for his hand, stopping him from bringing the phone to his ear. "My parents will kill me if I get arrested."

"Well, you should start talking then," Kevin shot back.

Unless she'd been involved in the theft, she wasn't going to be arrested, but Detective Francois would want to talk to her anyway once Kevin told him about their visit with the intern. He didn't share that piece of information with her.

"Fine," she huffed as if she were a five-year-old. "Look, all I was going to do was add a couple of names to the guest list for the donors' open house."

Maggie's forehead furrowed. "What names?"

Diyana rolled her eyes. "I didn't do it, okay? Like, you guarded that list like it was gold or something. I knew I wouldn't be able to sneak the names onto it without you noticing, so no harm, no foul, right?" She crossed her arms over her chest defensively.

"I don't understand," Maggie said. "Whose names were you going to add to the list and why?"

"Just a couple friends of mine. They wanted to get inside the party, and when the board members and whatnot started up with the speeches about how great it was to have the Viperé ruby at the Larimer, they were going to chant and stuff. Like just civil disobedience."

"What are these friends' names?" Kevin asked.

Diyana pressed her lips together again.

He waved his phone at her. "Detective Francois is not going to ask as nicely."

"Fine." She gave him two names. "You're making a big deal out of nothing. I couldn't get their names on the list, so the protest didn't happen."

"But the theft of the Viperé did," Maggie pointed out.

Diyana held her hands out in a surrender pose. "Hey, my friends had nothing to do with that. All they were going to do was, like, yell a little until security dragged them out. That's it."

If her friends were anything like Diyana, Kevin doubted very much they'd know the first thing about stealing a precious jewel. "Were you and your friends members of the AARP?"

Diyana shrugged. "We were but they do their own thing mostly now."

"Why did they leave the group?" Maggie followed up.

Diyana snorted. "I mean, Josh has been doing this work for, like, twenty years, and he isn't exactly getting it done. They felt like they could do better on their own."

"And you?" Maggie said. "Why did you leave the group? Or did you?"

Diyana shrugged again. "I don't know. I mean, I think that these artifacts should go back where they belong, but I also want to be a curator someday."

Welcome to adulthood, he wanted to say. One hard choice after another.

"Are you going to tell Robert what I almost did?" Diyana looked at Maggie with a plea in her eyes.

"I'm on leave from the museum right now, but I really think you should tell Robert. I can't promise you that things will work out for you the way you want them to, but I know that it would show a lot of maturity and integrity if you did. I think Robert would appreciate that."

Diyana chewed her bottom lip. "Maybe."

They left the young woman contemplating her next move.

"Are you going to tell your boss about Diyana's actions?" Kevin asked Maggie once they'd stepped back outside.

"Well, since I'm on administrative leave, I don't think there is any conflict in giving her a little time to work up the courage to do it herself. But if she doesn't—" Maggie nodded "—yeah, I'll have to."

"I think she was telling us the truth," he said, holding the passenger-side door open for Maggie.

She let out a deep, frustrated breath. "Yeah, unfortunately for me, I do too."

Chapter Twenty

Maggie followed Kevin into his house. She could feel a panic attack coming on. Her throat constricted, her lungs burning from a lack of oxygen. Kevin wanted to speak with the people Diyana had planned to get into the donors' open and confirm their alibis, but Maggie's gut told her that no graduate students were behind the Viperé's theft and Kim's death. And the two were connected. She was absolutely sure of that.

No. The things that were happening now had been orchestrated by someone who'd meticulously planned it out. Planned it to seem as if she'd played a part in the theft and in killing her friend.

She tossed her purse on Kevin's kitchen table and collapsed into a chair.

Breathe. Breathe. She gulped in air.

Kevin slid into the chair next to her. "Maggie, I know this is tough for you, but don't give up hope."

She stared into Kevin's eyes. "I don't know how much more of this I can take."

"Hey." He reached across the table for her hand. "You are one of the toughest people I know. You can do this. We are going to prove your innocence."

"How? Every lead turns into a dead end. Nothing makes

any sense. If the person who stole the Viperé ruby is behind this, why kill Kim? Why stick around and leave that note for me at the office?"

"I don't know, but we will figure it out." He squeezed her hand. "You're going to make yourself sick if you don't de-stress some. Why don't you take a swim?" He slanted his head toward the sliding glass doors and the pool in the backyard beyond.

Maggie shook her head. "I don't have a swimsuit."

"There should be a couple swimsuits in the dresser in the guest room. Tanya bought a few suits to keep here, and she's never used any of them. You two are about the same size."

She looked longingly at the crystal blue water in the pool. She loved swimming, although she rarely found the time to make it to the pool at her gym. Actually, she couldn't remember the last time she made it to the gym at all.

"Are you sure Tanya wouldn't mind me stealing one of her swimsuits?"

Kevin smiled and her heart did a flip-flop. "I'm sure Tanya won't even notice. And while you swim, I'll whip us up a late breakfast. I have to go into the office at some point this morning, but you're welcome to stay here as long as you want."

"Thanks. I'm not sure what I'll do with my time now that I don't have a job to go to. I guess I need to go to my place and check on the cottage."

"If what Francois said about Kim's will is true, the cottage and Kim's house are yours now. You'll have some decisions to make whether or not you go back to the Larimer."

A knot formed in her throat. No matter what happened, her life was never going to be the same again. She found Kevin's gaze and held it. No, too much had changed and too many feelings she'd thought were dead had been resurrected. Kevin was back in her life, and as much as she wanted to protect herself from the kind of hurt she'd felt when he'd walked away years ago, she could feel herself falling for him again. Falling just as hard as she'd fallen as a twenty-year-old coed, and she wasn't sure she had the strength to stop falling in love with him again.

She wasn't sure she wanted to stop falling in love with him again.

Maggie rose and went to the guest room, where her suitcase lay open on the bed just as she'd left it. A reminder that she hadn't slept in the guest bed at all the night before.

Memories of the prior night in Kevin's arms floated back at her as she changed into a swimsuit and headed out to the pool. The six-foot privacy fence on Kevin's side of the property line was buffeted by evergreen trees that towered at least three feet higher, giving the backyard the feel of a remote oasis.

She'd found a swim cap and goggles in the drawer, along with several swimsuits with tags still attached. She adjusted the swim cap and pulled the goggles down over her eyes before pushing off the side and gliding into the water. The water was surprisingly warm, and by the third lap, she could feel some of the stress she'd been carrying in her body easing. By the tenth lap, she was in a zone where there was nothing but the sound of the water and her breathing.

She knew the moment Kevin stepped out onto the patio. She finished her current lap then waded to the side of the pool. She pulled herself up and out. An innocuous move, but she watched desire flare in Kevin's eyes. He stood next to the chaise longue, backlit by the light coming from inside the house. His chest and feet were bare, a pair of nylon shorts hung low on his hips.

He grabbed the towel she'd left on the lounger and padded barefoot toward her. He dropped the towel over her shoulder then lowered his head and captured her mouth in a smoldering kiss that heated every inch of her skin.

His hands wandered to her hips, pulling her against him so she could feel how much he wanted her. She wanted him too. Even if she knew she shouldn't. Even if she knew it wouldn't last. She wanted him, and that was all that mattered at that moment.

He walked them toward the chaise and sat, pulling her onto his lap. The intensity of his kiss stole her breath. She thought she might like to kiss him forever. But then he pressed his hips to her, grinding against her core, and she wanted to do much more than kiss.

He shifted and flipped her so she lay on her back underneath him on the lounger.

She spread her legs wider, giving him space to seat himself comfortably against her.

She rubbed against him, rotating her hips, creating a delicious friction between their bodies. She rubbed her hands along his spine and broad shoulders, then down lower over the curve of his back to his firm behind.

His hands slipped under her bikini top. He kneaded her breast and pinched her nipple hard, sparking a pain that only heightened her pleasure. He moved on to her other breast, replaying the same movements.

It felt so good to have his weight on her body. His hands on her body. His mouth on her body.

They'd never had any problems in the bedroom. Their physical attraction had always been explosive. This was the part they always got right, she reminded herself. It was all the other stuff that they'd struggled with.

Kevin slid his hand under the fabric of her bikini bottom, stroking her core, and she stopped thinking at all and just felt. And it felt good.

She let out a little mewling sound, and Kevin smiled sexily in return.

His gaze slid down her body. He untied her bikini top and lavished each of her breasts with kisses now that they were free. His mouth on her sent sparks shooting through her.

He slid down her body, pulling the strings that held her bottoms together. Lifting her slightly, he pulled the bottom of her bathing suit free and tossed it on top of her bikini top. She flexed her hips, enjoying the sensation of the bulging erection under his shorts.

He groaned, his jaw tightening. "Maggie, you feel so good."

"I'd feel a lot better if you weren't wearing so many clothes."

He reared up, pulling protection from his pocket before shedding his shorts.

She marveled for a moment at his hardened body and his thick erection before reaching out to pull him back down to her.

Kevin fit his hips between her legs, his length against her thigh. He held her gaze as he inched inside of her, setting a slow rhythm that sent her heart racing. His tongue darted in and out of her mouth, mimicking the pace set by the thrusting of their hips in time with each other.

He increased his rhythm, surging in and out of her until her orgasm hit with a force she'd never experienced before. She panted, clinging to him as pleasure sparked through every inch of her body. She clung to him, her legs wrapped tightly around his waist.

Kevin didn't stop making love to her. He increased his pace, pushing her toward a second orgasm that threatened to be even more powerful than the first.

His body tensed in time with hers. They quivered in each other's arms, tipping over the precipice of ecstasy together.

KEVIN STRODE THROUGH the doors of West Security and Investigations' West Coast offices the next morning, shooting a smile at the receptionist and heading for his office. He'd been reluctant to leave Maggie alone, but he needed to give Tess an update on the Larimer case and to check on several other cases that he'd been neglecting while he'd been focused on Maggie. Making love had been a much needed stress release for both of them, but he knew that neither of them would be able to completely relax until they'd cleared her name. And Maggie was right about one thing: they were really no closer to doing that than they'd been when he'd started the investigation.

He wasn't surprised to see Tess's head pop around his doorframe before he'd even booted up his computer.

She gave a perfunctory knock on the frame, the keys in her hand jingling, before speaking. "Morning, Kevin. Do you have a moment to give me an update on Maggie's case?"

He waved his boss into the office. "Of course. I was planning on stopping by your office in a minute or two anyway."

He'd been keeping Tess updated via quick calls and text messages throughout the investigation, but now he filled in all the details he'd skirted over in those prior communications. He also told his boss about Maggie having found a photograph of Diyana at one of the Art and Antiquities

Repatriation Project's protests and the graduate students' thwarted plans to protest at the donors' open.

Tess massaged her temples. "This is a real mess."

"There's a logic to it," Kevin said, feeling his own frustration bubbling in his chest. "At least to our thief and killer. We just have to figure out what it is."

"I think it's safe to say that the theft of the Viperé ruby is certainly connected to Kim Sumika's death. Given the woman's gambling debt, it must have crossed your mind that she could have had a hand in the theft."

Kevin sighed. "It has, although I've been reluctant to share those thoughts with Maggie. But Kim had the same access to the ruby as Maggie did, and I do find it strange that Kim would miss the donors' open house."

"Migraines can be debilitating," Tess said, playing devil's advocate.

"Yeah," Kevin responded, his tone indicating that he still didn't buy it.

"Maggie seems to believe her friend and fellow curator was telling the truth about the migraine, and we don't have any direct evidence to the contrary. Although..." Tess shot him a pointed look. "Maggie is definitely too close to this case. I've given you wide latitude here, but do you think we should be letting her have a role in this investigation?"

"I don't think we have much of a choice. She's not going to sit back and stay out of it, and I don't think it's in her or our interest to have her out there trying to conduct her own investigation."

"Definitely not."

"She's been a help. Her dealer contact led us to Carter Tutwilder."

Tess twirled the keys. "Yeah, but so far I haven't been able

to dig up anything on him that would suggest he had anything to do with the theft or Kim Sumika's death."

"He has the money to hire someone to pull this kind of
thing off."

"Yeah, and if he hired someone, you can bet the money
trail is buried under dozens of layers. We'll never find it."

Kevin let out a frustrated sigh. "The same could be said
about Ivan Kovalev, although shockingly I believed Ivan
when he said that Kim paid off her debt."

"He doesn't have a reason to lie." Tess's keys jingled,
twirled and jingled again.

"No, he doesn't. But that raises another question. Where
did Kim get the money to pay off the loan from Ivan?"

"And we're back to the ruby's theft," Tess said, catching
the keys in the air and leaning forward in the chair. "If Kim
had a hand in stealing the ruby, maybe she used her cut of
the money to pay off her debt."

"And then what? Whoever she was working with killed
her?"

Tess shrugged. "It wouldn't be the first time. No honor
among thieves and all that."

He couldn't deny he had thought about this scenario.
Heck, it was the one that made the most sense so far. Maggie was going to hate it, but it seemed clear that Kim Sumika
had some role in stealing the Viperé ruby. How exactly that
had led to her death was still an open question.

Tess leaned back in her chair, twirling her keys again.
"You know I said that Maggie was too close to this case,
but I've also wondered whether you're too close to it as well.
You and Maggie? I haven't wanted to delve too much into
your personal business, but it's clear that your 'past relationship'—" Tess drew air quotes around the last two words

"—isn't so much in the past. Are you sure you can handle this case?"

His and Maggie's past relationship wasn't at all in the past anymore. And he planned to make sure a relationship with Maggie was his future, but he didn't tell Tess that. Not yet at least. He and Maggie still hadn't had a heart-to-heart, and despite the mind-blowing sex they'd shared, he didn't know what she was thinking. Heck, if he was being truthful with himself, he was afraid to find out exactly what she wanted. He could only hope she was feeling at least some of what he was feeling.

He realized he'd been silent for a beat too long. "I can handle it."

Tess cocked her head to the side and gave him a slight nod before rising. "Okay, then. Let me know if you need anything."

She turned back to him at the door. "Finding the ruby is why we were retained by the insurance company, and I don't think Maggie had anything to do with the theft. But we don't have unlimited time. If we don't find the ruby soon, the insurance agency will pull us and hire another firm."

He understood what she was saying. They'd lose access to the files and likely the people who could help clear Maggie's name. And another firm might think Maggie wasn't innocent.

"You need to find answers," Tess added. "Fast."

Chapter Twenty-One

"I can't imagine dealing with everything you've gone through in the last several days," Lisa said on the other end of the phone. "What can I do to help? Do you want me to come back down there?"

Maggie had just spent the last hour catching her best friend up on the events of the past several days and venting on the phone.

"No. I don't want to put you out." Lisa just having made the offer to drop everything and come stand by her side was enough to remind Maggie why she loved her friend. "I just needed someone to talk to."

"And I'm always here for that or whatever you need. You know that, right?"

"I do."

A beat of silence passed over the line.

"I feel like there's something else you want to say but aren't." Lisa always was perceptive.

"I slept with Kevin."

Lisa snorted. "That's not a surprise. I saw the way you two looked at each other."

"Yeah, it's not that simple." Maggie took a deep breath and told Lisa about her past relationship with Kevin while they were undergraduates and her miscarriage after they'd broken up.

"Maggie, I'm so sorry."

"I never expected to see Kevin again, but now that I have, I can't deny that there is still something there between us. But even if there is, does that mean it's healthy? Shouldn't I be looking forward, not backward?"

Lisa's sigh sounded through the line. "You know I don't believe in regrets or looking backward, but is that what this really is? I mean, you just said that there is something there between you two. Something in the here and now. I wouldn't necessarily say that it's unhealthy to explore what that might be."

"When has reuniting with an ex-boyfriend ever worked out in the end?"

"Frida Kahlo and Diego Rivera married, divorced and re-married, staying together until she passed away."

Maggie chuckled. "Of course you know that."

"What can I say? I know my art history."

Maggie couldn't help but be buoyed by Lisa's teasing.

"But really," Lisa said, becoming more serious. "I think you should think about what you really want. Forget the past. Think about the now and your future. And give yourself permission to forgive Kevin for walking away all those years ago. I'd hate for you to miss out on a good thing today because of choices you and Kevin made when you were just kids."

Maggie's phone beeped that she had a call coming in. She checked the screen and saw her father's photo.

"Lisa, I have to go. My dad is calling. But I heard you. I'll think about what you said."

"Good. Love ya."

"Love you too."

She ended the call with Lisa and clicked over to her father. She knew instantly that something was wrong.

"Dad?"

"Maggie?" Her father's words came out groggy.

"It's me, Dad."

"Maggie?"

"Dad? Are you okay?"

The silence on the other end of the phone spiked her anxiety.

"My head…my head hurts."

"Is Julie there, Dad?"

"Julie?"

Concern prickled at the back of her neck. Something was clearly wrong with her father.

She shoved her feet into her sneakers and grabbed her purse. "Did you fall? Dad, where are you?"

"Maggie, can you come over? My head hurts."

"I'm on my way, Dad. I'll be there in ten minutes. Stay on the phone with me, okay?" She was already moving to the front door.

"I think I need to lie down."

"Dad? Dad!"

The line went dead.

She dialed Kevin's number. The call went straight to voicemail.

"Kevin, something is wrong with my dad. I'm headed to his house now."

The drive from Kevin's house to her father's was fifteen minutes, but she made it in ten.

Her father's car wasn't in the driveway. She let herself into the house with her key.

"Dad? Julie? Anybody home?"

The house was quiet. Her heart galloped.

"Dad?"

A soft groan came from the back of the house.

"Dad?" She dropped her purse by the sofa in the living room as she hurried toward the back bedrooms.

Her father was on the floor of the main bedroom, next to the bed. She knelt next to him. "Oh my God, Dad. Here, let me help you up."

Her father gripped her arm tightly. "Hit me." His words slurred.

"Hit you? Did someone hit you, Dad?" Anger swelled in her chest. "Did Julie hit you?"

Her father shook his head. "Not… Julie. He hit me. From behind."

It was a struggle to get her father to his feet, but with his help she was finally able to get him onto the bed.

He rubbed the back of his head.

She put her hand to his head and felt a bump.

"He who, Dad?" she asked, panting slightly from a mix of exertion and rage. "Who hit you?"

"Ellison."

Her body went cold. "That's not possible. Ellison is dead."

Her father shook his head, but whether he was just trying to clear it, or he was disputing her claim about Ellison, she couldn't tell.

A thump came from the front of the house.

Her pulse quickened. Her father might have been confused about who hit him, but someone had. Someone who was still in the house.

She glanced around the room for a weapon but found

nothing. Her purse was in the living room where she'd left it after she'd entered the house.

"Dad." She lowered her voice to a whisper. "Where is your phone?"

Her eyes darted around the room. Her father had called her using his cell phone, but it was nowhere to be seen now. It didn't look like there was a landline in the house. At least, not in the bedroom.

The bedroom window was big enough for her to shimmy through. She could get out, run to a neighbor's house and call the police. But she couldn't leave her father.

She had to get to her purse and her cell phone.

"Stay here, Dad. I'm going to get my phone."

Her father gave a slight nod and squeezed her hand. She could tell he was in a lot of pain. Probably had a concussion. She needed to get him help quickly.

She forced herself to walk to the bedroom door and stuck her head out carefully, peering into the hallway.

It was empty.

She slid into the hall, closing the bedroom door after her. The hallway carpeting was the stiff, scratchy kind. It seemed to snap and crackle with each footstep.

There was a second bedroom across the hall from her father's room that was full of moving boxes.

Forcing herself to step as quietly as possible, she made her way down the hall toward the living room. Her father's house wasn't large. The living room could be seen from the kitchen and dining area. If the intruder was in any of those rooms, he'd see her as soon as she stepped out of the hall.

She stopped at the point where the hall opened onto the living room. Her heart hammered. She couldn't hear anything other than the sound of her own breathing, and that sounded like thunder rumbling through the entire house.

The living room looked to be empty.

She darted across the open space and grabbed her purse. She always kept her phone in the front pocket, but when she plunged her hand inside she felt nothing.

"Looking for this?"

Terror was a strange thing. Rationally, she knew she was more scared than she'd ever been in her life. Yet, at the sound of the voice that was almost as familiar to her as her own, a certain calmness washed over her.

She turned and, for the first time in three years, faced her ex-husband.

"ELLISON."

Ellison stood in the passageway between the living room and the kitchen, a misshapen smile on his face. In one hand, he held her phone, and in the other, a knife.

"Ellison." Although her eyes were telling her that he was there, alive, her brain was struggling to catch up with the sight.

She was looking at a dead man. A very alive, dead man.

He looked different. His blond hair was now dark, almost black. The piercing blue eyes were now covered by brown contacts. He'd aged far more than the three it had been since she'd seen him. His skin darkened by a tan, but leathery looking. It looked like he'd been living hard, but being on the run would do that, she supposed.

"Ellison." She said his name again in an effort to make it all make sense in her head. "What…what are you doing here? How are you here?"

"I'm here for you," Ellison said, the words sending a sliver of fear through her. "You and the ruby."

"You…you stole the ruby?"

Ellison let out a laugh that sent a shiver down her spine. "You can get away with so much when you are dead."

She swallowed hard, already knowing the answer to the question she was about to ask. "And Kim?"

"I needed her help to steal the ruby. Wasn't hard to convince her. But I couldn't take the chance that she'd turn on me later."

"You killed her?"

He shrugged, but it was more than enough of an answer. He'd killed her friend. And he planned to do the same to her.

She could make a run for the front door, but that would mean leaving her father, and she wouldn't do that. Even if she tried, she had no doubt that Ellison would catch her before she could get the door open. And he had a knife.

She looked into Ellison's eyes and saw a stranger. And hate. The man standing in front of her hated her. But why? She had to try to reach the man she'd married. He was still in there somewhere. At least, she hoped he was.

"Ellison, my father needs help. Let me call an ambulance for him."

"You want to help him? Where were you when I needed help?"

"I tried to be there for you."

"You tried? I lost my job. My reputation. My so-called friends. My home. You," he spat.

"We were divorced before the scandal."

"I never wanted that. I did everything for you. The money? That was all for you."

Maggie jerked with the realization of what he was saying. "I never asked you to steal for me. I wouldn't have."

"You didn't have to ask," he roared. "That's how much I loved you. And when I needed you, you deserted me."

"I tried to be there for you. I called. I reached out. But the pressure. The police suspected I'd helped you steal that money. The police and the press hounded me. I had to move to the West Coast to get away from it. Even after you died."

Ellison smirked. "Looks like that wasn't far enough." He tapped the knife against his thigh twice then flipped it, blade out.

"You don't have to do this. You have the money and now the ruby. Just take them and go."

"The money is gone. It takes a lot of money to live on the run. Why do you think I came for the ruby? And as for this?" He waved the knife at her. "I've had a lot of time to think about your betrayal. You have to pay."

She wasn't going to be able to reach him. If she wanted to get herself and her father out of this alive, she was going to have to fight.

She leaped toward the door, then as Ellison lurched after her, she spun, lashing out with a kick to his side. He hopped and stumbled backward, cursing. She pushed past him into the kitchen. There was another door there and, more importantly, a host of possible weapons she could use to defend herself.

She got lucky. Her father hadn't gotten around to cleaning up after lunch. The sink was full of dishes, including a large butcher knife. She grabbed it and turned just as Ellison stumbled into the kitchen.

"You're going to pay for that," he snarled, starting toward her.

Keys jangled in the front door.

Ellison froze.

"Boyd? Baby, are you okay?"

Maggie screamed, "Julie, run!"

She lunged at Ellison again, swiping out with the knife.

He jumped back, untouched. But the introduction of another person changed his odds. He swore then ran for the back door, shooting a venomous look over his shoulder at her before disappearing out of it.

"Maggie? What's going on? Are you okay? Where is Boyd?" Julie's eyes darted back and forth between the open back door and Maggie.

Maggie slid down onto the kitchen floor, her back against the lower cabinets.

Fire burned up her right arm. She looked down, catching sight of the bloody gash slashed there. He'd stabbed her.

She felt like she was going to throw up. Blood trickled from the wound on her arm and her head spun. "Dad, he needs help. Call 911," she stammered.

Then she passed out.

Chapter Twenty-Two

Maggie had regained consciousness by the time the EMTs arrived, her pride only a little worse for wear for having passed out at the sight of her own blood. She rode to the hospital in the ambulance with her father, Julie driving her car close behind. She'd called Kevin while the EMTs loaded her father into the ambulance and given him a quick summary of Ellison's attack on her father. Kevin was already there when the ambulance pulled up in the emergency room drive, standing next to his sister, Tanya.

She was relieved her father had a doctor that she knew cared. Tanya took charge immediately, barking out orders to the nurse and EMTs helping to move her father into the hospital. Kevin was by her side the moment she stepped out of the ambulance.

"I think my heart stopped when I got your message," Kevin said as they followed the gurney into the hospital. "Are you okay?"

"It's just a scratch." She held up her arm so he could see. The white bandage the EMT had applied in the ambulance was much bigger than was necessary. "I gave everyone a scare by passing out though."

A smile cracked through his worried expression. "Still can't stand to see your own blood."

"I'm not sure how anyone can."

She filled him in on her father's call and Ellison attacking her when she arrived at her father's house.

The shock she felt at seeing Ellison was mirrored on Kevin's face. "Ellison? How?"

"Apparently, he faked his death to get out of the embezzlement charge. I don't know how he did it, but, Kevin, I'm telling you he's alive." A tiny shiver shook through her.

"I'm not doubting you."

The doors to the waiting room opened, and Julie rushed through before he could say anything else. Julie scanned the visitors in the waiting room until her eyes landed on Maggie and Kevin in the far corner.

She rushed forward. "Has the doctor seen Boyd yet? Have they told you anything about his condition?"

Almost as if Julie had conjured her, Tanya stepped through the glass doors separating the emergency room from the waiting room.

"Maggie." Tanya stopped in front of the trio. "It's good to see you, although I wish it was under different circumstances."

"It's good to see you again too. I'm sorry to be so abrupt, but how is my father?"

"Nothing to be sorry for. Your father suffered a pretty serious concussion, but otherwise looks to be in good health. Because of his age, I want to keep him overnight just to keep an eye on him."

Maggie let go of the breath she felt like she'd been holding since she'd walked into her father's house and found him on the floor.

Julie squeezed her hand, tears of relief streaming down her face. "Can we see him?"

"You can see him now but only two at a time, and I'd suggest you keep the visit brief. He needs to rest, but I anticipate releasing him tomorrow."

Julie and Maggie thanked the doctor.

"You two go," Kevin said. "I'll wait here."

Maggie froze when she saw her father in bed. His eyes were closed, and he looked so small and frail. His face was gray and ashen. His mortality slapped her in the face. Ellison's attack could have ended so much more tragically, and no matter what, one day her father wouldn't be here.

Julie squeezed her arm and gently pulled her forward toward her father's bed. "It's okay. He's okay," she whispered, seemingly reading the angst on Maggie's face.

"Dad," Maggie whispered.

Her father's eyes opened. It took several seconds for him to focus, but when he did, a small smile crossed his lips.

Julie slipped to the other side of the bed. Each woman took one of his hands.

"Did somebody die?" he quipped, looking from Maggie to Julie and back.

"I'm so sorry, Dad." Tears pooled in Maggie's eyes.

Her father pulled his hand from hers and cupped her face. "Hey, hey. You have nothing to be sorry for. This is not your fault."

"But Ellison…he was using you to get to me. He…"

Her father's face darkened. "He's out of his mind, but that's not your fault. I don't want you to blame yourself."

Her father's eyelids dropped.

Maggie shot a glance at Julie, who gave a slight shake of her head.

"Dad, I'm going to go and let you get some rest."

Her father's eyes opened again. His hand slid down to the bed and grasped hers. "Be careful. Stay safe."

She returned her father's squeeze. "I will. I promise. You get some rest." Maggie's gaze shifted to Julie. "You're going to stay with him?"

Julie smiled, looking down at Boyd with so much tenderness and devotion that it made Maggie's heart clench. "You just let them try to put me out of here."

Maggie was pretty sure that nothing less than a small army would be capable of dislodging Julie from her father's side. Still, the hospital wasn't a bunker. If Ellison wanted to get in, there were dozens of opportunities.

"I'll be back to check on you later."

"No need. I'm just going to be sleeping anyway. You just stay safe."

She leaned forward and pressed a kiss to her father's cheek. "I love you, Dad."

"I love you too, honey."

Kevin was on the phone when she returned to the waiting room. He hung up as she sailed through the doors.

"How is your father?"

She opened her mouth to answer, but all that came out was a choked sob.

Kevin pulled her into his arms and let her cry for several minutes. Once the deluge of tears slowed, she pulled back.

"Feel any better?" He grabbed a tissue from the box someone had left on the waiting room's coffee table.

Maggie dabbed her eyes and blew her nose. "A little. It was just…seeing my father so helpless."

"It can be hard to see our parents in a vulnerable state, but he's going to be okay according to the doctors, right?"

She nodded. "Right. Julie is staying in his room with him, but I'm scared that—"

"Ellison might try to hurt your father again as a way to get to you. I thought of that too. Tess called Detective Francois, and she is sending one of our guys from West Investigations to guard your father until Ellison is in custody."

A boulder of stress rose from her shoulders. "Thank you." Ellison's screed at her father's house came back to her. "Ellison killed Kim," she said, a sob catching in her throat. "He admitted it to me."

From the look on his face, it appeared Kevin had already figured that out. He set his notebook aside and pulled her into another hug. "I know, sweetheart. I'm sorry."

"It's my fault. Ellison, he blames me. For the divorce. For pulling away during his embezzlement scandal."

Kevin lightly gripped her shoulders. "Hey, don't do that to yourself. You aren't to blame for any of this. He is. No one made him steal that money. Or the Viperé ruby. He took Kim's life. That's on him and only on him, understand?"

Her head understood, but her heart felt as if she should have known. The heavy weight of guilt wouldn't be lifting soon.

The doors to the waiting room opened again, and Detective Francois and Tess strode in.

"Ms. Scott, I'm happy to see you are relatively unharmed," the detective said. "Wishing your father a speedy recovery."

"Thank you, Detective," Maggie replied.

"Heard you kicked butt." Tess offered a tight smile. "Good girl."

Maggie sighed. "I don't know about that, but thanks."

"I know this is a trying time, but are you up for some questions?" Detective Francois asked, taking out his phone.

Maggie sighed. More questions were the exact opposite of what she wanted to do at the moment, but she knew the detective was just doing his job. "Whatever I can do to help."

She went through the details, reiterating everything she'd told Kevin only minutes earlier. Francois's questions were nearly identical to Kevin's, but worded differently enough that a few smaller details she hadn't recalled before came back to her.

Detective Francois finally put his phone away. "Well, we have one major problem here."

Kevin's and Tess's slight nods showed they'd picked up on whatever the major problem was, but Maggie found herself left in the dark alone.

"Anyone care to fill me in on the problem?" Maggie asked.

"Ellison has been living off the grid and hiding his tracks for a long time," Tess started.

"He's practiced at being invisible. That's going to make it harder for us to find him," Kevin finished.

"I had patrols out driving a ten-mile radius within minutes of the 911 call, but he got past us somehow," Francois said, the frustration in his voice evident.

"Like I said, he's had a lot of time to practice being invisible. And since we can be sure he isn't using his real name, but we have no idea what name he is using, we don't really have a place to start looking," Kevin said.

"He's planned this for a long time." Tess frowned. "Harbored anger toward Maggie. He's not going to stop until he gets her."

"Tess," Kevin hissed.

Maggie pushed back the fear bubbling in her gut. "No, Tess is right. There's no point in sugarcoating it. Ellison is obsessed. He took the ruby because he needed the money, but he's stayed because he wants me. Dead."

Their quartet was silent for a long moment.

"We need to draw him out on our terms," Tess finally said.

"No," Kevin barked.

"The brass would never sign off on something like that," Detective Francois said, shaking his head.

"So it doesn't have to be an LAPD operation," Tess shot back.

"I said no." Kevin's bark had turned into a growl.

"Excuse me." Maggie raised her hand as if she were a pupil in school. "Again, could someone tell me what it is we are talking about here?"

Tess looked at her. "Bait. Specifically, using you as bait to draw out Ellison."

"How many times do I have to say it—"

Tess held up a hand. "You didn't have to say it the first time. I know you're against it, but if we weren't talking about Maggie, would you be as opposed to the idea?"

"It's too dangerous," Kevin said.

"Not an answer," Tess shot back. "Maggie is already in danger, and we don't know when Ellison is going to pop up again. He's waited years to come out of the shadows. He could very well go back into hiding, wait until our guard is down and pop up again. We have an opportunity now, and we should press it."

"She's right," Maggie interjected.

"She is not right."

"Look, I don't like it either, but she's right about Ellison going back underground. I don't want to live my life look-ing over my shoulder. If we have the chance to grab him now, I say we take it. All the better if we can get the Viperé ruby back at the same time and save West Investigations' reputation."

"I don't give a damn about West Investigations' reputation," Kevin growled.

"Not the best way to get on your new boss's good side," Tess chided.

"He doesn't mean that," Maggie said, shooting Kevin a look.

"If I thought he did, I'd fire him," Tess responded.

Detective Francois took a step away from the group. "I need to get back out there and try to catch Ellison Coelho using less…radical means. LAPD can't be involved in dangling Ms. Scott as bait, but if I can be of any help, you have my number."

Maggie guessed that meant he didn't suspect her in the crimes any longer. That was some relief. "Thank you, Detective."

Detective Francois gave her a brisk nod then strode from the waiting room.

"This is a terrible idea," Kevin said.

"If you have a better one, I'm all ears," Tess shot back.

His frown said it all.

"I'm in," Maggie said. She reached for Kevin's hand and looked him in the eye. "I'm in. I trust you and Tess, and I want to end this now."

Kevin gripped both her hands and leaned down until his forehead rested against hers. He closed his eyes. Out of the side of her eye, Maggie saw Tess slide away.

"I don't want to lose you," he whispered.

"I don't want to lose you either. This is the best shot that we have right now."

They stood for a moment more before Kevin pulled back. His gaze tracked to Tess standing a polite distance away now. "What do you have in mind?"

Chapter Twenty-Three

Kevin sat in his office, frustrated. Detective Francois hadn't been willing to dangle Maggie as bait, but the police department was willing to bend the truth a bit to get the public off their backs. Francois put out a press statement saying the department believed they knew who the suspect was in the theft of the Viperé ruby and Kim Sumika's murder. The statement made it clear that the crimes had been targeted and that the police believed the culprit had likely fled the country.

And in the week since Ellison had attacked Boyd Scott, Kevin could almost convince himself that the police's statement was correct and that Ellison had done the rational thing and run. Neither West Investigations nor the LAPD had been able to find a single trace of Ellison.

But Kevin's gut told him that after everything he'd done, Ellison wasn't going to give up on getting to Maggie.

Despite his attempts to convince her not to, Maggie had moved back into her cottage. West Investigations had set up discreet surveillance on her at home and at work. Since Detective Francois had made it clear Maggie was no longer a suspect, Maggie was pushing to get her job back. Gustev and Tutwilder were both dragging their feet and resisting though. Neither were happy to have her back at the museum, but Maggie was determined to fight for her job. She wasn't going to allow Ellison's actions to ruin the life she'd built for a second time. Kevin admired her for that gumption.

There was a knock on the door to his office. Tess stood there, practically vibrating. "Hey, we have a lead on the ruby."

His pulse quickened. A lead on the ruby meant a lead on Ellison's whereabouts. "What's the lead?"

"A source tipped me to an underground auction for black-market art. My source says the guy running it was bragging about some, and I quote, 'big, honking gem that's going to bring in a boatload of money.'"

Kevin grinned. "LAPD?"

"I've already called Detective Francois, and he spoke to my source and found him credible. The cops are working on search warrants right now." Tess's smile grew wider. "And since I've been such a Good Samaritan, Detective Francois has allowed us to tag along."

Kevin rose, moving around his desk before she'd finished the sentence. "Let's go."

POLICE VEHICLES CROWDED the parking lot of the elementary school a half block away from the target house. They were lucky that the estate homes sat several yards back from the street. Kevin and Tess joined the half a dozen uniformed officers standing at the trunk of one of the patrol cars listening to Detective Francois give instructions.

"Okay," Francois said, fastening the strap on the bullet-proof vest he wore. "Our source says that there is a high-value auction of various stolen goods going on inside the property three homes down from here. The real estate records show it's owned by a foreign national from Sweden who is supposedly out of the country. We are going to breach quickly and detain everyone inside. We want to take everyone in safely and make sure we don't damage any priceless art or jewels or whatever else they are selling in there." Detective Francois gestured toward where Kevin and Tess stood at the back of the pack. "These two are headed in with us. They are on the trail of the Viperé ruby."

A ripple fluttered through the group as heads turned to check them out.

"We're going in as four teams of four. Two through the front and two around the back." Francois checked the magazine on his gun then looked up at the group. "Everybody ready?"

Kevin adjusted the bulletproof vest he wore and checked his own gun.

There was a ripple of agreement before everyone peeled off into groups of four. One of the officers carried a ram. The teams advance toward the house, quickly and quietly, the first two teams peeling off and heading around the house toward the back. The front rooms of the house were empty, the lack of lights making it appear empty, but the house was large, easily six to seven thousand square feet, with two aboveground levels.

Kevin and Tess's team brought up the rear heading to the front of the house. The two teams stopped on either side of the front door waiting for the breach signal. It was late, and the neighborhood was quiet. Cool air brushed over his skin, but adrenaline and anxiousness had beads of sweat forming on his temple despite the breeze.

"Team three and four in position," the radio on one of the uniformed officer's shoulder crackled.

Detective Francois held up three fingers. The first finger

dropped soundlessly. Then the second. With the last finger, Francois barked, "Go! Go! Go!"

The officer with the ram advanced, swinging it at the door at full speed. The door cracked under the force and swung open. The rest of the team wasted no time flooding through the open door, yelling out commands for the inhabitants of the house to "freeze" and "put their hands up." The other two teams flooded in from the back of the house.

The teams that had come through the back door moved forward, clearing the rooms on the main floor quickly. But it was clear from the angry shrieks and screams that came from the basement that was where the action was.

Kevin followed Tess, their team leader, and one of the other teams down the basement stairs. The basement was finished with marble floors, two chandeliers and a full bar running along one of the rear walls.

A small stage had been set up at the other end of the basement. People, most clad in business attire, were scattered in the rows of chairs facing the stage. Three paintings, abstracts that looked like nothing more than paint splatters, rested on easels in a semicircle on the stage. A gold statue of a dragon held a prominent place on a podium in front of the paintings. Anyone could be forgiven for thinking they'd walked into an auction house or gallery instead of the basement of a multimillion dollar home in the suburbs of Los Angeles.

"Nobody moves!" Francois called out. "Keep your hands where we can see them."

Two of the men in the crowd stood, but the third team of uniformed officers hustling down the staircase quickly snuffed out any errant thoughts of fleeing.

Kevin scanned the faces of the men in the crowd looking for Ellison, but Maggie's ex wasn't there.

"Lombard. Stenning. Over here. I think there's something you'd like to see," Detective Francois called.

He followed Tess. Detective Francois held back a curtain separating the front of the stage. Several more items waited behind the curtain for their turn on the stage. Kevin's eyes were drawn to one. One sparkling, large, red jewel. The Viperé ruby, nestled in a black velvet cushion in a locked glass case.

Tess turned to him with a grin. "Bingo!"

It wouldn't be official until the insurance company's gemologist evaluated and signed off on it, but it looked like they'd just found the Viperé ruby.

MAGGIE WAS FRUSTRATED. Without a job, she was listless and unsure what to do with her days. She couldn't spend every minute with Kevin, and wouldn't want to if she could. He had a job, and even though he was spending the majority of his time searching for Ellison, he had other cases he had to oversee for West Investigations.

Her father had been released from the hospital, and at her urging, he and Julie had gone to Julie's son's house in Arizona. Kevin assured her that he had a man he could trust watching over the family, although Maggie had chosen to keep that piece of information from her father. She didn't want to worry him more than necessary, but she was relieved that her father and Julie were safe. Both of them assured her that they didn't blame her for Ellison's attack, but Maggie couldn't shake the guilt. She'd brought Ellison into their lives in the first place, and it was her Ellison was really after.

Since moving back into her cottage, she was under constant surveillance by the West team, but so far Ellison hadn't taken the bait. With time on her hands, she spent it researching and racking her brain for where Ellison could be hiding out. In this day and age, it was nearly impossible for a person to go completely off the grid. They just had to figure out where Ellison would go. She knew him best, and she was their best chance of doing that.

The doorbell rang, and then someone pounded on the door. "Ms. Scott? It's Detective Decker."

"Yes."

"Ma'am, I received a call from Detective Francois. He believes Ellison Coelho is in the area. He'd like me to stick close to you until he gets here. Do you mind if I come in?"

Her pulse rate picked up its pace. Ellison was close. That meant they had a chance to catch him and end this nightmare tonight.

She looked out the peephole. The detective stood too close for her to see his face, but he held his badge up so she could see it.

She unlocked the dead bolt. As she opened the door, a hard push came from the other side, wrenching the doorknob from her hands and sending the door crashing open.

Ellison stood on the other side of the door, a gun in his hand. "Surprise."

She turned to run but didn't get far.

Excruciating pain vaulted through the back of her head. Then everything went black.

When she awoke, Maggie's head hurt worse than it ever had before. Her hands and feet were tied, and there was a piece of masking tape over her mouth. She was on her side, bouncing against a hard surface. In a car. The trunk of a car, to be specific.

Ellison had her. He intended to kill her.

And Kevin had no idea where she was.

Panic started to rise in her chest. She pushed it back down. She needed to keep her head if she had any hope of getting out of this alive. She needed a plan. It was dark in the trunk, but Ellison had tied her hands together in front of her.

She groped around the floor of the trunk hoping to find something, anything, to defend herself with. But there was nothing.

The car stopped abruptly, slamming her into the back of the trunk then rolling her forward.

She heard the car's door open then slam closed. Gravel crunched.

Ellison was coming.

The trunk popped open, and she blinked rapidly. Her eyes adjusted to the moonlight filtering in the open trunk, and she looked up into the mottled face of the man she'd once thought she'd loved.

"I'm going to get you out of the trunk. If you try anything, I will shoot you." He held up the gun to underscore his point. "Do you understand?"

She nodded.

Ellison grabbed her tied hands and yanked her up. He lifted her out of the trunk then roughly dropped her to the ground next to the back tires of the car.

She took the opportunity to scan the area. They were on a dock. Next to a warehouse that looked to be closed.

He slammed the trunk then reached for her again.

He pulled her to her feet, pushing her toward the warehouse.

Chapter Twenty-Four

He had her.

Kevin tried to control his panic, but it was a losing battle. It was all he could think about. Ellison had Maggie and was doing God only knew what to her. She might not even still be alive.

He pulled to a stop on Maggie's street, which was full of vehicles—squad cars, marked police sedans, black West Investigations SUVs and an ambulance.

Please, God, don't let that be for Maggie.

He got out of the car and ran toward Detective Francois.

"Maggie, is she—?" He couldn't bring himself to say the words.

The tech who'd been monitoring the security system at Maggie's house had called as soon as he'd realized the man at Maggie's door wasn't a police officer. He'd said that Ellison had knocked Maggie out and carried her out of the range of the camera, but what if he'd been wrong. What if Ellison had just taken her out of the range of the camera to—

"The ambulance isn't for Maggie," Tess said, stepping in front of him and stopping him from racing for the ambulance.

Francois radiated anger. "It's for the man I had on her house tonight. Detective Decker. He took one gunshot to the torso through the car window. The EMTs are preparing to take him to the hospital now."

As if they'd heard Francois's words, the ambulance's sirens whooped, and the vehicle lurched forward and down the street, increasing in speed as it went.

Kevin worked to slow his racing heart. It wasn't Maggie in the back of the ambulance on the way to the hospital. That was good. "What do we know?"

"Our cameras caught Ellison walking up to Maggie's door at 9:25 p.m.," Tess started in a calm, focused voice. "Kept his head down, but he had Decker's badge around his neck and a holstered sidearm, so our tech thought it was Decker at first. Maggie must have thought so too. She opened the door to him after he held his badge up to the peephole. It wasn't until he pushed open the door and clocked Maggie over the head with the gun that the tech realized something was wrong."

Kevin tamped down the anger that swelled in him at hearing that Ellison had hurt Maggie. He needed to remain professional, clearheaded, if he was going to find her in time.

"The tech tried to reach Decker, but he didn't answer."

The ambulance was gone now, but they all instinctively turned to look at the unmarked sedan with the missing driver-side window that CSI was now crawling over.

Tess cleared her throat. "When he couldn't reach Decker, he called Francois."

"I had a squad car dispatched immediately. The unit found Decker when they arrived, one uniform started CPR while the other went into Ms. Scott's house."

"Ellison and Maggie were gone by then." Tess picked up the story again. "He parked out of view of the cameras, so we don't have a tag, make or model."

"That suggests that Ellison knew where the cameras were. And if he was able to sneak up on a trained detective—"

"He's probably been casing the house and neighborhood," Tess finished his thought.

"How is that possible?" Kevin wanted to scream. The LAPD and West Investigations, one of the best security firms in the nation, were supposed to have been protecting Maggie, and they both failed?

Tess frowned. "There are always blind spots. You know that. We're doing the best we can, but Ellison has had years of practice being invisible. Hiding himself from people he didn't want to see him."

"I have officers canvassing the area for possible witnesses," Francois spoke up. "It's possible someone saw something or someone's security system caught the car."

"And if no one did?" Kevin asked although the answer was obvious. If they didn't get a break, they were screwed.

"Detective Francois, sir," a uniformed officer called. Francois ambled away.

"Kevin, I think you should head back to West headquarters," Tess said.

"The hell I will."

"You are too close to this. You've been too close to this case. I should have taken you off days ago. And now..." She shook her head. "I can't use you if your personal feelings for Maggie are going to cloud your professional judgment."

He glared at Tess. "I'm not going anywhere."

Tess glared right back. "I can make it an order—"

"Lombard. Stenning." Francois waved them over. "I think we got something here."

Kevin whirled away from his boss, stalking over to where Francois stood with the uniform. He hadn't noticed him earlier, but a teenaged boy stood with the two men. Long wisps of curly red hair fell in the boy's face, and he fidgeted from one foot to the other.

"This is Allan. Son, can you repeat what you just told me?"

The teen let out a heavy sigh. "Again?"

"One more time," Francois encouraged him.

"Okay, I mean, like, I was out, okay, I snuck out to see my girl, and I'm just walking, right?" He looked at the adults around him as if walking might not be familiar to the old folks.

"Got it, kid. You were walking," Kevin said, hoping to urge the story on faster.

"So yeah, I'm walking. My girl lives a couple blocks down that way." He pointed south of where they stood. "Then all of a sudden, I hear this lady scream, and then I see a man carrying a woman, like, fireman style over his shoulder and whatnot. And I'm like, whoa, that's probably not cool."

Kevin was finding it hard not to shake the story out of the kid to get him to talk faster. Tess must have sensed his agitation.

She gave a slight shake of her head.

"So then I was like, I can't let him see me, you know. So I ducked down behind that car there." The boy turned and pointed at a black Range Rover. "But like I said, something didn't seem right, so I snapped a picture of the car."

"You have a photo of the car the man put the woman in?" Francois said, testily.

"Oh, yeah." The teen reached into his coat pocket and pulled out his phone. "I must have forgotten to tell you that part. I got a photo of the tag and everything. Wanna see?" He held the phone up to his face to unlock it.

Maggie was in that warehouse. He could feel it.

Hang on, baby. I'm coming.

THE CONCRETE FLOOR was cracked, little more than rubble in several places, and the air was sour and smelled of mold. The space was mostly empty, but there were signs of the business that used to inhabit the space. Broken wooden pallets, a metal desk and office chair. Wires hung precariously from the ceiling, and most of the windows that lined the top of the wall had been broken, jagged shards of glass protruding dangerously.

She heard a squeak as they entered, followed by the pitter-patter of paws that signaled she and Ellison were not the only two animals in the space.

But rats were the least of her problems.

Ellison led her to the chair and pushed her into it. "Don't move. I'm going to take the tape off of your mouth. If you try anything…" He held the gun up.

She yelped when he ripped the tape off.

"Why are you doing this?"

He glared at her. "I already told you why."

"Ellison, this…this has to stop. I'm sorry if I hurt you. But s, you aren't going to get away with it. The police know 're alive. They know you stole the money, the ruby, that killed Kim and attacked my father." She said the last s with more than a little bitterness. She'd never forgive or hurting her father.

hortled. "Then what's one more notch on my record, was so much harder to live on the run than I expected. dred thousand dollars doesn't go nearly as far as I'd ed. New identities. Constant moving. Staying off It's expensive." He propped himself against the

Kevin didn't wait for the teen to find the photo. He snatched the phone from the boy's hand.

"Hey, man! That's mine."

Kevin ignored the teen, navigating to his photo gallery while Tess assured the boy that he'd get his phone back in a moment.

He found the photos quickly. A silver, four-door Toyota Corolla. A dime a dozen, but the teen had captured a clear picture of the license plate. He sent copies of the photographs to himself, Tess and Francois before handing the phone back to the boy.

"You did a good job," he said to the teen. "Stop sneaking out at night though. You're going to get yourself in trouble." Kevin turned and started after Tess, who, like Francois, was already on the phone probably having someone pull the registration for the license.

THE CAR BELONGED to Charles and Louise Bennett, a couple in their seventies. The computer guru at West Investigations tracked down an address and phone number for the couple, worried that they might have become Ellison's victims too. Luckily, they were out of town in their winter home in Florida. As far as they knew, the car was parked in the garage at their San Pedro home.

The Bennetts had given permission to search their property. They had a larger home on several acres that afforded them the privacy that was elusive in much of Los Angeles. Ellison had to have spent a significant amount of time formulating his plan. If they dug deep enough, they'd probably find some connection between him and the Bennetts, even a tenuous one. How else would he know that they spent part of the year in Florida? He'd had years to come up with a nearly foolproof plan. Who knows how much time they had to find Maggie before it was too late for her? It might already be too late for all they knew.

Kevin, Tess, Detective Francois and several other officers fanned out in the house. Despite the size of the home, it didn't take long to determine that Ellison and Maggie weren't there. It was equally clear, though, that someone had been living in the house while the Bennetts were away. Dishes cluttered the countertops. The bed in the main bedroom was unmade. Wet bath towels lay on the bathroom floor. A dark blue Tucson was parked in the garage, but the silver Toyota Corolla that should have been next to it was gone.

"Damnit! Where are they?" Kevin's chest felt as if it were caving in on itself. He'd never been more afraid.

Tess clasped a hand on his shoulder and squeezed. "Keep your head in the game. We'll find her."

He nodded, taking several deep breaths then joining the search of the house for clues to where Ellison may have taken Maggie.

He crossed the sunken living room to the home office. One long wall was a floor-to-ceiling bookcase that matched the oversize walnut-colored desk that dominated the room. A sleek silver computer sat on the neat-as-a-pin desk.

Kevin sat in the leather executive chair and turned on the computer. The login and password were taped to the monitor. What better way for Ellison to stay off the grid than to use someone else's Wi-Fi and login information.

Kevin opened the browser and went to the history, frustrated to find that it had been deleted.

"Try the cache," Tess said, coming up behind him at the desk.

"The cache?"

"Move." She shooed him out of the chair, taking the seat for herself and clicking the mouse. "Everyone knows to clear their browser history if they don't want someone to come behind them and see what they've been searching. But most people don't think about the cache. That's where the computer stores certain data—images, fonts, that sort of thing—that make it easier for you to download the same pages again later. That can tell us a lot too."

Tess clicked the mouse a few more times, and a logo popped up on screen.

"MaxPrint," Kevin read the name off. "Never heard of it."

"Let's see." Tess opened a browser and put the name of the company along with "Los Angeles area" into the search box.

The search engine returned a webpage. Bright red letters at the top of the page screamed that, as of a few years ag MaxPrint had closed its doors permanently. Tess copie address for the company and pasted it into a map searc

A map pinpointing the defunct business's location up in a new tab. She zoomed in on what looked l dustrial area of mostly businesses.

"That must be where he took her." Tess loo from where she sat. "The building is proba Ellison would have made sure of that. A he'd have all night before anyone from ing businesses showed up."

"Francois!" Kevin yelled, already

The detective met him in the quickly explained what he and theory.

"I'll get squad cars rollin already dialing a number

"Tess and I are on our wa

side of the desk. "When I saw that the Larimer would be exhibiting the Viperé and that you were curating the exhibit, well, it had to be a sign."

"A sign?"

"Yes. The ruby is priceless. And if I could steal it and make it look like you'd done it then disappear, well, that had a certain symmetry to it, don't you see? Only you wouldn't just be pretending to be dead like I was."

"No one will believe I stole the ruby now, and if you kill me, Kevin will hunt you to the ends of the earth."

Ellison's laughter grew louder. He threw his arms out wide and tipped his head back. "Let him come." He looked her in the eyes. "I lost everything when you walked out on me. I have nothing left to lose."

They were the words of a man who was lost to madness. There was nothing behind Ellison's gaze. She knew he would kill her if she didn't do something.

She lunged up out of the chair at him, ready to fight for her life.

Luck was on her side. She caught Ellison off guard. By the time he thought to raise the gun, she was driving her shoulder into his stomach.

He yelped and staggered backward.

She'd never punched anyone in her life, didn't know the first thing about doing it properly, but she made a fist and swung for Ellison's face, catching him on the chin. He had four inches and at least thirty pounds on her, but she knew that if she lost this fight, it would be her last. She used that knowledge, that fear, as fuel, punching and kicking like a wild animal.

Ellison put his hands up in self-defense, the hand with

the gun coming around in a circular motion and catching her in the temple.

Now she staggered, falling down to her knees.

She looked up to find Ellison pointing the gun at her. His lips moved, but she couldn't hear him. It sounded like the world had exploded into screams.

All she could see was the gun pointed at her.

Then Ellison jerked backward, the gun flying out of his hand.

Thunder rolled over the warehouse, and it took a moment for her to realize that it wasn't thunder but a helicopter. The screams had come from the police officers that had stormed into the warehouse.

Then Kevin was there, on his knees beside her.

"Maggie, baby, are you okay? Talk to me."

She looked past Kevin to where Ellison lay on the floor. She couldn't see him because he was surrounded by half a dozen armed officers. "Is he dead?"

"Don't worry about him." Kevin slid one arm around her waist and another under her legs. "Let's get you out of here."

She rested her head on his shoulder and let him carry her to safety.

Kevin didn't wait for the teen to find the photo. He snatched the phone from the boy's hand.

"Hey, man! That's mine."

Kevin ignored the teen, navigating to his photo gallery while Tess assured the boy that he'd get his phone back in a moment.

He found the photos quickly. A silver, four-door Toyota Corolla. A dime a dozen, but the teen had captured a clear picture of the license plate. He sent copies of the photographs to himself, Tess and Francois before handing the phone back to the boy.

"You did a good job," he said to the teen. "Stop sneaking out at night though. You're going to get yourself in trouble." Kevin turned and started after Tess, who, like Francois, was already on the phone probably having someone pull the registration for the license.

THE CAR BELONGED to Charles and Louise Bennett, a couple in their seventies. The computer guru at West Investigations tracked down an address and phone number for the couple, worried that they might have become Ellison's victims too. Luckily, they were out of town in their winter home in Florida. As far as they knew, the car was parked in the garage at their San Pedro home.

The Bennetts had given permission to search their property. They had a larger home on several acres that afforded them the privacy that was elusive in much of Los Angeles. Ellison had to have spent a significant amount of time formulating his plan. If they dug deep enough, they'd probably find some connection between him and the Bennetts, even a tenuous one. How else would he know that they spent part of the year in Florida? He'd had years to come up with a nearly foolproof plan. Who knows how much time they had to find Maggie before it was too late for her? It might already be too late for all they knew.

Kevin, Tess, Detective Francois and several other officers fanned out in the house. Despite the size of the home, it didn't take long to determine that Ellison and Maggie weren't there. It was equally clear, though, that someone had been living in the house while the Bennetts were away. Dishes cluttered the countertops. The bed in the main bedroom was unmade. Wet bath towels lay on the bathroom floor. A dark blue Tucson was parked in the garage, but the silver Toyota Corolla that should have been next to it was gone.

"Damnit! Where are they?" Kevin's chest felt as if it were caving in on itself. He'd never been more afraid.

Tess clasped a hand on his shoulder and squeezed. "Keep your head in the game. We'll find her."

He nodded, taking several deep breaths then joining the search of the house for clues to where Ellison may have taken Maggie.

He crossed the sunken living room to the home office. One long wall was a floor-to-ceiling bookcase that matched the oversize walnut-colored desk that dominated the room. A sleek silver computer sat on the neat-as-a-pin desk.

Kevin sat in the leather executive chair and turned on the computer. The login and password were taped to the monitor. What better way for Ellison to stay off the grid than to use someone else's Wi-Fi and login information.

Kevin opened the browser and went to the history, frustrated to find that it had been deleted.

"Try the cache," Tess said, coming up behind him at the desk.

"The cache?"

"Move." She shooed him out of the chair, taking the seat for herself and clicking the mouse. "Everyone knows to clear their browser history if they don't want someone to come behind them and see what they've been searching. But most people don't think about the cache. That's where the computer stores certain data—images, fonts, that sort of thing—that make it easier for you to download the same pages again later. That can tell us a lot too."

Tess clicked the mouse a few more times, and a logo popped up on screen.

"MaxPrint," Kevin read the name off. "Never heard of it."

"Let's see." Tess opened a browser and put the name of the company along with "Los Angeles area" into the search box.

The search engine returned a webpage. Bright red letters at the top of the page screamed that, as of a few years ago, MaxPrint had closed its doors permanently. Tess copied the address for the company and pasted it into a map search box.

A map pinpointing the defunct business's location opened up in a new tab. She zoomed in on what looked like an industrial area of mostly businesses.

"That must be where he took her." Tess looked up at him from where she sat. "The building is probably still empty. Ellison would have made sure of that. And since it is late, he'd have all night before anyone from one of the surrounding businesses showed up."

"Francois!" Kevin yelled, already heading for the door.

The detective met him in the foyer of the house. He quickly explained what he and Tess had found and their theory.

"I'll get squad cars rolling that way now." Francois was already dialing a number on his phone.

"Tess and I are on our way," Kevin said.

Maggie was in that warehouse. He could feel it.

Hang on, baby. I'm coming.

THE CONCRETE FLOOR was cracked, little more than rubble in several places, and the air was sour and smelled of mold. The space was mostly empty, but there were signs of the business that used to inhabit the space. Broken wooden pallets, a metal desk and office chair. Wires hung precariously from the ceiling, and most of the windows that lined the top of the wall had been broken, jagged shards of glass protruding dangerously.

She heard a squeak as they entered, followed by the pitter-patter of paws that signaled she and Ellison were not the only two animals in the space.

But rats were the least of her problems.

Ellison led her to the chair and pushed her into it. "Don't move. I'm going to take the tape off of your mouth. If you try anything…" He held the gun up.

She yelped when he ripped the tape off.

"Why are you doing this?"

He glared at her. "I already told you why."

"Ellison, this…this has to stop. I'm sorry if I hurt you. But this, you aren't going to get away with it. The police know you're alive. They know you stole the money, the ruby, that you killed Kim and attacked my father." She said the last words with more than a little bitterness. She'd never forgive him for hurting her father.

He chortled. "Then what's one more notch on my record, huh? It was so much harder to live on the run than I expected. Five hundred thousand dollars doesn't go nearly as far as I'd have hoped. New identities. Constant moving. Staying off the radar. It's expensive." He propped himself against the side of the desk. "When I saw that the Larimer would be exhibiting the Viperé and that you were curating the exhibit, well, it had to be a sign."

"A sign?"

"Yes. The ruby is priceless. And if I could steal it and make it look like you'd done it then disappear, well, that had a certain symmetry to it, don't you see? Only you wouldn't just be pretending to be dead like I was."

"No one will believe I stole the ruby now, and if you kill me, Kevin will hunt you to the ends of the earth."

Ellison's laughter grew louder. He threw his arms out wide and tipped his head back. "Let him come." He looked her in the eyes. "I lost everything when you walked out on me. I have nothing left to lose."

They were the words of a man who was lost to madness. There was nothing behind Ellison's gaze. She knew he would kill her if she didn't do something.

She lunged up out of the chair at him, ready to fight for her life.

Luck was on her side. She caught Ellison off guard. By the time he thought to raise the gun, she was driving her shoulder into his stomach.

He yelped and staggered backward.

She'd never punched anyone in her life, didn't know the first thing about doing it properly, but she made a fist and swung for Ellison's face, catching him on the chin. He had four inches and at least thirty pounds on her, but she knew that if she lost this fight, it would be her last. She used that knowledge, that fear, as fuel, punching and kicking like a wild animal.

Ellison put his hands up in self-defense, the hand with

the gun coming around in a circular motion and catching her in the temple.

Now she staggered, falling down to her knees.

She looked up to find Ellison pointing the gun at her. His lips moved, but she couldn't hear him. It sounded like the world had exploded into screams.

All she could see was the gun pointed at her.

Then Ellison jerked backward, the gun flying out of his hand.

Thunder rolled over the warehouse, and it took a moment for her to realize that it wasn't thunder but a helicopter. The screams had come from the police officers that had stormed into the warehouse.

Then Kevin was there, on his knees beside her.

"Maggie, baby, are you okay? Talk to me."

She looked past Kevin to where Ellison lay on the floor. She couldn't see him because he was surrounded by half a dozen armed officers. "Is he dead?"

"Don't worry about him." Kevin slid one arm around her waist and another under her legs. "Let's get you out of here."

She rested her head on his shoulder and let him carry her to safety.

Chapter Twenty-Five

Maggie didn't complain when Kevin insisted she go to the hospital and get checked out this time. Ellison faking his death, stealing the Viperé ruby and attempting to kill her had made international news. She'd had to turn off her cell phone, and Detective Francois had stationed several officers at Kim's house, her house, to keep the vultures off the property.

Ellison was dead. The police were still searching the home he'd been hiding out in, but it appeared he'd documented his plan to steal the Viperé and his growing hatred for Maggie in a journal. From what the police had already been able to piece together, it appeared that Ellison had decided that the best way to avoid the consequences of his embezzlement back in New York was to fake his death. He'd done a sufficiently good job at hiding most of the money, so he had the means to live comfortably if he scaled back his lifestyle. Unfortunately, scaling back was the opposite of what he'd done. In less than three years, he'd blown through almost all of the half a million dollars he'd been able to squirrel away. With no money and nothing but time, his thoughts had turned to how to get his hands on more money.

The browser history on his computer showed that he'd

been keeping track of Maggie and her new job, his bitterness toward her perceived slight of him during the embezzlement investigation growing. When he saw the announcement for the upcoming Viperé ruby exhibit, a plan to steal it began to take shape in his head. Being dead allowed Ellison a lot of latitude for sneaking into Maggie's life. He discovered Kim's gambling habit and debts and, using a fake persona, convinced Kim to give him the security code for the museum's cameras as well as details about the donors' open house. Maggie wasn't initially a target. Ellison had no idea she would still be there on the night of the theft, but seeing her ignited all the animosity he'd built up toward her, and his rage had taken control. He'd decided that she had to pay for what he saw as abandoning him. He was the one who had broken into her house and attacked her father.

There was a knock on her hospital room door. She looked up to find Kevin standing in the doorway. He held a white paper bag in one hand and a coffee cup in the other.

Her stomach growled, and she realized that she was starving.

Kevin put the bag and coffee down on the bedside table then leaned over and kissed her lightly on the lips. "How are you feeling?"

"Like I'd like to get out of this hospital bed and into my own bed."

Kevin kissed her again. "Soon. Let the doctors run all their tests then I'll take you home."

She smiled up at the man she'd loved since she was twenty, the man she now knew she'd always love. "That sounds good." She wiggled her eyebrows.

He laughed. "I wasn't suggesting anything." He sobered a touch. "But I do think it might be a good idea if you stayed with me. Just for a few days. It's a bit of a madhouse at your place right now."

She sighed. "So I've heard. I talked to my father and Julie and let them know I was okay."

Kevin nodded. "I know. Tess agreed to keep a man from West on them for another day or two. Just to be on the safe side."

Maggie let out a breath of relief. "Thank you. I know Ellison is no longer a threat to me or my dad, but…"

"But you need time to process everything. I get it." Kevin reached for her hand. "Take your time. I'm not going anywhere."

She squeezed his hand, for the first time in days feeling light, despite being in a hospital bed. "That's a promise I'm going to hold you to."

Kevin leaned down, his lips grazing hers. "Hold me tight."

Epilogue

Maggie stood in the small party room with Julie and Julie's daughter, Sara. She felt butterflies soaring in her stomach. She could hear the sound of the harpist and the buzz of the wedding guests floating on the breeze being carried in from the garden. Everyone was waiting.

She looked in the mirror, touching her hair, which had been twisted into an elaborate updo with curls falling forward to frame her face.

"You look gorgeous," Julie said from the other side of the room.

Maggie turned and smiled at the bride. "We're supposed to be telling *you* that."

Julie really did make a beautiful bride. She wore a champagne-colored tea-length dress and red satin heels with a sparkly buckle. She'd spent the last three months all but glued to Maggie's father's side, nursing him back to health. Her father and Julie had decided that they didn't want to wait any longer than necessary to make their relationship official, although as far as Maggie was concerned, Julie was already officially part of their family. There was no need for a quick wedding, but since that was what her father and Julie wanted,

Maggie made it her mission to make it happen. She'd thrown herself into wedding planning with gusto.

Kevin had gently suggested, more than once, that her enthusiasm for wedding planning might be an offshoot of the lingering guilt she felt over Ellison's attack on her father. It was true that she still struggled with guilt from having brought Ellison into their lives, but she was working through it. And she did want her father and Julie to have the wedding of their dreams. Even if they only had three months to make it happen.

Thankfully, Julie's daughter and sons had also been on board with making their mother's wedding everything she wanted. And Boyd and Julie wanted to keep the nuptials small and intimate. They'd divided up the to-do list, and together they'd been able to get the flowers, cake, food, venue, dresses, tuxedos and musicians on board in less than ninety days. And in the process, Maggie had begun building the first threads of a bond with her soon-to-be stepsister and stepbrothers.

"My hands are shaking," Julie said.

"Here, Mom," Sara said, thrusting a champagne flute in her mother's hand. "Drink this. It will calm your nerves."

Julie took a long sip and pressed her palm flat against her stomach. "Whew. I don't want to be tipsy going down the aisle."

Sara waved away her mother's concern with a laugh. "Don't worry. Rick can carry you down the aisle if he has to."

Maggie joined her soon-to-be stepsister and stepmother in laughter. At six three and built like a professional football player, Julie's oldest son, Rick, would have no problem carrying his mother down the aisle. But Julie dispelled that notion quickly.

"No way." Julie set the half-full champagne glass down on a side table. "I want to get to the end of that aisle on my own steam and greet my groom."

Maggie's heart swelled with the love she saw in Julie's eyes. "Well, let's get this show on the road then."

The women shared a quick three-way hug before marching into the anteroom where Rick, Julie's younger son, Thomas, and one of Boyd's friends from the senior center waited to escort them down the aisle.

Maggie slipped her arm through Thomas's and grabbed her bouquet of pink and off-white roses. Together, the wedding party stepped forward as the harpist began playing the wedding march. They walked into the garden, which was full of colorful flowers, and faced the sparkling manmade lake that was the centerpiece of the resort's attractions. It was the perfect backdrop for Julie and her father to exchange their vows, but all Maggie could see was Kevin.

He looked more handsome than she'd ever seen him in a dark blue suit that looked as if each thread had been spooled just for him. His smile lit up his face, and his eyes never left hers as her father and Julie pledged their undying love to each other. Maggie was ridiculously happy. Not just for her father, but because she and Kevin had decided to give their relationship another shot. They'd both been through a lot and made mistakes when they were younger, but she knew that they were wiser and stronger as individuals now. They'd spent a lot of time talking, about what they'd done wrong and about what they wanted out of a relationship and life now. She felt in her heart that it would last this time. They'd agreed to take it slow, but she knew Kevin was the man she was supposed to spend her life with. He'd always been that man.

Later that night, with the reception in full swing, Kevin

swept Maggie outside onto the patio where her father and Julie had exchanged their vows just hours earlier. They walked hand in hand to the edge of the lake, a bottle of champagne in Maggie's hand and two champagne flutes in Kevin's.

She tapped her glass against Kevin's before taking a sip. "It was a beautiful wedding, wasn't it?"

"I don't know," Kevin answered. "All I could see was you."

She set her champagne glass on the patio and kissed him.

After a long moment, Kevin broke off the kiss. "I worried that it was too early, but I don't think I can wait any longer." He fell to one knee and slid a little black box from his trouser pocket. "I want to spend the rest of my life with you. Marry me?"

A single tear fell from Maggie's eye, but her heart swelled and the smile she wore lit up her insides. "Yes," she answered, gazing down at the man she loved.

Kevin slid a brilliant square-cut diamond onto her finger then stood, sweeping her into his arms. "Since you're now an expert in pulling together beautiful weddings quickly, how about we set the wedding day for three months from now?"

Maggie laughed, her insides flip-flopping at the thought of another wedding. "I'm not sure I can wait that long to be your wife."

Kevin's grin spread from ear to ear. "That's just what I hoped to hear."

* * * * *

THE SILENT SETUP

KATIE METTNER

For Tom

Chapter One

*The radio crackled to life, and Eric Newman reached for it.
His army team brother, Mack Holbock, climbed from the car
ahead of him. "We've got him covered from the front," their
team leader, Cal Newfellow, said over the radio. "What do
you see from your vantage point?"*

*Eric brought the radio to his lips. "We're in position. Gun-
ner ready to engage." Motion caught his attention, and he
noticed the back door of the diplomat's car crack open. A
little foot came out, and his breath caught. "The back door
of the car is openin—"*

*He never finished the sentence. An explosion rocked
the air, and he was blasted backward in his seat. His head
smacked the side of the Humvee from the percussion wave,
and his gunner fell into the back seat. Just as the acrid scent
of war reached his nostrils, Eric slammed down the accelerator and whipped around the raging fireball of the diplomat's car. He had to get to the rest of his team. There was
no way anyone inside the car had survived the explosion.
He could only pray his team wasn't dead alongside them.*

*"Do you see the team?" Eric shouted to his gunner, but he
got no response. He skidded to a stop when he saw the bod-*

ies. His three brothers had fallen alongside each other but were all moving. Crawling. Clawing their way toward him.

Roman Jacobs was first to open the door, helping Mack and Cal into the Humvee, all three bleeding and covered in soot. Eric hit the accelerator and tore away from the carnage before Roman had closed the door. There was no need to render aid to the family in the car. They'd been vaporized the moment the bomb had gone off. They could do nothing for them, and it was time to get out of Dodge before someone decided they were a target too.

Eric pulled alongside the helicopter in a matter of minutes, slammed the Humvee into Park and jumped out, nearly falling when his world spun in one direction before it flipped to the other. Doggedly determined, he helped Roman carry an injured Mack to the chopper, both of his legs a bloodied mess from flying debris. Roman's lips were moving, but all Eric heard was the buzzing in his ears. He was used to that after an explosion. It had happened more times than he could count, but it was frustrating when he couldn't communicate with his team. Cal, Roman and Eric piled into the chopper as it lifted off the ground, the sandy hellscape growing distant with every spin of the helo blade. Eric worked with Cal to stabilize Mack on a gurney so they could take stock of his injuries.

Cal tried to wrap Mack's legs with gauze but kept dropping it. It was what Eric noticed when he went to pick it up that had him shouting for Roman. "His hand!" he yelled at the man who had grown up with Cal as his foster brother. "I've got Mack. Help Cal!"

Roman nodded and said something, but Eric couldn't make out the words. He was dizzy and fell twice while trying to get Mack's legs covered to protect the wounds. He

*would not be the reason his buddy became a double ampu-
tee. Mack gave him a thumbs-up, his lips moving, but Eric
couldn't determine what he said. He turned to face Roman
when there was a tap on his shoulder. Roman had wrapped
Cal's hand in a beehive fashion to hold it all together, but
Eric had seen the truth. He no longer had five fingers on
that hand. Roman was saying something, but the only thing
Eric heard was silence.*

"Can't hear you!"

*Roman handed him earphones, and Eric threw them on,
forcing himself to concentrate on listening below the ringing in his ears. That was when the truth hit him—under the
ringing in his ears was nothing but radio silence.*

A TAP ON his shoulder made him turn, arm up, ready to
block a blow. He was face-to-face with Efren, who took a
step back. "You okay, man?"

Eric dropped his arm and sighed. "Sorry—I got distracted
by something."

"Hey, I know that kind of distraction," Efren said, shaking his head. "Sometimes you can't avoid it."

Efren had lost his left leg during the war. He knew how
easy it was to get trapped in those flashbacks, which was
one reason he fit in so well at Secure One—the team understood being in a war zone, foreign or domestic. No one
judged you for slipping into the past when the conditions
were right. Thankfully, the team was always there to bring
you back to the present.

Eric pointed straight ahead. "The car reminded me of the
one that blew up the day everyone at Secure One got hurt."

The mission had gone perfectly wrong. Their team might
have reached their destination, but the horrors that had trans-

pired after were burned in Eric's memory forever. Every night for the last fourteen years, he watched the replay of a little foot coming out of the door and then it falling to the ground, unbound by its body. He watched the horror show of Mack walking a few feet away from the car before he was tossed forward in slow motion and fell to the ground. He was alive, but the debris had hit his lower legs and severed the nerves beyond repair. He wore braces on both legs to stay upright now, but he was lucky to be walking at all. Cal, their team leader and owner of Secure One, had nearly lost his right hand. They'd salvaged a few fingers, but the hand was grotesquely disfigured. Cal wore a unique prosthesis to compensate for the fingers he'd lost that day, and it shocked Eric every time Cal pulled out a gun and pulled the trigger with precision.

Eric had gotten the silent injury, literally and figuratively. By the time they'd gotten to the hospital, the ringing had started to subside, which had made how silent the world was even more evident. The doctors had told him that percussion injuries like his often resolved within a few days to a few weeks and to wait for his hearing to return slowly. After four months, they'd admitted that maybe there was a problem and ran some tests. They'd discovered he'd had severe sensorineural hearing loss, which meant his hearing would never return. While he wore top-of-the-line hearing aids, at the end of the day, when he took them out and set them on the bedside table, his world was silent again. It had been fourteen years, and he still wasn't used to it.

"Do you think we have a situation?"

Eric's gaze drifted back to the car parked in front of a darkened storage unit. "Time will tell."

"Should we call Cal?" Efren whispered from behind.

"Whatever for?" he asked defensively. "I'm team leader while he's in DC, and I've worked here as long as Cal and Roman. I can handle this."

Efren held up his hands in defense. "You're right. I'm sorry. I'm so used to Cal standing over my shoulder that I don't know what to do when he's not. I'm surprised he even went to DC with everyone."

"It took some convincing," Eric admitted, his gaze trained on the car in front of them as it sat idling by an empty unit at the back of the storage buildings.

Convincing was an understatement. Eric had to threaten to leave Secure One for Cal to listen to his complaints. For years, Eric had diligently worked to level up Secure One in the security industry, but the team never seemed to notice. If it hadn't been for him installing the latest technology and integrating their clients' information into the computers, it wouldn't have mattered that Mina was a world-class coder and hacker for the FBI. If he hadn't found the adaptive outerwear and clothing for uniforms to help Mack, Efren and Mina change quickly while on the job, the team wouldn't have been prepared when things went sideways. Ultimately, Eric was in the background, ensuring Secure One ran smoothly and efficiently. His ego didn't require recognition for that. He'd been a member of an elite team of army police when he'd served, and there was no place for ego there. All he wanted was to be on a level playing field with Cal, Mack and Roman—just as they had been when they'd served together.

Last spring, Secure One had been involved in a case that had gained national attention. Mack and his fiancée, Charlotte, had been responsible for finding and arresting the Red River Slayer, a serial killer terrorizing the nation. Charlotte was receiving a medal for bravery in DC, and Cal wanted to attend the event, so he'd asked Eric to lead the team in his absence. He had been stunned by the request since Roman wasn't going to DC with them, and Roman had always been Cal's right-hand man. Eric had jumped at the chance—but not to prove to Cal that he was capable. He'd proved that in the field time and time again in much more dangerous situations than surveilling a storage unit.

Eric wanted—no, he needed to prove that he could still be an effective leader who others respected. If he didn't, all the years he'd spent being a silent leader had been wasted—at least in his eyes. The rest of the team would say otherwise, but they were all coming from a place of leading the team in front of the public, which was an opportunity Eric had yet to have. He wouldn't waste this chance to show his boss his leadership skills were sharper than ever.

"I readily admit that I don't understand all the dynamics between you, Cal, Roman and Mack. That said, I'd trust you to have my back any day on the battlefield. You and Selina are the two most underappreciated members of this team," Efren said.

"I can't fault your observation skills, that's for sure. I'm surprised you noticed Selina's contributions, considering her prickly attitude toward you."

"Probably why I noticed," he said, chuckling as he shook his head. "That said, it would be hard to miss. She's putting on Band-Aids when she should be out in the field. Don't get me wrong—she's great at what she does, but I think she's underutilized for her talents."

"I get the feeling you aren't the only one who feels that way," Eric said with a nod. "Selina may need to have a day of reckoning with Cal too. As for you, I don't know what you did, but you sure rubbed her the wrong way. Usually she's the sweetest, most easygoing person at Secure One."

"I wish I knew too. Selina has been prickly since the moment they introduced me to her. If you want my opinion, I think she's hurt and angry that Cal hired me when it should have been her."

"That's possible, but we needed help at the time, and Cal couldn't worry about whose toes he stepped on or who got their feelings hurt. We were hunting a serial killer."

"I can agree and disagree on this one," Efren said. "Yes, you needed help, but an EMT or nurse is easier to find than someone like me."

"Fair." Eric was forced to agree with his logic, especially since they'd only procured him because he was a friend of Mina's. "All I'm saying is I don't think that crossed anyone's mind. Mina knew you and said you'd come in fast." He sighed and shook his head. "I guess I'm just as guilty as Cal for not suggesting he bring Selina in and hire a new nurse. I hope Selina sticks around long enough to have it out with Cal. She deserves her day in court."

"I hope she does too, and hey, if it takes the heat off my back, you won't hear me complaining," Efren said, tongue in cheek.

The dome light came on inside the car, and Eric crouched low—Efren sat since his above-knee prosthesis didn't allow him to crouch. "Get this on video, and make sure to get the make and model of the car and the plate," he whispered, motioning for Efren to use the app on their tablet. It wouldn't be fantastic quality, but it would give them something to go on.

Two men climbed from the car, and Eric leaned in for a closer look. He had no doubt a crime had been committed or was about to be committed, and he wanted to see it go down in real time just in case he could still help the victim. Fettering's was a self-storage for the rich and famous, but it was the middle of the night, and the rich and famous didn't casually drop by their storage unit in the cold rain to pick something up. Efren and Eric were there to find holes in the client's security and close them before bad things happened. He knew they'd just found a hole and a bad thing was about to happen.

He motioned for Efren to pull on his night-vision goggles before he did the same. The lighting was nonexistent, which was another issue for Fettering to address, but the goggles would keep them from missing anything. He kept his gaze trained on the two guys opening the storage unit door while he pondered if what Efren had said was true. If it was, then he did owe Selina an apology. He knew what it was like to be constantly overlooked as an asset to the team, even when you were working your tail off every day. He'd chat with her and let her know that feeling hurt for being overlooked was okay. Then he'd encourage her to talk to Cal and demand the respect she deserved.

"What are they carrying?" Efren whispered as the guys grabbed something from the car and carried it into the storage unit.

"Whatever it is, it's heavy," he answered. The men shifted, and he caught a glimpse of the item. "It's a trunk." The two guys lowered it to the unit's floor and then stood. They turned to face each other for a moment before they pulled the door back down and locked it. "I don't feel good about it," Eric said as the car pulled out the back exit.

What he didn't tell Efren was that he could read their lips. Whoever the Winged Templar was, that was who these guys worked for. Their expressions had told him they also feared him. Eric ran a hand along the back of his neck to see if the hair was standing up. His ingrained military intuition told him what those guys had just dropped inside the unit wasn't seasonal clothing.

"My gut is clenched as well," Efren agreed.

"First of all, two guys don't go out at midnight to drop off something at a storage unit unless they want to be certain no one is around."

"True," Efren said, moving his goggles to the top of his head to check his tablet screen. "What's second of all?"

"Second of all, because of the first of all we're going to search that unit."

"Sure, it's unusual for two guys to drop something off late at night, but I don't know if it's break-in worthy."

Eric slid his goggles to the top of his head. "The property management has a right to search any unit that displays suspicious activity. It's in the lease they signed."

"And didn't read."

"Bingo," Eric said before he pointed at the tablet. "Are they gone?"

"Sure are. They drove out of the gate and headed down the road. I still don't understand why Fettering, who has more money than Heinz has pickles, put a storage business on his property. The clientele can be rather sketchy, and it's a lot of coming and going at all hours of the day and night," Efren pointed out.

"All true, but believe it or not, there are a lot of rich people in Minnesota who need a place to store their off-season toys and goodies. Dirk Fettering is one of those rich people. He built these units to cater to his kind of people. Classy, not sketchy."

"Well, that felt sketchy," Efren mumbled, motioning at the storage unit.

"Exactly," Eric agreed, taking his bolt cutters from his belt. "And that's why we're going to take a look."

Efren hoisted himself to standing and grabbed the tablet. "What does your gut say?"

"I give it fifty-fifty odds that it's either money or a body."

"A body doesn't make sense. Eventually it would start to smell."

"Then let's hope it's money," Eric said, pushing himself away from the building. He knew full well it wasn't money. He was almost certain it was a body. The men had struggled under the weight of it, and you didn't dump money in a storage locker and drive away. Why they'd dump a body here, he couldn't say, but this was his chance to prove himself to Cal, and he wasn't going to sleep on the job.

"This is the perfect example of why that back entrance and exit is a problem. The lack of security back here is disturbing," he said over his shoulder.

"They have to swipe their card to get in, right?" Efren asked.

"They have to swipe a card. It doesn't have to be theirs. It's easy to dupe a card with no one the wiser." There was a guard at the front entrance to check people in, but not the back one. It had been their first suggestion when they'd taken the job, but Fettering had refused to consider closing the back entrance and exit from 8:00 p.m. until 7:00 a.m. He'd said as long as the person had a card, they had every right to be there. Eric knew that wasn't the case, and after their initial walkthrough tonight, he'd put it back on the list as number one. What had just happened had proved his point.

The two men reached the storage unit, and Eric glanced

around the space. "We need better lighting and cameras back here too. We just lucked out that we were back here when they pulled up."

"Agreed," Efren said. "Fettering built a state-of-the-art storage facility for big-name clients and then slacked on security measures. It feels a little suspicious to me."

"You'd be surprised how often that happens," he said. "They get so caught up in the idea of what they're offering people that they forget about the logistics of how to protect it. Got gloves?"

They each tugged black leather gloves from their waistbands and pulled them on. Eric inspected the lock and chuckled at the simple padlock you could buy at the local hardware store. As if that would stop anyone who wanted to get inside. Sometimes people were far too trusting of other humans. He cut the metal band quickly and rolled the door up. Efren flashed his light into the cavernous space, and Eric wasn't surprised to see the unit was empty other than the giant trunk.

"Something feels off. Why do they have this giant storage unit for one trunk?" Efren asked.

Eric shook his head as he stood with one hand planted on his hip. "I would guess that whatever is in that trunk is the answer. This was likely a drop, and someone else will come to pick it up."

"And if it's not a drop?"

"Then it's a body, and the climate control will buy them a few extra days before it starts to smell."

"Are we going to open it, or are we going to call the cops?"

"Oh, we're going to open it," Eric said, "and depending on what we find, we'll call the cops."

He knelt, inspecting the locks on the trunk. They were

surprisingly easy to get open with his lock-pick set. Once the three locks were popped, they lifted the lid. A smell hit him that he knew all too well. Copper.

"Well," Efren said as he stared at the dead body inside the trunk, "you called it. Last time I checked, a man's head doesn't belong in the middle of his chest."

"Nope," Eric agreed. "Sure doesn't. It looks like a call to the Bemidji PD is in order."

Efren flicked off the flashlight. "This is gruesome."

"Yes, removing someone's head and sitting it on their chest to fit them in the trunk is a bit gruesome, but the manner of death also indicates—"

"A mob hit," Efren answered, and Eric tipped his head in acknowledgment.

"That or a gang killing. Either way, this guy is not a Secure One problem. He's a police problem." Eric pulled out his phone to call the police, but internally he was cussing out the universe. The first time Cal trusted him with a solo job and he found a body. Not that he had any control over that other than how things went now.

"Maybe we should wait and see if someone comes along to pick up the trunk," Efren suggested.

"We don't know for sure that anyone is. Now that I know it's a body, I'm legally obligated to report it. We'll leave it to the PD to sort out. A dead guy in a trunk is above our paygrade."

"Fair point. If nothing else, a dead guy in a trunk is also incentive for Fettering to tighten security."

"We can only hope." Eric's tone was dry and nonbelieving as he connected his hearing aids to his phone via Bluetooth.

After reporting the body to the police, they settled in to wait for a squad. Eric would update Cal as soon as he turned this over, and then he'd sit down with Dirk and find out exactly what kind of business he was running out here. Eric had every intention of proving he could do the job, even if it was the last thing he did.

Chapter Two

Sadie Cook pulled the curtain on a front window back slowly. She liked working the night shift because it was quiet and it was easy to finish her tasks, but tonight was anything but quiet. The rumor was they'd found someone dead by the storage units. She wouldn't be the least bit surprised if the rumor was a fact. It was only a matter of time before someone figured out that the lighting was nonexistent in the back of the units, and with an exit built right in, it was bound to happen. Maybe now Mr. Fettering would stop telling them, the housekeeping staff, that it was perfectly safe to park back there. Safe or not, she didn't have a choice but to stay and work for him as a housekeeper. The pay and the hours were what she needed to survive, but a dead body gave her pause. The last thing she wanted was to end up a dead body simply because she worked for Dirk.

The flashing lights made her anxious, so she let the curtain fall and turned away from the window. She wanted to head home, but no one was allowed in or out until the police had taken everyone's statements. She deduced that trying to sneak out would be an excellent way to end up in the interrogation room of the Bemidji Police Department. With a resigned sigh, she grabbed her phone. Since she had no idea when she could leave, she'd better make a call. She plastered herself along the wall farthest from the door before she dialed, just in case someone happened to walk past while she was talking.

"Hello?"

Sadie let out a pent-up breath with relief. "Julia? It's Sadie."

"What's up, girl?" her friend of five years asked.

"I've been held up at work. Can you keep him a little longer?"

"Of course. He's sleeping anyway, so there's no need to wake him. Everything okay?"

"I don't know," Sadie admitted, a shiver of undefined fear running down her spine. "The Bemidji PD showed up after the security guys were here. Rumors are floating around that they found a body, but I can't confirm. I also can't leave until I talk to the cops."

"That sounds ominous, Sades. Time to pull the rip cord?"

"I don't think I'd get off this property without being stopped by someone, nor do I want to end up in the clinker for leaving the scene of a crime. I'll be first in line so I can get home though."

"I meant in general," her friend said in the kind of voice that told Sadie exactly what Julia thought about Dirk Fettering.

"You know I can't quit this job yet, Jules. Once we find Kadie, then I'm out. I promise."

"Okay—be safe. No need to worry about our little guy. He's fine here. Take your time, and while the cops are there, ask them if they have any new leads on Kadie's whereabouts."

Sadie grimaced at the thought as she told her friend goodbye. After stowing her phone back in her pocket, she picked up her cleaning supplies and left the bedroom. Julia was right. She would have to face the same detectives who kept telling her that her sister hadn't disappeared but had left of her own free will. Sadie knew that wasn't true. Her sister loved her baby boy more than life itself and would never willingly leave him. Something had happened to her, but the police refused to listen, much less look at the evidence.

In fairness to them, there had been a note that said single motherhood was too much for her and she was leaving town, but it wasn't real. Sadie knew her sister's handwriting, and what was on that paper wasn't it. If Kadie had written it, she'd done it under duress so Sadie would recognize the stilted writing as something other than her usual beautiful flowing penmanship. She'd even shown the police other samples of Kadie's handwriting, but they still refused to help her.

In the meantime, Sadie was trying to take care of Kadie's eight-month-old baby boy, Houston. Thank heavens Julia could keep him while she worked because there was no way he was going into the foster care system, even temporarily. It was her job to keep him safe until Kadie returned. Since Kadie had never named a father, Houston had no one but Sadie to protect him.

"Sadie Cook?"

She jumped and spun, her cleaning kit tumbling to the floor as she stumbled backward. Strong, warm hands grasped her arms and kept her from falling at the last second. The man who had called her name, and kept her upright, was the epitome of *tall, dark nd hnd some*. His skin was perfectly tan, he had black hair in a crew cut that said *military turned civilian* and coffee-brown eyes that were pinned directly on her lips. Her skin heated from his touch, and whispers of a sensation she hadn't felt in too long spiraled through her.

"I didn't mean to scare you. Are you okay?"

"Fi-fine," she stammered. "Sorry—I was lost in thought when you called my name."

"Are you Sadie Cook?"

"That depends on who's asking." She noticed his nose had a misshapen bump near the top, telling her without telling her that he'd broken it once or twice in the past. The bump added character to his already intriguing eyes. Both were overshadowed by his lips though. Full, plump and pink, they'd make any woman yearn for a kiss. The way he stared at her lips made her wonder if that was what he was thinking about right now. How would she feel if this man planted them on hers out of the blue? *Not even upset* was the answer.

Stop, she scolded herself. *You have a baby to take care of now. You don't have time for kisses from hot guys.*

After her internal chastising was over, she stiffened her spine and raised her chin as a slow smile lifted his lips. It was the kind of smile meant to be sly, but on this guy, it just screamed *bedroom sexy*. The worst part? He knew she was lusting after his lips.

"My name is Eric Newman. I'm part of the Secure One security team."

Well, she wasn't expecting that. She'd had the security guys pegged as much older and far less of a male specimen than the one before her.

"I noticed a bit of commotion."

"You could say that," Eric said with a chuckle. "I'm helping the police question the staff. Since I witnessed the incident, I know you had nothing to do with it, so don't worry about that. I do have to ask the staff if they saw or heard anything unusual over the last few days."

Unusual? Like her sister disappearing into thin air? She resisted the urge to give this man more than he'd bargained for in answer to his question.

"I don't know what you mean by *unusual*."

Casually, he let go of her arms and placed his hands on his hips. "The same vehicle coming and going. People on the property you had never seen before. That kind of thing."

Sadie thought about it for a moment but finally shook her head. "That's the problem, Eric. There are always people coming and going in the house, but I don't know all of Mr. Fettering's friends. You'll have to ask him."

"I believe the Bemidji PD is doing that now." The tone of his voice was patient, but she could tell he was on edge.

"Something bad happened, right?" she asked. "Probably by the back exit." She gauged his reaction and noticed his eyes dilate for a moment. Her words had hit the way she'd hoped.

"What do you know about the back exit?" His tone told her this was no longer a friendly question-and-answer session. Now he wanted information.

"That's the exit Mr. Fettering makes us use, but I hate it. The lack of lights back there makes it unsafe as soon as the sun goes down, and I always told my friend if anyone wanted to commit a crime, that was the place to do it." A shiver racked her body, telling the man in front of her just how much she believed that statement to be true. "I knew it was only a matter of time, but Dirk didn't want to hear it."

"You're observant," Eric said. "Have you seen any suspicious activity back there before?"

"No," Sadie said, taking a step back. He was one of those

men who pulled you into his atmosphere and held you there. It was disturbing and wonderful simultaneously, but Sadie knew she had to get out before she wanted to stay. "Can I go now?"

"You can. I'll check you off as having been questioned. You'll need an escort to your car."

Sadie nervously swallowed before she answered, "That's okay. I'll be fine, but thanks." She turned away to gather her supplies when he tugged on her apron.

"No, I mean you'll have an escort. No one is allowed in the storage area without a security guard. The back exit is closed, so everyone has to show identification and exit through the front. Are you working tomorrow?" Her nod was short. "When you arrive, someone at the entrance will direct you to the new parking area. I'll take you to your car now if you're ready."

Sadie frowned. They must have found a body. It was the only thing that made sense if they were being this cautious and demanding at the same time. Kadie's face skittered through her mind's eye, and she fought the urge to ask him if they had found a woman's body. The way he looked at her, she wondered if he suspected she was hiding something. She had to stay off this guy's radar if she wanted to find her sister and bring her home. "I just need to grab my coat."

He turned and motioned for her to go ahead, and that was when she noticed the device behind his ear with a thin wire attached to a translucent earpiece. It wasn't a security piece. It was a hearing aid. A second glance told her he wore one on the other side too. The memory of how he'd stared at her lips brought heat to her cheeks when she realized he'd simply been reading her lips and not thinking about kissing her.

Embarrassed, she grabbed her coat and keys from the

closet and followed him out the door. After some fancy security talk and flashing her identification, they made it to
her car without incident.

"Head to the front of the units and exit there. Another
guard will be there to check your identification," Eric said,
holding the door open for her while she climbed in.

"Wow, you mean the help gets to leave through the front
door tonight?" she asked, her words laced with sarcasm so
he knew she was kidding.

His sly smile told her he was amused. "Don't get used to
it. I'm sure by morning you'll be parking at the pavilion and
ridesharing on the back of a mule if Fettering has anything
to say about it."

He shut the door on her laughter and waved her off as she
headed for the front of the storage unit. She comforted herself with the knowledge that she may have to work tomorrow, but at least she wouldn't have to see Eric or his kissable
lips ever again.

ERIC WATCHED SADIE drive off in a red Saturn that was probably as old as she was but showed no signs of rust from the
Minnesota winters. The memory of her warm skin beneath
his skittered heat through his body, sounding his internal
alarm. Their short encounter had been enough to tell him she
was a flame he'd better stay far away from to avoid getting
burned. If this were a different time and place, he wouldn't
have let her drive away without getting her number, but he had
no time for this now or ever. He had a job to do, which didn't
include wishing he could kiss those lips he'd read to the letter.

He'd had to read her lips, so he was grateful that she had
the perfect set. His hearing aids were good, but background
noise was impossible to control in some situations, no matter how good your aids were. He'd learned quickly to read

lips if he wanted to concentrate on the conversation. It was easier than asking *What?* all the time. Sometimes it was the only way he could follow a conversation or even have a conversation if he wasn't wearing his aids. People took communication for granted until it became difficult. He'd been just as guilty of that sin until the moment it had happened to him. His experiences in the sandbox had taught him to take nothing for granted.

He couldn't stop thinking about Sadie though. Not just her girl-next-door looks or how tiny she'd been under his hands, but how he'd noticed a flicker in her eyes when he'd told her who he was. She'd been skittish, and his years of working security told him one thing—she was hiding something. If he had time to spare, he might look into her and her background, but he didn't, and by the looks of this place, he wouldn't have time for a while.

The trill of his tablet stiffened his shoulders. He'd been expecting the call, but that didn't mean he was prepared for it. He stepped into the empty guard booth at the entrance and answered the video call.

"Secure two, Echo," he said to the black screen, waiting for his boss to answer.

"Secure one, Charlie," Cal said, and then his face flashed on the screen. "Eric, what the hell is going on there?"

"Cal," he said, noting his boss's mood. "I wasn't expecting to speak with you until morning. It's late in DC."

"Or early, depending on how you look at it, but I got your message and wanted an update."

"Bemidji PD is here, and they've taken over the investigation."

"Of a body dropped in a storage unit? You and Efren witnessed it?"

"We did," he confirmed, his attention pulled away for

a moment by the ME van as it rolled slowly toward the exit. "We were walking the property looking for security breaches. The suspects didn't know we were there when they pulled up. They unloaded a trunk that was a little too suspicious to be clothing or home goods. That was confirmed when we opened the trunk and found a dude with his head sitting on his chest."

"Mob hit?"

"Or gang. Either way, it was odd to dump him there and leave. Unless it was a matter of convenience for these guys." The name he'd seen on the guy's lips ran through his head and he said, "I was watching them with our night-vision goggles, and one of the guys said the name Winged Templar. Have you ever run across that name before?"

"Winged Templar?" Cal was silent for a moment and lifted his eyes toward his hairline while he thought about it. "No, but it sounds like a code name to me. If this is a mob hit, that could be the name of the hitman."

"Exactly what I was thinking," Eric agreed. "I suppose I should tell the cops about it?"

"Probably. At some point. Keep it under your hat for now. In case it has something to do with Dirk's place rather than the dead guy."

"Heard and understood," Eric agreed. "We always knew that the back exit was a problem, and tonight proves it. Maybe now we can convince Fettering to fix it. He's not happy being the center of an investigation."

"That's your job now," Cal said. "But if it matters, I agree. He needs to close off that back entrance onto the property and add more lights. People should only be allowed to enter and exit through the front gate that's staffed."

"With cameras that record and hold the data for thirty days."

"Agreed. What is your plan moving forward?"

He asked the question in a way that told Eric to read between the lines. It was a test, and he'd better have the correct answer if he wanted to remain in control of the situation.

"Tomorrow I'll talk to Fettering regarding the security issues we discovered and how to fix them. After we go over all of the weak points of his property, Efren and I will head back to Secure One and let Fettering think about it for a few days. Once you're back, we can implement the most important changes, like lighting and cameras. That will make our lives easier back at headquarters as well. Right now, he only allows one camera at the guard booth that saves the data for twenty-four hours. That doesn't help us much."

"You know how hard I fought him on that. He hired us to be his security team and then tied our hands at every turn."

"True, but I've seen no less than five high-profile people in and out of the units over the twelve hours we've been on the ground. He promised discretion, and that's what he gives them."

"Maybe, but the time for all of that has passed. Now it's time to let us do our job properly. Besides, *discretion* is our middle name."

"As well it should be, but getting Fettering to believe that will be a much tougher sell. Anyway, don't worry about us here. We've got this."

"I have no doubt that's true, Eric. We planned to be home in three days, but if you need us sooner, just say the word."

"We'll be fine. Roman and Mina are keeping things humming in the control room, and there isn't much to handle here outside the scope of our business. The cops will deal with the body, and Efren and I already gave our statements. Just enjoy your trip, and know that I'll reach out if something comes up that I need approval on."

"We'll be back in seventy-two hours. I'm counting on you to have everything ready to go for when Fettering decides to let us add additional cameras and security measures. I want to move on it the minute he gives us the go-ahead, so he doesn't have time to change his mind."

"Ten-four. Echo out," Eric said before ending the video call.

Eric let his shoulders relax and started a mental list of the equipment they'd need to do the job right this time. Unfortunately for him, his mind was focused on Sadie Cook and nothing else. She intrigued him, which was a rare occurrence when it came to women. He'd never been one to worry about what a woman was thinking when he was looking for a good time, but Sadie was different. He'd only spoken with her for a few short minutes, but that was all he needed to know she was the whole package. That was when he reminded himself that made her a woman he would never have.

Chapter Three

Why did I go this way? Sadie was kicking herself for taking that exit without checking if there was a way back onto the highway. The long, dark, winding road she'd been on for the last twenty minutes did accomplish one thing—it told her the SUV in her rearview mirror was following her. It had been behind her on the highway, and she'd convinced herself it was headed in the same direction until she'd taken the exit and they'd followed.

She was exhausted after back-to-back shifts. She only had a few hours of sleep after getting home late the night before and heading back there this morning to do the work she didn't get done last night after the body was found. Sadie would do whatever she had to do to protect Houston though.

Now she was utterly alone on a dark road in middle-of-nowhere Minnesota, with a baby in the back seat. To add insult to injury, it had started raining about an hour ago, leaving the pavement covered in wet leaves and making it almost impossible to see. She couldn't stop or even think about pulling over until she was somewhere safe and she'd lost the SUV behind her. Houston was who she had to protect right now, so she'd take it slow and easy but wouldn't pull over. Pulling over was certain death, she had no doubt.

If only she knew why. She hadn't done anything but work hard to keep Kadie and Houston in her life. Now someone wanted to end hers.

Sadie grasped the wheel tightly and accelerated, her gaze jumping to the rearview mirror. The other car was keeping pace. "Now what, baby?" she asked the sweetheart in the back. She'd planned to pull over and give him a bottle, but she hadn't bothered to stop when she'd noticed the black SUV follow her down the exit. She'd fished the bottle out of his bag and propped it against the edge of his car seat. The clock was ticking down to when he needed to be changed and fed again. She couldn't do that on the side of the road, so she had to find somewhere safe sooner rather than later.

Her gaze focused on the horizon, and she searched for the lights of a city. There were none. All that stretched out before her was desolate darkness without an end in sight. She should have turned around and returned to the highway, but she'd been afraid the SUV would overtake her if she'd tried that. With dread, her gaze dropped to the gas gauge. It was down to a quarter of a tank. The last road sign she'd seen had said the next town was fifty miles. She had to have gone at least thirty by now. If she could keep the SUV behind her, she'd make it to a well-lit and populated area before she pulled over. It wouldn't save her, but it might buy her time. She cursed the fact that she'd had to leave her phone at home and hadn't bothered to stop and pick up a burner phone immediately. Without one, she couldn't even call up Google Maps.

With it, they might find you.

Not that she knew who *they* were. Sadie had been minding her own business at work when she'd been called to the office and handed an envelope. The secretary couldn't tell her who had delivered it, but her name had been on the front. Sadie had thanked her and tucked it into her apron until she'd had time to read it on her break. Inside the envelope had been three letters cut from a magazine and glued to a notecard. It had said *RUN*. After what had happened the night before, Sadie had heeded the warning. She'd grabbed Houston and done just that.

With no idea where she was going, Sadie had made the short-term plan to get to Minneapolis and blend into the city for a few days until she could figure out what was happening. Did this have something to do with Kadie being missing or something to do with the body they'd found last night at Fettering's place? Or was this someone playing a game because they had Kadie and wanted Sadie vulnerable so they could get Houston too?

The truth stuck in her chest, and her hands tightened on the wheel a hair more. Suddenly, she wished she'd listened to Julia when she'd begged her not to go off alone with Houston. She'd said the note could have been a practical joke, which was possible, but Sadie knew better. The person who'd sent her that note knew something she didn't and wanted to warn her. In hindsight, it could have been sent to isolate her. If that was their goal, they'd succeeded.

Her mind drifted to that pair of lips she saw every time she closed her eyes. Was it Eric who had warned her? He ran security for Fettering's complex. He could have insider information. If he wanted to warn her without compromising the investigation, an anonymous note was the only way. That was a bit farfetched, but nothing was off the table when you worked for a celebrity.

Sadie had learned that truth several times over the last few years. Dirk had made his fair share of enemies. Some would even consider him cutthroat. Maybe he was in his business, but not in his personal life. Fettering was essentially a forty-year-old college frat boy who thought he knew everything but also wanted to be everyone's friend. Sadie had served at and cleaned up enough of his parties to know who he was when the cameras weren't on him. Working at his private parties put her on a different plane of household importance than others. Not that she wanted even an ounce of that hierarchy, but she had been eager and energetic when hired. That was her way of saying she'd been naive to the ways of some peoples' worlds.

Headlights filled her car, and a glance behind her showed the SUV coming up fast on her. Maybe they wanted to pass. Crazy to do it on a curve, but she slowed, hoping they'd go around her and leave her in peace. The car swung into the left lane, and she eased off the gas more, relief filling her chest. They were following her, but not for nefarious reasons.

"We might make it after all, Houston," she whispered, holding tight to the wheel as the car came up on her left on the curve. "We'll find somewhere to stay and ditch this car," she promised, wishing the SUV would get past her before someone came at them from the other direction. She eased down on the brake as the SUV accelerated, giving them space to clear the lane.

Sadie sighed with relief when they swung over until she realized they wouldn't clear her. She slammed on the brakes, but it was too late. She heard the crunch of metal as her head whipped to the side. The car spun, and she screamed, the sound bouncing around as they twirled at a dizzying speed toward the edge of the road. Sadie desperately grabbed the wheel again and twisted it to the left. It didn't respond. Houston cried, glass shattered and then there was nothing but the rhythmic swish of the windshield wipers.

ERIC RUBBED HIS eyes with one hand while he gulped coffee from his mug with the other. He'd been back at Secure One for less than four hours and was already covering a shift in the control room. Mina wasn't feeling well, and Roman didn't want to leave her alone. Eric had told him not to worry about it, but now, two hours later, he regretted his decision. At least he and Efren were in the same boat. Neither of them had gotten much sleep after dealing with Fettering last night, and the trip back to Secure One only added to their fatigue.

"When is Cal coming back?" Efren asked.

The person who answered surprised the hell out of him. "Tomorrow late afternoon or evening," Selina said as she entered the control room. "He wants to get home sooner, considering the situation at Fetterings'. He'll file a flight plan once he knows for sure."

"Hey, Selina," both guys said in unison.

She had a pot of coffee in one hand and a tray of sandwiches in the other. "I thought you might be hungry," she explained as her gaze drifted across the monitors in front of Efren. "Everything status quo?"

"Quiet, just how we like it," Efren said, snagging a sandwich. He held it up. "Thanks."

"Don't get used to it, Brenna. I'm not a waitress."

"I wouldn't, and I'm aware," Efren said when he swallowed.

"Maybe you could cut Efren a little slack, Selina," Eric said, grabbing a sandwich. "If you've got a beef, it's not with him. It's with Cal."

Selina spun on her heel and gave him a look that would

wither weaker men. "I didn't ask for your opinion, Eric. Nor his, for that matter. I was going to offer to take a shift so you guys could sleep, but I think I just changed my mind."

She stalked out in a way that left no room for argument.

Efren whistled and shook his head. "I don't even know what to say."

"Neither do I," Eric admitted, turning back to the screen. "That's not the Selina I've known for the last seven years. I wish she'd stop taking her angst out on you. It's not right."

The phone rang, so Efren picked it up, answering with mostly *yes*, *no*, and *are you sure?* When he hung up, Eric eyed him. "Who was that?"

"Bemidji PD. They have a warrant out for a suspect. That was a courtesy call to let us know they hope to have her in custody soon."

"Her?" he asked, and Efren shrugged.

"That's what they said. Apparently she works for Fettering."

Eric sat up straighter and leaned toward him. "What's her name?"

Efren glanced down at his pad and then back to Eric. "Sadie Cook? I have no idea who that is."

Eric's heart pounded, and his mind spun a mile a minute. What on earth? There was no way Sadie Cook had anything to do with that body drop.

"Efren, I interviewed Sadie. She's this tiny little thing who was terrified of me! There is absolutely zero chance she has anything to do with that murder. I'd stake my career on it. We were there when the two guys dumped the body." For a moment, he remembered that look of fear in her sweet blue eyes. Was it fear that she'd been discovered? No matter how hard he tried, Eric couldn't get there with it. It didn't make any sense whatsoever. There was no way she would order a hit and then have them drop the body at her place of employment. She drove a car almost as old as she was, which was a good indication that she didn't have a lot of cash to throw in on a murder-for-hire plot. Something was going on with Sadie Cook, but it had nothing to do with the murder last night.

"According to the PD, the dead guy was Howie Loraine." Eric leaned back against the chair with a groan, and Efren paused. "What?"

"A Loraine? They were involved in a multistate counterfeiting scheme about eight years ago. Last I heard, Dad was doing life, the stepmom was dead, and Randall Junior and Howie were running the legal business. Everyone suspected Randall Junior was also running a not-so-legal business, but no one could prove it. Howie was the youngest son and, shall we say, the most free-spirited. It still doesn't make sense that they suspect Sadie."

Efren held up his finger. "Except that they pulled in one of the guys from our video. His version goes that Sadie is the one who hired him."

"This makes less sense now than it did last night," Eric growled, turning to face the computer screens again. "Why would Sadie order a hit on Howie Loraine? Does she even know him?"

"According to the chief, the dude refused to answer that question."

"Well, of course he did! You know damn well someone sent him in there to say that. It's too clean and neatly drawn. The only way that guy got caught was if he wanted to—"

A blur caught his attention on the screen. Before he fully

registered what he saw, he was on his feet and grabbing Efren's shirtsleeve on the way to the door. "Let's go!"

"What grid was that?" Efren asked as they ran out the door, weapons at the ready.

"Lake side, northern edge!" Eric yelled back as they ran toward what he thought was a car driving onto the property.

"Should we call Roman for backup?" Efren asked as he pulled up next to him.

"No, let's see what's going on first. I don't want to pull other guys from their grids until I know if this is a threat. If it is an attack, we can't leave those areas vulnerable for them to infiltrate."

They both knew all too well about people trying to infiltrate Secure One. The last few years had been one attempt after another. Roman's FBI partner and now wife, Mina, had been hunted by a madwoman and ended up at Secure One for protection. The Madame had then infiltrated Secure One and snatched Mina from under their noses. Cal had sworn that would be the last time Secure One was vulnerable to an outside force. They'd learned about the vulnerabilities of their property the hard way but put those experiences to good use. Secure One now had one of the most protected perimeters in the country. That said, they couldn't stop someone with an axe to grind from trying. He was in control of this base now, and this was his chance to prove himself to Cal. Eric couldn't risk taking the wrong action too soon. Once he assessed the situation, he'd make the call.

They closed in on the grid section that wasn't surveilled other than in the control room. It was outside Secure One property and owned by the county, which tied their hands. "It looked like a car driving into the ditch, but it's raining, so it was hard to tell," Eric said as they ran. What he didn't say was that he thought he recognized the car. "That bank is steep. The only way down it is to roll. I'm worried someone's hurt."

They reached the fence, and he grabbed his walkie. He'd set off the all-hands-on-deck alarm before he'd left, so he hoped Selina was in the control room by now. "Lights on, fence off," he requested.

Relief flooded him momentarily when the spotlights came on and the gate clicked open. Selina still had his back. His relief was short-lived when they ran through the gate and found the car. It rested on its side with a tendril of white smoke whispering its way through the bent hood. His fears were realized—he knew the car. An older-model red Saturn that, unlike last night, was now crumbled stem to stern as one wheel spun lazily in the air.

Eric paused for a moment. "Is that crying?"

"Sounds like a baby to me," Efren agreed.

They sprinted forward, reassured that this was an accident, not a planned attack.

"Help!" a woman screamed as their boots crunched through the leaves. "Help! I can't get out!"

"We're coming! Don't move!" Efren called out as they rounded the back of the car.

"Houston! You have to get Houston out of the car!"

"Sadie, it's Eric from Secure One. You're okay. Just let us assess the baby."

Glancing at each other, the men peered through the back windows. Sure enough, there was a strapped-down car seat holding a crying infant.

"Are you hurt, Sadie?" Eric called to her.

She pointed at her right leg. "My leg is stuck! Don't worry about me! You have to get the baby out!"

Efren grabbed Eric's shirt. "The same Sadie the cops are looking for?"

"It appears so," he said. "We need to get her out of the car before we worry about her legal situation."

With a nod, Efren called out to Sadie, "Just take a deep breath. We're going to help you. How old is your son?"

"Almost eight months, but Houston is my nephew."

"Call Selina. We might need her," Efren said before he ducked low again.

Eric hit his walkie and requested Selina's help at the grid. A medical professional would be helpful if they needed an ambulance, and if they couldn't get Sadie's leg free, they'd need to call the fire department. His gaze drifted to the smoke billowing from the engine, and he hit the walkie again, requesting fire extinguishers.

If his luck held, they'd be able to free Sadie and get her inside the confines of Secure One. If he could talk to her about what had happened last night before too many people realized she was here, he might be able to run interference for her. Why he cared so much about what happened to her, he didn't know, and he wouldn't—couldn't—take the time to figure that out right now. They had a job to do, starting with rescuing a baby and his aunt. Eric forced his gaze away from the baby's chubby legs as they pumped against the seat. Another baby wasn't going to die on his watch. He had enough to atone for. He didn't need to add more to his already full dance card.

The truth settled low in his gut. Sadie had been running. He didn't know if that made her guilty or scared until his gaze flicked to hers for a millisecond. Scared. Terrified, actually, and they had to help her. She believed their lives were in danger. There was no other reason she would be out driving in the rain with a baby.

Efren was walking around the car and pointed to the wheel well on the passenger side. "I think our best bet is to lower it back to four wheels and then try to get them out through the door that isn't smashed." He put his hand on top of the door facing up. "Opinions?"

"That's our only choice. Let's do it now before the engine decides to go up."

The car was a lightweight sedan made of more plastic than metal. The two of them easily lowered it back into position, and once the wheels touched the grass, they tried the back door. Locked.

"Can you hit the Unlock button?" Eric called out to Sadie. She said something he couldn't hear. The rain and the wailing infant had rendered his aids useless.

"She said it's not working," Efren said right next to his ear. Eric hated that the guys knew how much he relied on them to fill him in.

"Give me your shirt," he demanded, and Efren stripped off his sweatshirt and handed it over. Eric wrapped it around his arm and ran to the other side of the car. "Protect your head," he yelled to her. She turned away, and Eric smashed his elbow into the cracked driver's-side window. It fell inward, and he cleared away the extra glass to stick his head inside. "We're going to get you out. Others are on their way to help."

"The baby first!" she cried.

"I'm going to hand him out to my friend. His name is Efren Brenna. You're on Secure One property, which was a handy place to crash."

"I didn't crash. Someone followed me and then ran me

off the road!" Sadie's eyes were wild, and her chest heaved from adrenaline.

Someone had run them off the road? Son of a... "We're going to help you—just take long, slow deep breaths so you don't hyperventilate." Eric kept talking to her while he cleared glass off the seat and then turned to Efren. "I'm going to climb in and unlock the door that isn't smashed. We need to take the baby out that way."

"Got it," Efren said, lopping to the other side of the car to wait for him.

Eric carefully slid into the car, pulling his legs into the tight space. At six-four, he wasn't made for cars this size. "Everyone is going to be just fine. I've got a nurse on the way to check on the baby, so hang in there."

He finally got the door unlocked, and Efren pulled it open immediately. "How do I unlatch the car seat? I want to leave him in it until I'm sure he isn't injured." The baby had cried himself out and just whimpered as they worked to free him. He didn't look injured at first glance, but Selina Colvert, their on-site nurse, would be the one to determine that for certain.

"Pull the handle forward, and there's a red button on the back."

Efren followed directions and had the baby out in no time. When Eric knelt in the front passenger seat, he realized freeing his aunt—and wanted murder suspect—would be a lot more complicated.

Chapter Four

Air hissed between Sadie's teeth when Selina touched the wound with antiseptic. Selina glanced up and frowned. "I'm sorry. I know it sucks, but I'm almost done."

Sadie worked up a smile and waved her hand in the air. "No apologies. I appreciate you fixing me up so I don't have to go to the hospital. I don't know who's after me, but I can't risk taking Houston back out on the roads right now."

"You're absolutely certain that someone ran you off the road?" Eric asked as he walked around the med bay with Houston, jiggling and patting the baby as though his life depended on it. Despite the seriousness of their situation, she couldn't help but smile. He was terrified of hurting him—that was easy to see. Then again, she might be afraid of the same at six-four and over two hundred pounds. Eric's arms swallowed up Houston, and Sadie struggled not to love the whole image. Houston's father had been a no-show, so the baby had never had a man in his life. She wondered what it must be like for him to be held in the strong arms of a man who cared, even for a little while. Was Houston afraid, or could he sense that everyone here had protected him?

"I'm positive," she said. "I took the exit to look for a place to feed and change Houston but noticed a dark SUV follow me down the exit ramp. I was already paranoid, so I kept driving rather than stop at the gas station. They stayed behind me, which could have been innocent."

"Until it wasn't," Eric said just as Houston started to cry again.

Selina didn't say anything, but she grimaced, which worried Sadie. They knew something she didn't, but everyone refused to answer her questions.

Sadie knew things didn't look good for her. She was on the run with a baby that wasn't hers, his mother was missing and she'd been run off the road. She couldn't help but feel like the ante had just been upped and that her sister was in more danger than ever before. She had to find Kadie soon, or she worried her sister could be gone forever.

"This needs a few stitches." Selina broke into her thoughts, and Sadie snapped to attention. The plastic under the dashboard had crushed into a V during the accident and trapped her inside the car. They'd gotten her out, but not before a jagged piece had sliced her lower leg open. "I'm afraid it won't heal if I don't close it up."

"Do what you have to do," she said, gritting her teeth and waiting for the burn of the needle. Everyone at Secure One seemed to trust Selina Colvert with their life, so she was grateful she didn't have to leave the security Secure One offered right now. Selina set about her work, and Sadie was pleasantly surprised that she felt nothing but the sharp prick of the needle to numb it.

"All done," Selina said, applying a bandage to the wound before removing her gloves. "It only needed five stitches, but you're going to feel it in the morning," she explained, cleaning up her tray. "I'll give you antibiotics to ensure it doesn't get infected. It's safe to shower since I put the waterproof cover over it. We'll have to take them out in about a week."

"Thanks, Selina. I appreciate the help. Is there somewhere I can go to warm a bottle for Houston? He's going to start screaming if I don't."

"Sure, Eric can take you down to the kitchen. There's no high chair, I'm afraid."

"No problem," Sadie promised, standing and fixing her pants. "I can feed him in his car seat."

"Eric, can you take Sadie to the kitchen?" Selina asked as he continued to walk around the room with Houston, but he didn't respond. Selina held up her finger and walked over to them, tapping Eric on the shoulder. He turned, and she signed something to him, to which he nodded and walked over, handing Sadie the baby.

"Hi, Houston," she cooed to the little boy. She watched as Eric fiddled with his ears and gave them a rueful smile.

"Sorry—I turned my ears off when he cried and didn't hear you. Selina said you need to go to the kitchen?"

"Yes, please," Sadie said, standing and setting Houston on her hip while she tried out her leg. It was sore, but she could walk with no problem. "He'll need a bottle and food before I do anything else."

Eric exchanged a glance with Selina, who nodded, and then he ushered her out of the room and down a long hallway. "Sorry about back there," he said, walking beside her while carrying the car seat.

"Don't apologize," she said with a shake of her head. "Sometimes I wish I could shut my ears off when he's crying. I never thought of it when I asked you to take him. I should be the one apologizing."

"I didn't mind. He's a good boy, just scared and confused."

The shrug he gave at the end of the sentence told her that Eric had liked his babysitting job more than he wanted to let on.

"Once he eats, he'll be off to dreamland, which is good. I need to figure out what's going on."

"I can probably help with that." She glanced at him, but his face was a mask of neutrality. "Let's get him fed first, and then we'll talk."

He flipped the light on, and they walked into a large commercial kitchen big enough to feed a small army. Then again, this place looked like it housed a small army, so it was probably needed. Sadie busied herself getting Houston's food made and heating his bottle, but the whole time, her mind was racing to figure out who wanted her dead and why.

ONCE HOUSTON HAD been fed and changed, Eric brought Sadie and the baby to the meeting room. He'd said he wanted to tell her what was happening but hadn't divulged anything so far. After the long day, she was starting to fade, but Houston wouldn't settle down like she had expected him to after dinner.

"Give me the baby. You need to rest that leg." He held his arms out for the little guy who practically threw himself into them.

Sadie collapsed into the nearest chair while he tucked Houston into his arm and grabbed the half-finished bottle, popping it into his mouth. Houston sucked at it hungrily, which offered blessed silence to the room.

"You look like you've done that a few times," she said, her keen eye ensuring he was doing everything correctly.

"I had six younger brothers and sisters, so I was feeding babies by the time I was seven."

"Wow," she said with a shake of her head. "I can't imagine having that many siblings. It must have been chaos."

"There were days I'm sure my mother drank once we were in bed." His smile was rueful, so she knew he was joking, and she cracked a smile herself.

"I would be surprised if she didn't too. It was only Kadie and me in our family. Kadie is older by barely a year, and Mom called us her Irish twins. That's why our names rhyme. Mom wanted us to be as close as real twins so we always stuck together in life. I have to find her."

Eric tipped his head in confusion. "Wait, find her? Is she missing?"

Sadie nodded and swallowed hard around the panic clawing at her throat. Pushing back the tears was much more challenging, but she managed to say the words that terrified her. "Kadie's been missing for almost ten days now. I told the police, but they don't believe me."

"They think she ran away?"

"Yes, but she didn't! I swear to you she didn't!"

He rested his hand on her shoulder to calm her. "I'm listening, Sadie. You're positive she didn't get overwhelmed taking care of Houston?"

"I have no doubt in my mind. Kadie is an excellent mother, and she has a strong support system. There was never a time that she couldn't tell me she needed a break, and I would take over care of Houston. Something happened to her, I'm telling you!"

Eric squeezed her shoulder to calm her, but it wasn't working. She was barely holding it together. Then again, maybe he was why she was still holding it together. By rights, she should've been in a bed nursing her leg wound.

"I'm listening," he promised. "Walk me through it."

She held her arms out for Houston, and he gently laid the babe in her arms. Houston immediately rubbed his face against her shirt while she stroked his head. Sadie loved him like a son; she'd do anything for him, including risking everything to find his mother.

"Kadie and I live together. I'm the younger sister but also the one with the most common sense. Kadie was always the fanciful child and the free and easy adult. At least until she had Houston," she added quickly, so he didn't think Kadie didn't take care of the baby. "When she found out she was pregnant, I convinced her to move into my apartment so I could help her with the baby and she could save money. We worked opposite shifts, so while I worked, she had Houston, and while she worked, I took care of him."

"Where does she work?" Eric asked. "At Fettering's?"

"No, she's a dental hygienist." She gave him a crooked grin. "I know, a strangely responsible career for someone as free and easy as Kadie, but it worked for her. She finished school first since she was the oldest, and then I was supposed to go."

"Supposed to?"

Sadie was embarrassed, so she kept her gaze glued to Houston rather than the eyes of the man who was too nice to her in her time of need. She couldn't stand to see pity or disgust in his eyes. "Life kept getting in the way and I kept putting it off. Then Houston came along. He was more important. I'm only twenty-nine. I have plenty of time to go back to school."

He lifted her hand and squeezed it. "You're a good aunt to that little boy. He's lucky to have you."

"That's why I worked nights," she said, finally glancing

up at him. There wasn't pity or disgust in his eyes, just an earnestness to help.

"Why did you work the day shift today then?"

"Since Kadie disappeared, I've had to work my schedule around my friend Julia's since she watches Houston for me."

"Which means you worked back-to-back shifts."

"He's worth it."

"We do what we have to do, right?" She nodded rather than answer and kept her face turned to Houston's. Soon, he was tipping her chin up to face him. "I need to read your lips while we're talking, okay?"

"So-sorry," she stuttered, forgetting herself for a moment. "I'm tired and sore."

"Scared and hungry too?" he asked, and she nodded. "I'll get you some food once Houston is asleep. In the meantime, tell me what happened the day Kadie disappeared."

"It was like any other day," she said with a shrug. "I came home from work and took over Houston's care while she went to work. It was about an hour after she left when her work called to find out if she was coming in. She had never missed a day of work, and they were worried. Since I knew she'd left an hour earlier, I was frantic, thinking she'd been in a car accident or something dreadful like that. I drove her route to work, but she was nowhere to be found."

"Her car is missing too?" he asked, and she nodded. "You know that's a pretty good sign that she did run, right?"

"The note would also lead a person to think that," she added, chewing on her lip. His brow went up, and she sighed. "I found the note in my room later that morning."

"A note that said she was overwhelmed and leaving town?"

"Yes, but here's the weird part. It wasn't there when I changed my clothes after I got home from work, but it was there when I returned from searching for Kadie." His brow went up higher. "That freaked me out because someone was in our apartment. I immediately loaded up Houston and went to stay with my friend Julia. Here's the other thing. Kadie didn't write the note. It's not even close to her handwriting."

"Maybe she was in a hurry?" he asked, and she shook her head, setting her jaw.

"Listen to me," she hissed as she leaned toward him. "I know my sister and her handwriting. If she wrote that note, she purposely wrote it so I would know she was being forced. I showed the police. I even showed them samples of her real handwriting, but they aren't listening!"

He held his hand out, and she took a deep breath before she upset the baby. "I believe you, Sadie. You know your sister better than anyone, so if you say this is completely out of character for her, we work the case until we find her. Mina Jacobs, one of our operatives, could analyze the note's handwriting." He paused and grimaced. "I bet you don't have it with you."

"I do," she said with a nod. "It's in my luggage. I took everything I thought I might need to find her."

"Good. Efren brought everything in from your car, so we'll get Mina on that once Houston is settled."

"We need to call a wrecker for the car, right? I'm afraid it's done for after that crash."

Eric smiled. "Oh, that car has carried its last passengers. We've moved it to one of our equipment sheds for now. You don't need to worry about it until you're feeling better."

Houston let out a wail, and she rubbed his soft head to soothe him. "I'm worried about him," she said as he continued to fuss. "He was jostled in the accident. What if we're missing something, and that's why he's so fussy? Maybe he did get hurt in the crash."

"I'm sure he's got bumps and bruises the same as you do."

"I know I could use some Tylenol." Her tone was joking, but he could tell she was serious.

Eric turned, grabbed a black phone off the wall and then punched a button. "Hey, Selina," he said when she answered. "Could you come to the meeting room with some Tylenol or Advil? Sadie is hurting." He hung up the phone and swung back to her. "Selina is on her way."

"You didn't have to do that," she said in frustration. "I think I have some in my purse."

"Selina was on her way down anyway. She wants to check on you and Houston. Do you have any pain reliever for him?"

"In his diaper bag," she said, chewing on her lip. "I should give him some, but I don't want to mask any problems we don't know he has yet."

Eric was about to speak when Selina entered like a whirlwind. She handed Sadie a small cup with pills and knelt to check the bandage over her wound. Once she was satisfied, she stood up and glanced between them.

"How is everyone?"

"Houston is fussy, but hopefully he'll fall asleep now that he's had a bottle," Sadie said, swallowing the pills with the water she'd grabbed from the kitchen.

"I think he needs some Tylenol too," Eric gently said. "Sadie is worried about masking any injuries we don't know he has, which is a legitimate concern. What do you think?"

"I think if we don't, we'll have an unhappy boy on our hands all night." She turned to Sadie. "How about I take him to the med bay, give him the Tylenol and observe him for the evening? He can sleep on the gurney with side rails or in his car seat, whichever you think is better."

Sadie rubbed her palm on her thigh a few times before she answered. "I'm okay with that. I don't want him to suffer all night, but I'm worried about him."

"Completely understandable," Selina promised, kneeling next to her. "You love him and feel guilty about the crash, right?" Sadie nodded with half a shrug at the end. "Remember that someone ran you off the road. We don't know why, but this wasn't your fault. You had him buckled in correctly, and because of that, he wasn't severely injured. I'm sure he has some sore muscles like you, but he'll bounce back by tomorrow. I also have a heated blanket system to offer him some relief from those sore muscles if he sleeps on the gurney. I'll be right there by him, so you don't have to worry about him falling."

"Okay," she said with a grateful smile. "Houston needs to sleep, and if you can offer him some comfort while keeping an eye on him, I would be forever grateful."

"I'm more than happy to," Selina promised, patting her knee before she stood and gathered Houston's diaper bag. "Would a bath be okay? It would allow me to look him over head to toe for large bruises or bumps without scaring him."

"He loves his bath time," Sadie said, pushing herself up. "I'll help you."

Selina held her hand out and motioned at the chair. "You have things to discuss with the team. I'll get Houston settled for the night while you do that. Then, when you're ready to sleep, you're more than welcome to join him in the med bay."

Sadie chewed on her lip for a moment before she spoke, her gaze glued to her nephew in her arms. "Call me with any problems?"

"Without question," Selina promised.

With a kiss to Houston's head and a whispered I love you, Sadie handed him over to Selina.

After they left, Sadie leaned back against the chair with a sigh. "Selina is an angel."

"Truer words were never spoken," he agreed. "When you meet the rest of the team, you'll see we all specialize in certain areas of the security business. That's how we work cohesively as a team."

"Everyone I've met so far has been wonderful, you included. Thanks for all your help, Eric. We'll get out of your hair as soon as I can figure out how to get a car that runs."

"I don't think so, Sadie," he said, sitting across from her. "Why were you running in the first place?"

Her shoulders were hunched, and she stared at the floor rather than make eye contact, remembering at the last minute to look up so he could read her lips. "I was at work, and my boss gave me a note someone had left for me."

"What did it say?"

"Run."

"That's it? Just *run*? So you did?"

Her nod was punctual. "My sister is missing, and they found a body the night before at my workplace. I don't need a college degree to know something is off. I grabbed Houston and left town."

"Where were you going?"

"I don't know!" she exclaimed, jamming her hands into her hair. "I don't know, okay? I just got in the car and drove."

"It's okay," he promised, awkwardly patting her shoulder. "Just take a deep breath." She did, and he patted her shoulder again. "Good. You picked up Houston and took the back roads to avoid the highways?"

She glanced up at him in question for a moment before she shook her head. "No, I was on the main highway headed to

Minneapolis. I planned to get lost in the city for a few days until I figured out what to do. It was getting late, and Houston needed a bottle and food, so I took an exit, thinking I would stop at the gas station and take care of him. That's when things changed."

"That's when the SUV started following you?"

"Yes, but I wasn't sure if they were actually following me, so I drove past the gas station thinking maybe that's why they took the exit. If they stopped at the station, I'd turn around and go back."

"But they didn't."

"Nope," she said, shaking her head. "They stayed behind me, so I kept driving. After an hour, I thought they'd decided to pass me, so I slowed down in hopes they'd go around me and I could finish the twenty miles to the next town in peace."

"That's when they attacked?"

"Yep," she said with a sigh. "They swung the back of their SUV into my car, and you saw the result."

"If it makes you feel any better, slowing down probably saved your life."

"I'm glad I did something right tonight." She added a wink and a smile, so he offered her a smile back.

"You did many things right, including taking that note at face value. Are you aware there's an arrest warrant out for you?"

"What?" The gasped question was loud in the quiet room. "An arrest warrant? Why on earth would they put out an arrest warrant for me?"

"For ordering the murder of Howie Loraine."

Sadie gasped, her mouth open, but no words came out. She blinked twice and then crumbled into Eric's arms.

Chapter Five

Sadie blinked several times until she realized the man holding her was not a figment of her imagination.

"Welcome back," he said, helping her to sit up.

She accepted the water he offered and sipped it, her body zinging with the electricity of being touched by a man for the first time in too long. Sadie smoothed her hand down her neck and cleared her throat. "I don't know what happened. The last thing I remember is you saying there's a warrant out for my arrest, which is obviously a joke."

"I wish that were the case, but it's not. The cops picked up one of the men who dropped the body in the storage unit. He told the police that Sadie Cook hired them to put Howie Loraine in the grave."

Her head swam again, but she took a deep breath and let it back out. "There must be another Sadie Cook because I don't know who Howie Loraine is, Eric. You have to believe me!"

He put his finger to her lips to hush her. "I do believe you. We did some digging into your records and can see that you live paycheck to paycheck and have minimal savings."

"I help my sister care for Houston and pay all the rent." Her tone was defensive, and he took her hand.

"And that makes you a wonderful aunt and sister. I wasn't

judging you. I was pointing out that there is no way you paid anyone to commit a crime. Do you know the Loraines?"

"Again, I don't have a clue who Howie Loraine is," she said, rubbing her temple with the hand he wasn't holding. She liked how his hand encapsulated hers. It made her feel safe as her entire world fell apart.

"The eldest Loraine, Howie's father, Randall, was arrested and jailed for a counterfeiting scheme he ran about eight years ago."

"I moved to Bemidji from Minneapolis five years ago, so that was before my time here. This Howie was his son?"

"Yes, his youngest of three. Let's just say Howie liked to play it fast and loose. Chances are whoever killed him was someone he owed something to."

"If that's the case, why frame me?" she asked. "They don't even know me."

"At least not on the surface—"

"I don't know them!" she exclaimed, jumping up and planting her hands on her hips.

Eric stood, making her feel diminutive as he gazed down at her. "I believe you," he said again, taking her hand. "What I'm trying to say is we can't say that your sister didn't know them."

Sadie tipped her head in confusion. Kadie? Her head started to shake before she even spoke. "No. Kadie tells me everything. I know everyone she knows and who she dates."

"Good. Then we need to start with Houston's father."

"Okay, so that's one thing she didn't tell me," Sadie admitted with a grimace.

"You don't know who the baby's father is?"

"No, but I assure you, it's not someone with the last name Loraine. She never dated anyone by that name. Full disclosure?" she asked, and he nodded. "I'm not proud to say this, but Kadie told me she isn't sure who Houston's father is. She had a one-night stand and never got the guy's name. About three months later, she found out she was pregnant."

"This is not an untold story," he said, probably to make her feel better. It didn't work. "That happens a lot. I'm saying that until we know why they accused you, we need to protect you and Houston."

"I don't know how we would find out why they accused me if I don't know who *they* are, Eric."

When he squeezed her hand again, a jolt of electricity ran up her arm to lodge in her chest. What was happening to her? She didn't have time for entanglements or romance while running for her life alongside Kadie's and Houston's. Maybe that was why she reacted to the tall, dark and handsome stranger. He offered her a small light in the darkness, and she was grateful to him. Sure. That was it. Once he dropped her hand and never touched her again, she'd be able to convince herself of that.

"That's what we do here at Secure One." When she raised her brow, he chuckled for a moment. "Okay, so that's not our purpose, but we've been involved in some high-profile cases that we solved because of the targets on our backs."

"But you don't have a target on your back. I do. I'm no one special."

"Never say that," he insisted, squeezing her hand tightly. "The moment I met you at Dirk's, I knew you were someone special. The moment you walked through the doors of Secure One, you became family. That's how Cal runs this place, so you may as well know that right now. You aren't leaving here until we clear your name and find Kadie."

"Those are a lot of promises when you don't know if

you can keep them," she whispered, her gaze on his lips as he focused on hers. That was when she remembered not to whisper. She lifted her gaze until he held hers, and she was drawn to place a finger against his lips. "Remind me to speak louder if that's what you need. I don't want to make life harder for you."

When she dropped her finger, he cleared his throat as though he were as surprised by the contact—and her words—as she was. "Will do. You're observant, which is good. That will help us with this mess. As for making promises I can't keep, that statement proves that you don't know what we're capable of at Secure One, but you'll learn. For now, you must put your leg up with some ice and rest until morning."

Her head shake was frantic. "No. There's no time to rest. We have to start searching for Kadie."

"There is time for you to rest while I fill the team in on what's happening. While I do that, Mina will look at the note. Our boss, Cal, flies back tomorrow afternoon or evening with the rest of the team. Once they're here, we'll have enough people to help us search for answers. We'll find Kadie and clear your name, but we can't do that if we're exhausted. You included." He stood and held out his hand to her. "Houston needs you to be strong enough to care for him while you're here too."

Tentatively, she placed her palm into his. His hand was so warm that it instantly calmed her and made her feel like everything might be okay. "Don't you have to turn me over to the police?"

"Should I? Yes. Do I *have* to? No. We don't have to do anything."

"But there will be repercussions for you if you don't,

right?" she asked, following him to the door. He took her elbow so she could lean heavily on him as her leg started to ache now that the local anesthesia was wearing off.

"Only if we can't prove that you're innocent. Once we do, we'll hand over the evidence and you to the police, and you'll be cleared. That won't happen until your sister is safe and the threat has been mitigated. The events of this evening are enough to tell me that whoever has decided to set you up plays to win. Do you understand what I'm saying?"

Sadie's throat was too dry to speak, so she just nodded. She understood that she could have died tonight, and if she wasn't careful and didn't listen to everything this man told her to do, she could still find herself dead and unable to protect Houston. As they walked down the hallway to the med bay, she had to ask herself if all of this had to do with something she'd seen, heard or done at Dirk's house. Nothing else made sense. Had she seen or heard something odd or unusual at work that she hadn't registered?

She begged her tired, concussed mind to think, but all it did was pound. The answers to the thousand questions running through her head would have to wait until she'd had some sleep and the headache dissipated. With any luck, her head would be clear by morning, and she could help the team sort out all the moving parts of this mystery. A glance at Eric told her that a guardian angel had been watching over her tonight when that car had tried to take them out. Both by keeping them alive and having them land on the property of a team that fought for the underdog, no matter the evidence stacked against them.

"WHAT DO WE KNOW?" Mina asked as soon as everyone was gathered in the conference room.

"Cal called and they're flying back in the morning," Eric said to open the meeting. "They should be here no later than nine. He knows we need help."

"Good. We need the entire team back here if we're going to have enough staff to go around," Mina said.

He pointed at her. "Exactly what I told Sadie before I forced her to rest with Houston. I got as much out of her as I could tonight. She was exhausted and in pain."

"How did she react when you told her there was a warrant for her arrest?" Efren asked.

Eric lifted a brow at him. "She became so overwrought that she passed out in my arms."

"Hard to fake that," Mina said. "Not impossible, but hard."

"She wasn't faking," Eric said between clenched teeth. He wanted to jump down Mina's throat but held himself back. He had to play it cool, or they would start to think this was about more than just helping the underdog. "Once she came to, it was easy to see that she had no idea what was happening." He walked to the whiteboard where he'd written a list of information and tapped it with his finger. "This is the timeline of events since a few weeks before I met her at Dirk's."

"Wait, her sister is missing?" Mina asked, pulling a notepad in front of her. "I didn't see a missing person report on our basic background check of Sadie."

"The police blew her off. Kadie left a note, but Sadie says there's no way her sister wrote it." He turned to Efren. "Sadie said the note and a sample of her sister's handwriting were in her car."

"I put everything in the guest room since I didn't know where they'd be staying," Efren confirmed.

"I'll get to work on running those samples through my programs in the morning," Mina said, and Eric turned to her.

"If we can prove without a doubt that two different people wrote those notes, that's another point on Sadie's side of the column that she's being set up."

"I don't need columns to tell me that," he said, leaning on the table. "The woman has no idea what's going on. She's just trying to care for her nephew and keep them alive. We need to do a deep dive on both Sadie and Kadie to see if they're tied to the Loraines in a way even they aren't aware of on the surface."

"Where is the baby's father?" Roman asked from where he sat at the table. "He might be our best place to start."

"She doesn't know. All Kadie would say was that she wasn't sure who the father was. She had a one-night stand and never got the guy's name."

"Do you think Sadie would agree to a DNA swab of Houston?" Mina asked, and everyone turned to her expectantly. "If we run the baby's DNA through CODIS, it's possible the father could be in the database."

"Or a family member," Roman said, standing and leaning on the table like Eric. "Good thinking, babe."

Mina smiled, but Eric could tell she still wasn't feeling well. Her face was drawn, and her skin had a pallor. It was time to wrap up the meeting so everyone could sleep.

"That's a great idea, Mina," Eric agreed. "I'll talk to Sadie about it in the morning. It might take some convincing, but I'll do my best."

"In the meantime, I'll do the handwriting analysis and start a background search on Kadie," she said, writing on a pad.

"In the morning," Roman said firmly, glancing at her, and she nodded. "We all need to call it a night and start fresh tomorrow."

"Agreed," Eric said, his frustration mounting at the lack of information and the late hour. "Efren and I will do shifts with the rest of the guys to cover all the accounts. I'll turn everything over to Lucas at 5:00 a.m. when he comes on shift. We'll reconvene when Cal is back and Sadie is rested."

Everyone agreed and they gathered their things before they left. Eric insisted on taking the first shift so Efren could take his leg off and rest his limb. There was no sense in trying to sleep right now. If he did, his mind would conjure up the horrors he'd already lived through once. Better to keep his mind busy trying to help Sadie.

When Eric strolled into the control room, he stopped short. Lucas Porter was at the monitors with his trusty companion, Haven, under his feet. "Lucas? What are you doing here? Your shift doesn't start for a few more hours."

The man turned to him with an easy smile. "I know, but after all the commotion, I couldn't get back to sleep, so I thought I'd help out with the accounts so you guys could rest."

"That's appreciated, Lucas." He pulled out a chair and fell into it. "I'm exhausted, but my mind is swirling. I'll sit here and stare at a computer monitor until I fall asleep or the sun rises."

Lucas chuckled as he hit a toggle switch to flip his screen to a different camera. "I've been there. I'm so lucky to have Haven to keep me on the straight and narrow now. Ever think about getting a service dog?"

Eric glanced at him for a moment and shrugged. "I have, but my lifestyle doesn't lend itself to caring for a dog. I'm often off on jobs that wouldn't work with a dog in tow."

"They're trained animals, Eric," Lucas said with an eye roll. "They can be away from their person. They don't like it, but they can. They can also be invaluable in the field because, again, they're trained animals."

Eric ran his hands over his face a few times and slowly leaned back in his chair. "I don't need a dog as much as better hearing aids."

"I wasn't talking about your hearing loss."

Lucas fell silent, and Eric held his tongue. He knew Lucas was talking about his PTSD. After all, that was why Lucas had Haven, but Eric preferred to pretend he hadn't seen the horrors of that day every time he closed his eyes. Pretending was more manageable than admitting he had no control over anything that happened in this world. His chuckle was sardonic when it left his lips. It wasn't but a few months ago that he'd been telling Mack he needed to find help for his PTSD from that day when their worlds had exploded. Talk about the pot and the kettle.

"If the team needs extra hands, Haven and I are in," Lucas said. "Whether in the control room or the mobile command station. I joined Secure One because I believe in what you guys do."

Eric nodded once. "Noted, but now that you're here, it's because you believe in what *we* do. We're a team, and you're part of that team now. Once Cal arrives, we'll meet with all the big names. You want in?"

"Absolutely," the man said, sitting up straighter. "Anything I can do to help."

Eric thumped his back and nodded. "We're lucky to have you, Lucas."

They were lucky. They all knew it. Lucas had been working as the head of security for Senator Ron Dorian's estate when they'd crossed paths. After Secure One had saved the senator's daughter and taken down a serial killer terrifying the nation, Lucas had emailed to ask if they ever hired other disabled veterans to join the team. The email had come at an opportune time for both of them. With all the press they'd gotten starting with taking down The Madame and The Miss and solving the Red River Slayer case, they'd had more clients than manpower. Cal had pulled Lucas in for an interview immediately.

The fact that Lucas had severe PTSD from his time in the war wasn't a sticking point for any of them. Everyone on the team had it to some degree. When a human experienced war, it changed them on a molecular level. No one left their time in the military without some form of PTSD, whether they'd served in peacetime or wartime. Lucas controlled his with medication and by keeping Haven by his side. He was also meticulous, insightful and eager to prove himself as a team player. Cal had hired him immediately after his background check had cleared, so he'd been working for them for almost six months. Eric had been the underdog enough times to know what Lucas was feeling now that he had his feet under him.

"It's time for you to spread your wings around here," Eric said, pushing himself to stand. "In fact, since you took the initiative to cover for me, I'm going to bed. The main team will be back in play at 9:00 a.m. I'll get you in on the meeting. Good enough?"

"Better than good enough. See you then."

He held his fist out for a bump, which Eric delivered before he turned and left the room. Suddenly, his burdens didn't seem so heavy. It was time to lay his head down before the start of what was sure to be another busy, confusing day.

Chapter Six

Houston banged on the table and squealed with the glee of an eight-month-old with scrambled eggs. Through the large serving window, Sadie watched one of the men refill his plate from the chafing dishes and sit beside Houston to eat. She liked that the kitchen was set up so the cook never had their back to the dining room.

"What is going on in here?" Eric's voice boomed through the kitchen, and Sadie spun away from the stove, spatula still in hand, as her heart pounded against her ribcage. She couldn't be sure if it pounded from the scare or from having his voice surround her again.

"Uh, breakfast," she said, remembering to speak clearly since there was so much noise in the other room. "Are you hungry?"

"You're supposed to be resting."

She returned to the pan and stirred the eggs momentarily before facing him again. "Where did you get the idea that a woman with a hungry infant gets to rest?"

Eric smiled, and she did an internal fist pump to get that much out of him. He was always so stoic. Maybe he came by it naturally or maybe it was the job, but seeing his smile at the start of the day was lovely.

"That's a fair point, but why are you feeding everyone?"

Rather than answer, she turned to the stove, flicked the heat off and made him a plate. She answered as she handed it to him. "Because everyone was hungry?" His brow lowered to his nose, and she bit back an eye roll. "I made Houston breakfast, and one of the guys wandered down when they smelled food. Before long I had an entire pack of hungry men lining up for breakfast. It's like no one ever cooks for them."

Eric was already shoveling food into his face, but when he swallowed, he grinned at her again. "It's been a long time since we've had a cook here. Cal has been buying premade meals for the freezer and someone cooks something every few days, but it's not like when Charlotte was cooking."

"Who's Charlotte?" she asked, checking on Houston over her shoulder. He was strapped securely into a chair with his baby sling, but with so many people telling him he was cute and making sure he finished his breakfast, she had no worries he'd get hurt.

"Mack's fiancée. Charlotte is the reason they're in DC. She received an award at the White House for the Red River Slayer case."

Sadie snapped her fingers when she remembered. "That's right. She started working here as the cook?"

"She started as a sex-trafficked woman who found refuge here during a case. When she stayed on at Secure One, she replaced Marlise in the kitchen when Marlise was promoted."

"Who's Marlise?" She felt like she was playing *Who's on First?* with this guy.

Her confusion made him laugh, and he shook his head as he set his plate down. "In fairness, you haven't met the whole team yet. Marlise is Cal's wife. They should be back any minute."

"Thanks for the information. I would hate to put my foot in my mouth. That said, if they're on their way, I'd better clean up this mess so we can get to work."

"We?" he asked, raising a brow.

"You don't think I'm going to sit here meekly while you rescue me, do you?"

"The thought had crossed my mind—not rescue you so much as help you out of this jam."

Sadie worried her lip between her teeth as she watched Houston blow raspberries at Mina. "I do need help out of this jam. I have no idea how to keep Houston safe and clear my name at the same time."

"That's why we're going to fight for—"

"Secure one, Charlie," came a voice from the doorway.

Eric snapped to attention and turned to the giant of a man blocking the door. "Secure two, Echo."

"Secure three, Romeo," Roman said from the dining room.

And so it went around the room as it appeared to be how they welcomed their team back into the fold. When everyone started talking at once, Sadie grimaced as the decibel level climbed. She couldn't help but wonder how Eric even functioned in that environment. Then she noticed him flick his finger near his ear before he did some fancy handshake with the man in the door. It was impressive, considering the steampunk-looking prosthesis Cal wore on his hand.

"Glad you're back, boss. How was the flight?"

"As gentle as dove's wings," the man said, his eyes crinkling as he smiled.

Something told Sadie this man could be as sweet and loving as your nana, or as hard and mean as an assassin. She hoped she never saw the latter.

"Good to hear. I'm glad you're back. We need the manpower."

"As always," Cal said with a chuckle and a shake of his head. "You must be Sadie?"

He stepped around Eric and stuck his hand out for her to shake. It was a unique experience when his three prosthetic fingers wrapped around her flesh. "I am. It's nice to meet you, Cal. Eric was schooling me on the who's who of the Secure One team."

"Good to hear since you'll see these faces for the next few days. I need to get settled, and then we'll meet in the conference room in thirty?"

"I'll be there. Do you want breakfast? There's plenty here," Sadie said, motioning at the warming dishes on the counter.

"You made breakfast?"

"The baby was hungry," Eric answered, and she pretended not to notice his eye roll.

Cal's laughter cut above the din of voices, making Sadie smile. "One thing led to another" was her only explanation.

Cal grabbed a plate and dug into the eggs. "I'm not one to turn down good home cooking. We've missed it around here. Thank you for feeding everyone."

"It was no problem," Sadie said, knowing she wore a ridiculous smile. Seeing someone appreciate her work was gratifying, and she tossed a withering look of *I told you so* at Eric. "I work as house staff for Dirk, but I often help out in the kitchen when there's a big party. I love it when I get a chance to stretch my cooking wings. Anyway, I'll clean up the baby and meet you in the conference room in a few minutes."

She tried to walk past Eric, but he grabbed the crook of her arm. "I'll be down to your room to escort you in ten."

"I don't need an escort," she said, shaking her arm free of his grasp. Every time he touched her, electric heat slid through her belly. That needed to stop if she was going to get out of Secure One with her life and her heart intact. He lowered his brow and waited until she sighed. "Fine. See you in ten."

Sadie plastered a smile on her face and walked into the dining room to collect Houston. She didn't like being ordered around by a man, even if he was trying to help her, but she forced herself to remember she had bigger problems. Eric was trying to keep her out of jail so nothing happened to Houston. She would lose him to CPS if they took her into custody, which was out of the question. Her only objectives were to find Kadie and keep Houston safe. She'd do whatever she could to make that happen, even if it meant being bossed around by a tall, dark, brooding stranger. She would go as far as making the ultimate sacrifice so Kadie and Houston could live. Sadie had already come to terms with the idea that she might not walk away from this situation alive, and she was okay with that as long as Houston was safe.

After wiping Houston's face and freeing him from the sling, she swung him into her arms and waved as she left the room. It was time to start the day and stop thinking about the man who had an unseen power over her after such a short time. When they were together, his warm hands and the look in his eyes didn't help matters. She had to focus on her goals, to clear her name and bring Kadie home. Anything else was a distraction she couldn't afford.

AFTER A SHARP rap on the door, Eric dropped his hand to his side and shook out his shoulders. He was steeling himself for the fight to come, but there was no choice. If Sadie didn't agree to the DNA swab for Houston, it would cut them off at the knees when it came to finding Kadie. He'd convinced Sadie to trust them when she was skeptical and untrusting of everyone and everything, so he hoped for that reason she'd listen to the reasons why they needed Houston's DNA to find his mother and keep her nephew safe.

The door cracked open, and Sadie stuck her head out. "Hi, I'm almost ready to go. We'll be out in a few minutes."

She went to close the door, but he held it with his palm. "I need to talk to you privately first." Fear skittered through her eyes. "Don't worry," he whispered, stepping closer to the door. "It's not Kadie."

The door swung open for him to enter, but not before he noticed her shoulders relax a hair. Once he was inside, she pushed the door shut and walked over to the floor, where Houston was playing on a blanket. She picked him up and tucked him into her arms as though she alone could protect him. She couldn't, and he hated to be the one to prove that to her, but he'd have to if she wanted to get out of this alive.

"You're not taking Houston from me."

He took a step closer and cocked his head. "I have no plans to do that. Why would you think I would? You're both safe here until we sort out how you're involved in this mess. Just take a deep breath and hear me out."

She nodded once, but he noticed she didn't let go of the baby. "Usually when someone says *hear me out*, they have something bad to say."

"Not so much bad," he said, lowering himself to the bed to sit. "Maybe uncomfortable for you, but I want you to understand why we need to do it." She motioned for him to explain, so he did. "We need to take a DNA sample from Houston.

It's just a swab of his cheek. Once we have his DNA, Mina can run it through CODIS to see if there's a match."

"What is CODIS, and why does it matter?"

"CODIS is a DNA database that the FBI developed. It's filled with DNA profiles from all over the country. If you have a sample from a crime scene or victim, you run it through the database to see if it matches anyone's profile already on file."

Eric watched her eyes and waited. Since losing his hearing, he'd mastered the art of hearing what a person said with their eyes. He saw the moment the ball dropped. "You're trying to find his father." Eric tipped his head in agreement. "No. It doesn't matter who his father is. He's not going to help us find Kadie."

"You can't say that with certainty since you don't know who Houston's father is yet. If we can find his father, that gives us a new path to try to trace your sister's whereabouts. It will also help us see if there's a connection between your family and the Loraines."

"I'm telling you, Eric, we don't know the Loraines!"

He held his hand out to calm her so she didn't upset the baby. "I know what you're telling me, but my job isn't to take your word at face value and stop looking. That doesn't do anyone any favors. For all you know, you ran into one of the Loraines at Dirk's, had an interaction with him and never even knew who he was. If we can tie you to a Loraine, then we have better insight into why the cops think you wanted one of them dead. Does that make sense?"

"I understand why you want me to do it," Sadie said, walking up to him. This time her eyes yelled the fierce determination of a mama bear. "But I am not this baby's mother, and I cannot give you permission to find the man my sister has decided won't be part of his life. If she wants to find out who the father is, she can run the DNA test once we find her."

"That doesn't help us now, Sadie. You're not hearing me," he said, frustration filling the room so much so that Houston started to whimper. "Taking Houston's DNA may be the only way to find his mother. We have nothing to go on, the police refuse to look for Kadie and with the arrest warrant active, we can't even take you outside the compound. If you don't agree to this, our hands are essentially tied. Every minute that we don't do something is another minute that Kadie is in danger." He'd tried to deliver that harsh reality with kindness, but he saw the grimace of pain on her face before she turned away.

Sadie kissed the top of Houston's head to calm him as she paced around the room. Every time she looked at the baby, Eric noticed her eyes overflowed with the love of a mother despite not having given birth to him. He had to respect that she was Houston's protector, but at the same time, he had a job to do. There was a woman missing and in danger and another woman being accused of a crime she hadn't committed. Secure One was the only protection Sadie had, and he prayed she saw that before it was too late.

When Sadie turned back to him, she had a mask of neutrality firmly in place. "If I agree to this DNA swab and you find Houston's dad, can you promise me we can go down that path without contacting him? There's no way I'm going to introduce Houston to his father without my sister's permission. Do you understand me?"

Eric held up his hands in defense. "I read you loud and clear. There's no reason we have to contact Houston's father in a public fashion. Mina needs a name, and then she can find everything we need to know."

Sadie brushed another kiss across the top of Houston's tiny

head, and he reached up and patted her face as though he was giving her permission to do the test. She laughed, though Eric could tell she wanted to cry, and kissed the baby's palm.

"You have my permission, then. The only thing that I want is to get Houston's mama back. Whatever happens to me is inconsequential as long as he's with Kadie."

"Never say that again," Eric said, standing and stalking across the room. He stood in front of her as white-hot anger tore through him at the thought that she would sacrifice herself for her sister. Did she think so little of herself that she believed no one would miss her? He'd only known her a few days, but when she left Secure One, he knew she would leave a gaping hole in the part of him that he hid from the world. "What happens to you is consequential, both to this little boy and your sister. Never, ever let yourself believe that you're inconsequential, sweet Sadie. That's a good way to give up when the going gets tough. I don't know you that well, but I do know that's not your constitution, so get that straight in your head this instant."

Her eyes widened at his tirade, but he noticed her spine stiffen when she raised her head and gave him a jaunty salute. "Sir, yes, sir," she said with a small smile on her lips.

"Good," Eric said with a nod. "We'll make sure nothing happens to either one of you while you're under Secure One's roof. With any luck, we'll reunite your sister with both of you in seventy-two hours. First, we need to give Mina a path to follow."

"Then let's hit the woods," she said, taking a step back as though being that close to him was unnerving. Maybe it was. In fact, he hoped it was. Because as long as she was unnerved by him, she would keep her distance. If she came too close, he couldn't promise that the mutual heat flaring between them wouldn't consume them.

Chapter Seven

Sadie walked through the door of the conference room with Eric and came face-to-face with the full force of the Secure One team. She stopped short at the end of the long table, and Eric put his hand to the small of her back.

"Thanks for joining us, Sadie," Cal said from where he stood at the whiteboard.

Sadie glanced around the table with a nod. "Thank you for trying to help me with the nightmare my life has become. I'll make breakfast, lunch and dinner for two weeks if you can find the reason someone wants me dead."

"Don't say that too loud," Lucas said with a chuckle. "It's been months since we've had anyone to cook for us. Everyone sure did love a hot breakfast this morning."

"I'm glad it made them happy, and I'll gladly make dinner tonight too. We all have to eat, and it makes me feel like I'm contributing to the team while I'm here."

"I can't argue with that," Cal said. "Unnecessary, but if you want to, no one else will argue either." He winked, and she blushed, glancing down at the table for a moment until Mina spoke up.

"Where's Houston?"

"I left him with Selina," Sadie explained. "Eric suggested it would be easier without him here."

"She needs to focus on the plan without worrying about the baby," he explained before turning to Efren, who sat on the left side of the table. "I told Selina you'd be down later to fill her in on the plan."

"Great," Efren muttered. "It's like you enjoy throwing me to the wolves or something."

Sadie was confused why everyone was snickering, but she figured that was a story for another day. "Selina did the DNA test for Houston before we left. We have to find my sister, and if that's the only way to do it, then it was a chance I had to take."

Mina motioned Sadie over to an empty seat next to her. "It may be the only way to find her, which sounds dramatic, but when someone disappears into thin air—not even leaving a digital trail—it's nearly impossible to find them. Houston's father is the only unknown in her life, correct?" she asked.

"At least to us," Sadie agreed. "She swears she doesn't know who he is, but I wonder if that's true. Either way, that doesn't help us now."

"Exactly," Mina agreed. "If we can find Houston's father, there may be a connection there that we don't have right now. Every second we waste is another second Kadie is in jeopardy."

Sadie took a quick glance around the room. "You mean, you all believe me? You believe that Kadie didn't run away?"

"I looked at Kadie's note this morning," Mina said, slipping it out from the folder on the table. "I believe Kadie wrote this because she left you a secret message within the note. She purposely wrote it so you would question the authenticity of it. At least the authenticity regarding her intentions."

"I don't understand what you mean," Sadie said, her gaze sliding to the note. "I read that one hundred times and never saw a secret message."

Mina held up her finger and pulled out a copy of the note with most of the words blanked out. "It almost escaped me, but when I scanned it into the computer, I noticed that some of the words were darker than the others. It was hard to see with the naked eye, but the computer magnified it. I concentrated on just those letters and got the message she wanted you to know."

"I didn't run. Taken. Protect Houston. Find me," Sadie read, her eyes filling with tears as she gasped for breath. Her world started to spin, and Eric grasped her shoulders and squeezed, bringing her back to center. "I knew it." Her voice gave out, and she closed her eyes, resting her forehead on her palm. "I knew she'd never leave Houston that way."

Eric rubbed her shoulders as the room fell silent and she worked to keep it together for both Houston and Kadie. "Do you need a break?" he asked, resting his warm hand at the base of her neck.

Sadie lifted her head and wiped a wayward tear from her cheek. "No, I'm okay. This makes it clear that she's in danger and we can't waste a minute."

"Give us a timeline on how long she's been missing," Cal said from the board, making a new column to write in.

"It's been ten days now. Kadie went to work like any other day. I know my sister, and there wasn't a hint that anything was different that morning when she kissed Houston goodbye. An hour later, her work called to see if she was coming in. They told me she hadn't arrived and wasn't answering her phone."

Cal wrote *October thirteenth* on the board. "Okay, so you went looking for her on the thirteenth?"

"Immediately. I put Houston in my car, and I followed her route to work. She wasn't anywhere along any of the routes she would normally take."

"You didn't find her car abandoned either?"

"No," Sadie said, sucking in a breath. "That part worried me the most and was another reason the cops wouldn't look for her. They said she had to have run if she had her car."

"Not necessarily," Lucas said from across the table. "If enough people were in the car that stopped her on the road, it would be easy to take her and her car."

Cal pointed at him and wrote *Multiple attackers* on the board. "What did you do after you went looking for her?"

"I went back to my apartment hoping she was there. She wasn't, and that's when I found the note on my bed. It hadn't been there when I left to look for Kadie."

"Is the building open to anyone?" Cal asked.

"No, you need a key to get in the front of the building and another key for the apartment. The apartment was locked when I got home."

"Which means they had Kadie's keys at that point to get in and out without being noticed."

"I didn't even think about that, to be honest. It's possible the apartment complex still has the security footage!" Sadie said with excitement.

"Lucas," Cal said from the board. "After the meeting is done, take Sadie to the control room and work with her to contact the apartment management about security footage?"

"You got it, boss," Lucas answered, shooting a smile at Sadie.

She felt better knowing that all of these people had her

and Kadie's backs. "Should we ask for as much footage as we can get?" she asked, turning to look at Eric. "Just in case they came back?"

"That's not a bad idea," he agreed, glancing at Cal for confirmation. "You haven't been back since you found the note from Kadie?"

Sadie shook her head and turned back to face Cal. "After I found the note, I was super freaked out. I gathered all of our things and took Houston to my friend Julia's. We've been staying there ever since. She watches him while I work."

"I agree with getting as much footage as possible, then. If you haven't been back, you don't know if they came looking for something in the apartment or left a ransom demand," Cal pointed out.

"I never thought of that!" She gasped the words more than she spoke them. "I should have stayed at the apartment, but I was so scared for Houston that I didn't even think!" Tears filled her eyes again and she choked on a sob. "I'm a terrible sister!"

Eric's fingers squeezed her shoulders. "You're not a terrible sister. You did the right thing. Staying in the apartment was dangerous when you knew they could get to you there. You had no other choice."

"Eric's correct," Cal said as Mina handed her a tissue. "We just have to consider all possibilities when it comes to why these people took Kadie."

"But if they left a ransom demand and I never got it, they may have hurt Kadie!"

"No," Eric said, squeezing her shoulders again. "It's not a secret where you work, correct?" Sadie shook her head no. "Considering the note you got yesterday telling you to run, we all know someone else is aware that you work for Dirk. I would venture a guess it's not hard to ask around in Bemidji for directions to Dirk's place. If they wanted ransom, they'd know where to find you."

Cal motioned for Eric to stand next to him at the whiteboard. Sadie didn't know if that was because he wanted his help or if it was because that way Eric would be able to hear him better. If there was one thing she noticed about this team, they all worked together to support each other and work around their disabilities.

"I didn't think of that, to be honest. Mostly because I wasn't part of the events at Fettering's place, but I think we're all on the same page now," Cal explained. "Sadie, did Kadie act normal during the weeks leading up to her disappearance?"

Sadie appreciated that he'd said *disappearance* and not that she'd run. She paused to think about his question, recalling the last month before Kadie had been taken. "For the most part."

"But?" Eric asked, drawing out the word.

"It's probably nothing."

"Give it to us," Cal encouraged her. "You never know what might be important."

"Well, she started taking Houston out every night for a walk. Even if I offered to keep him for her on my nights off, she insisted on taking him. She claimed she was trying to lose the baby fat, but she had no baby fat. She barely gained any weight with Houston."

"How long were the walks?" Eric asked, while Cal had the marker posed on the board.

"Hours? She was gone so long a few times that I got worried and called her. She didn't answer the calls but texted me she was fine and would be home soon. How long she was gone on the nights I worked, I can't say."

Cal wrote it down on the board. "Which means she could have been trying to get in shape or she could have been secretly seeing someone?"

"Again, yesterday I would have said no, but today I can't say that and believe it."

"Anything else?" Mina asked, taking her hand in hers. "A change in eating habits, sleeping habits or attitude? Anything she may have said that made you wonder at the time but then you forgot about?"

Sadie racked her brain to come up with anything that might help them find Kadie. "There were a few times she was late getting home from work last month. I mean like hours late, not just a few minutes."

"That had never happened before?" Mina asked, and Sadie shook her head.

"No, and she used to always text me to let me know if she was going to be late. She didn't do that those times. I called her work, and they told me she'd left at her normal time."

"Did you confront her when she came home?" Cal asked.

"No. Kadie always apologized and said she lost track of time at the grocery store or running errands. I took it at face value since she'd come in with bags."

"And she had no excuse for not letting you know?" Eric's question was curious but also moody—as though it made him angry that her sister would disrespect her.

"Her phone was dead both times."

"Or that's what she told you," Mina said, and Sadie answered with a shrug.

"Is it fair to say that Kadie's personality had changed over the last month?" Cal asked, and this time Sadie nodded.

"I never really thought about it, to be honest, but it had changed. I would say for the better, actually. Kadie was a new mom, working and trying to juggle everything on little sleep, so I was happy when she started walking with Houston. It got them out of the house, and Houston slept better, so she got better sleep as well. I wasn't home at night, so I couldn't get up with him to give her a break."

"I just have one question," Mina said, her brow lowered. "How did you work all night and then take care of Houston during the day? When did you sleep?"

"In bits and pieces," Sadie answered with a chuckle. "I napped when he napped, and when she got home at three, I slept until nine and then went to work. Working the night shift for Dirk meant tasks that took longer but were less physical. If I had an evening shift for a party, Julia would watch Houston until Kadie got done with work." She paused and then sucked in a breath. "Julia could be in danger if anyone figures out that she knows me."

"I have surveillance on her," Cal said. "She hasn't been approached by anyone as of yet."

"I need to let her know I'm okay," Sadie said, but Eric shook his head.

"Can't happen. Too risky."

"She could call using a Secure One line. They can't be traced," Mina gently said.

"No," Eric said again, taking the same stance he had earlier in her room. It screamed dominance. "Any contact with Julia could put the woman at risk if they think she knows something she doesn't."

"If that's the case, it's already too late," Cal said. "By way of association, if anyone discovers they're friends, she's going to get a shakedown for information. Sadie needs to call

Julia and let her know she's safe but give her no information about where she's staying. It's all over the news that Sadie is wanted for murder, so I'm sure Julie has to be shocked and worried, right?"

"Absolutely, but she won't believe it," Sadie said with conviction. "She's probably terrified though."

"Does she work somewhere during the day?"

"Yes, she's a receptionist at a staffing agency."

"You'll call her there. There could be a listening device at her home, so it's smarter to call her where she can't be overly loud about who is on the phone. The call will put her mind at ease and also get us information. We'll give you a list of questions to ask her, but we need to know if anyone has contacted her about you in a way we can't surveil."

Sadie could tell that Eric didn't like it, but he finally gave his boss one stiff nod.

"Do we have everything up on the board that we know so far?"

Eric held up his finger and grabbed a marker. He wrote the words *Winged Templar* on the board and circled them. "This name is still an unknown entity. Mina, have you had any luck tracking down that moniker?"

Mina shook her head. "No. I couldn't find anything connected to the mob, but we both know that means nothing. I'm still working on it. Don't give it to the cops yet."

"I have no intention of doing that," Eric said with an eye roll. "They'll assume it's Sadie's mob name or something equally ridiculous."

Sadie couldn't help it. She snorted with laughter, slapping a hand over her mouth. "Sorry, but this whole thing is outrageous."

Cal was grinning when he spoke. "The update I got from

the Bemidji police earlier this morning was that Howie Loraine was killed in typical mob-style pointblank range before his head was removed to sit upon his chest. They are currently doing a deep dive into Sadie's life to see how she's connected to the mob."

"For heaven's sake!" Sadie growled, anger and righteous indignation filling her. "I'm not connected to the mob in any way, shape or form. I'm an underemployed maid trying to help my sister raise her son. I didn't put a hit out on anyone! Like, how does one even go about that? Is there a number in the phonebook? Do I google 1-800-HitsRUs?"

Mina slipped her arm around her shoulder. "We know, Sadie. Cal is just telling us what the police are doing in their investigation. It's important to know if they're keeping you as a suspect or tossing out the warrant."

"Mina is correct. We know you have no connection to the mob," Cal said. "We've already done backgrounds on you, but we'll let the police busy themselves looking for a connection that isn't there while we do the hard work of solving the case." Everyone around the table chuckled at that comment. "You see, the Bemidji police are missing the most important person that Secure One has, and that person is Mina. She will find the important connection if there's a connection to be found."

Eric must have noticed she was confused because he returned to the whiteboard and pointed at a picture on the board. Below the picture were arrows, one going to the name *Sadie* and one to the name *Kadie*. "If Mina can find a connection between Howie Loraine and you or Howie Loraine and your sister, then we can trace where the interaction occurred. Once we know the point of contact, we can dive into

Howie's life at that junction to see why someone set you up to take the fall for his murder."

"Wait," Sadie said, standing from her seat. "Is that a picture of the Loraines?"

"Of the three boys, yes," Cal said. "This one here," he said, pointing to the middle man in the picture, "is the victim, Howie, this is Randall Junior." He pointed to the man on Howie's left. "And this is—"

"Vic." Sadie walked up to the whiteboard to peer at the image. How could this be possible? Her heart pounded in her chest as she stared at the image. She had to be mistaken. There was no way the answer was this simple. She put a shaky finger on the man to the right of Howie. "I think this is Vic."

"Victor Loraine?" Cal asked with surprise.

She spun toward him with her breath quick in her chest. "Is that his name? We only knew him as Vic."

Eric came up behind her and grasped her shoulders almost as if he knew she needed the warmth of his hands to ward off the chill of the truth. "You knew him as Vic? How do you know him?" he asked as Cal picked up the marker again.

When Sadie spun around to face him, she was immediately pulled in by the intensity of his gaze. "Um…" She forced herself to look away for a moment. If she didn't, she'd never finish a thought. "I… We…met him at a Halloween party."

"How long ago was that?" Cal asked.

"I want to say it was, like, two years ago? I know it was before Kadie got pregnant. She had an instant crush on him, and they danced together at the party. He asked her out before the night was over."

"You're saying Kadie went out with Victor Loraine?" Eric asked.

"She went out with this guy," Sadie said, pointing at the man in the picture again, "but he told us his name was Vic Larson."

"We just found our connection, people," Eric said. "Mina—"

"Already on it," she answered as she started typing into her laptop.

"Why would he lie about his name?" Sadie asked.

Eric met her gaze again and held it. "I can't say for sure, but he's the only Loraine son who has stayed above the law. He may not like to associate with the name."

"He's the family's black sheep, so to speak," Cal explained. "I imagine using his real last name in this state is difficult. *Larson* gives him anonymity."

"Okay," Sadie said, "even if that's true, what good will it do him to lie when he eventually has to come clean about it?"

"I can't say, but we found our connection regardless." He turned to Mina. "Can you work with this?"

"Are you kidding me?" she asked with a chuckle. "You're making this too easy on me. I'll update you soon." She stood and walked over to the board. "Sadie, do you remember how long Kadie dated Vic?"

"As far as I know, they only went out once."

"Do you think this could be the one-night stand Kadie was referring to?" Eric asked as Cal wrote on the whiteboard.

"No," Sadie insisted. "It was long before she got pregnant with Houston."

Mina dropped her hand from the board. "As far as you know, Kadie only went out with Vic once? You can't say for certain that they didn't go out more than that and your sister didn't tell you?"

"Honestly, three weeks ago, I would have told you no. But today, I can't say that and believe it. I'm starting to think Kadie kept more secrets than I realized. We always vowed to tell each other everything, but clearly I'm the only one who stuck to that vow."

"Listen," Eric said, catching her eye again. "It's possible that the secrets she kept were to protect you and Houston. Don't assume the worst until you know why she did what she did, okay?"

Sadie nodded, trying to break their connection but was unsuccessful. She was connected to him if he was in the room, like it or not. When Eric stared at her lips like he wanted to kiss them senseless, she didn't want to break the connection. *He's reading your lips, Sadie. Nothing more.* She kept telling her brain that, but it wasn't listening. She wanted him to kiss her senseless, which was a bad idea when she was up to her neck in deception. At this moment, she didn't know up from down, and allowing Eric to get close would only complicate the situation. Sadie swallowed hard and reminded herself she had to be strong for Houston. She had to concentrate on finding Kadie before it was too late.

A phone went off and everyone checked theirs, but it was Efren who was being paged. He stood and grabbed his notepad. "I'm needed on the west side of the property. There's a section of the fence that's offline. Are you guys okay here?"

"Go," Cal said with a nod. "When you're done, we'll hopefully have footage to watch from the apartment building. Find me in the control room."

"Ten-four. Tango out."

"Let's adjourn for now," Cal said, putting the marker back

on the whiteboard. "Once Mina has time to run some of this information down and we get some of the footage from the apartment building, we'll come back together. In the meantime, you know how to reach each other if situations arise."

Everyone nodded and stood, leaving the conference room for their stations. Sadie still hadn't broken her connection with Eric.

"Are you ready to call the apartment management?" Lucas asked when he stood.

Without taking her gaze off Eric, she nodded once. "I have to check on Houston first though."

Eric grasped her shoulder and squeezed it. "I'll check on him when I go down to fill in Selina since Efren got called away. If he's sleeping, we'll leave him alone. If he's happy, he can stay with Selina until you're done on the phone. Here," he said, turning and grabbing a black box off the table. "Take this walkie. I'll keep you updated on his status."

Sadie slid it from his hand, his warm skin brushing across hers with just the hint of warmth and tenderness. She wondered what it would feel like to have him caress her face, her body or to have him hold her through the night.

Stop. Focus.

She held up the walkie. "I'll be waiting."

Chapter Eight

Eric stuck his head inside the door of the med bay and noticed Houston asleep on the gurney. Selina stood from the computer and walked over to the door, motioning him outside to talk.

"You must have eyes in the back of your head," Eric said as a greeting.

"I saw you on the computer screen. Is there a problem?"

"No, why would there be?"

"Because you're here instead of Brenna."

"He got a call to fix a fence. I told Cal I'd fill you in."

"Any day is a lucky day when I don't have to deal with that guy," she said on an eye roll.

Eric bit his tongue to keep from popping off on her. Whatever was going on with her had nothing to do with Efren Brenna. He was just the unfortunate person she'd picked to wear her target and take her bullets.

"How's the baby?" He held up the walkie. "I promised Sadie I'd let her know as soon as I saw him."

"Sleeping like one." Selina glanced back to the gurney for a moment, and a smile filled her face. "He's such a good boy. As long as he's fed and dry, he never makes a peep."

"That's helpful considering what we're dealing with right

now. I'm glad he can be away from Sadie for a bit while she helps us with the case. She's calling the apartment management now to see if there's any security footage from the day Kadie disappeared."

"Someone did deliver the note to her room," Selina agreed.

"And that someone had a key, which means it's possible they were caught in the lobby somewhere. Will you keep Houston until she's finished working with Lucas?"

"Houston is not a problem. What can I do to help while he's asleep?"

"Keep working on the DNA, and let us know the moment it's available so Mina can get it into CODIS. We found a connection to Sadie and the victim from the storage unit."

"Do we have a name for the victim? I've been down here since they showed up, and no one has filled me in."

"Howie Loraine. Mob-style execution before his head was removed and put on his chest to fit in the trunk. They're claiming Sadie paid for the hit."

Selina said nothing, but her eyes were wide as saucers. Eric wasn't sure she was breathing so he grasped her arm. "Selina?"

She jumped and took in a quick breath. "Did you say Howie Loraine?"

"Yeah, the youngest of the Loraine brothers...do you know them?"

"N-no," she stuttered. Her lips said one thing, but her eyes said another, and Eric was instantly on edge. "I just remember when their dad was arrested. That was messy."

"Yeah, and the fact that one of Randall Loraine's sons was killed mob style tells me they're still somehow wrapped up with them."

"So how are Sadie and this Howie kid connected?" Selina asked, her shoulders straightening as she dropped a mask down again. Her reaction to that name was visceral and something Eric couldn't ignore, but for now, she had slipped back into operative mode.

"They don't, but Houston's mom, Kadie," he explained, pointing at the baby, "dated Howie's middle brother, Victor. Mina is running that down for us right now to see how long they dated and if Kadie ever met any of the other brothers."

"Do you think Vic—Victor is Houston's father?"

He saw a bit of fear on her lips when she said the name before she locked it down again.

What was going on with her? This wasn't the same woman he'd worked with for years. Something had changed during the Red River Slayer case, and she hadn't been the same since.

"Sadie doesn't think so, but I'm planted solidly in the other camp. I think there's a good possibility that Houston is a Loraine. If Mina finds a timeline of how long they dated and when they were last seen together, it could line up."

"If that's the case, we have to protect this little boy, Eric. No one can know he's here. No one." Her hands were shaking, and he held her shoulder to calm her.

"What am I missing here, Selina? What do you know that I don't?"

She glanced around the hallway, her eyes filled with fear and worry. There was something else there that Eric couldn't put his finger on, but he was deeply concerned for the woman in front of him.

"Just take my word for it. If that boy is a Loraine, they'll do anything to get their hands on him. No one can know he's here!" she hissed, her voice low enough he couldn't make out her words clearly and had to read her lips.

Before he could say another word, her face changed again and she was back to the calm, organized Selina he recognized. "I'll get the DNA to Mina for upload. If Houston is related to the Loraines, we'll know soon enough since Randall will be in the system as a convicted felon. I'll keep you posted."

With that, she turned, slid the med-bay door shut and walked over to Houston. Eric noticed the shudder that went through her as she stroked the baby's downy head. That left him to wonder just what Selina was hiding from the rest of the team.

LUCAS SHOULDER BUMPED Sadie when she hung up the phone. "That was tough, but you pulled it off."

She let out a breath while she nodded. "For a minute there, I didn't think they bought the story. I'm glad they finally agreed to send the footage over."

"I'm going to let Cal know we were successful, and then I'll set us up in command central to watch the footage. You'll have to be there in case we find something."

"I need to check on Houston," Sadie said, eyeing the black box Eric had given her. He'd messaged that the baby was sleeping, but she wanted to check on him herself. Everything about this was scary, but Houston grounded her. He motivated her to fight to find her sister and bring her home.

"That's fine. It will be at least thirty minutes before the footage arrives by email. Go check on the babe and bring him to the control room if you have to. We'll make it work."

"Okay, thanks, Lucas," she said, standing and stretching. "I'm going to grab a bite to eat too since I missed breakfast."

"You cooked breakfast," he said with a chuckle.

"Doesn't mean I remembered to eat it." She winked as she turned and walked toward the door.

The truth was she hadn't forgotten to eat. She just hadn't been hungry. The moment her sister had disappeared, so had her appetite. Add in the responsibility of Houston and now an arrest warrant for murder hovering over her head, and she was a hot mess. Sadie would force herself to eat and sleep so she could be there for Houston, but the idea that Kadie was in danger while she went about life as usual made her sick to her stomach.

Sadie stepped into the hallway and walked straight into a wall. She glanced up when she heard his exhale of breath. Their gazes met, and for a moment neither of them spoke, both too consumed by the electricity zapping through the air.

"Where are you going in such a hurry, Sades?"

Sades? When did he start calling her Sades?

"To—to check on Houston." She hated how tongue-tied she got around Eric. He unnerved her in the best and worst way possible. She forced her mind to take a step back from his intensity so she could think straight. "We're waiting for the apartment manager to send over the footage. It should be here within the hour."

"Excellent news. I'm glad you could convince them to turn it over."

"It wasn't easy, but I could tell they didn't know about my 'legal troubles'—" which she put in air quotes "—so they bought my story about an intruder."

"I hope it helps us move this along. Every second we search for Kadie is a second Houston doesn't have his mother." His words hit her like bullets. She closed her eyes and sucked up a breath. "I'm sorry. That was insensitive."

"But true," she whispered, knowing he wouldn't hear the

words, but he'd read them on her lips. Her tiny pink lips would melt under his if he ever kissed her. Before she could open her eyes, he'd pulled her into a hug. She stiffened at first, unsure how to feel about being in his arms, until his heat relaxed her and she sank into him. She'd longed for a hug of reassurance but had no one to ask—until now. She was sure that was all it was until he started to rub her back with his warm, gentle hand.

"We're going to find her," he promised, and she slid her arms around his waist and held on for dear life.

"We have to," she said, remembering to speak clearly since he couldn't read her lips. "She didn't do anything wrong. I don't understand the game being played, so I'm taking my toys and leaving the sandbox."

The rumble of laughter from his chest ran the length of her, the sound warming her head to toe while the sensation made her feel like she had a home and a family. She hadn't felt that way in far too long. Sure, Houston and Kadie were her family, but having someone of her own to lean on, depend on and laugh with was what she yearned for more than anything.

But it couldn't be Eric Newman. He was off-limits physically, logistically and emotionally. Physically he was standoffish. It was understandable. He lived a different life than she did and always would. Emotionally he was unavailable. There was no question he'd brought demons back from war—and that was expected, but he still let them control him. She saw it every time he held Houston. A shadow would cross his face that said his time at war had been ugly. Sadie wanted to ask him about it but was afraid he'd never speak to her again if she did.

This hug doesn't feel standoffish, that voice inside said.

She sighed internally. The hug was nothing more than a moment of comfort. Her sanity depended on believing that, but when Eric leaned out of the hug and captured her gaze, he made that impossible.

He zeroed in on her lips and then licked his, narrowed the gap and brushed his against hers. It was soft, tender and too quick, but it told Sadie he experienced the same heat and magnetic pull between them. She wondered if he'd felt the same electric spark she had when their lips had touched.

She didn't have time to ponder the question before he spoke. "Speaking of Houston," he said, clearing his throat though his gaze was still on her lips. "I just checked on him. He's fine."

Sadie blinked several times before she could respond. Her body was on fire with need and desire, and her brain had stopped functioning the moment his lips had touched hers. Why had she been cursed with poor timing? She hadn't found anyone who was interesting or engaging for years, and the one time she did, her life was a hot mess.

He's off-limits. Kiss or no kiss, that voice reminded her.

"I'm happy to hear that, but I can't leave Selina to take care of him. She has a job to do too. I'll go get him, and he can sit on my lap while we watch the footage."

"Right now, Selina's most important job is to take care of the baby."

"Houston is not her responsibility," Sadie said with a shake of her head. "I know I haven't been here long, but I get the vibe that she has more to offer the team than what anyone allows."

The corners of his eyes crinkled from a grimace. "Is it that obvious?"

"It is to someone who lives the same kind of life. Being

underemployed puts you on the defense and the offense at the same time. You want to defend your skills and prove them. You have to keep your boring, unchallenging job while looking for opportunities that would put your real skills to the test. I won't let Houston get in the way of Selina being able to flex her skills."

Eric slung his arm around her shoulders, leaving a burning trail of desire across her still-heated nerves. "You don't have to worry about Selina or the team. Your only focus is on yourself, your sister and your nephew. You let us worry about Secure One as a whole. That said, I have it on good authority that Selina is waiting for Houston's DNA from the lab. Once she has it, she'll get the report right to Mina who will run it through CODIS. If he's related to the Loraines, we'll know soon enough since Randall's DNA is in the database."

"He's not a Loraine," she said, immediately on the defense.

"Maybe not, but it makes the most sense to start at the beginning of the path, and right now, that's with the Loraines. If there's no connection to them then we'll pivot."

Sadie noticed Eric was working too hard at keeping his expression neutral when he spoke. He believed Houston was a Loraine too. It wasn't like she hadn't considered it, and while there was always a chance that Kadie had slept with Victor Loraine, she didn't believe he was the father.

"I was going to ask you how Mina does all of this hacking without getting caught. She's hacking government websites."

"You really want to hear that story?" Eric asked, walking them into the kitchen and flipping on the light.

"I do. I'm fascinated by what Mina can do with a computer. If she can trace Kadie down using a mouse and a keyboard, I'll forever be grateful to her."

He pointed at the coffeepot across the counter. "Better fire that up, then. We're going to be here awhile."

Sadie took the opportunity to break their connection and prepare the coffeepot. Once it was gurgling, she couldn't help but touch her lips. Eric had kissed her and then pretended as though it hadn't happened. Maybe he'd realized it had been a mistake the moment his lips had touched hers and wanted to move past it? That was probably what she should do too, but that was easier said than done when living in close proximity.

"Don't overthink it." He came up behind her and plastered his body the length of her back as he leaned into her ear.

"It's kind of hard not to," she answered, her eyes closed since he couldn't see her face. She swallowed around the dryness in her throat and took a breath. "I can't explain the draw between us."

He turned her and grasped her shoulders. "Neither can I, and we don't have time to unpack what's happening between us. We have to concentrate on finding Kadie."

"I agree," she said with a single nod.

"Once Kadie is safe and reunited with Houston, then we can concentrate on this draw between us."

He dropped his hands and slid a stool out to sit. While Sadie prepared mugs for the coffee, he gazed at her with an intensity that left her nerve endings singed. In the next breath, he launched into how Mina had found her way to Secure One via the FBI, as though anything mattered but the promise he'd just made.

Chapter Nine

Eric stood behind Sadie and Lucas, arms folded across his chest with his eyes focused on the screen in front of them. They had the footage from the morning of Kadie's abduction, which he was now convinced was the case, and had found the moment Sadie had left with Houston to go look for her sister. If they were going to catch the guy on camera, the time was coming soon.

"I find it hard to believe they wouldn't know there were cameras in the building," Sadie was saying as Lucas ran the recording. "Everyone has cameras these days."

"There," Lucas said, pausing the video on a guy who had walked into the lobby. He wore black jeans, combat boots and an army-green jacket. "Is he wearing a mask?"

They all leaned in together to get a closer look. "Looks like it," Sadie agreed, and Eric could hear the disappointment in her voice. "A mask of Richard Nixon."

"Original." Lucas huffed the word more than he said it. Disappointment was evident in the room.

"He's wearing gloves," Eric noted while they watched the suspect approach the apartment door. "And he's got a key."

"Those are Kadie's keys," Sadie whispered. "She keeps

a little teething ring on them for Houston in case they get stuck in line somewhere."

They waited, and in less than thirty seconds the masked man had walked into the apartment, returned, relocked the apartment door and slipped out the side door.

"I wish they had cameras on the outside of the building," Eric growled. "If they did, we could trace the car he gets into."

"We asked, but they said they don't have them outside other than at the doors. I'm making some calls to see if there are any cameras on other buildings that might capture the parking lot," Lucas explained.

"Good—stay on that. We know this guy is young, just by the way he moves, average height and white by the color of his neck where it meets the mask."

"That's not much to go on." Eric heard the weight in Sadie's words. He couldn't help but wish he could do something more than stand there.

"No, but at least we know that she was absolutely abducted and forced to write that note. Let's keep watching and see if they come back."

Lucas hit the Double Speed button, and they watched people come and go, but no one other than Sadie approached the apartment door. Eric's phone rang, and he motioned for them to keep going with the video, then stepped out the door to answer the phone. He could see who it was on caller ID, and he needed to take the call.

"Dirk," Eric greeted the man on the other end of the line. "How are things over there?"

"Things would be better if the cops could find my former employee and arrest her."

Eric was going to pretend that he hadn't heard the word

former in that sentence. He didn't want to break the news to Sadie that her boss had abandoned her. "I don't know how I can help with that, sir. Secure One is not the police."

"You seem to solve more cases than they do," he snapped, and Eric had to bite back laughter. He wasn't exactly wrong, but wouldn't he be surprised to know Sadie was in the other room.

"Is there something you need in regard to your security at the property, Dirk?" Eric asked, using the placating tone he had perfected for working with demanding clients.

"Yes! You can find Sadie! Are you listening? The cops won't let anyone near the storage units, and I'm losing business!"

"Again, I remind you that we aren't the police and we have no say over what they do or don't do. I can call the chief at the Bemidji PD and find out when they'll release the storage units, but that's as far as I can go in my role as your security expert. It hasn't been forty-eight hours yet, so I'm not surprised they haven't cleared the units. It should be within seventy-two hours."

"I can't wait another day! Find out how much longer," Dirk snapped, his usual snippy tone firmly in place. "People need things from their units, and this is making me look bad!"

Eric opened his mouth to speak, but the phone went dark. "Nice. He hung up on me." With an eye roll, he opened his phone app and clicked another number. Since his hearing aids were already connected to Bluetooth, he might as well follow through on his promise, even if his client was annoying.

"Chief Bradley here."

"Chief, it's Eric Newman from Secure One." He went on to explain what he needed and listened to the heavy sigh of the chief before he spoke.

"Fettering has made it very clear how he feels about this investigation, but I can't have other cars in that storage unit until I'm sure that the evidence response team has everything they need. I predict we'll be able to clear the area by the end of the day, but I won't rush it."

"I don't expect you to, Chief. I am simply touching base on the request of my client."

"More likely he yelled at you and then hung up."

Eric couldn't help but smile. "Seems you're familiar with Mr. Fettering. I'll let him know to cool his boots for a few more hours. Any luck on finding Miss Cook?"

"None. She's fallen off the face of the earth with that baby. Almost as if someone was offering her protection…"

"That is odd," Eric said, stopping himself from saying *just like her sister* since he wasn't supposed to know that Kadie was missing. "Would you do me a favor?"

"Depends on what it is. I'm rather busy trying to solve a murder over here."

"This has to do with the murder. It might even help you find the actual killer because I sure as hell know it's not Sadie Cook."

"So you say. If I could get a warrant, I'd be running my people through Secure One to look for her, but I have no proof to show a judge."

Eric's grin grew wider. "No, you sure don't, and she's not here anyway, so you'd be wasting your time. That said, I was thinking about the way Howie Loraine was killed."

"What about it?"

"I'm sure you're familiar with what happened eight years ago with the Loraines?"

"I've read the reports. I was chief of police in Iowa at the time, so I was rather removed from it."

"Then may I suggest you look into Medardo Vaccaro's organization."

"The Snake? What does he have to do with this?" Eric heard the skepticism in the chief's voice loud and clear.

"Let's not split hairs here, Chief. What happened to Howie was a mob hit, and we all know that Vaccaro and the Loraines used to be tight. It's not outside the box to think they still are and Howie crossed a line Vaccaro didn't like."

"You're suggesting the mob is framing Sadie Cook to take the fall for a hit?"

"It's possible," Eric agreed, his chest tight as he worked to convince the chief there were other avenues to explore when it came to who'd killed Howie Loraine.

"Aliens are also possible."

Eric bit back the sigh and flexed his shoulders. "Chief, something reeks, and it's not Howie Loraine's dead body. You can't tell me you don't feel the same way."

"I do," he agreed slowly. "None of it makes any sense, which is why I'd really like to speak to Miss Cook and try to clear her as a suspect. I don't suppose you happen to know her whereabouts at this point in time?"

Eric's gaze drifted to the control room where Sadie sat holding a toy for Houston while she watched the footage. "I do not, but with or without Miss Cook, concentrating on the right avenues—the ones that make sense—should clear her name and reveal the real killer. That's all I'm saying."

"You're saying a lot for a guy who just works for a security company."

"Sir," Eric said, biting back the disrespect that sat on his tongue. "I may work for a security company now, but the core group of us were MPs in the army. We know when something stinks of a setup."

"I'm busting your chops, Newman. I know you have a unique history with the law. I will try to clear Fettering's units today. I'll keep following my other leads in hopes something pops up to clear Miss Cook. Until that time, or until I can speak to Miss Cook, the warrant will remain active."

"Ten-four," Eric agreed before hanging up.

The phone fell to his side with a sigh of frustration. They needed that warrant canceled. At some point, they'd have to move Sadie and Houston out of Secure One, and they couldn't afford to get hit with a charge for harboring a fugitive. His mind's eye drifted back to the moment his lips had touched hers. He realized that he wanted her name cleared for other reasons too. Reasons that he shouldn't even have been considering but couldn't banish from his mind.

A rush of air swooshed past him, and he glanced up to see Sadie as she ran into the bathroom and slammed the door. Lucas, now holding Houston, ran to the door calling her name but stopped short when he saw Eric.

"What happened?" Eric asked, torn between talking to Lucas and going after Sadie. He settled for taking Houston from Lucas and cuddling him into his chest.

Lucas motioned him into the control room after giving Haven a command to rest. "We found something on the footage."

"Show me." He sat and waited for Lucas to load the video. When he hit Play, Eric leaned into the screen, trying to get a better look at the guy approaching Sadie's door. "Wait. Is that…"

"Victor Loraine," Lucas confirmed.

Eric's whistle was long and low. "What is he doing?" Lucas held up his finger for him to wait, and sure enough, Victor knelt and slid something under the door. "Dropping a note. I think it's fair to say he knows Kadie better than her sister thought."

Lucas pointed at him in agreement. "She called the apartment manager on-site and asked them to go into the apartment, get the note, take a picture and send it to us. When she hung up, she took off."

"I would imagine she's stressed and near her breaking point," Eric said, glancing at the door to see if she had returned. "Sadie is coping with a lot right now, including taking care of her nephew without knowing when or if her sister is coming back." He stood and pushed the chair in. "I'm going to check on her. Let me know when the letter comes in, and we'll reconvene." Eric picked up a walkie-talkie and clipped it to his belt.

"Ten-four," Lucas agreed as Eric left the room.

First, he'd leave Houston with Selina for a few minutes so he could find Sadie. He reminded himself she was a woman in need of a friend and nothing more.

Maybe one day, he'd believe it.

Chapter Ten

Sadie sat on the toilet in the small bathroom and tried not to hyperventilate. This was too much. She could only imagine what Eric would think when he found out Vic had come to their apartment. She was ridiculously naive for not knowing that her sister was involved with this guy. She'd honestly had no idea. Kadie had done a fantastic job keeping her in the dark about Vic, but now Sadie wished she hadn't. A little part of her worried that Victor Loraine was Houston's father, and if that was true, life just got dangerous. It would be disastrous if they couldn't find Kadie before Vic learned he was Houston's father.

"Oh, no," she groaned aloud. "What if he already knows?"

There was a knock on the door, and she snapped her head up, holding her breath so they would go away and leave her to freak out in peace.

"Sadie? It's Eric. Come out so we can talk."

"I don't want to talk," she said and waited to hear his footsteps moving down the hallway.

"I can't hear you through the door, Sades," he said, and she suspected his lips were pressed to the door. "We need to talk."

With a heavy sigh, she pushed herself up off the toilet and

threw the door open. "Can't a girl have an existential crisis without an audience?"

"Not here," he said with a grin. "Here we approach the problem head on and find a way to fix it."

"I don't know that there's any fixing this," she said with a shake of her head. "What's that saying? You can't unscrew what's already been screwed?"

Eric's snort made her smile. "Yeah, something like that. Let's go talk."

"I want to see Houston."

"Okay, we'll talk on the way to the med bay," he agreed. They started walking, and he waited for her to speak, but she wasn't going to. The less she said, the better right now. It didn't take them long to get to the med bay, and Eric pressed his thumb on the fingerprint reader. When the door slid open, he announced himself. "Secure one, Echo."

"Secure two, Sierra," Selina said, spinning around in her chair with a happy Houston on her lap.

As soon as Sadie saw her nephew, she ran to him, scooped him into her arms and hugged him. "I'm sorry I ditched you, baby." She kissed his cheek noisily, and he giggled, his belly jiggling with the motion. Sadie noticed Eric smile at Houston, and soon he was tickling his belly as she held him.

"He's a good boy," Selina said, and Sadie couldn't help but notice it was the first time since she'd been here that the woman looked happy. "We were watching *Sesame Street* and playing pat-a-cake. He's probably getting hungry and then will need a nap."

"I'll feed him," Sadie said before Eric suggested anything else. "We're waiting for some information to come in anyway."

"Sure, that would be great. I'll do some work while you're

gone. When Houston's ready for a nap, bring him down and he can stay with me so you can work."

"Thanks, Selina," Eric said with a pat to her shoulder. "I'll bring you some lunch too. How's everything coming along?"

"I've sent the information to Mina. If the father's DNA has been stored in a database, we'll know soon enough."

Sadie swallowed over the nervous bubble of fear that lodged in her throat. "I'm embarrassed to say that I think Kadie does know who Houston's father is and purposely kept me in the dark."

"There's nothing to be embarrassed about, Sadie," Eric said, resting his hand on her back. It was warm, and she focused on that rather than the fear spiraling through her. "You had no reason not to take Kadie at her word. You're a wonderfully supportive sister, and that's what you should focus on."

"He's right," Selina said, standing and handing her Houston's blanket. "Kadie may have been trying to protect you from the truth."

"That Victor Loraine is Houston's father?" she asked, and both Selina and Eric tipped their heads in acknowledgment. "That's my worry right now. Especially if he knows he's the father. A part of me wants that note to tell us he is the father, and part of me wants it to be something dumb about how much he adores Kadie and wants to be her boyfriend." She waved her hand in the air. "Or something meaningless to the investigation, I guess."

"Note?" Selina asked, glancing between them with confusion. Sadie couldn't be sure, but she swore she noticed a look of panic on Selina's face when she'd mentioned Victor's name.

"Lucas and Sadie were watching the footage from the

apartment building. About three days ago, Victor Loraine showed up and shoved a note under the door," Eric said to fill her in. "We're waiting for the apartment manager to get the note and take a picture for us."

"Which means a Loraine is still in your lives. And no one knows you're here, right?" Selina asked. Sadie noticed a tremble at the end of the sentence and she glanced at Eric in confusion, but he was dialed into Selina and not paying her any attention.

"No one," Sadie repeated immediately. "I don't even have a phone or any way to contact the outside world. Well, I guess the apartment manager knows I'm still around, but he's sending the information to my regular email, not the Secure One email, and I called from the untraceable phone."

"Good," Selina said with a jerky nod. Sadie could see the relief flow through her. "You'd better get the baby fed before the note arrives."

There was no question that Selina was dismissing them, so she nodded and left the med bay with Eric's hand resting at the small of her back. She grabbed on to the sensation of warmth that it offered and focused on it. She didn't want to need this man, but the longer she remained at Secure One, the more she wanted him.

The kitchen was empty when they walked in, and she flipped Houston to her hip and opened the fridge. "We're out of baby food," she said over her shoulder. "It might be eggs again."

"Give him to me," Eric said, pulling Houston from her arms and holding him against his chest so he could see what she was doing. "Now you don't have to work one-handed."

"Thanks." She smiled at his thoughtfulness—and at the way he looked holding a baby. He was a big, bad security operative until you put a baby in his arms. The baby softened him and made him approachable as a person rather than a guard.

"You're welcome, and we're not out of baby food." He pointed at the counter where jars were stacked. "Mina had more baby food and formula delivered this morning. They also dropped off a high chair. We want him safe while he's here."

"Bless her," Sadie said, her hand to her heart as she shut the door and grabbed some jars. "I was wondering what I was going to do when I ran out."

"Now you don't have to worry. Houston won't suffer for something that isn't his fault. It's not your fault either."

She shrugged as she made his bottle. "Maybe not, but I still feel as though we're putting everyone out here. Maybe I shouldn't feel that way, but I do."

She shook the bottle until it was mixed and then handed it to him. "He will drink some of that while I make his food."

She watched as Eric handed Houston the bottle and he sucked at it hungrily, his hand patting the bottle as he lay cradled in Eric's arms.

"Do you see your family often?" she asked, smiling at her nephew as he hummed with happiness.

"No. They didn't support my choice to join the military."

"No offense, but that's kind of a crappy thing to do to someone you love."

"Offense taken," he said with a smirk, and she grimaced. "People always say that as a precursor to something that's true but pointed. You're correct though. I still talk to one of my brothers and one of my sisters. My parents are already gone, so at least they don't have to watch the destruction of the family unit at my expense."

"Not really," she argued, spooning baby food into a bowl to warm it. "They're using you as an example in a twisted, misaligned way. You aren't the enemy and didn't start the war."

"True, but my participation in it made me the enemy in their eyes. Especially after…"

She spun and waited for him to answer, but when he didn't, she raised a brow. "Especially after what, Eric?"

She waited, but the only thing she heard was silence.

Chapter Eleven

Sadie remained quiet, hoping that he'd finish his thought, but he didn't. The longer he gazed at Houston, the paler he became. She couldn't decide if she was seeing a ghost or if he was channeling one.

He stroked Houston's leg absently, his breath heavy in his chest. She was about to speak when he did. "I'm sure you noticed that we all have battle scars?" She nodded but didn't speak. "There was a mission. We were moving a diplomat's family to a safe house. Mack was with the family, Cal and Roman in the lead car, and myself and a gunner in the rear. I'm sorry—I don't talk about this. Ever."

She stopped his hand from caressing Houston's leg. "I didn't ask you to talk about it, Eric. You don't have to show me your demons for me to trust you."

He glanced up and captured her gaze, then flipped his hand until he was holding hers. "Mack keeps telling me to talk about it more to help it fade. Lucas says I should get a dog like Haven so I have something else to concentrate on."

"What do you believe?" she asked quietly. "That's what matters more than anything."

"I believe that people died that day for no reason," he answered, his eyes flashing angrily. "People were injured for no reason. Cal almost lost his hand. Mack can't walk without braces, and I can't hear a thing without these pieces of plastic." His words were growled and angry. Houston looked up, and his tiny hand patted Eric's chest twice as though he alone could comfort him.

"I'm sorry that you had to go through that, and still have to deal with it, when it wasn't your war to fight."

"We were supposed to save that family, but we didn't. We didn't," he said with a shrug, dropping her hand to stroke Houston's leg again. "We didn't save them, and it ended our careers in the military. In hindsight, I'm glad I got out, but I would have preferred it had been on my own terms."

"I'm sure every disabled veteran feels the same way." She leaned her hip on the counter and held his gaze. "But you know you were never going to save them, right? If the terrorists wanted them dead, there was no stopping them. Unfortunately you were in the way of them completing their mission."

He pointed his finger at her and then let it drop back to Houston's leg. "Cal, Roman and I know that without question. It took Mack much longer to understand that he wasn't to blame. I get it. He drove the car and felt responsible for them but still couldn't change or stop it. Charlotte helped him see that in the end he saved a lot of lives by what he did do."

"I'm not going to say *no offense* because you will take offense at this without a doubt. You still harbor a lot of anger about it, right?"

"We all do. We always will. What happened might fade into the background of our lives, but it will always be there. We will always carry the ghosts of the people we lost. That comes with the territory of being special ops for the military. Will I always be angry about it? Yes. I accepted that

I could end up on the battlefield when I joined the special ops team. I accepted that I could end up dead. I can't accept that a little boy died a horrible death and I couldn't stop it. Do you know what I see every night when I close my eyes?"

She shook her head, but didn't speak, hoping he'd pour out some of his anger for her to carry.

"I see his tiny leg," Eric whispered, his fingers gripping Houston's leg again. "It came out of the door." His voice was choked when he lowered his arm to imitate what he'd seen. "This tiny, innocent leg sticking out of the door, and then just a ball of flames. That little leg is burned in my memory forever as the symbol of an unwinnable war with tragic consequences that were too high. I lie in bed at night in silence, but in my head, I hear it all again."

"I'm sorry," she said, remembering not to whisper or he wouldn't hear her. "I'm sorry I can live in total oblivion because you can't."

He tipped his head in confusion as he straightened Houston in his arms. "I don't understand."

"I was here when you were there. You saw things over there that I'm oblivious to because you waded into that battle. I'm free to walk around and live my life." She paused and shook her head. "Well, you know what I mean. You carry the horrific memories of freedom so I don't have to."

His breath escaped in a whoosh, and he held Houston closer as though he was taking comfort from the tiny being in his arms. "I honestly never thought of it that way."

"You should," she said, resting her hand on Houston's belly. "He's safe and happy with food in his tummy because you held the line for him without ever knowing him. To me, that's a hero. That's selflessness I don't have within me. You carry burdens you shouldn't have to, but you do it so Houston and I don't know the horror of war firsthand."

"And I would never want you to," he said, holding her gaze. "Ever. Not you, my nieces or nephews, or even my siblings who think I'm the enemy."

"It's gotten worse, hasn't it?" she asked, and the look in his eye told her she was correct. "Since Houston got here, I mean. The memories have been harder to suppress."

"The boy who died, he was older than Houston but just as innocent. That leg…" he said, only a puff of air coming out as he stroked Houston's tiny foot. "I just… I need to stop seeing that leg."

"I wish I could carry that memory for you, Eric. I can't, but I can make sure that Houston doesn't make it worse. Give him to me."

"No," he said, tightening his arm in the cradle where he held her nephew. "While he's made the memories more frequent, I think in a way he's also offering me a chance to heal from it. I don't know if that even makes sense." He gazed up at her from under his brows, and she nodded slowly.

"He's giving you a second chance to keep a child safe from harm."

"I need that second chance," he agreed, a small smile on his face as he tickled Houston's belly. "I need to prove to myself that my ears don't override my instincts."

"Your ears?" Sadie put the food in the microwave and waited for him to answer.

"When you go from sound to silence in the blink of an eye, you struggle to compensate for it with your other senses."

"I can't pretend to understand," she said, stirring the baby's food. "If it matters, I think you do an excellent job of communicating. I'm sure that's little comfort when you're the one who deals with the frustration of communication every day." She took Houston from his arms and fit him into the high chair, where she spilled some cereal onto the tray for him to eat. "Maybe instead of compensating for the loss of your hearing, you should use it to your advantage."

"Maybe you don't know anything about it," he growled.

She heard the offense in his words, and she held up her hand. "I'm not saying I do, Eric. It was only a suggestion and not meant to upset you. I care about you, and knowing that you live in a state of frustration makes me sad."

"You care about me?" he asked, watching her spoon sweet potatoes into Houston's mouth. "We've only known each other a few days."

"The length of time we've known each other doesn't preclude me from caring about you, Eric. You're a good man with a kind heart. You're dedicated to helping people, which is something few people can say these days. I'm forever grateful to you for taking the risk of protecting me and Houston when you didn't have to."

"You're innocent, and we'll prove it," he said, his words gentler now. "For the record, I care about you and Houston." He fell silent as she fed the baby, his happy squeals and babble filling the empty kitchen. "Just out of curiosity," he finally said, "how would I use being deaf to my advantage?"

"In a way, you already do it. You just need to decide it's an advantage instead of a disadvantage."

"Which is?"

"Lipreading," she answered, wiping Houston's face and kissing his cheek. "You see it as a necessary evil right now rather than a skill the other men don't have." She motioned at the door behind him. "Efren didn't know that the guy in the car said the words *Winged Templar*. You were the only one there with the skill to see that. Do you see what I'm saying?"

He was silent for a long time but finally nodded. "I never thought of it that way. I do have that advantage when my position allows it."

"You're good at multitasking with it too. I've watched you the last couple days and noticed your gaze is always tracking other people in the room. You're always taking in other conversations by reading their lips."

"True," he agreed, lifting Houston from the chair while she washed off the tray. "That's an interesting take on it. I'll think about how to incorporate it. You're observant, Sadie."

Her shrug was nonchalant, but on the inside, she was cheering that they'd had a breakthrough. "I try—"

"Secure one, Whiskey." The black box on Eric's belt crackled with Mina's voice.

He grabbed it and held the button down. "Secure two, Echo."

"Conference room in five," Mina said. "We have the letter, and you'll want to see it."

"Ten-four. Echo out." He stuck the box back on his belt and shifted Houston to his hip as he raised a brow. "Ready to take one step closer to finding your sister?"

She set the towel down and took a deep breath before she followed him out of the kitchen. Like it or not, she was going to learn what her sister was hiding. If it helped them find her, then she'd swallow her embarrassment in front of the team and do anything to bring her back to Houston. As she followed Eric back to the med bay, she couldn't help but think how good he looked with a baby in his arms. She watched the muscles of his back ripple as he shifted his load, and she wondered what they would feel like under her hands as he lifted her and carried her to his bed.

Her eyes closed, and she shook her head—*Focus, Sadie, and not on the man before you. Your sister is in danger, and you are being accused of an atrocity you didn't commit.*

She heard the internal chastising and made note of it, but the man she followed was too enigmatic to ignore. She wanted to know what made him tick, and that drew her to him like a moth to a flame. Sadie was sure she'd get burned, but in the end, the pain would be worth it.

Chapter Twelve

The conference room lacked most of the big players when Eric walked in. It was just Lucas and Mina waiting for them, which told Eric things were about to get real. Sadie had been quiet since they'd left the med bay, but he supposed he had been too. Every time they talked, this tiny woman gave him too many big things to grapple with in his mind. It almost felt to him like she could see inside him and read the list of people and events that haunted him. It freaked him out if he was honest, but he didn't have time to fixate. There were steps to follow in this investigation, and none of them included kissing Sadie Cook. He had to keep his mind on the steps. Learn what Vic Loraine knew, apply it to find the missing mother, bring her home and move Sadie out of Secure One and his head for good. His inner demons laughed. Fat chance of that ever happening. He'd have to try though.

"Mina, Lucas," Eric said as they walked in. "Where is everyone? I thought we were having a meeting."

"Cal and Efren will be down shortly. Everyone else is tied up with other clients."

"Should we call Elliott and see if he's available for extra work?" Eric asked.

Mina tossed her head back and forth a few times. "That's

not a bad idea. Maybe we could have him take over a couple of our clients closer to him. Let me talk to Cal."

"Who's Elliott?" Lucas asked, glancing between them.

"He's one of our guys who installs and maintains security systems closer to the border," Eric answered.

"Of Wisconsin?"

"Canada," Mina said to clarify. "He's near International Falls. He hadn't worked here long when an old friend needed help in his hometown of Winterspeak. He went up to help her develop a security plan for her tree farm, but—"

"They fell in love," Lucas said with a groan. "Why does that always happen here?"

Mina's laughter filled the room. "Well, in fairness, they had been best friends through high school, so it wasn't completely unexpected. Anyway, he helps Jolene on the tree farm and with their new baby but has stayed on the payroll. I'll talk to Cal about reaching out to him. If he's interested, it might be a good way to take some of the everyday strain off our shoulders for clients he's closer to."

"I'm sorry this is taking up resources and adding strain to the already thin staff," Sadie said, lowering herself into the chair. "Maybe you should just turn me over to the chief in Bemidji. All I request is that you keep Houston until I'm released again."

"No." The word left his lips without conscious thought. "That's not going to happen. Don't worry about our team. We've proved time and again we're strong enough to handle the most ruthless criminals. Protecting a baby and his aunt is like a cakewalk for us."

"He's right," Lucas said, pointing at Eric. "We got you and Houston. We'll keep you safe until your name is cleared. You can trust Secure One. Just ask Mina."

Mina nodded at that statement—she'd been the one to steer Secure One into the personal-protection arena they'd gotten so good at in the last few years. Lucas patted Haven to settle the dog on the floor. "If we turn you over to the police, you could end up in jail, where you're vulnerable to the person who set you up in the first place. Eating a bullet for something you didn't do isn't fair, so it's not going to happen."

Eric motioned at Lucas before he sat. "What he said. Besides, we're up to our neck in this case as Fettering's security team." He turned to Mina. "Have you found anything on the Winged Templar yet?"

"No, but," she said, holding up her finger, "I am layers deep into the organization now. I have a good feeling that I'm getting to the bottom of it. From what I can see, the mob bosses of their different divisions, which is what they call their regions, use code names. Makes sense, right?"

"Generally speaking," Eric agreed. "If they have a code name, it's so no one knows their real one."

Mina pointed at him. "Which means we'll always be one piece short of a full puzzle, but if I can build the rest of the picture around that missing piece, we might be able to find the Winged Templar's image and then run that through facial recognition."

"You're saying it's nearly impossible," Sadie said with a shake of her head.

"Nearly, yes, but not completely. There are ways—I just need a bit more time."

"Take all the time you need," Cal said, walking into the room with Lucas. "We're not sharing the name with the cops anyway. Do we have an update?"

"Yes," Mina said, grabbing a remote and aiming it at the

projector. "We have the note that Vic left for Kadie. I'm going to warn you, Sadie, the revelations in the note are jarring."

Sadie set her jaw. "I'm prepared for anything."

With a nod, Mina flipped the note up on the screen and started to read aloud. "'Kadie, are you avoiding me? Did I do something wrong? I love having you and Houston with me at night, but I haven't been able to reach you for days. I'm scared that you've taken Houston away from me but also scared you weren't given a choice. I love you, Kadie. I love our son. I want nothing more than to be a family with our baby boy. I know you're still scared about my family, and I hope they aren't the reason that you left, both figuratively and literally. Please, if you get this note, at least let me know you're okay. I love you. Vic.'"

The room was silent as Sadie stared at the note. Eric could tell she was trying to process all of the information and stay detached from it at the same time.

"Essentially, he knows his family is capable of making someone disappear," Eric said, his tone angry.

"No," Sadie said. "He knows his older brother is capable of making someone disappear because he's all that's left of his family now."

"Unless their father is pulling the strings from prison," Cal pointed out. "He was one of Vaccaro's top guys before he got pinched."

"Also a possibility," Mina said. "I'll put my ear to the ground on that one."

"Maybe Vic warned Kadie about his family and what they were capable of and it spooked her," Lucas suggested. "Maybe she did take off in the hopes of protecting Houston, you and Vic?"

Sadie shook her head immediately. "No, she wouldn't do

that. I know I've said that before and been wrong, but I'm not about this. She was taken. We already have evidence to prove she didn't leave by choice. Now we need to figure out where she is."

"We need to talk to Victor," Cal said, motioning at the note. "He doesn't come right out and say it, but it gives me the impression that he knows there are reasons why someone would go after Kadie."

Sadie spun on him and stuck her finger in his chest. "You promised! You promised we wouldn't contact the father."

Her growl was cute, but he didn't laugh or smile. He just wrapped his hand around her finger and held her gaze, closing out everyone else around them. "That was when we thought the father didn't know Houston existed. Clearly that's not the case." He motioned at the note still up on the screen. "The man knows Houston is his son, and he's worried about them. Yes, we need to talk to him to find out what he knows, but we also need to let him know his son is safe. That's the very least we can do."

Eric noticed Mina grab her tablet and start punching buttons. "What's up, Mina?"

She popped her head up. "Before I came down, I started running Houston's DNA against the samples we have from the Loraines." She turned the tablet around for them to see. "I just got a hit. Randall Loraine Senior is not excluded as the grandfather of Houston and has a 99.998% likelihood of being the paternal grandfather. Likely, a son of Randall Loraine Senior is the father of the sample submitted and the results support the biological relationship. That combined with the note is enough for me to call him the biological father of Houston Cook."

"Me too," Eric said with a nod as he rested a hand on Sadie's shoulder. "I know that's not what you wanted, Sadie, but we have to play the hand we're dealt."

She rested her forehead in her palm and sighed. "It's not that I don't want Kadie to be happy or Houston to have a father if they've found a life with Victor. If Victor Loraine is his father, then Kadie is in real danger and Houston could become a pawn in a dangerous game."

"Agreed. That's why we need to pull this guy in and talk to him," Cal said, leaning on the table. "He could have information about where they may have taken Kadie."

Sadie motioned at the note still up on the board. "Clearly not. If he knew where she was, he wouldn't have left that note."

"Cal means he may not know he has the information," Eric patiently explained. "When asked the right questions, he may provide an answer that even he didn't know he had."

She worked her jaw around and finally nodded. "Okay. I follow that train of thought. He knows his family better than anyone, so he's a valuable resource. Let's pull him in and have a chat."

"Not here," Cal said. "I don't want a Loraine to know where my property sits—right side of the law or not."

"That's smart," Eric agreed. "We need a neutral location, and we're not bringing the baby."

"Then he may not come," Sadie jumped in. "He's going to want to see Houston."

"When he pats our back, we'll pat his." Cal set his tablet down on the table and leaned over it. "I'd rather keep the baby tucked away with Selina here. If we take him out, there's a chance that whoever took Kadie tries to grab him. We could be under surveillance since they know we're Fettering's security."

"I didn't think of that." Sadie chewed on her lip. "How are we going to convince Victor to meet with us if we can't bring Houston?"

Eric straightened his shoulders before he spoke. "His brother just died, right?" Cal and Efren nodded, then waited for him to finish. "We contact him as the security team for Dirk Fettering. We tell him his brother had a storage unit at Dirk's place and we need his help to open it and clear it out."

"I'm listening," Cal said, sitting on the edge of the table and crossing his arms.

"We lure him to a unit that will serve as a meeting space. We bring a video of Houston playing happily but with no identifying features of his location."

"I like it." Cal pointed at Sadie. "Take her, or leave her here?"

"Pros and cons?" Eric asked, glancing at Efren and Mina.

"Excuse me, but *her* is right here," Sadie said with enough force to own the room. "There are no pros and cons. I'm going. He knows I'll always protect my sister and nephew. If I'm there, he'll talk."

"She's not wrong," Eric said, lifting a brow at Cal.

"She's not, but it's about moving her safely. It's ninety minutes to Bemidji. That's a lot of exposed time, even if she's hidden in the back of a van. It's risky since we don't know if someone is watching us."

"We take mobile command." Eric waited for Cal's reaction and noticed his lips pull into a tight line.

"Still risky."

"Roman and I will leave at the same time in a distraction car," Mina said. "We can even put a baby seat in the back as added incentive." She glanced over at Sadie for a moment. "With a wig and a hat, I could be Sadie from a car length away."

Efren nodded. "Absolutely. I'll drive a follow car just in case they're approached. Once you're at Fettering's, we'll circle the wagons back here and decide what kind of manpower you need there."

Cal raised his hands in the air and let them drop. "All right, let's do it. Who's going to call Vic?"

"I'll do it," Eric said. "Since I'm running point on the team at Dirk's."

"Good. Line him up. We'll get you a fake contract for a storage unit in Howie's name while you get ready to roll."

Eric held up his finger. "I'm rethinking this. How quickly can Marlise get me that contract?"

"Minutes. Why?"

"We should have mobile command in place before I reach out to him. We need to be on-site so if he shows up immediately, we're there. If he asks anyone else about the unit, he's going to learn there isn't one."

"I see your point," Cal said. "Be ready to roll in thirty?"

"I need to check on Houston," Sadie said as she jumped up from her seat.

"A fast check, and then get a bag packed. We won't be back until tomorrow at the earliest. Be prepared to stay longer," Eric instructed.

"But Houston…"

"Will be fine with me and Selina," Mina assured her, squeezing her hand. "We'll be his stand-in aunts and take good care of him. Remember, you're leaving him here for his safety but you're going so you can bring his mother home to him, right?"

Sadie nodded, and after a smile and a thank-you, she headed to the med bay.

"Do you think she's ready for this?" Mina asked.

Eric stared out the door for a moment before he turned back to his team. "I don't know Sadie that well, but I do know one thing—she would do anything for her sister and that baby. She'll roll with the punches like a pro because she's motivated to bring her family back together."

Cal tapped the table. "Let's try to keep the punches to a minimum this time around." He grabbed his tablet and walked to the door. "I'll get everyone else updated. See you in the garage in thirty. Charlie out."

Eric glanced at Efren and shook his head. "Keeping the punches to a minimum will be easier said than done."

Chapter Thirteen

Sadie paced around the small office in the back of mobile command. Any minute now, Vic would knock on the door to the RV. When that happened, she could no longer deny the truth. Houston was a Loraine, and that meant one thing for her little family—danger. With her sister still missing, Sadie knew that to be the absolute truth. They had to find Kadie, and if they had to use Victor Loraine to do it, so be it. Her mind immediately flew to the worst-case scenario—finding Kadie dead. The thought sent a shiver down her spine, and she lowered herself to the couch to rest her stressed-out body.

"You can't think that way. Kadie is alive and waiting—no, depending on you to find her." She said it aloud as though that might manifest it into being.

They had to find her because there was no way she'd be able to turn Houston over to his father and walk away. Anger bubbled up inside her. Anger at Kadie for not telling her the truth about Houston's father when they'd had a chance to work through it together. What did she think Sadie was going to do? Disown her?

Sadie's shoulders slumped forward, and she forced herself to face the truth. Kadie had been protecting her. She was the older sister, and she always tried to keep Sadie safe. If she knew Victor's family was dangerous, she would keep whatever secrets she had to in order to protect her sister.

The knock sounded loud on the RV door, and Sadie stood instantly, fear rocketing through her. She had to face Vic and tell him the truth about where his son was. Eric would be beside her, but getting a lead on where Kadie might be would be up to her. Vic had to trust her before he'd trust Secure One. If he didn't trust Secure One enough to tell them his family's secrets, they had no hope of finding Kadie. Sadie focused on the goal and forced everything else from her mind. She had to play this exactly right if they were going to find her sister. That meant sharing Houston with his father, and she hoped Vic would sacrifice just as much to keep him safe.

She could hear murmuring in the central part of mobile command. The two bedrooms had been soundproofed to allow better sleep for the operatives who weren't on shift. She glanced around the office she stood in, which was about the size of a closet but had been optimized for Cal's disability. The computer equipment and setup made everything accessible when he wasn't wearing his prosthesis. The sofa against the other wall opened into a bed, though she couldn't picture a guy the size of Cal sleeping on it.

The core team dynamic of Secure One was unique. Cal, Roman, Eric and Mack had all served on the same special ops Army Military Police team for years before being injured together on a mission. They anticipated each other's weak points and made sure they were filled so everything went along like clockwork. The men were all different, but they all had one thing in common: integrity. Her own experience told her that. Before the accident, Eric had only met her for a brief snapshot in time, but he refused to let her face any of this alone. That said something to her.

There was a knock on the door, and then Eric said the phrase she'd been waiting for. "Time for a chat," his deep voice said, and she inhaled a breath, steeling herself for what was to come.

Sadie grabbed the door handle, blew out her breath and pushed it open to come face-to-face with the man she had come to rely on in just a few short days. It wasn't a hero-worship thing either. They had a profound connection that she couldn't explain. She was drawn to him, and when they were together, Eric made her feel like everything would be okay. And not just about Kadie and Houston, but for her. There was an emotional connection she had never experienced before—and wasn't sure she ever would again.

She'd been with several men, some longer than others, but none of them had made her feel the way Eric did with a simple look or brush of his hand against her back. He made her feel like she was the most crucial person in the room and he would do anything to keep her safe. When he looked at her, his expression said he'd do anything for her, but Sadie knew the truth—the one thing Eric wouldn't do was consider a relationship with her.

She flashed back to the story of what had happened the day he'd lost his hearing. He still hadn't come to terms with it, and until he did—and accept how it had changed his life—he never would. Until he learned how to move his life forward while carrying that burden, there would never be room in his heart for anyone else. In fairness, he carried the atrocities of too much war and the faces of too many who he couldn't save, so learning to live again with those souls now part of him might be too much to ask.

"Ready?" he asked, grasping her shoulder in a sign of solidarity and strength.

"As I'll ever be."

Eric led her down the hallway to the front of mobile command that housed their complicated visual command center. Vic sat in a chair, his elbows braced on his thighs and his hands folded together as though he were praying. She took a split second to take in his side profile. He was different from the other Loraine brothers. He wasn't all muscle and hard lines. He was young, wore a baby face like none she'd ever seen before and had a dad bod before he even knew he was a dad. There was something about him that was genuine and honest though. Sadie could understand why her sister had been drawn to him.

"Sadie!" Vic said, jumping from the chair and running to her. He had wrapped his arms around her before Eric could even move. "I'm so glad you're okay! What are you doing here? Have you seen Kadie? Where is Houston? Why are they saying you killed my brother? You didn't, right?" he asked as he took a step back.

"Of course not!" Sadie exclaimed. "I don't even know your brother. I didn't even know your name until they figured out your real identity."

He held up his hands in defense. "I wasn't saying that you did kill my brother. I'm just so confused right now. Hold on a minute—Howie doesn't have a storage unit here, does he?"

"No," Eric answered. "But we needed to talk to you without tipping off anyone else in your family."

"Which means you know about my family."

"It would be hard not to," Sadie said. "But we're not here about your family. We're here about my family."

"Your family is now my family, Sadie. I love Kadie. Before she disappeared, we were putting together a plan to be a family somewhere away from the tentacles of the Loraine dynasty. She was going to talk to you about it as soon as we had everything in place, I swear. Do you know where she is?"

"We were hoping you could tell us that," Eric said.

"If I knew where she was, don't you think I would have gone to her by now? I've been worried sick! Does she have my son with her?"

"No," Sadie answered quickly. "I have Houston."

"Is he here? I want to see him!" Vic demanded.

Eric stepped between them. "Houston is tucked away safely and well cared for. Right now, we need to focus on where his mother is and how to get her back to him. Once we do that, you can see your son."

Vic glanced between them in defiance for a moment but finally relented. "I've had a bad feeling in the pit of my stomach since she missed our usual nightly visit. What happened, Sadie?"

She ran him through what had happened the day Kadie had disappeared and the events that had transpired since. "We have no idea where she is, Vic. Once we discovered that you're Houston's father, you were our only hope of finding a lead to follow."

Vic slowly lowered himself back to the chair and rubbed his forehead. "The first night she didn't show up at our apartment, I thought she just needed time to think." He turned to face them, and Sadie noticed the look on his face was part rapture and part pain. "I asked her to marry me the night before she disappeared."

"And what did she say?" Sadie asked.

"Yes, but that was followed by an immediate question about how my family would be involved."

"Why was she worried about how your family would be involved?" Eric asked.

"She was worried they were going to come after Houston once they found out he was a Loraine. Let's not split hairs here—we all know who my father is and who he worked for. Let it be said that Loraines raise Loraines no matter what."

"Even so," Sadie cautiously said, "you're a Loraine. If you and Kadie are together, then a Loraine is raising Houston. Why would that be a problem?"

Victor rubbed his palms on his pants for a moment, and Sadie noticed his Adam's apple bob before he spoke. "The problem is I'm not just the black sheep of the family—I've been disowned. And as far as my family is concerned, I don't exist as a Loraine anymore."

"Our intel indicates you aren't involved in the family business. Either the legal or illegal one," Eric said. "Is that accurate?"

"Accurate to a *T*," Vic promised. "I've had nothing to do with my family since my father was arrested and put in prison. I didn't have much to do with them before that either. When my mom died, I lost the only person who defended me in that family. I didn't know exactly what my dad was doing, but I knew he was working for The Snake. It wasn't hard to figure out that it wasn't on the right side of the law. Once I left for college, I never looked back. I'll work sixty hours a week if I have to just to make sure every penny that I earn is honest."

"Yet despite all that, my sister is still in danger because she chose to be with you. It's easy to understand why she was worried being with you would be dangerous for Houston."

"But nobody else should know that Houston is my son!" he exclaimed, standing from the chair.

Eric made the *calm down* motion with his hands. "We understand your frustration, Vic. We're all stressed, but we have to approach this in a logical manner. Is it possible your family is responsible for Kadie's disappearance?"

Sadie noticed he had asked the question deliberately, as though his precision would net them the answer they desperately needed.

"Absolutely. There isn't a doubt in my mind."

"Okay, second question. Assuming they're the ones who have her, would they set up Sadie to take the fall for your brother's death just to get their hands on Houston?"

"Why do you think I sent that note to your work? I didn't know if you were with Kadie, but I was worried you were in danger. I remembered Kadie saying you worked for Fettering, so I sent the note just in case you were still in town." Vic put his hands on his hips. "My family would literally do anything you could conjure up in your mind, and worse, to remain in favor with Vaccaro. Do I think that they would try to steal Houston away from me? Absolutely. That's why I rented an apartment under an assumed name just so I could see Kadie and my son."

"Despite all of that, my sister is still missing."

"Sadie got the note," Eric said, his jaw ticking, "and she ran with Houston. Someone followed her and ran her off the road."

"Luckily I ended up on Secure One property. I don't know where I'd be if I hadn't."

"You'd be dead," Vic said, his words defeated. "You and Kadie would both be dead, and my son would be in the hands of evil. Thankfully they failed to bring you and the baby to Randall Junior that night. That means Kadie's still alive. We have to find her. I don't want Houston to grow up without a mother. We have to find her, and then we have to take Kadie and Houston somewhere safe. Somewhere my family and Vaccaro can never find them or hurt them again."

"How do you know that Kadie is still alive?" Eric asked, taking a step forward to put himself between Vic and Sadie.

"She's still alive because you have Houston. Until they have the baby, they won't kill her. They might need her for leverage. I should have known this would happen. I wanted Kadie and Houston in my life, and I didn't take enough precautions. We should have left town immediately. That's on me. Truthfully I don't know why it matters so much that I have a son. I never had anything to do with Vaccaro. He doesn't even know who I am."

"Oh, don't fool yourself," Sadie said, her hands in fists at her sides. "Vaccaro knows everything about you, right down to your underwear size. He knows what you do, where you go and who you see. Why? Randall Senior was running one of Vaccaro's biggest operations. Just because your father is in prison doesn't mean you're not being watched. In fact, they probably saw you come here tonight!"

"I—I should have considered that," Vic said. "Did I just put everyone in more danger?"

"No," Eric said stepping in and placing a hand on Sadie's shoulder. She tried to concentrate on the warmth it offered while she took some deep breaths. "Your brother was found on this property, and if anyone looks, they'll find a contract between him and Dirk for a storage unit. They'll also see that I called you to come look at the unit."

"So, what happens now? How do we find Kadie while we keep Houston safe?"

"When you leave here tonight, you're going to call Randall Junior. You'll request an audience with him," Eric instructed. "You'll insist you need to see him tomorrow, and when you're in the house, you're going to look for any possible evidence that your brother has Kadie."

Vic took several steps back until he bumped into the command console. "I haven't been in that house in over twelve years. I have no intention of breaking that streak. Think of a new plan."

"Not even if you could save my sister's life?" Sadie demanded.

He shrunk back, his eyes filling with tears. "I'm sorry— you're right. It's just that I wasn't made the same way my brothers were. I'm not good at deception and games. I'll do anything for Kadie though, and that includes taking on my own family."

"Good," Eric said with a head nod. "As long as you're in, Secure One will keep you safe. Are you ready for a fast lesson in how to be an operative?"

Vic stiffened his shoulders and pushed his chest forward. "Where do we start?"

Eric turned to Sadie and grasped her shoulders gently. "Are you okay with this?"

He asked the question as though there was no one in the room but them. As though nothing mattered more than her answer.

"Just like Vic, I'll do anything I have to do to save my family," she said.

"Even when it scares you?"

"Especially when it scares me."

Her answer brought a smile to his lips, and he gently chucked her under the chin, his thumb caressing her jaw as his hand fell away. "That's because you're a warrior."

Eric turned away to address Vic, but Sadie didn't notice. She was too busy replaying the way his touch had left trails of heat along her jaw and the way his kindness with her and Vic touched her heart. Eric Newman was becoming less of a mystery she needed to solve and more the man she wanted in her life with every passing second.

Chapter Fourteen

"I can't believe I left a defenseless baby alone." Sadie paced the small hallway as though every step would bring her closer to Houston.

"You didn't leave him defenseless. He's with trained operatives, one who also happens to be a nurse."

"I know, I know," she muttered, rubbing her forehead. "I'm still trying to wrap my head around Kadie having a second life that I knew nothing about, Eric. It's not something I ever thought she'd keep from me. What did she think was going to happen if she told me she was in love with Vic? None of it makes sense."

"It does make sense," Eric said gently. "Kadie was protecting you."

"I'm sorry," she said, as she turned to face him. "Kadie had months to get used to the fact that Vic was a Loraine, now I'm left to play catch-up while trying to keep it together for Houston's sake. He's coming here tomorrow?"

"That's the plan," Eric agreed. "Cal will bring him and the rest of the team. Selina will monitor mobile command and help you with Houston. When Vic is done at the homestead, he will come here and let us know if he saw any sign of Kadie. We'll be monitoring him the entire time he's inside the Loraine mansion too. If he hits on anything, we'll know immediately."

"I wish we didn't have to wait until morning."

"Me too, but we have to protect Houston. I want to make sure we're safe here before they bring him."

"The mansion," she said, as she started pacing again. "Only Randall Junior lives there now, correct?"

"Now that Howie is dead, yes, besides the hired help. Vic hasn't lived there since he left for college. When his father was arrested, he never went back. That decision probably saved his life. If he had returned home, he could have been dragged into Vacarro's shenanigans without even knowing it."

"Don't get me wrong," Sadie said, turning to make eye contact with him. "I'm glad that Kadie found Vic and not one of the other Loraine boys. Vic loves my sister and his son—I can see that when he talks about them. I may not like that she kept secrets from me, but I also understand why she did it."

"She's the big sister. It's her job to protect you," he said with a nod.

"True, at least in her mind, but I don't have to like it." She started pacing again, and he snorted, the sound loud in the quiet space.

"I can't make you like it, but I can help you see it's time to accept it."

"That's going to be about as easy as me convincing you that the car bomb wasn't your fault."

He couldn't hide his sharp intake of breath. "That's not a fair comparison," he said through clenched teeth He hated that he couldn't hide the hurt that laced his words.

"I didn't intentionally mean to hurt you when I said that, Eric. I did though, and I apologize. I shouldn't have compared the two." She reached out to touch him, but he spun away from her.

He walked to the front of mobile command, where a panel of bulletproof sheeting closed off the cab and protected the team from unexpected attacks. The cameras on all four corners of the vehicle also gave them a bird's eye view of the area. They'd parked mobile command inside the gated storage-unit area, so they should be safe tonight. Dirk was reopening the units tomorrow for clients, but the security measures would be considerably tighter than in the past.

"During the day, I don't think about what happened. I'm busy enough that I can keep those memories at bay. It's only when I take my hearing aids off and lie down to sleep that the torment begins," Eric said. "Since you and Houston arrived, I haven't been able to keep those memories at bay during the day. It's overwhelming to get hit both day and night. I used to allow the memories to wash over me while in bed, as a way to make it through the next day. Now it's wave after wave all day and night. I'm always on edge and find it hard to relax."

She walked toward him, and he could feel her heat and energy as though he were a magnet and she was the metal. In a beat, her soft, warm hands caressed his back and then up over his shoulders in a pattern that relaxed him and put him on edge simultaneously.

"I'm sorry, Eric. We inserted ourselves into your life in a way that's uncomfortable and makes your life harder. That's not fair. I'll go back to Secure One and keep Houston there while you're here."

He turned, ready to agree. If he banished Sadie to Secure One, he wouldn't have to face the trust he saw in her eyes—trust that he would bring her sister home. If she wasn't here, he could force himself to work relentlessly, shoving the memories back where they belonged for another decade. Before he could speak, his lazy gaze ate her up head to toe. Dammit, how did she have so much power over him in such a short time? He didn't know the answer, but he knew she wasn't going anywhere. "I don't want you to go. It's not your fault that I can no longer control the memories. That's my fault. I refused to deal with what happened because I thought it would be easier to pretend it didn't happen. All that's gotten me is fourteen years of suffering. You brought it to a head in an irrefutable way, and that tells me my life needs to change. If I don't do something, it will eat me alive."

"Do you know how to do that?" Her question was soft and gentle, but it was also heavy and loaded. He struggled to answer it since he didn't know how.

"Maybe I'll take Lucas's advice and look for a service dog."

"For your PTSD, or to be your hearing guide dog?"

"Both?"

Sadie's smile brought one to his lips too. "If you take the question mark off that answer, it's a solid plan. Not that what I think matters. I think what you think is the only thing that matters."

"That was quite a sentence," he said with a chuckle. "I understood what you meant though. This is what I know—I've spent too many years trying to bury a ghost rather than exorcize its demon. I watched Cal and Mack go through it all while trying to pretend the same didn't apply to me. My learning curve is high, but the events of the last few days have leveled out the curve for me."

Sadie's laughter was soft when she nodded. "We all have to take our own path with things, Eric. If we aren't ready to make a change in our lives, it will never truly stick. It happens for each one of us at a different time and place in our lives. It's about having the wisdom to know when the time has come and grab onto whatever rope is dangling there for us to hold."

"Houston gave me the wisdom to see the time has come, but oddly enough, he was also the dangling rope," he said. "When I picked him up for the first time and stared into those little eyes, I realized he had his entire life ahead of him, and I didn't want anything to mar it. That's what I've been doing by pretending those people didn't mar a part of my life. They existed. They were real. Their trust was mine for just a hairsbreadth in time, but they weren't mine in being. It was because they belonged to someone else that we all suffered that day. No amount of wishing or denial will change that, right?"

"You're exactly right, Eric, but also, trying to face a situation like this head on without any help could make things worse. I'm worried about you," Sadie said, resting her hand on his chest.

"I wish I could benefit from talk therapy," he said, cupping her cheek to caress her chin with his thumb. "Unfortunately it never worked for me in the beginning."

"Maybe because you weren't ready to face it yet? Would trying again be worth the risk?"

"That's possible," he agreed. "Here's the thing—talking about it won't make it go away. PTSD doesn't go away. We all know that. Sometimes talking about it, keeping it all mixed up and frothy week after week, just makes it worse. I need to find better ways to cope so the memories slowly fade and become less tangible over time. From what Lucas tells me, Haven has helped him do that. He has something else to focus on when the memories overtake him. Haven is there to pull his focus back to the present immediately. That's why I was thinking about getting a dog that could help me with both my hearing disability and the PTSD."

The admittance forced a heavy breath from his chest, and he closed his eyes for a moment. "I wasn't expecting to have this conversation tonight, but the truth is it's the most important conversation I've had in years. You've only been part of my life for a short time, but you're the only person I could trust with the truth, Sadie. You're the only one I trust not to judge me."

"I would never judge you, Eric. It feels like I've known you—"

"Forever," they said in unison.

His gaze held hers, and what he saw in her blue eyes said they shared a connection neither had been expecting. He lowered his head until their lips were only a breath away. Rather than pull away, she closed the distance and brushed her sweet lips against his. His chest rumbled with pleasure, so she lifted herself onto her tiptoes and turned her head—permission to take the kiss further.

He cupped the back of her warm neck and pulled her against him until their bodies connected. Her heart pounded against his chest when she dropped her jaw and let his tongue take a tour over the roof of her mouth before it tangled with hers. He was sure his lungs would explode from lack of oxygen, but he didn't want to stop. He didn't want to break the spell. He didn't want to think about anything else when his lips were on hers. When his lips were on hers, he thought about what life might be like with her if he could take that leap of faith. Desperate for air, he ended the kiss but rested his forehead on hers.

"What is this connection between us?" The question was asked in desperation, as though she wouldn't live to the next minute without knowing the answer.

"I wish it made sense to me. If you're in the room, I can't help but react to you. I want to tell you things I've never told anyone else before. Being in a combat zone didn't scare me as much as my reaction to you has the last few days. I was prepared for a war zone. I wasn't prepared for you, Sadie Cook."

"I'm not staying. Maybe that's why?"

"No." One word that held fervent denial. "Because I want you to stay. For the first time in fourteen years, I want someone to stay. That in and of itself is…" He put his hands to his head and made the *mind blown* motion.

"I've never met anyone like you, Eric Newman. Maybe I can't explain the connection yet, but I do know that it has nothing to do with my situation and everything to do with who we are as individuals. The way you hold Houston, the way you take care of me and the way you sacrifice for your teammates tells me that you care. It tells me that you're protective but in a positive way. Growing up, we never had a father figure in our life," she said. "As an adult, I've realized that not having a male presence in my life has made it not only difficult to date but to know when I'm being taken advantage of. I've never been able to discern when someone likes me for me or when someone wants something from me. I never have to worry about that with you. You are you, and you are real all the time, no matter what is going on around you. I can trust you to keep me safe, but you're also teaching me how to love and be loved."

"Love?" he asked, a brow in the air.

"Figure of speech, but you know what I mean, right?" she asked, nervously flipping her hand around in the air.

He caught her hand and held it to his chest. "I do know what you mean, Sadie. I don't want you to think I'm making light of what you're saying because I'm not. I'm struggling to wrap my head around this too. What I see in your eyes when you look at me…it makes me want to be a better man. It makes me want to change the things that I can change and cope better with the things that I can't—"

Before he could finish the thought, her lips were on his. She owned the kiss in a demanding yet gentle way. She took his face in her hands and stroked his five-o'clock shadow tenderly, all while she kissed the lips right off him. When they broke for air again, she took his hand, turned and walked toward the bedroom. Enchanted by her beauty and confidence, all he could do was follow.

Chapter Fifteen

Sadie's heart was hammering in her chest as she walked through the bedroom door and he followed. What was she doing? This was so not her MO. She didn't have casual sex with men who she'd only known for three days.

But is this just casual sex? that voice asked. *Or is this going to be something more?*

She couldn't speak for Eric, but she knew in her heart it was something more. It was also something that likely would not end in her favor. Once they cleared her name and brought Kadie home, she would have to leave Secure One. It wasn't hard to see that none of the guys at Secure One had time to date. How could they when they were always working? Cal, Roman and Mack made it work because their significant other also worked at Secure One. Sadie didn't work there. She had to remember there was an end date on this thing between them. She could move forward and take everything from him until that day arrived, or she could play it safe and walk away from this now.

Eric slid his warm hands up her back to knead her neck. "Everything okay?" He leaned in to ask the question, his breath hot against her ear, running goose bumps down her back. The sensation told her that while none of this would last, she could enjoy a moment of pleasure during a time of uncertainty and fear.

"Everything's fine," she said. "I paused when I remembered we didn't have any protection."

His strong hands gently spun her around to face him. "You're serious about this?"

"I mean, only if you want to." She hated that he could hear the waver in her voice.

Without breaking eye contact, he pressed her hand to his groin. He didn't say a word, just lifted his brow.

"Well, hello, big fella," she purred, taking a tour of him until his breath hitched and he grasped her hand. "We still don't have protection."

"Oh, sweetheart, I'm always prepared." He held up a finger and darted to the med bay, returning with a handful of condoms.

"Looks like someone has plans. Did you buy a case?"

"Yes," he answered, walking toward her until the backs of her knees hit the bed.

"You get that much action in mobile command?"

"No." This time his answer was low and growly. "We use condoms for other things besides raincoats."

"Oh, really?" The question was more a breath than words. "Water balloons?"

He slid his hands up under her shirt from her waist to her ribs, gripping them gently. "Makeshift water canteens," he said, blowing lightly on her neck as his hands worked their way to the edges of her breasts. "Waterproof phone bags." His thumbs stroked her nipples until she lost track of the conversation. She wanted to touch him, so she ran her hands across his chiseled, warm chest and back down to his hips where she rested her hands. "Fire-starter protectors."

"They sound versatile."

"They are," he agreed, taking a nip of the skin across her collarbone before he kissed the same spot to wash away the pain. In one fluid motion, he pulled her shirt over her head and took a step back. "Gorgeous." His voice was low and filled with desire as he ate her up in her lacy bra. "Pretty bra, but it has to come off."

It was a flurry of hands as they tore their clothes off, throwing them into a pile on the floor. Barely naked, Eric was already kissing, sucking and tasting Sadie's skin in a slow but deliberate trail down her chest.

"If you're trying to turn me on, it's working," she moaned as he dipped his tongue into her navel.

When he raised his head, he fiddled with both hearing aids before he lifted her by the waist and set her on the bed.

Sadie grasped his face and trailed her thumbs over the tiny wires and down to the earpieces. "You can take your ears out if that's more comfortable."

"Take my ears out? Oh, no, darling, I was turning them up. I want to hear every moan and squeak you make as I make love to you."

With a smile she lowered herself to the mattress and crooked a finger at him until he followed her down. He kissed his way across her left breast and up her chest to her chin.

"I'm not very good at this," she said, her hands buried in his hair. "You could say my experience is advanced-beginner level."

Eric lifted his head to meet her gaze. "But you've been with a man before, right?"

"Yes. I just meant *experienced seductress* isn't one of my titles."

His laughter was loud in the room as he kissed his way back to her navel and dipped his tongue in to take a taste. The sensation covered her in goose bumps, and her hips bucked for what was to come. "I don't want an experienced seductress, Sadie." She spread her legs, and he moaned as he kissed his way down to her center. "You're already better at this than you think."

She hummed when he kissed his way up her thighs. "I'm still willing to learn."

"Then let me teach you how I make love to a woman," he murmured, setting his tongue on her swollen bud.

Sensations overtook her, and her hips bucked at the sweet, sweet torture he doled out until she couldn't stand it a minute longer. "Eric, I want you," she cried, pulling him to her mouth by his hair. "Please." The word was a begged prayer against his lips. She grasped him in her hand, and he pulsed hard against her grip. Captivated by the feel of him in her hand, she slowly rolled on the condom he'd handed her.

Once protected, he poised himself at her opening and grasped her face to make eye contact. "We're at the *no going back* moment. If we do this, there's no going back to the people we were yesterday."

"I don't want to go back, Eric. I want to go forward with you."

Permission granted, he entered her on a gentle thrust, and she cried out from the pure joy and pleasure of being complete. Something had been missing in her life all these years, and now she knew what it was—Eric. He was her destiny and always would be, regardless of how long they were together.

"God, Sadie." He sighed into her neck as he carried them both up to sit on a cloud of pleasure. "It's never been like this before."

"Eric," she moaned, her mind overflowing with so many emotions and sensations. "I want to take this leap with you."

With a guttural yes, he shifted and together they jumped into an oblivion where they could have a life together, if only for a moment in time.

ERIC WONDERED IF this was what it felt like to be a caged animal. He hated having to wait for someone else to do a job he could do faster and better. Except this time he couldn't, and the wait was killing him. It didn't help that Selina had arrived at mobile command before sunup with Houston—and with an attitude that grated on his last nerve.

To add to his living hell, he couldn't stop thinking about the woman he'd made love to for half the night. She was incredible, and he did not deserve her in any way, shape or form. He turned and noticed her bracketed in the doorway with the sun streaming in to highlight her golden hair. She rocked Houston side to side as he slept, occasionally kissing the top of his head. The scene was so sweet that it broke his heart. He knew he could never give her that life. She deserved a husband, two-point-five kids and a white picket fence. He couldn't offer her that. All he could offer was too much time away, too many memories that wouldn't go away and no chance of having babies with the job and lifestyle he lived.

Could he live a different lifestyle for her? The answer to that was complicated. He probably could, but what he would do he didn't know. He'd graduated high school and within two weeks had been at basic training. He'd been trained as a special ops police officer, but after losing his hearing, being a civilian cop was out. That was why he'd worked at Secure One since leaving the army. Secure One was safe. It was a place where everyone understood him and the things that he went through, but they also knew there was nothing he could do to change the things he'd brought back from the war.

To put it another way, they all carried the same ghosts. Those ghosts were stacked by the years, not months, that they'd done bad things to protect good people. It was hard for any civilians to grasp the magnitude of their service, both good and bad, but somehow Sadie did. She understood that he fought a battle every day even all these years later. Most people would jump ship and run, but Sadie had simply picked up a bucket and helped bail.

Sadie glanced up and met his gaze. She offered him a shy smile, and he turned away. He couldn't do this right now. He had to focus on her sister and bring her home safe. Then he had to free Sadie of this murder charge so she could go on with her life. The sooner she left Secure One, the sooner she could find someone who deserved her love, devotion and desire. His body tightened at the thought of it. She was all sweet curves and soft edges in a way he had never experienced before. Sure, he'd been with plenty of women, but none of them had made him feel the way Sadie did. None of those women had made him want to leave his current life behind and go anywhere with her. That was the truth of it, even if it could never be reality.

Eric turned his attention to Selina and the computer screens in front of her. She had agreed to help him in mobile command while the rest of the team dealt with Dirk and the issues surrounding the security at the storage units. He should have been running point on that, but he couldn't be in two places at once. Since he had been the one to talk Vic into visiting his brother at the Loraine mansion today,

Cal had insisted he remain in mobile command with Selina, Sadie and the baby.

Vic was inside the Loraine mansion. He sat on a couch in the living room across from Randall Junior. Vic's button camera on his jacket showed them everything he saw in real-time. He had refused to wear a microphone, afraid Randall would see it and know he wasn't there just to grieve their brother.

"How long are they going to sit there and talk?" Selina asked. It was more like a grumpy growl, and it drew Eric's attention from the screens.

"They haven't seen each other in a long time, so I explained to Vic that he needs to make it look like he's there for a reconciliation. Anything else will raise Randall's suspicion, and Vic will be the next dead body on our hands."

Selina didn't respond. She kept her gaze on the screens with her jaw clenched tightly. Eric could not figure out for the life of him what was going on with her. From the moment she'd arrived at mobile command this morning, she'd been skittish, standoffish and downright rude to Sadie when she'd asked how Houston had done during the night. He walked over and knelt next to the bank of computers so she didn't have a choice but to make eye contact with him.

"Selina, what is going on?"

"Nothing is going on." She said the four words with such disdain that it made him snort.

"Nice try. There isn't one of us here who can't see that something has changed with you. Efren has been your punching bag, but I'm starting to think this has nothing to do with him and everything to do with you. Or something you don't want to tell us that is happening in your life."

"You can think whatever you'd like, Eric. I'm here to do my job, which lately has been undefinable."

Eric had already suspected that was part of the situation, but it certainly wasn't all of it. "Then I say it's time you talk to Cal about your job and your hopes for your future at Secure One, and see what he says."

"What if I don't like what he says?" she asked, side-eyeing him.

"Then you counteroffer or you give him your notice. But one way or the other, at least you know. The animosity you're carrying about the situation has to be exhausting."

"That's rich coming from you."

"Meaning what?" He didn't like the barb at the end of that sentence, but he couldn't take it back, nor would he. He wanted an answer.

"It means that you carry plenty of animosity. You wear it like a cloak of armor, reminding everyone that we're so lucky because we can hear. You never take into consideration the fact that we know that and we all have your back. It's easy for you to sit there and call the kettle black, but you forget that you're the pot." She snapped her lips closed, focused her attention on the screens and refused to say anything more.

Rather than respond to her catty observations, he stood and watched the screens for a few more seconds. Vic was still sitting there talking to Randall, and every so often they caught a glimpse of his beer bottle going to his lips. He'd been there for over an hour now, and Eric hoped he was still nursing the first beer. They couldn't risk he would get tipsy and give up his reason for being there. An hour was long enough to chew the fat anyway. It was time to start looking for Kadie.

He walked over to Sadie in the hallway and leaned against

the wall to talk to her in low tones. The baby was sleeping on the floor of Cal's office on a giant bed of blankets. Sadie was watching over him, but she turned, knowing instinctively, as she always did, that he would need to read her lips.

"What's going on with Vic and Randall?" Her gaze flicked to the front, but she was too far away to see the screens.

"Right now, Vic is still talking to Randall in the living room. I wish he'd taken a microphone with him so we could hear what they're saying."

She rested her hand on his chest, and her warmth spread through his body, automatically relaxing him. He loved it and hated it at the same time. No woman had ever done that to him before, and it was likely no other woman ever would.

"It would have been nice," she said, "but I understood where Vic was coming from. If for any reason they found a microphone on him, not only would Vic be in terrible danger, but so would we and Kadie. We have enough bad vibes to carry right now—we don't need to add more."

"I know you're right, but it's still frustrating for someone like me to sit around and wait while someone else gets the answers I need to do my job."

"It's equally as frustrating for me when I know my sister could be in that house somewhere, scared, hurt and wondering if we're ever going to find her. All I can do is trust in the process and trust that you know the best way to find her and bring her home to her son. If I could, I would take her place and let them do whatever they wanted to me if it meant Houston had his mother."

"No." The word came out in a way he hadn't been expecting. It was forceful and, if he was honest with himself, possessive. "Don't even think that way, much less say it aloud.

We will find Kadie, bring her home to Houston and keep you all safe in the process. It's what we do. You have to trust me."

"I do trust you, but I don't trust the Loraines. Any of them."

He didn't need to hear her words to read the meaning behind them. "Listen, I know where you're coming from, but I think Vic is on the up and up."

"I'm reserving my opinion on Victor Loraine until we get Kadie's side of the story. Right now, we're taking the word of someone I don't know with ties to a family that doesn't know how to do anything but lie. Forgive me if I can't trust him at first sight," she said.

"No apology necessary, Sadie. I know where you're coming from, and I understand how you feel. We did a deep dive on Victor Loraine, and there is nothing—at least nothing anywhere on the light or the dark web—about him. I've had a lot of experience on making snap first impressions about people. Sometimes it was a matter of life and death, and I can tell you if Victor Loraine had walked into our camp unannounced, I would have pegged him as an ally and not a foe. That said, I respect how you feel and I ask that you reserve judgment until we know if Kadie is in that mansion."

"This is a terrible thing to say, but I actually hope she is at the mansion," Sadie said. "If she's not, I don't know who took her or why."

He grimaced before he could stop it.

"What? You promised to always be honest with me, Eric."

At that moment, he wished she had never uttered those words, but he had and he was a man of his word. "It's entirely possible if Randall Loraine doesn't have Kadie that The Snake does."

"Vaccaro? You think a mob boss has my sister?"

Her voice was loud enough now to wake the baby, and he put a finger to her lips. "All I'm saying is with Howie Loraine involved, there's more than a fifty percent chance that The Snake has something to do with it. We have our ears to the ground, but so far we've heard no chatter about The Snake picking up a woman in Bemidji."

"Your ears to the ground? You mean Mina?"

He winked and smiled, enjoying the moment of levity in a tense situation.

"We have movement," Selina called out, snapping them both to attention.

Sadie glanced at Houston, who was still sound asleep, and then motioned for him to go. They stood behind Selina, watching the bank of computers in front of her.

"What's going on?" Eric asked.

"Randall got a cell phone call, so Vic made a motion that he was going to the bathroom, I have to assume, and Randall nodded. Now Vic is wandering the hallways."

"He's looking for something," Eric said.

"He's looking for some*one*," Sadie said. "Kadie."

"I hope so. That's what he's there for. Otherwise this has been a waste of precious time."

The camera went screwy and out of focus momentarily before Vic's face filled the screen. He had twisted the camera toward himself like a selfie and started to speak. Eric immediately said, "Office. He's going to the office." The camera shifted again, and then Vic was moving down a hallway.

"You have to give them credit—the place is pretty swanky," Sadie said as Vic passed expensive artwork on the walls. "I'm surprised that lure of the place didn't suck Vic back in after college."

"Once you escape a place like that, you never go back,"

Selina said. "Ever. This is a big ask. I hope you appreciate what he's doing for you."

"You mean what he's doing for his family, right?" Sadie said, her tone of voice an obvious challenge to Selina. She glanced at Eric, who shook his head no and darted his gaze to Selina for a moment. Thankfully Sadie backed down just as Vic walked into a home office fit for the Godfather.

"Hey, honey, I'm home," Selina sang. "Show us the goods, Vic," she cooed to the screens, widening and tightening different views and angles in front of them.

They all leaned in while holding their breath. None of them knew what he was looking for, but it was evident that Vic did. He had a plan that he was hoping would lead him to his future wife.

"How long has he been gone from the living room?" Eric asked Selina, who punched up a timer on the screen.

"Only two minutes. Vic should have at least three more before Randall gets suspicious." She pointed at the camera still monitoring the living room that Vic had so kindly tucked under the couch cushions. Randall was talking on the phone, his head nodding.

Eric slid his gaze back to the computer screen where Vic was searching the office. He had lowered himself to the executive chair and was going through the desk. There was a monitor on the desk that was off, but no computer could be seen anywhere. He couldn't hear Vic, but he could sense his desperation as his motions grew frantic. Eric prayed he was still being quiet.

Selina had her eye on Randall, who still sat on the couch seemingly laughing along with whatever the caller was saying on the other end.

"He needs to hurry up in there," Sadie said. "I doubt his

brother is going to leave something out that will point him directly to where his girlfriend is being held hostage."

"Nothing ventured, nothing gained," Eric said. "You're probably correct, but he's still got to try. That's why we sent him in. He knows his brother better than any of us, and he can think like a Loraine. We can't."

The camera got a shot of Vic running his fingers along the edge of the desk. Suddenly the computer monitor came to life and the camera jerked. That was the moment Vic laid eyes on the woman he loved. He held the camera up, scanned the screen and then turned it to show his face.

"'Help! I don't know where this is,'" Eric read as he watched his lips move.

A sharp intake of breath had Eric's head swiveling. Sadie had turned white as a ghost as her knees collapsed. He scooped his arm around her waist so she didn't fall and held her to his side.

Vic was still talking to the screen. "'We have to find her! We have to get to her! She needs help!'"

"There's nothing we can do," Selina said without turning. "He needs to follow the plan and rendezvous with the team before we try to save Kadie. We don't even know if that feed is from inside Randall's house."

"Of course it is!" Sadie exclaimed. "She's right there on the screen!"

"Selina's right, babe," he gently said, trying to soothe her. "It could be a remote feed from somewhere else."

"We also can't go in alone," Selina pointed out. "We're not the cops."

Vic still had the camera up to his face. "'Remote feed?'" Eric read. "He's asking that as a question," he told them. "Which means he doesn't know if she's on-site either."

"Oh, we've got trouble," Selina said, pointing to the monitor and the empty chair where Randall had been sitting.

"Get out, get out," Eric chanted, hoping Vic would sense the danger coming at him.

Vic must have heard his brother coming or calling for him because he reached out, searching for a button to turn off the monitor. It was too late. His brother stood in the doorway wearing a satisfied yet smug grin. Eric leaned in as Randall walked toward his brother. Vic's coat camera was pointed directly at Randall now, and Eric didn't want to miss a word Randall had to say. He tightened his grip on Sadie and waited while the two men faced off.

"'What are you doing, little brother?'" Eric read on Randall's lips.

He couldn't see Vic's response, so he waited for Randall to speak again.

"'You didn't think I'd believe you were here to mourn our lost brother, did you?'" Eric read slowly. "'You…years.'" Eric paused. "He probably said he hasn't seen him in years."

Vic slid out from behind the desk and inched toward the door. Whatever he said made Randall laugh.

"'I don't know what you're talking about, Vic,'" Eric read. "Something about the computer." He was frustrated but watched as Randall approached Vic, who tried to skirt past him to make for the door. Then a gun appeared, aimed directly at the camera.

"Dammit!" Selina exclaimed.

"Vic better do some fast talking," Eric muttered. "We can't save him at this point. He's got to save himself."

He leaned closer to the monitor, hoping Randall would give them enough information to find Kadie. Eric also hoped he didn't shoot his brother. Randall stood still while wearing that smug smile on his face. They could only assume Vic was speaking to him.

"'This will be touching,'" Eric read, breaking the silence when Randall spoke. "'I can see the headlines—Loraine brother dies wrapped in his lover's embrace.'"

The gun waved toward the door, motioning Vic to start walking. Terrified to the point of shaking, if the camera was any indication, he had the wherewithal to walk backward so they could still see Randall in the camera.

"'It's a secret,'" Eric read. "'I'd kill you now, but The Snake wants no dead bodies to deal with unless he orders it.'"

Vic visibly started and must have said something to his brother because Randall sneered. "'Enough talk,'" Eric read. "'Time to see your lover girl.'"

Vic turned slowly to walk down the hallway, allowing them to see the direction he was going. Hopefully he'd be able to show them where to start looking.

"For not being an operative, this guy is intuitive," Selina said as she typed a message to Cal.

The two men paused near a door while Vic turned the handle. He took a step forward, and immediately the camera went dark. Before Eric could say anything, the door to mobile command nearly flew off its hinges, announcing the arrival of the cavalry.

Chapter Sixteen

Eric hung up the phone and disconnected his hearing aids from the Bluetooth. "Cal and the guys are digging into Howie's financials." He offered the information to anyone in the room who was listening, but Lucas and Mina had their heads buried in their computers.

As soon as it had become evident they wouldn't see more from Vic, they'd circled the wagons as a team to make an extraction plan. To do that, they needed more space, so Dirk had given them a heated storage unit to use so they could spread out the team between there and mobile command. Eric wasn't letting Sadie out of his sight, so he moved her and Houston into the storage unit with him until they had a better plan to keep them safe.

His gaze traveled to the woman he had too many feelings for in such a short time. He couldn't stop thinking about how she'd made him feel last night when she'd offered him her body and her heart. Maybe she hadn't come right out and said *I love you* with words, but she didn't need words when she trusted him with her body. Eric swore internally. He never should have allowed himself the pleasure of being with her. It would be impossible to let her go once they had Kadie back safely. He knew and accepted that he would have to let her go, despite wanting to keep her close to him.

The thought gave him a jolt. He'd never thought that about a woman before. All the women he'd been with had been well aware they were there for a bit of fun and nothing more. They'd all been okay with that. Sadie said she was okay with it, but Eric knew she wasn't so much okay with it as accepting of it.

"We have a hit," Mina said, jumping up from the desk and giving him a start. "Roscoe Landry, age fifty, is a mob boss for Vaccaro. It's said his underlings call him the Winged Templar."

Eric did a fist pump. "We have another connection. The guy who dropped the trunk said they had to follow the Winged Templar's orders."

"Which to me sounds like the person responsible for the hit."

"Yes," he agreed, "but we can't prove it. How do we prove it?"

"I wish I knew who these guys were. I'd trace them back until I found the original hit order. We don't know if the guys who dumped him also killed him. They could have just been on disposal duty."

"We tried running facial recognition on the video we took, but it was too dark and far away. Wait." Eric clapped his hands together. "We need to use the victim."

"Use the victim?" Mina asked for clarification. "You mean trace Howie back until we find a connection to Roscoe?"

Eric pointed to her, and she ran back to the computer to start typing.

"What does any of that mean?" Sadie asked, pacing the

small area around the playpen where Houston sat happily, babbling at his toys.

"If we can find hard evidence that Howie and Roscoe are linked, you're off the hook."

"Just because they knew each other?"

"No," Eric said with a head shake, "because Howie was killed in a mob-style execution, and Roscoe is one of The Snake's top bosses. Once we know if Howie and Roscoe are connected, we look for a double cross by Howie. I assure you there is one. If Howie crossed him, Roscoe would order the hit and deflect the blame."

Sadie's head tipped to the side in confusion. "If that's the case, maybe he shouldn't have had him killed execution style." Her eyes rolled, and she mumbled what he thought was the word *men*.

"I never said he was smart." Eric winked and turned to Lucas. "Anything from Vic?"

Lucas shook his head. "Nothing usable. I know he's got the camera because it keeps shaking, but there's nothing other than blackness."

"Have you found the blueprints for the Loraine home? We need to know where that door leads to. If we have to go in, I want everyone to have the floor plan memorized."

The team knew Vic, and likely Kadie, were still inside the Loraine mansion. The GPS tracker in his shoe told them that much. What it didn't tell them was where inside, which was the reason they needed the blueprints.

"I'm working on it," Lucas answered, but Eric could hear the frustration in his tone. "Mina might have to make a go of it. Trying to get them through legal channels isn't working."

There was a knock on the door. "Secure one, Sierra."

Eric walked to the door and answered. "Secure two,

Echo." Then he opened the door to allow her in. They were working out of a corner storage unit with a small side door, so they didn't have to open the main door as people entered. Selina had been their go-between for information, but when she burst through the door this time, her arms were loaded with long cardboard tubes. She dumped them onto the table in the center of the room and stepped back.

"What's all this?" Eric asked, homing in on her stiff shoulders and fisted hands.

"The blueprints for the Loraine mansion."

"What? How?" Lucas asked, standing immediately. "I've been working on getting those for hours."

"Don't ask questions I can't answer," she said through clenched teeth. "Just help me get these up on the wall."

Lucas glanced at Eric, who gave him a slight head tilt to go ahead and help her. He waited while Selina tacked the blueprints to the wall in an order that only she understood. She gave Lucas one-or two-word directions until all the prints were up. They stepped back, and Selina grabbed a marker. She started writing and marking things on the blueprints while everyone stared in stunned silence. Eric sensed the entire room was wondering the same thing—how had Selina gotten the blueprints, and how did she know the things she was writing on them?

"No way," Mina said to break the silence. "That was way too easy."

"What was too easy?" Sadie asked, handing Houston his bottle before walking over to Mina's station.

"I found the connection between Howie and Roscoe. Howie Loraine was engaged to Roscoe's daughter."

Eric stepped forward, certain he had misheard. "Say that again?"

"Howie was engaged to Roscoe's daughter, Lydia."

"Is there any evidence that Howie was working for Vaccaro?" he asked, an idea beginning to take root in his mind.

"Not that I can prove yet, but if he was engaged to Roscoe's daughter, the likelihood is high that he was working for Vaccaro."

Sadie put her hand on her hip. "If Howie was engaged to Roscoe's daughter and possibly working within the organization, the next question we have to answer is why did Roscoe have him killed?"

Eric couldn't stop the grin that lifted his lips. "She's good. It's like she's always been part of this team. That was my exact thought. Do you have any theories, Sadie?"

"I don't know much about the mob," she answered, "but I have watched a lot of mob movies. And it seems like the only thing that gets you killed in the mob is a double cross or personal affront."

Mina pointed at her. "What she said. Being engaged to the mob is a dicey place to be. It's highly possible there was a personal affront, especially with a guy like Howie. There could also be a double cross, which might be harder to track down. I'll keep looking." She went back to her keyboard, and Eric turned to Sadie.

"Things will move quickly once we figure out the connection between Howie and Roscoe. You'll return to mobile command and stay locked up tight with Houston."

"I won't stand around while someone else saves my sister! I'm going with you."

"No, you're not." This time it was Selina who answered. "You know absolutely nothing about an operation like this, which makes you more hindrance than help. If you go out there with no idea what you're doing, you will end up dead."

"She's not wrong," Eric said with his brow in the air, "and I can't allow that. You need to be here with Houston to keep him safe until we bring Kadie back."

He had to bite the inside of his cheek when Sadie planted her fists on her hips, puffed out her chest and jutted her chin in a sign of fierce determination. She clearly wanted to help save her family, no matter what they said.

"No," Selina said again. "The Loraine mansion is complicated, has too many entrances and exits, and is no place for someone without formal security training. We bring you along and the next thing we know, Randall will have three hostages. That simply cannot happen. Besides, I'm going with the team, which means someone must be here to care for Houston."

Eric turned on his heel to face her. "Are you going to be able to work with Efren?"

She took a step forward and stuck her finger in his chest. "For your information, I can work with anyone on this team. I don't appreciate the insinuation that I'm not a team player. I have always been a team player and will continue to be one. Now, let's step over to the blueprints and devise an attack plan."

"Well, well. Someone has decided to stop waiting to be told she's part of the team and just be part of the team. I like it. Keep it up."

Before he could say more, Cal announced himself.

"Secure one, Charlie."

"Secure two, Echo," he responded, then opened the door for Cal, Mack, Efren and Roman. "You're just in time to get the lowdown on the mansion's layout," Eric said, motioning at the wall where the blueprints hung. "Mina is following up a lead on the connection between the Winged Templar and Howie."

"You found one?" Cal asked with his brows up in surprise.

"It was too easy," she said without breaking stride on the keyboard. "Howie was engaged to Roscoe's daughter."

Efren's whistle was long as he set his hands on his hips. "Hell hath no fury like a woman scorned."

"My thought exactly," Mina said, her gaze never leaving the screen. "If it's here, I'll find it."

"While she's doing that," Cal said, motioning to Mina, "let's break down the mission. Regardless of the connection, we must get Kadie and Vic out of that mansion."

Selina motioned them toward the blueprints spread across the wall. "This is Randall's office," she said, pointing to a room she circled in blue. "This," she said, pointing at a small opening she had circled in red, "is the door they walked through."

"Where does it go?" Roman asked from where he stood by Mina, a hand on her shoulder.

"According to the blueprints, it's a closet. Unless you have this set of prints." She pointed at the bottom row. "They show the tunnels. If I were a betting woman, I would say they're in this area somewhere."

"Tunnels?" Cal asked, stepping forward and letting his gaze wander the blueprints.

"We already know Kadie's at the mansion since Randall Junior told Vic he was taking him to see her. That said, he won't keep a hostage anywhere the hired help can happen upon her."

"He needs a secret room?" Sadie asked, and Selina gave her the so-so hand motion.

"Something like that."

"Do the tunnels go to a secret room?" Cal asked, pointing at a long, narrow hallway on the blueprint.

Her finger went up one blueprint and pointed at the room to the left of the door Randall had taken Vic through. "This is Daddy's private library. Here—" she moved her finger to the end of the room "—is a trapdoor with a ladder."

"And you know this how?" Efren asked, his head cocked as he stared at the blueprints.

"Because I do my job," Selina answered, her teeth clenched together.

"No, there's more to this than just doing your job, Selina," Cal said. "How did you get these blueprints?"

She spun on the group and walked up to Cal, sticking her finger in his chest. Eric grimaced. No one was insubordinate to their leader without suffering the consequences. "I will not answer any questions about what I know and how. I will share my knowledge with the team on how to stay safe and accomplish the mission. Is that clear?"

Eric stood frozen, as did the rest of the team. Even he could have heard a pin drop until Cal spoke. "Clear. For now," he added. "But we will address all of this," he said, motioning at his chest with his prosthetic finger, "when this case is resolved."

Eric stepped forward, the peacemaker in him wanting to settle things down for everyone. "Listen, Selina, we're grateful for any information you can give us about the mansion." Her shoulders were stiff and unyielding as she faced them. It was never more apparent she was hiding something, which didn't come as a surprise. Everyone knew that Selina's past was a dark hole she never discussed. But none of that mattered right now. "We have to move if we want to find Kadie and Vic before they're moved or killed."

"And we can't count on the cops," Efren said, stepping forward. "They still believe Sadie ordered the hit on Howie. They're going to be no help."

"Agreed," Selina said turning back to the plans on the wall. "Since we can't involve the cops, this will be considered breaking and entering."

"Considering we're rescuing hostages, I'm sure such a minor charge will be overlooked. Were anyone to learn of the mission, that is," Lucas said, his arms crossed over his chest.

She stiffened her spine and raised her chin. "If we're all in agreement, then what I'm about to tell you will make this job twice as easy but twice as dangerous. Are we all in?"

"Secure one, Charlie," Cal said.

"Secure two, Romeo."

"Secure three, Mike."

"Secure four, Echo," Eric said with a wink at Sadie.

"Secure five, Whiskey."

"Secure six, Tango."

"Secure seven, Bravo," Marlise, Cal's wife, said.

"Secure eight, Lucas."

"Secure nine, Sadie."

Eric reached out and took Sadie's hand, squeezing it.

"Secure ten, Sierra," Selina said, and then with a respectful nod, she turned back to the blueprints. "I can't confirm but I do suspect that this doorway is a set of stairs that goes to the same place the trapdoor does in the library," she said, pointing at that long empty space again. "Otherwise, it's another entrance to the library. Either way, it will take them to the tunnel."

"What do they use the tunnel for?" Cal asked.

"Escape," she answered immediately. "That said, there are also storage rooms on each side of the tunnel."

"Storage rooms?" Eric asked, releasing Sadie's hand and walking to the front so he could hear and see Selina better. "Can you explain?"

"More like cubbies, I suppose," she answered. "Places to store off-season sports equipment, clothing and household stuff."

"Or perfect for stashing a woman away for a few days," Eric said.

"Yep," Selina answered, pointing at the tunnel again. "There's plenty of space for Randall to hold Vic and Kadie while he waits for orders from The Snake. We now have confirmation that's who he's working for since he came right out and told his brother. Thanks to Eric's lipreading skill, we know that Vaccaro is pulling the strings. I assure you, where the mob is involved, danger quickly follows, so we need to get into that tunnel and get them out of there before The Snake gives an order we can't stop."

"How do we do that?" Cal asked. "Better question is once we get into it, how do we get out?"

Selina returned to the table and unrolled a smaller blueprint still waiting to be opened. "Tunnels always have an entrance and an exit, right?" she asked, getting head nods from the crew. "So does this one. The exit, or what we'll make our entrance and exit, is next to the garage in the back of the house. It's hidden in plain sight as an egress window. This is all the information I have on security around the yard," she said, passing out a paper packet to everyone.

"Hello, connection, my name is Winner," Mina gleefully said as she spun in her chair to face everyone. "Howie Loraine was engaged to Roscoe's daughter but was playing Hide the Salami with a model in Chicago."

"Hide the Salami?" Cal asked with his brow up.

She just laughed and clapped her hands. "Once a playboy, always a playboy where Howie Loraine was concerned. In their eyes, the only answer was to fix the problem."

"That made a bigger problem for us," Selina said with a shake of her head. "Knowing that, we have to move. You get five minutes to read that, ask questions and start your mission prep. I want to be rolling as soon as it's dark. That gives us—" she checked her watch "—an hour and twenty-two minutes to have our ducks in a row."

"Who's running this mission anyway?" Cal asked, taking a step toward the table.

"I am," Selina answered, leaning forward on the table. "Trust me when I say if you all want to walk out of there alive with our two hostages, not a soul around this table will argue with me."

Eric waited while Cal debated his next move. The Selina of the last thirty minutes was someone he didn't know, and he suspected he wasn't alone in that feeling. That was confirmed when Cal took a step back and nodded once. "Mission leader is Sierra. Mission foreman is Echo. Mission communication manager is…" He turned to Lucas and gave him a finger gun with his prosthesis. "Lima."

The unexpected declaration of a call name brought a smile to Lucas's face as he nodded at their leader. Lucas had officially been accepted onto the elite team at Secure One, and Eric knew he'd work twice as hard to prove that he deserved that distinction.

Cal turned to the rest of them. "Everyone else, get your assignments from Sierra. Let's get this couple back to their baby." Selina might've been running this mission, but he still ran the show.

Chapter Seventeen

Sadie paced the room, anxiety and the need to do something filling her to the breaking point. Houston slept in the playpen, blessedly unaware of how dangerously close he was to becoming an orphan. He'd become Sadie's responsibility forever if his parents didn't make it out alive. It also meant she'd have to run far and fast to keep him out of Randall Loraine's hands. Could she handle being a single mother of an infant? Absolutely. Did she want to? No. She wanted her sister home, alive and raising her son. Sadie couldn't fathom life without her sister in it.

"Secure one, Echo."

Sadie walked to the door, unlocked it and let Eric into the tiny room at the back of mobile command. "Hi," she greeted him after she closed the door.

"Cal got a call from the chief of police in Bemidji. You've been cleared of Howie Loraine's murder."

"What? How?" She took a step closer to him, desperate for the news to be true.

"We tipped them off to the Winged Templar. Once Mina had his real name, the Chicago police raided his home and found the contract paperwork on the hit."

"Did the paperwork show that I didn't order the hit?"

Eric nodded, and she let out a sigh, her shoulders slumping. "I'm so glad to be out from under that suspicion."

"You're one step closer to getting your life back."

She fisted the front of his shirt in her hand. "What's happening tonight, Eric? I need to know the plan."

"Nightfall is here, so we're gathering our final supplies to approach the mansion and enter the tunnel. If our luck holds, that's where we'll find Kadie and Vic and get them back here safely."

"I'm going," she said, her tone no-nonsense and forceful.

"Absolutely not," Eric said in a tone of voice that to anyone else would leave no room for argument.

"Listen to me, Eric! Kadie is my sister," Sadie hissed, stabbing herself in the chest with her finger. "I need to be there when she comes out of that mansion! She doesn't know any of you!"

"Vic is with her. I'm sure he's filled her in on who we are and that we're working to rescue them. He'll also tell her that you are keeping Houston safe. Once we get them out, the team will bring her right to you and Houston."

"You don't know that Vic is with her! You don't know that she's even in that mansion! What if she's injured and needs a hospital? I have to be there, Eric!"

"Listen to me, baby. It's too dangerous. We've talked about this. If you're there, then I'm worried about you and I can't afford to have my attention split that way. It's hard enough to make sure that I'm communicating and getting all of the information correctly from the rest of my team. If my mind is partially focused on your safety too, the mission will fail."

"You don't have to worry about me. I will stay wherever you tell me to stay."

"I'm telling you to stay here," he said. "I'll be brutally

honest with you, Sadie. The idea of having you there where I can't protect you terrifies me. I've never felt this way about anyone before. That also terrifies me, but in ways that I can't put into words."

"Maybe you can," she said, taking a step closer and putting her lips on his for a brief moment. "Maybe you can put it into three words."

"That's the problem," he said, his forehead balanced on hers. "Putting it into those three words is dangerous."

"That makes it real?" Sadie asked, her heart pounding at the idea that he loved her too. "Is it possible to fall in love in less than a week?"

"If I've learned one thing working at Secure One, it's that it's possible to fall in love in one breath. I've seen it happen multiple times. But I never expected—"

"It to happen to you?" she asked, her voice soft and tender. The brush of his forehead against hers when he shook his head told her more than any other answer he could have given her. "You're afraid to be vulnerable again, right?"

This time he nodded and took a step back. She reached up and flicked the button on his hearing aids until they were off. His eyes widened, and she held her finger up. Then she said those three words. She waited while his eyes did the hearing for him. "I love you, Eric Newman. That may complicate life, but it also completes it. I'm not letting you go out there without telling you how important you are to me."

She flipped the switches back on his aids and waited for him to speak. "Why did you turn my hearing aids off?"

"I wanted there to be no question about what I said. You trust the things you see more than the things you hear. I wanted you to see that I love you and that I'll always find a way to show you as much as tell you."

Before she could say another word, he pulled her into a tight hug, both arms wrapped around her and his lips against her ear. "I love you too, Sadie Cook. Oh, boy, does that complicate things, but I've never felt like I needed someone else to breathe. Then you came along, and suddenly I needed to see you morning, noon and night. That's why it terrifies me even to consider putting you at risk. Anything can happen out there, and you could get hurt."

"I could say the same about you," she said, leaning back so he could read her lips. "I'll do whatever you think is the best, but Kadie has to know that I've been looking for her and that I've kept Houston safe."

He grasped her shirt and pulled her to him, kissing her in a frantic tangle of tongues that neither of them would forget anytime soon. "Those will be the first words out of my mouth," he whispered against her lips. "I want you here, locked safely behind these doors where there's not a chance you can get hurt."

His lips attacked hers again, and she leaned into the kiss, dropping her jaw so he could drink from her the courage he would need to go out and face the risk for both of them.

When the kiss slowed, she said those words again so he could feel them. "I love you, Eric. Do not get yourself killed out there, do you understand me?"

"Loud and clear." He leaned back and tucked the hair back behind her ears. *I love you too.* He mouthed the words this time so seeing was believing. "We should keep how we feel about each other under our hats for now. I don't want any distractions within the team tonight."

"Agreed," she said with a head nod.

As though the idea of keeping it between them was too powerful for him, he walked to her, grasped her chin and laid a kiss on her that would carry her through until he was back in her arms.

ERIC TIGHTENED THE straps on his bulletproof vest, checked his gun and tucked it into his holster at his side, and flipped his night-vision goggles down over his eyes. He forced himself to put Sadie from his mind and concentrate on nothing but the mission—find Kadie and Vic and bring them out safely.

"You're sure about this?" he asked Selina, who stood next to him. "You're positive there's a way in from the back?"

"There's no question in my mind that we can get into the mansion this way. I know it's hard for you to trust me, but I promise you if we're going to find them and bring them out, this is the only way."

"Are the cops in position?"

Selina pushed the button on her earpiece. "Secure one, Sierra. Do we have a go?"

"Secure two, Charlie. Detectives are approaching the door as we speak. Hold your position."

"Ten-four."

He pulled his gun and waited. "I don't want the cops to screw this up," he growled.

"There's a fifty-fifty chance," Selina agreed. "But we didn't have a choice. If we didn't bring the cops in on this, we'd get hit with more charges than we could wiggle out of without damage to the business. Once I showed the chief the video of Randall holding his brother at gunpoint, they decided maybe they should take a second look at the brother. We've only got one chance at this while he's distracted by the cops. We need to make this happen."

"If they can keep Randall Junior busy for a few minutes, we can do the rest."

"I hope they have more than just detectives approaching that door. I hope they have the SWAT team. There are way too many exits to cover here. Not to mention Randall's personal bodyguards won't favor the cops arresting him."

"That confuses me," Eric admitted. "Why does Randall Junior need bodyguards if he's not doing anything illegal?"

Selina snorted to hold back her laughter. "Randall Junior obviously took over the business when Randall Senior went to prison. That's why he needs bodyguards. Of that, I have no doubt."

"How do you know so much about the Loraine case?"

She flipped her night-vision goggles down over her eyes and pulled her gun from her holster, pointing it at the ground. "I told you before that I won't answer questions. That still stands."

"I hope you realize at some point that excuse won't hold water and Cal will demand answers. Keep your secrets— I've got other things on my mind tonight."

"Like the woman back at mobile command who's waiting for you to be her hero."

"I'm not her hero, Selina." Eric's gaze darted around the yard, searching out danger.

"It's okay to love her," she said.

"Who said anything about love?"

"One doth protest too much, if you ask me. I'm happy for you, Eric. Sadie is your perfect match. You don't have to confirm that for me to know I'm right. All I'm saying is don't be afraid to take that chance. Real, all-encompassing love like that is hard to come by in life. Don't pass it by just because you don't think you deserve it."

"Why would I think that?"

"Oh, I don't know, because of what happened in the sand-box? We all know that you haven't dealt with your ghosts from that time. Maybe it's time to let somebody help you carry the burden."

"This still feels a lot like the pot and the kettle," Eric said.

"Except it's not," Selina pointed out. "You have someone within your reach who wants to be part of your life. Don't blow it, Eric. You might not get a second chance."

"Noted," he said through clenched teeth. "Be ready—we've got to be close to go time."

She nodded, pulling her gun close to her vest and crouching in the shooter's position. He'd go first, covering the open ground while she covered him. The empty stretch of grass ahead of them felt one hundred miles long. He reminded himself it was his job to get across the space, find Kadie and bring her back to her sister, and then walk away. While he absolutely loved Sadie and she made him feel things he had never felt before, they could never be together. There was no way he would drag somebody as sweet and innocent as Sadie into his life just to poison her too.

"Secure one, Charlie." His hearing aid crackled to life with Cal's voice. "The detectives have made contact with Randall Junior. It's go time."

"Ten-four. Echo and Sierra out."

Eric fiddled with his hearing aid for a moment. The ear-pieces kept them connected, but the app that ran it to his hearing aid couldn't have full control. Once he had surround sound again, he glanced at Selina, who gave him a nod. He took off in a runner's crouch, his gun pointed at the ground as he ran. He could bring it up and get off a shot in a split second, but he hoped he'd get across the yard to the safety of the brick garage without notice. Selina had assured them the backyard didn't have motion-sensor lights or alarms. How she knew that they weren't allowed to ask, which meant they were putting trust in her word against their better judgment.

He had no doubt Selina was already following him, even though she should've been waiting for him to cover her. She knew this property too well for her to have learned it all by studying the blueprints. There was a reason she had this much knowledge about the Loraine mansion and the people inside. At this moment, he didn't care what Selina's secret was. They all had secrets, and no one had the right to judge someone else for theirs. That said, if they were going to get out of this alive with their hostages, he was going to have to offer blind trust in a way he never had before.

Once his back was plastered along the cold brick of the garage, he spotted Selina moving toward him. The night was silent, which meant thus far, Randall was cooperating with the detectives. They just had to avoid any motion sensors they didn't know about, Selina's assurance or not, and they had to be sure if they ran into any SWAT members they made it clear they were friend and not foe.

His mind slid to mobile command, where the woman he loved was waiting for him to be the hero. That was a heavy load to carry. Even heavier than when he'd been in the army and carrying the load of a country on his shoulders. Back then, the people he was protecting had been nothing more than an idea of the larger picture. Tonight, the idea was concrete, and he remembered every curve of her body and the feel of her soft skin under his.

Selina slipped through the night and up alongside him, snapping him from his thoughts of Sadie and bringing him back to the present situation. Selina crouched as she assessed the backyard with her night-vision goggles. She whispered, but he didn't hear a thing.

He tapped her on the shoulder. "You can't whisper. Look at me when you speak."

She turned and nodded. "Sorry—forgot. From what I can see, everything looks clear. Do you see anything?"

"Negative," he replied.

"Are you ready to go in?"

"Let's do it. Eyes forward, guns ready, be prepared for anything."

Her laughter took him by surprise. "Oh, you don't have to tell me that. I know how things can turn on a dime when it comes to the Loraine mansion."

Before he could reply, she was motioning him forward along the back of the garage until she came to a halt and knelt.

I had to find the opening, she mouthed, pointing at the ground.

Eric aimed his gun at the ground and waited while Selina pulled back the 'grass' to reveal an egress window cover.

"You can't even tell it's there," Eric whispered. The glass had been covered with artificial turf to make it blend in.

"Once we're down there, we have to make quick work of that window. It will be locked from the inside."

"Ten-four," Eric whispered, then waited as she lifted the glass and it rose on hinges. He pointed his gun into the hole, and his night-vision goggles revealed a short metal ladder that led to the window below. "You go first. I've got you covered," he said, motioning at the ladder with his gun.

Selina hesitated for only a moment before she slung her gun into the front of her pants, backed up to the opening and descended the ladder within a matter of seconds.

Silence was of the utmost importance now, so she made the hand motion for him to follow. Before he ducked under the cover, Eric did a full sweep of the yard in front of them. He saw no one moving nor any lights in the distance. He quickly descended the ladder far enough to grab the cover and pull it closed. He didn't want a surprise attack. At least Selina would hear someone opening the cover above them.

The window keeping them from the tunnel looked like a simple double pane side slide open, but he suspected it was something far more secure than one of those. Selina confirmed that when she lined the window with duct tape and used a center punch to break the pane. She quickly did the same thing with the second pane, making a hole just big enough to reach the levers to unlock the window.

"I have to admit this is too easy," Selina said, making eye contact. "As soon as I open this, be ready to fire. There could be a silent alarm on it or they could be waiting."

"Ten-four," he said, standing to the side of the window. He expected her to slide it open, but instead, the window swung open into the well. He swept the area below them, surprised when there was another ladder that they'd have to descend to reach the floor of the tunnel. How deep did these people need to bury their secrets?

With a nod, he motioned Selina down the ladder. When she hit the bottom, she immediately pulled her gun and swept the area ahead of her. In a moment, she motioned him down, so he followed her, being sure to pull the window nearly closed to prevent sound traveling down the tunnel.

Once he was standing next to Selina, she pulled out a folded paper from her chest pocket. It was a map of the tunnels, and she held it out for him to see with his goggles. She pointed to where they were and where Vic and Kadie might be tucked away. The tunnel was easily the length of a football field and originated in the main house library. The several closet-sized storage rooms along the way held their interest. If you were going to squirrel someone away for an extended period, this creepy dungeon would fit the bill.

They moved forward, but Eric didn't like that they were heading toward the house rather than away from it. The air was thick with intense fear. Eric had felt this kind of fear before. He tried to focus on this mission rather than the ones that had failed. There were twice as many humans in the world doing evil as those doing good. That made it impossible to win every time.

Immediately, his mind's eye went to the woman waiting for him to return. She was everything to him, even if they couldn't be together. He would do anything to bring her family back to her. At the end of the day, her family would be the only thing she would have, so he owed her that. Eric understood that he could love someone, but he lacked the ability to love someone unconditionally. No, that wasn't true. He loved Sadie unconditionally. He lacked the ability to love her freely because he knew he could lose her in the blink of an eye.

He'd seen that happen so many times during the war. One minute he'd been talking to his buddy, and the next minute his buddy had been gone. Vaporized. Shot down. Bleeding out. Asking him with a waning, gurgling voice to pass those last words to their wife or girlfriend. Those words had been burned into his soul and always would be. Sadie shouldn't have to suffer the scars too. She said she understood what he'd been through, and maybe she did to a degree, but at the same time, she didn't. She'd never been there at 2:00 a.m. when he was drenched in sweat and covered in scratches from his fingernails or curled into a ball in the corner of the bed sobbing into a pillow. She'd never seen that, and he didn't want her to. Sadie deserved the kind of man who could offer her stability in life. That would never be him.

Selina held up a fist, telling him to halt. She motioned to the left with two fingers, reminding him that was the first room they had to clear. The door was solid wood and locked from the outside with a padlock like one used to lock up athletic equipment or bicycles. He waited while Selina cut the padlock, and then they both took a deep breath before she swung the door open. His night-vision goggles showed him winter skis. His heart sank.

Selina closed the door, pulled her gun back to her shoulder and motioned forward. He followed with his gun aimed at the ground as they approached the next door. This one was also padlocked, but it only took Selina a moment to cut it loose. With a nod, he crouched and aimed his gun at the door. When she pulled the door back, it revealed a woman with her hands tied to her feet and a gag in her mouth.

Kadie Cook was alive.

Selina put her gun behind her back and walked into the room while Eric covered her. Selina whispered into Kadie's ear, and the woman began nodding frantically. She was trying to hold her hands up, so Selina quickly cut through the ropes and let them fall to the floor before she removed the gag. She held her finger to her lips and motioned out the door. Kadie nodded her understanding.

Selina approached Eric and knelt, pulling her Secure One phone from her vest. She typed something in and held the screen out for him to read.

We're near the end of the tunnel. Randall could be right above our heads. Time to go silent mode. She doesn't know if Vic is here, but she did hear a commotion a few hours ago. We have one room left to check. If he's not there, we take her out and regroup?

Eric gave one nod, confirming the plan. His left hearing aid gave a warning beep in his ear that the battery was almost dead. Frustrated, he reached up and shut down the aid, leaving the right one on. Selina motioned Kadie behind her, and they sandwiched her as they moved toward the final padlocked room. Eric knew they were dangerously close to the stairs and the library. He held his breath when the bolt cutters loudly snapped on the last padlock. Selina motioned for Kadie to take a step back, and then with one motion, she opened the door and brought her gun up to her shoulder.

Vic was draped across a chair, his hands and feet tied and a gag in his mouth. His head listed to the side while he blinked his eyes repeatedly. Randall had clearly knocked him around before putting him in the room. His limp posture worried Eric, and he prayed the man could walk. The one thing he did notice was the relief in Vic's eyes when he saw them. Selina quickly cut the ties from his hands and feet and then removed the gag. Surprise and fear bloomed across Vic's face when he got a good look at her. He stood on quivering legs and stumbled backward away from Selina, mouthing something Eric struggled to read.

He swore he'd said *Ava Shannon*. Before Eric could step in, Selina leaned forward and blocked his view of Vic's lips. Whatever she said to Vic made him nod with excitement. She put an arm around him and helped him out of the room where Kadie, to her credit, was silent when she ran to him and slid under his other arm to help hold him up. Selina motioned to Vic's head, and Eric immediately noticed the bloodied mat of hair. She gave him the good-to-go sign, so they turned back toward the trapdoor.

If everything had gone to plan, Cal and Efren would be waiting to help them bring out the hostages while Roman and Mack worked the perimeter to ensure they all got out safely. He grabbed his Secure One phone and punched in the agreed-upon Morse code he would use if they found the hostages. He waited and was rewarded with the reply telling them everyone was in position. With a nod at Selina, he picked a steady but slower pace than he liked as he headed for the trapdoor. Vic needed both women to support him, which meant they could only go as fast as their slowest member. He tossed around helping Vic but decided they were all better off with both hands on his gun if confronted. After a tense few minutes, they reached the ladder, and Eric punched a code into the phone again. The window swung open to let in a bit of the night sky, and he tipped his head up.

Cal's hand lowered into the hole, and he made a fist and then held out a finger—*Secure One*. They were good to go. He whispered into Kadie's ear that it was safe and urged her up the ladder. Eric waited as Efren helped her, but he held the stop fist up to Selina as she tried to get Vic to climb the ladder. Eric could see he would never make it up on his own. They needed another team member to come down and help him up. Within seconds of helping Kadie out, Efren was climbing down the ladder. As an above-knee amputee, Eric didn't want him trying to help a half-conscious man up a vertical ladder. He wanted him to cover their butts with his gun. He'd been a sharpshooter in the army and could take out a threat in the dark with one hand tied behind his back.

"Cover me," he whispered to Efren as he helped Vic toward the ladder.

"No, she's dead. I know she's dead. She's dead." Vic was rambling as though the knock on the head had done more damage than they'd thought.

Eric didn't have time to worry about it, except that he was too loud. He leaned into Vic's ear and whispered, "It's Eric from Secure One. If you want to see Kadie and Houston again, you must quiet down and climb this ladder. They're waiting for you."

"Kadie? Is Kadie safe? Houston? Houston is my son. Why is she here? She's dead."

They were out of time, so he took one of Vic's hands and placed it on the metal, hoping the unexpected chill would clear his head a bit. It seemed to work as he immediately put the other one up and slowly climbed the ladder even while murmuring. It wasn't ideal considering the situation, but if they could get him out into the fresh air, that might help clear his head and quiet him down.

"You should stop right there," a voice said from their left. Eric spun slowly and came face-to-face with Randall Loraine Junior. "Since you're holding the next Loraine heir hostage, I was planning to exchange his mother for my nephew. There is a low likelihood of you getting out of here alive until you tell me where he is."

"You're outgunned, Loraine," Eric said in the voice he reserved for dire circumstances. "It's three against one down here. My team will shoot first and ask questions later." Their semiautomatic rifles were pointed at Randall, who carried only a 9 mm.

"We'll see about that," he said and pushed a button on his watch. The tunnel lit up, blinding Eric and Selina for a moment until they ripped their night goggles off. Thankfully, Efren still had the man in his sights.

"You can't win here, Loraine!" Efren yelled as Eric got his bearings back.

Selina lifted her head and pointed her gun at Randall's center mass. "You heard him. Back away."

"No!" He jumped backward, tripped and fell, then crab-walked to get away from the woman in front of him. "You're dead! They said you were dead!"

Before anyone could react, Randall brought his gun up and got off a shot. Selina's pained grunt filled his ears as she fell to the side just as Efren's shot rang out. The sound blasted through his aid, and Eric struggled to clear his head as the tunnel went dark. On instinct, he flipped his goggles back down and located Randall as he limped down the tunnel. He aimed but didn't pull the trigger. He couldn't shoot the man in the back as he ran. They'd have to leave him to the cops. "Randall is headed to the library! Selina is down! Need medic!"

He turned to Efren, who was tending to Selina on the ground. "What's her status?"

"Looks like a belly wound. Loraine got her under the vest—we need to get her to a hospital ASAP!"

"I can walk," Selina grumped, but Eric wasn't sure if he'd heard correctly. "I said I can walk!" She pushed at Efren until he stepped back.

That brought a smile to Eric's lips. A man couldn't count Selina down and out yet.

Efren helped her to her feet, her arm across her belly as she walked to the ladder. "It's just a flesh wound," she insisted as she put her foot on the first rung of the ladder.

Eric glanced at Efren. "Help her up. I'll cover your back."

With only a few moans from Selina, Efren was able to get her up the ladder where Roman and Mack helped her through the opening. Eric wasted no time on the ladder and joined them at the back of the property.

Flashing lights filled the backyard as a medic team ran toward Selina, who was now lying on the ground. Her bulletproof vest was open, her black T-shirt now silky with her blood.

Eric knelt next to her and leaned into her ear. "Who is Ava Shannon? Why do they think you're dead? How do you know Randall Loraine?"

Selina met his gaze, and a whimper left her lips. "I told you there are questions I can't answer. Those are three of them." Then her eyes drifted closed.

Chapter Eighteen

Sadie ran down the hallway carrying Houston, the nurse having pointed her in the right direction to find her sister. "Kadie!"

A curtain was thrown back, and a face so much like her own stared out. "Sadie!" her sister cried as soon as she saw her. "Houston!" The baby let out a squeal, and then they were together, hugging, laughing and crying as Kadie kissed her son's head, checking him over for injuries. "I knew you'd take care of him."

Sadie ended the hug and helped her sister sit with Houston on her lap before she dropped his diaper bag. "He's fine," she promised, hugging her sister again. "I'm so happy to see you," she said through her tears. "When they told me they had to take you to the hospital, I imagined all the worst scenarios."

"I'm okay," she promised as Sadie lowered herself to another chair. "That was a precaution, but the doctors said I'm fine and don't need to be admitted. I'm waiting on Vic to come back from the CT scanner."

"Kadie, what happened? How did you end up at Randall's?"

Kadie rubbed her cheek against Houston's as he snuggled

in against her neck. "I was driving to work, and two SUVs boxed me in and forced me off the road. I didn't even have time to grab my phone before I was tossed in the back of one of the SUVs and they all drove off. One of the guys even took my car. I have no idea where that is."

Sadie didn't have the heart to tell her it was probably in a chop shop somewhere and she would never see it again. "Did they take you right to the mansion?"

"I don't know. They blindfolded me, and eventually we stopped somewhere dark. Maybe a garage? That's where they made me write that letter. Did they send it to you?"

"I found it on my bed when I came back from searching for you," Sadie explained. "I knew it wasn't your handwriting. Mina, from Secure One, said you wrote it but you did it in a way I'd know you didn't want to."

"Yes!" Kadie exclaimed quietly so not to scare Houston. "I knew you wouldn't believe I wrote it, and I hoped you'd run."

"I did, after Vic sent a note to my work. That's how I ended up with Secure One. They've been protecting me and Houston since someone ran us off the road near their property. Randall treated you good?" Sadie asked, afraid of the answer but also needing to know.

"He didn't have a choice. I refused to tell him where Houston was. To be honest, that dude isn't the smartest guy I've ever come across. He was so mad when they brought me to him and Houston wasn't along. He also doesn't have the stomach for violence. He wouldn't let his bodyguards slap me around and insisted putting me in a dark room alone would break me."

"I'm so sorry, Kadie," she whispered, squeezing her hand.

"There were so many times I wanted to break down and cry, tell him everything if he'd let me out of that room, but then I pictured this sweet boy. I would live through anything, or die trying, to keep him safe."

"How did they know who you were or that you even had Houston?"

"I'm afraid that's all my fault," Vic said as they rolled him back into the room still on a gurney. "Houston, my sweet boy."

The baby leaned back at the sound of his voice and let out another happy squeal. Kadie stood so they could hug as a family. Sadie's heart broke from the sweetness of the reunion. If she had doubted Vic's love for her sister and his son a few days ago, she no longer did. Tears ran silently down his cheeks as Kadie stroked his forehead, being careful of the stitches in his head from the beating he'd taken. Houston clung to him like a spider monkey, so Kadie left them locked together while she kept her hand on the baby's back.

"Randall told me while he was walking me to the dungeon that Dad has kept someone on me since I left for college. He suspected I would try to have a family outside the family." Vic's eyes rolled, and he shook his head. "We were careful, but a few days before Kadie disappeared, his guy saw me open the door for her and Houston. It wasn't hard to do some research and find out who Kadie was, and even without solid proof, they suspected the baby was mine."

"Then why put me in the crosshairs with the note?" Sadie asked. "Why didn't they leave the note for you?"

"Randall said he knew Kadie lived with you and not me. He thought if they left the note for you, you'd run straight to me with the baby and they could grab him. They didn't realize that you didn't know who I was. When you disappeared completely, they had to do the legwork to find you."

"Which they did when they ran me off the road?"

"No," Vic said, shaking his head. "They still didn't know where you were. That's why I got a beating from his bodyguards. They wanted me to tell them. I passed out and woke up in that room."

"Do you think it was just a coincidence with an impatient driver?" Sadie's world spun to the side, and she was glad she was sitting down. If it had been an accident that put her on the course to fall for Eric while they'd worked to rescue her sister, that told her how truly special it was to have him in her life.

"In the rain, it could have been," Vic said, rubbing his forehead. "So many things had to come together to save this little boy. It was all my fault to begin with by thinking my family didn't care what I did. I put everyone I care about in danger."

"Will it continue to?" Sadie asked, her brow in the air. "I doubt The Snake is going to go away just because your brother and father are in prison."

"My brother and father were the ones who didn't want me to raise a Loraine, not The Snake. The problem is my brother won't stay in prison. The Snake will get him out, but I have a plan to make sure they all leave me, and my new family, alone."

"How?" Sadie and Kadie asked in unison.

"Through lawyers and mediators, I plan to approach Vacarro about a protection order, so to speak. I don't know him well, but I do know that he doesn't put time or energy into anything that doesn't serve him. Our little family doesn't serve him, which means he'll be happy to have this black sheep out of his hair."

Kadie wiped the rest of his tears from his cheek and then kissed his forehead. "We can worry about that once you're feeling better. Your brother is in jail for shooting a security officer, so we're safe for the next few days. Try to rest."

Sadie stood and squeezed her sister's shoulder. "I want to go check on Selina. Are you guys okay if I leave Houston with you?"

"Of course," Kadie said, turning to hug her. "We'll be fine."

"Okay, let me know when you need a ride home and I'll get it arranged." Sadie kissed the top of Houston's head and waved as she left the little family to spend some time together alone. Her first stop would be to check on Selina, and then she was going to find the man she loved.

THE HOSPITAL NOISE was a buzz saw to Eric's head. There was so much happening at once that he had to shut his only working aid down or lose his ability to focus on anything. Selina had been rushed into emergency surgery the moment she'd arrived at Sanford Hospital. Randall's bullet had lodged somewhere in her abdomen, and it was going to require exploratory surgery to remove it and ascertain what damage had been done.

Cal grabbed his shirt and pulled him into a room off the waiting area. "What the hell happened out there?"

Eric held up his finger and turned his aid back on. "I missed something." The words were spit out hard and fast as his fingers raked his hair. "He shouldn't have been able to get the drop on us, but I didn't hear his approach!"

"From what the team tells me, no one heard his approach. It was like he materialized out of thin air."

"But he didn't," Eric growled. "He was there. I missed him." He jabbed himself in the chest and forced the truth from his lips. "The battery died on one of my hearing aids.

It hasn't been holding a charge and it was my fault for not checking them before we left!"

Cal grabbed his shoulder and squeezed it. "It had nothing to do with your aid being down, Eric. We all missed him moving out of the main house. I was running point on the scout team, and I watched him escort the detectives to the door. He was in the basement with you in a quarter of the amount of time he should have been when we calculated it. That means there's another door to that tunnel somewhere. A door Selina didn't know existed."

Eric was still shaking his head. "I'm resigning effective immediately," he said, lowering himself to a padded chair. The weight of the last few hours sat heavy on his shoulders, and he couldn't bear knowing that his friend had been injured because of his failure.

"You're absolutely not doing that." Eric turned to see Sadie blocking the doorway, her eyes firing daggers at him. "Nothing that happened out there tonight was your fault."

"You can't tell me what to do," he said, his voice harsh in the quiet room. "And you don't know anything about what happened out there tonight. You weren't there!"

"I wasn't there, that's true," she agreed, stepping inside the room. "But you brought my sister home to me, and that's what I'll remember about tonight. Am I upset, sad and feeling guilty that Selina got shot? Yes, but it wasn't your fault. If anything, it was my fault for pushing you guys into trying to save my sister! I will owe Secure One and Selina for the rest of my life for what the team did to help my family when the cops wouldn't lift a finger. What I won't do is allow you to blame yourself for what happened as a way to push me away."

"It was no one's fault," Cal said with exasperation. "Eric,

you know we all accept the same risk when we run these operations. Did I think we'd be rescuing hostages when I started Secure One? No. I had no idea we'd be rescuing women and taking out serial killers, but here we are, aren't we? You have skills beyond being a security guard—don't think they haven't been noticed. I've seen what you've done to integrate technology into the team to accommodate us better as we do this job." Cal held up his prosthesis. "My hand, Mack's legs, your ears, Mina and Efren…we all benefit from the perceptive changes you've made on the team. I'm guilty of not saying it enough, but what we did tonight would not have been possible without the technology we have because of you. So, no, you're not resigning. You can be mad about it, but you've worked too hard to use your disability as an excuse to avoid living. Does living real hurt sometimes? It sure does, but that doesn't mean it's not worth the pain."

"Living real?" Eric asked in confusion. "I don't think I heard you correctly."

"You did. I said living real. What that means to you is up to you. To me, it means giving myself grace again. It means enjoying life and accepting love from a woman who understands that some days will be harder than others. It means letting the rough days be rough so that rough day doesn't turn into a rough week or month. Marlise taught me that accepting love doesn't make me weak. It means I'm strong enough to ignore the doubts and let someone else see all my ugly."

"And there's always plenty of ugly to see in my soul," Eric hissed, his gaze drifting to Sadie, who still stood in the doorway. "You're too pretty for that kind of ugly, Sadie Cook."

"I don't remember any ugly, Eric Newman," she said, her finger pointing at him as she walked toward him. "All I remember is the sweet way you held my nephew when he was crying, swaying him back and forth to offer him a safe place to be frustrated about life. I remember the way you shielded me from danger and the way your lips feel on mine when we kiss—"

"That was a mistake," he ground out, interrupting her. There was no way he could sit there and listen to her tell him all the ways they were perfect together. Not when he knew he had to let her go. "We were a mistake. I never should have gotten involved with you and Houston. I should have turned you over to the police. If I had, our friend wouldn't be in surgery right now!"

"And my sister would be dead." Her voice was so quiet if he hadn't been watching her lips, he wouldn't have heard her.

"You don't know that. What I do know is, this—" Eric motioned between them with his hand "—is over. I can't protect you, and as you learned, the world is dangerous, even in small-town Minnesota!"

"I don't need you to protect me, Eric Newman. I need you to stop pretending that this—" she motioned between them with her hand the same way he did "—isn't right. You're a big, bad security guy, whoopie! I'm not scared of your world, and I don't need protecting. I need someone to love me. Someone like you—"

"I've got an update on Selina," Mina said, racing into the room and interrupting Sadie.

Eric braced himself for the news while pretending he didn't want to pull Sadie into his arms forever. "How is she?"

"Out of surgery. She's going to be okay," Mina said, her folded hands near her lips. "The doctor couldn't tell me much since I'm not her medical power of attorney, but he did say she's going to be fine in a few weeks."

"Thank God," Cal and Eric said in unison.

"Cal, the doctor wants to speak with you," she advised. "He's at the nurses' station."

"On my way," he said, skirting past Mina and Sadie and jogging out the door.

"I'm so glad she's going to be okay," Eric said, his hand in his hair as he turned to pace away from the two women. When he turned back, only Mina stood before him. Good. It was time Sadie hit the road. She had a life that no longer included him. He had nothing to offer her. He never made that a secret—she just wasn't listening. Ironic, considering.

"In the FBI, we had a word for guys like you, Eric."

"Excuse me?"

"Is there one?" she asked, hand on her hip and her nose in the air. "I heard what you said to Sadie. Real jackhat move, Newman."

"Jackhat?" He was throwing every defense he had her way to shut her down. The last thing he needed was a lecture from Mina Jacobs about his love life or lack thereof.

"Would you like me to write down what I have to say so it's extremely clear and you can refer to it when you're alone in your cold, empty bed?"

"That's low, Mina," he said, crossing his arms over his chest. "I can hear you."

"I never said you couldn't. I was implying that you won't, and there's a difference. *Couldn't* means you have no ability to. *Won't* means you refuse to. Sadie is the best thing to ever happen to you, but you act like she's putting you out by existing."

"I'm no good for her, Mina!" he exclaimed, throwing his arms up. "I have nothing to offer her in the emotional department or for her future. She's better off without me."

"So that's it? You get to make that decision for her? You

get to be the judge and jury of her life? How would you feel if someone said you couldn't be with Sadie because you deserve better."

"There is no one better than Sadie Cook!"

"You made my point. You'd be angry, upset and sad if someone said that and then took away your chance to change it. That's what you just did to Sadie."

"I don't know how to have someone else in my life, Mina. Sadie is young and innocent and deserves a life outside the walls of a compound that exists to protect the protectors."

"Yes, protection from harm. Not from love. Look around you, Eric. Love comes in all different ways. It's up to you to recognize it when it comes your way."

The chair was there for him when he fell into it, his limbs heavy with sadness and dread. "I don't know how to love, Mina. Not anymore. It's been too long."

"Nice try, but love is like riding a bike. You never forget how even if you're a little rusty initially. You have to oil up the chain, straighten the brakes and set the seat to the right position. Once you've done that, it's smooth sailing, even over the bumpiest road." She motioned at her left below-knee prosthesis as though to prove a point. She had been through a lot, and Roman had been by her side for all of it.

"I'll think about it."

"While you're thinking about it, think about how to apologize to that girl. Think about groveling and begging for her forgiveness. If she does forgive you, then she's a better woman than I because I'd kick you to the curb."

He frowned and ran his palms over his legs. "I'm scared, Mina."

"I know you are, Eric," she said, dropping her arms and walking over to him. She squeezed his shoulder to remind him that she was still his friend. "But that's not a reason to treat someone cruelly. You tell them the truth and let them make their own choices."

"That's what I'm scared of," he admitted, staring at the empty doorway.

"That she won't choose you?"

"Yep," he answered with a sad chuckle. "I know if I were Sadie, I'd run."

"But you're not her, so you owe her an apology."

Her words were valid, and guilt filled him. The same guilt that filled him every night when he lay alone while wishing he wasn't. The guilt that a little boy had died before he'd ever had a chance to live and that he wanted to live even though the little boy couldn't.

"The doctor said she's going to need some time to recover," Cal said, walking into the room and breaking the silence. "But physically, she'll be fine. It's time to regroup with the team."

Cal and Mina turned to go, and Eric knew this was his only chance to bring up what had happened in the tunnel earlier. Selina was going to be okay, but if they didn't figure out her secrets, she wouldn't stay that way for long. It was time to follow his instincts again and be the leader the team needed.

Chapter Nineteen

"Wait." Eric stood and rubbed his hands on his pants when his friends turned back to face him. "What I say here needs to stay between us." They both nodded, so Eric turned to Mina. "I need you to do a deep dive on a name for me."

"What name?"

"Ava Shannon."

"Where did you hear that name?" Mina asked, shifting so she could look between him and Cal.

"I saw the name on Vic's lips during the raid. I wondered if it was pertinent." He didn't say that the name had been directed at their friend.

"It's weird that he would say the name in that setting," Mina said. "Ava Shannon is dead. I ran across her when I was researching Howie Loraine. She was Randall Senior's second wife. Some say an arranged mob marriage to offer him up as the family man again as they started their counterfeiting business. She was killed eight years ago during the raid on the mansion."

Eric lifted a brow in part confusion and part surprise. Interesting that both Vic and Randall Junior had thought Selina was Ava. It had to be a bad case of the doppelgänger among us. Eric wondered if it was a mistaken identity, but instinct told him Selina was in danger even if she wouldn't tell them why.

"How does this apply to the team?" Cal asked, stepping forward to stand behind Mina.

"I don't know that it does."

"Listen, I'm tired of people trying to hide stuff from me. I've got Selina in a hospital bed with a huge chip on her shoulder and closed lips. I don't need the same from you."

Eric's gaze flicked to the door, and then he took a few steps closer to the only people he trusted in his world. "Vic was looking at Selina when he said the name. She's lying in that hospital bed because Randall called her that right before he shot her."

Mina glanced up at Cal, and Eric could read the surprise on their faces. "That's more than a little weird," she said.

"And considering Selina's behavior since Howie Loraine landed on our radar, I think it's pertinent," Cal added.

"I don't know why," he said, uncomfortable with what he was about to admit, "but my instincts tell me Selina is in danger. Serious danger." Cal did a fist pump that made Eric pause. "What was that?"

"Me rejoicing. That's the first time you've listened to your instincts since we left that sandbox over a dozen years ago."

"That's not true." His words were defensive, but on the inside, he wondered if they were true. Had he shut out his instincts along with everything else?

"Believe what you want, but I know what I know," Cal said. "As for Selina, I agree that she's in danger. What's our plan?"

Cal and Mina looked to him for the answer, so he straightened his spine and inhaled. "We do a deep dive on Ava Shannon. I'm talking right down to the kind of underwear she wore," he said, glancing at Mina, who was smirking while she nodded. "And while we're doing that, we keep someone on Selina. She's never alone."

"She's going to hate that," Mina said with a chuckle.

"She's not going to have a choice." Cal's words left no room for argument. "There's no way she can fight anyone off in her condition. She's defenseless right now."

"Can we spare Efren?" he asked.

Cal lifted a brow in amusement. "You want to put Brenna on her?"

Eric held up his hands in defense. "He's trained in guarding bodies, that's all. I'd trust him with my life, which means, in my opinion, he's the best choice to keep Selina alive until we figure this out."

"Or she talks," Mina said.

"She's not going to talk," Cal argued. "She's had plenty of chances to talk. She'll keep her secrets until she's scared good and straight."

"Or she's tired of having a babysitter. Especially one she can't stand," Eric finished.

"She will be out of it for a few days, so you run point with Efren. Let him know what's going on and facilitate whatever he needs," Cal said to him. "Mina and I will do the deep dive and see what we can come up with on Ava Shannon."

"Hopefully it's not what kind of underwear she buys," Mina said with laughter as she turned to go. "Now that we know Selina will be okay, Roman and I will head back to Secure One. I'll sleep on the way so I can start searching when we get there. I'll keep you posted. Whiskey out."

They watched her go, and then Cal turned back to him. "I'm following behind them. You got this?"

"Absolutely, boss."

Cal grasped his shoulder for a moment and squeezed it. "For the record, you did exactly what I would have done out there tonight. We can't predict everything that might happen when we're out in the field. All we can do is be prepared and react to them, which is what you did. Tonight you listened to your instincts and you saved lives. That's what you should focus your thoughts on. Nothing else."

"Easier said than done, but I'll work on it."

Cal slapped him on the back gently. "That's enough for me. Charlie, out."

Alone in the room, Eric took a deep breath and stretched out his neck. It was time to talk to Efren and do what he could to protect a friend. He forced the image of Sadie's sadness from his mind as he walked to the waiting room and found Efren. With a crooked finger, he motioned him into the hallway.

"I need a favor, but you aren't going to like it."

"Hello to you too," Efren said with a chuckle. "Not the best way to start a story, bruh."

"I wish I had a story, but I don't. Right now, I've just got a gut feeling, and my gut tells me Selina is in danger."

Efren tipped his head to the side as though he agreed with him. "My gut may be saying the same thing. That or I shouldn't have had coffee from the cafeteria."

The comment lifted Eric's lips briefly before they fell again into a tight line. "I want you to stay here with her until she's released. Don't take your eyes off her until I get back to you with more information."

"Done. I'm not sure how Selina will take the news though."

Eric imagined her reaction to Efren being her bodyguard and it dragged a chuckle from his lips. "She'll be on pain meds, and her IV tube will only reach so far. You should be safe."

"Fair point. I'll need some things if this will be an extended stay." He motioned at his leg. He was wearing his running blade rather than his day-to-day leg.

"Of course. Text me a list. I'll head back to the mobile command center and gather it. We'll also get you a vehicle."

"In case I need to make a quick getaway from Selina?"

Eric's gut twisted. "No, in case you need to make a quick getaway *with* Selina. I'm not certain, but I will tell you that Vic and Randall recognized Selina tonight. They thought she was their long-dead stepmother. Considering his head injury, I could ignore Vic's mumblings, but Randall was of sound mind when he thought he saw a ghost and shot her. Understand?"

"Understand," Efren said, biting his lip. "I'll work on getting answers from her, but I doubt they'll be more than a hand gesture or two."

Eric couldn't help it. He smiled. "You might be new here, but you do have her pegged. Give me an hour to gather what you need, and then I'll be back to check on our mystery patient. In the meantime, if you need anything, you know our numbers."

"You got it, brother," Efren said, giving him a fist bump before he walked to the nurses' station to inquire about Selina's room.

Eric jogged to the elevator and stepped in. As the doors slid closed, he couldn't help but wonder if they were also closing on his time with Sadie.

HOURS LATER, Eric sat in his vehicle at the exit of the gas station. He'd just left the hospital again after checking on

Selina. It had been a long night, but in the light of the morning, she would be fine. She'd have a few new scars, and not all of them physical, but she was just grateful to be alive. She'd stopped talking to him the first time he'd mentioned the name Ava in their conversation. She'd feigned weakness and closed her eyes as though she had passed out. He knew better, but he couldn't make her talk. Instead, he'd left her in the capable hands of Efren in hopes that she'd eventually get sick of having a babysitter and fill them in on her past.

Cal had been right about one thing—he'd always had good instincts. It was time for him to start trusting them again. What had happened that day on their mission had been out of his control. He knew that even if it wasn't easy to remember or believe. Those people had died, but not because his instincts had been wrong. In fact, that day his instincts had told him nothing was as it seemed, but he hadn't been in charge of that mission and had had no say over when it happened. Even though his instincts had been correct, he'd stopped trusting them. Last night, when he'd watched Vic and Selina interact, those instincts had kicked back in and hadn't given him a choice but to listen.

Nothing was as it seemed with Selina Colvert. He had plans to find out what the truth was and make sure she was protected until it was resolved. That was what they did at Secure One. They worked together as a team, but they were also family. Family took care of family. Mack had dropped off a vehicle for Efren to use and collected the mobile command to drive back to Secure One.

Eric had texted Cal that he was on his way back, but Cal had other plans. He told Eric he had to stop pretending he didn't care about Sadie and follow through on the apology he owed her. Then he texted him Sadie's address.

Taking another swig of the gas-station coffee, he didn't even recoil at the battery acid as it slid down his throat. His taste buds had quit after the third cup of bad coffee at the hospital, but he needed the jolt of caffeine to help him think. He focused on the pros and cons of turning right versus left.

Right would take him back into Bemidji, where he could find Sadie's apartment and talk to her. Maybe. If she was there. He didn't know because he hadn't seen or heard from her since he'd told her to go away last night. Everyone on the team had found a way to call him on his bad behavior toward Sadie, leading him to believe they hadn't done a stellar job hiding their feelings for each other.

Left would take him back to Secure One, where he could keep living life fake, as Cal would say. Eric preferred to call it living safe. He was good at doing his job while holding people at arm's length. At least he had been good at it—until he'd met Sadie. Now he wasn't sure about anything in his life.

That was a lie. Eric was sure of one thing—he'd fallen in love with Sadie the moment he'd laid eyes on her. He was also sure she deserved better than he could offer her, but Mina had pointed out he didn't get to make that decision. Sadie had to do that for herself.

He watched a Lexus pass him going north and let his mind wander to Sadie. All he could see was the look in her eyes when he'd told her they were over. There had been hurt and sadness but also determination to be the strong one in the situation. She wouldn't cry or scream or curse him out. His instincts said she was going to fight. She would regroup and give him time to face what had happened to his friend.

He gasped, leaning back in the seat as though the weight of the entire world was on his chest. Sadie had shown him with blinding clarity that he hadn't just lost his hearing—

he'd lost his ability to listen. He shut everyone out, including his own instincts, and pretended he'd lost those in that war zone too. The truth was just the opposite. Losing his hearing had let him hear his instincts. Now it was his job to *listen*.

Eric punched a button on the car's display. 1786 W. Moreland Road was programmed into his GPS thanks to Mina. Cal had said Sadie lived in apartment 124. A quick glance at the clock told him it was only 6:00 a.m. and she was probably sleeping. He should take the left, drive the ninety minutes home and do the same thing. Sleep would help him put things right in his head before he saw her again.

He let off the brake and flicked his signal light on, waiting for a bakery van to pass before he turned…right. "She deserves more than you, man, but Mina's right. You can't make that decision for her. Regardless, she deserves an apology from your lug head."

The drive to Moreland Road wasn't long or complicated. Too quickly, Eric was parked in the lot of Sadie's apartment building. He knew she was home since Cal had dropped her off when he'd left the hospital to head back to Secure One and she hadn't had time to replace the Saturn.

He climbed out of the car and walked to the door, taking a deep breath before he pushed the button for apartment 124 and waited for someone to answer. Silently, the door clicked open, so he pulled the handle and stepped into the vestibule of the building. He followed the signs and walked down two hallways to find her apartment. When he stopped at her door, he took a deep breath and raised his fist to knock.

The door swung open, and Sadie stood before him wearing buffalo-plaid sleep pants, a white T-shirt and fuzzy slippers. She was the most gorgeous woman he'd ever laid eyes on. At that moment he knew he'd do anything to have her, even if that meant he had to live real. Fear rocketed through him, but he tamped it down. He had been in a war zone and survived. With Sadie's help, he could survive the first few months of living real. That is, if she was still willing to give him the time of day.

"Hi," she said, leaning against the door. "How's Selina?"

"She's out of recovery and in her room. She's grateful to be alive and happy Kadie and Vic are okay. Efren is with her. Can I come in?"

Sadie stepped aside and held the door open, motioning for him to enter. Once he was inside, she closed the door and leaned against it as he took in the space.

"You're packing?"

"Usually what you do when you have to move."

"What about Kadie and Houston?"

"Kadie and Houston are with Vic at his apartment. The doctors would only release Vic from the hospital if he had someone to stay with him. After her ordeal, there was no place else Kadie wanted to be. She planned to sleep for hours with her baby and the man she loves. Mack drove them home before he headed back to Secure One."

"She's decided to make a go of it with Vic?"

"She has," Sadie agreed, sitting on the couch, so he had to sit as well if he didn't want to be leering over her. "She understands now that Vic has nothing to do with his family, but she will try to convince him to move somewhere far away from Bemidji."

"Probably a good idea for their future," Eric agreed. "If he lives here, he'll always be known as the other Loraine brother."

"Which shouldn't be derogatory considering he has moral character, but somehow it would be," Sadie said with an eye roll. "He's decided to contact Vaccaro through a lawyer and strike a truce deal with him. He wants to live a normal life and raise his son without The Snake or his brother watching over him."

"I hope he can achieve that type of life. Randall was arrested, but you know he'll be cleared of the charges as soon as The Snake sends in a lawyer. Hopefully if Vic strikes a deal with Vacarro, Randall also falls in line and leaves his brother's family alone. It will be difficult to get free of them, and I feel bad that you and Kadie got wrapped up in that mess."

Sadie shook her head at his words. "I don't. If Kadie hadn't fallen for Vic, we wouldn't have Houston. He's worth every bit of trouble we must endure to raise him to be a good, caring, loving man who does the right thing, just like his father. I never realized how much Vic went through at the hands of his family, but his life hasn't been easy. He deserves happiness now."

"I agree, and I hope you'll get to see them often," Eric said with full sincerity.

"We'll work it out," she answered, but he heard how unsure she felt about the situation. "I'll always be part of Houston's life."

"What about mine?"

"I got the general impression you weren't interested in me sticking around." Her words this time were haughty, and he heard the anger underlining them even if she was trying to keep it light.

"That's why I'm here."

"To make it clear that you aren't interested in me sticking around?"

"No," he said, standing and walking to her before he fell

to his knees to take her hands. "To make it clear that I'm interested in you sticking around. I want you to stick to me like glue."

"You have a weird way of showing it, Eric Newman."

"I know." He gazed at her sweet face and brushed her hair behind her ear. "Mina made that very clear."

"Why does that not surprise me?"

"She was right though. You do deserve an apology and the independence to make your own decision. I don't have the right to tell you what you want or don't want. All I can say is I'm sorry for being a jerk the last few days. You came into my life and flipped it on its ear. I couldn't keep up with the emotions swirling inside me, and I got scared. Those emotions made the ghosts I live with pop up when I least expected it—"

"I understand, Eric," she said, running her finger down his cheek. "I understand that you can't control those ghosts and it's terrifying when they pop up unexpectedly."

"Yeah," he said with a breath. "But you've shown me that I must find a way to keep them buried, even if that means seeking outside help."

"You're tired of living with them unchecked. That's understandable. It must be torture to relive it over and over."

"Living fake," he said with a nod, and she tipped her head in confusion. "Cal told me it was time to live real. That all these years, I've been living fake, meaning that I shut my emotions down. I finally figured out that doing that also silenced my instincts until the day you walked into my life. Meeting you was the first time those instincts wouldn't be quiet."

"You knew I was in danger."

"Yes, that, but also my instincts told me you'd change my life."

"Clearly not for the better," she muttered, but he read the words on her lips.

His fingers grasped her warm chin, and he forced eye contact with her. "You're wrong. My life is so much better because I met you. I sat in a gas-station parking lot for far too long when I left the hospital this morning. It gave me time to think where it was quiet." He chuckled and pointed at his ear. "I guess I could have shut these off and gotten silence, but that wasn't what I needed."

"You needed clarity."

Eric pointed at her. "Yes, it made me realize that my soul fell in love with you when our eyes met. It was that simple. The rest is what's complicated."

"If you believe in love, and trusting in each other, then the complicated parts become a little less complicated each day."

"That's what I want to believe, but it's going to take me some time to learn how."

"I know," she agreed with a soft smile.

"Please don't move. Please stay and teach me how to uncomplicate the complicated parts of life."

"They didn't tell you, did they?" she asked, a smirk on her lips.

"Tell me what?"

"I quit my job at Dirk's and took a new one. I'll be working as a chef, where I can stretch my wings and finally do what I love."

His shoulders deflated, and he hung his head momentarily before glancing up at her. "Congratulations. You deserve it, Sadie. You're an excellent chef, and the guys will never let me forget it."

"Thank you," she said, her face beaming from his compliment. "Unfortunately I have to move for the job. Cooking for all those hungry operatives will have a learning curve, but from what I'm told, they're tired of the MREs. Even if they're better than the ones they got in the army. Something tells me they'll be pretty easy to please."

Eric's heart pounded hard as he lifted himself onto his knees. "MREs? Army?"

"Secure one, Cook."

A smile lifted his lips, and his heart slowed to a normal rhythm as he gazed at the woman he loved. "Cook isn't part of the phonetic alphabet."

"I know, but it is my last name, and from what I hear you have to be part of the team for a bit before you get a code name. I'll be starting tomorrow morning as the chef in residence, but a little stork told me that in about seven months, I may also be pulling in some hours as the nanny."

"Stork? Nanny?" He paused, and his eyes widened. "Mina?"

A smile lifted Sadie's lips when she shrugged. "We'll wait for the official announcement, but I have it on good authority that Secure One will need that high chair Mina ordered."

"You're going to work with us at Secure One?" His words were more of a plea than a question.

"You didn't think I would let you off the hook that easily, did you? I'm prepared to dig in and prove to you that not only do you deserve love but you deserve happiness and a better way forward."

"You've already proved that, Sadie. I need help learning to accept it."

"Learning to accept love or happiness?"

"From my viewpoint, they go hand in hand." He took hers

and twined their fingers together. "Once I accept your love, happiness will follow."

I accept you, Eric, she mouthed, stroking his cheek. The warmth of her love warmed more than his skin. It reached his heart and wrapped around that too. To be loved by someone who wanted nothing from him was magical. "I accept your pain, sorrow, challenges and strengths." He opened his mouth, but she put her finger against his lips. "And I know that your challenges may get worse over time. I also know that you'll adapt to whatever comes along because that's who you are, Eric. You adapt in ways that even you don't notice. I don't have my head in the sand about the challenges we'll face in the future, but my heart still beams at the idea of spending my life with you. That feeling," she said, shaking her fist near her chest, "is what tells me I have to fight for you."

"No, you don't," he promised, leaning forward and placing his lips on hers for a moment. "I'm done arguing. I want this. I want you. I want a life that's real, even when it's messy. You understand a messy life, but you keep returning to help clean it up. I love you, Sadie Cook."

"And I love you, Eric Newman. I have since the moment my heart told me I could trust you to keep us safe. You didn't let me or anyone else down. I know you think you did, but there was nothing you could have done differently."

Was that true? His analytical mind ran everything backward in a heartbeat, offering only one conclusion. "There were things I could have done differently, but that doesn't mean the outcome wouldn't have been the same."

"Or worse," she said, her words defiant. "The outcome could have been much, much worse."

"I need to help Selina with what she's facing, even if that takes me away from Secure One."

"We do," she said, emphasizing *we*. "And we will—together. You didn't think I would walk away because you scowled at me, did you?"

A smile lifted his lips. "It would have been easier if you had, for both of us."

She plastered her lips to his and kissed him like a woman who knew what she wanted. She kissed him like a woman who wanted him and no one else. "Would it be easy to walk away from that?"

"No," he whispered, grasping her face and returning the kiss. He climbed onto the couch to straddle her lap and pressed her head into the back of the couch with his kiss. She whimpered—from pleasure or pain he didn't know, so he eased off. "You were going to be impossible to walk away from. I knew that from the start. I don't know how things will go at work, but I know I want to give us a chance."

She popped open the first button on his shirt but held his gaze. "To start," she said, pausing to open another button. "You'll drive me to Secure One, and I'll put my suitcase in your cabin. Then we'll crawl into your bed and sleep for twelve hours. When we wake up, I'll work my magic."

"In my bed or the kitchen?" he asked, one brow raised as she pushed his shirt off his shoulders and onto the floor.

"Can it be both?"

"Nothing would make me happier."

"Then I say, secure one, Cook," she whispered, trailing kisses down his chest.

"Secure two, Echo," he whispered as her love filtered into his heart to heal it a little more.

* * * * *

COMING SOON!

We really hope you enjoyed reading this book.
If you're looking for more romance
be sure to head to the shops when
new books are available on

Thursday 21st November

To see which titles are coming soon, please visit
millsandboon.co.uk/nextmonth

MILLS & BOON

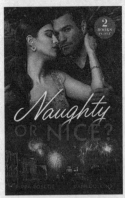

LET'S TALK
Romance

For exclusive extracts, competitions and special offers, find us online:

- **f** MillsandBoon
- **𝕏** @MillsandBoon
- **◉** @MillsandBoonUK
- **♪** @MillsandBoonUK

Get in touch on 01413 063 232